THE
HEALER

THE CROWN ROSE
Fiona Avery

THE HEALER
Michael Blumlein, MD

GALILEO'S CHILDREN: TALES OF SCIENCE VS. SUPERSTITION
edited by Gardner Dozois

THE PRODIGAL TROLL
Charles Coleman Finlay

PARADOX: BOOK ONE OF THE NULAPEIRON SEQUENCE
John Meaney

HERE, THERE & EVERYWHERE
Chris Roberson

STAR OF GYPSIES
Robert Silverberg

THE RESURRECTED MAN
Sean Williams

THE
HEALER

MICHAEL BLUMLEIN, MD

an imprint of **Prometheus Books**
Amherst, NY

Published 2005 by PYR™, an imprint of Prometheus Books

Inquiries should be addressed to
PYR
59 John Glenn Drive
Amherst, New York 14228–2197
VOICE: 716–691–0133, ext. 207
FAX: 716–564–2711
WWW.PYRSF.COM

09 08 07 06 05   5 4 3 2 1

Library of Congress Cataloging-in-Publication Data

Blumlein, Michael.
    The healer / Michael Blumlein.
        p. cm.
    ISBN 1–59102–314–9 (hardcover : alk. paper)
    1. Healers—Fiction. I. Title.

PS3552.L855H43 2005
813'.54—dc22

                                                                    2005007021

Printed in Canada on acid-free paper

ACKNOWLEDGMENTS

I owe a debt of gratitude to Carter Scholz, Richard Russo, Karen Fowler, Pat Murphy, Mike Berry, Angus McDonald, Dan Marcus, Eileen Gunn, and Steve Crane, all of whom read an early draft of this work and offered invaluable criticism and advice. I also am indebted to Philip Pullman, an inspired and inspiring writer. *His Dark Materials* was, at times, a lifeline during the writing of this book. Hilary Gordon, as always, was a rock. My debt to her is ongoing. Finally, I would like to thank my brother Steven, without whom it's impossible to imagine what this book would have been.

PROLOGUE

His Daddy was Grotesque. His Momma was a half. His brother Wyn had the gift, and at the age of fourteen was taken, schooled, and never seen again. Payne was eleven at the time. He felt left behind and excluded, which happened often with his brother and made him mad. The other things he felt he didn't have names for.

For a long time after that he thought about his brother. Sometimes he heard him in his room, but when he looked, the room was empty. Sometimes he saw him on the street, but it always turned out to be another boy.

His Daddy said that he'd get over it, and after a while he told him that he had to. Missing someone was one thing, but pining for something you couldn't have was a sorry waste of time. Gone for Grotesques was a fact of life. Gone was one in ten. Better that he get his mind on something productive and useful.

His Momma put up pennies. Pared down, scrimped and saved.

Preparing for the day of Payne's coming-of-age, in case that he, against all odds, be similarly gifted. To bribe whoever needed to be bribed. Or failing that, to send the boy away. Anything to keep him from being taken from her. Her one remaining child. Her baby.

怀怀怀

The day that Payne turned fourteen was hot and windy. It was summer, and in summer the air in Gode was never still. It blew across the desert plain from sunup to sundown and often through the night, sometimes gently, sometimes fiercely, stirring up the earth, raising whirlwinds of dust, shifting sand. It was a moody wind, and on this day it couldn't seem to make its mind up, alternating ferocious gusts that seemed intent on wiping out the ancient city with periods of tranquility and calm. The night before, Payne hadn't slept, anxious and excited for the day to come. Now that it was here, he was as restless as the wind, and he was scared.

He liked his life the way it was, loved his parents, felt loved and secure in return. He liked his room, which, cramped and tiny as it was, was his. The cracks and patches in the walls were familiar and comforting to him. The dirt floor he hated sweeping was cool underfoot, and it helped him sleep in the hot nights, for his bed was pitched on top of it. And his treasures—the stick that his father had carved and painted to help calm his fear of snakes, the skull-shaped rock that Wyn had bequeathed to him, the book of birthday portraits his mother added to every year—how could he leave these behind? And his other treasures, the odds and ends a boy his age collected and spun stories about, the toys whose lives depended on him as much as he did them . . . they'd be lost without his guiding hand and presence. Parting with them would be like parting with himself. He could not do it.

He felt fortunate, then, that he wouldn't have to. The chances were so very slim. One in ten, or nine in ten in his favor. And two children in a single family, two in a row, two of two, was practically unheard-of. And that was only going by the numbers. More importantly, his os melior showed no signs of life. For the past six months his parents had asked him about it nearly every day, and every day his answer was the same. This lifelessness was possibly the result of the herbal decoction his father brewed for him and diligently made him drink each week. Or maybe the heated pebbles his mother gently piled atop the opening. These were measures to disable the os, for while his parents hoped for the best, they did not rely on hope. And as for chance, they were not gamblers.

As his birthday approached and their anxiety naturally grew, he had taken to telling them first thing each morning. No, he'd say before they even asked, it's fine, there's nothing happening. It's nonfunctional, like yours. It's not like Wyn's was. He made a point not to mention the faint, fluttery sensation and tiny wave of warmth he felt on rare occasions near the opening. It was so brief and evanescent that it didn't seem worth calling attention to. It would only make them more anxious. He knew how much they suffered from his brother's loss, and he wouldn't have caused them further grief for anything.

From time to time, however, he wondered what it would be like to have an os like Wyn's. A fully functional, healing os. He thought of all the people he would help. And the physical sensation of being alive that way. And to follow in his brother's footsteps, that would be a dream come true. He'd make his brother—or his brother's memory, since that's all that was left—proud.

His mother hadn't slept the night before, either. She'd tossed and turned and lain awake for what seemed an eternity before finally rising at the coming of the day. Immediately, she started in on housework. She swept the floor of the common room and dampened it with water. She wiped the chairs and dining table of dust. She built a fire and put a pot up to make the sweetened tea that she would offer the examiners. She unwrapped the cakes that she had baked the previous evening and arranged them on a tray. These chores helped calm her nerves, like little prayers. For a few precious minutes they allowed her the illusion of control.

When she was done, she turned her attention to herself, bathing, then changing her clothes. Normally, she wore her long hair braided, but for these visitors, who would prefer not to have to look at the bubble of bone at the top of her head, she put it up.

Now she looked positively human. She added earrings. Absent-mindedly, she fingered her neck, touching naked skin where her heirloom necklace, her most treasured possession, had been. She had sold it and felt bereaved, not for having had to part with such a treasure but for being powerless to protect her son. Bribery hardly ever worked with the examiners, although sometimes it did. Especially if a child's gift was minimal. If it weren't, if like her Wyn's it was strong and promising, then it was useless trying to intervene. The examiners were on the lookout for such children, who were feathers in their cap. Reputations and careers could be made on finding them.

She had given up the thought of sending Payne away. No one dared to take him, and even had there been someone, where would they have gone? Rampart was out of the question. The only other road from Gode petered out in the desert. There had once been a city farther south, but it had long ago fell to ruin. Except for those poor children who had the misfortune of passing the examination and being torn from their families, people born in Gode remained.

After dressing and finishing with her hair, she fetched the money she had put away. Most of it was in the form of coins, which were tightly stuffed into a leather pouch that she'd kept hidden in the toe of an old boot. To her the pouch felt heavy, although she worried that to a hand accustomed to receiving bribes, it would feel light. On the chance that it did not suffice she considered other measures she might take, measures that other mothers had taken. In preparing for this day, she had talked to countless women and heard countless stories and pieces of advice. Some were shocking. Others literally defied imagination. And while she had been unable to substantiate the rumors of success of any of these interventions, she kept an open mind. She had lost one son already, and if it came to it, she would take whatever means were necessary to prevent the same from happening to the other.

She slipped the pouch into the bodice of her dress, then went to wake up Payne, pausing at the curtain that separated his room from the common room to peek past its edge and gaze on him unobserved. He was lying on his bed, awake, staring at the ceiling. She knew that he was nervous about this day and also knew that he would try to hide it. He was a quiet boy, reserved and thoughtful, unlike his brother, who had been impetuous, outspoken, and sometimes brash. She missed her firstborn more than she had words for, but she drew strength from knowing that he had the tools to look out for himself in whatever way he could. Her younger son, by contrast, was a dreamer. If there came a time that he had to defend himself, she feared he wouldn't know where or how to begin.

The sound of the front door opening startled her, but it was her husband, not the other ones, not yet. He'd been gone since nightfall, in search of a plant that grew only in a certain distant wash and bloomed by night but was best harvested at dawn. She hadn't known how worried she was if he would make it back in time until, on seeing him, she felt a wave of relief. He quickly closed the door to keep the sand and dust from blowing in, removed his robe, then crossed the room and embraced her. Over his shoulder he carried a woven bag, and in it was a scraggly bush of the plant he'd sought. One drooping white-petaled flower poked out of the bag's mouth, but the rest of it was tucked inside and wrapped in a cloth. She kept her distance from the bag, and he was careful not to let its contents prick her.

She asked if he was hungry. He was, but food would wait. He took a moment to look at her. Very nice, he said. Very human.

In reply, she kissed the pleated ridge that swept across the side of his skull, silently praising him for being who he was. Not once had he mentioned the necklace so conspicuously absent from her neck. Nor had she seen fit to call attention to the wedding ring missing recently from his finger. Some things were better left unsaid, and these required no explanation.

Together, they drew aside the curtain to their son's room. He was sitting up in bed, half-dressed, waiting for them. His father knelt beside him on the floor, removed the bundle from his bag and carefully unwrapped the cloth. The long gray stalks of the desert plant were studded with thorns; its leaves were small and inconspicuous. Silently, Payne watched his father take a knife from his belt and slice and chop the stalks into smaller pieces. His mother also watched, but after a while she gathered her dress, knelt down and took her son's hands, commanding his attention.

They might not have another chance to talk before the examination, she explained, and she wanted to let him know how much she loved him and how proud she was of him. And to thank him for understanding why, despite the fact his os posed no danger, they felt it necessary to take such precautions. It wasn't easy being saddled with such worriers for parents. She said this with a smile and a look of deep affection, and ended by telling him how confident she was that everything would turn out fine. The examination was a mere formality. It would be over quickly, and then life would return to normal.

Midway through the morning the examiners arrived. They knocked then entered swiftly, relieved, it seemed, to be out of the now raging wind. There were three of them—two men, one woman—all humans. One of the men was a doctor. He wore the mantle of the office, had oily hair, a fleshy mouth, and a portly build. The other was an enforcer. He carried a variety of shiny weapons and implements of restraint and kept his face expressionless. The woman was elderly, maybe even ancient. She was short and bent, and her face was hidden by a cowl. She dragged her feet across the floor in a shuffle.

Once inside, the doctor made perfunctory introductions. He was Valid, Doctor of the Mental Latitudes, and would be in charge. The woman was Unerrant Sorly, Class and Figure Five. The enforcer was Lieutenant Crisp.

Dr. Valid explained their purpose in coming and what they hoped to achieve. The speech, which he gave by rote, was a mandate of the law. Once he had dispensed with it and settled the Unerrant and then himself into a chair, he asked to see the boy.

Payne's mother gave a cordial nod. The boy would join them shortly. But she had to apologize, for he was sick. Always sick. Her son was a sickly boy.

Meanwhile, would they like some tea and cake? It was a thirsty day, and selecting children to be taken from their families for the honor of serving humans was a hungry business.

"It is an honor," answered Dr. Valid. "Make no mistake. And your offer is a kind one. But if we stopped to eat each time that food was offered us, we'd not get far. Fat, though. We would get fat."

He stole a glance at the tray of cakes perched atop the dining table, and this was followed by a sigh and then a reconsideration. While it was an indulgence to eat, he noted, it was a discourtesy to be ungrateful. In the interest of good manners, then, he'd have a nibble.

She served each of them, first cake and then the sweetened tea. The Unerrant's hand trembled like a leaf, and her cup and saucer rattled as she lifted them. Dr. Valid ate with relish. He cleared his plate of every crumb, complimented the cook, had a second helping, then fastidiously wiped his lips and repeated his request to see the boy.

Payne's mother promised to produce him. First, though, might she have a word in private with them? With all due respect, for it was certainly not her place to judge, they were the authorities, she a mere mother, but her son was a clumsy, slow, dull-witted child. And prone to illness and bouts of deep depression. He was difficult to manage. A trying, taxing boy to be around. To be quite blunt, and here she dropped her voice in strictest confidence, he'd be a waste of their time and effort. She truly wished that it were otherwise, but he wouldn't last a week away from home.

Some examiners were amateurs, some frankly doltish, but Dr.

Valid was neither of these. While he much preferred to speak, listening was a part of his job, and he did what was required of him, hearing her out. When she was done, he replied that at least in one respect he agreed with her. It was not her place to judge.

"You are his mother. Mothers are made to love their children, not judge them. That's why we are here. So if you please, leave that task to us."

She started to reply, but he halted her. "Madam, I've heard every manner of excuse you could imagine. Every entreaty, every flight of fancy, every plea. So please, spare yourself the trouble. Spare all of us." He paused, holding up a finger to keep her from interrupting.

"I understand how difficult it is to stand by and not interfere. To hold your peace when all you want to do is speak out. What parent would not want to stand up for their beloved child?" He paused again, this time, it seemed, more for the effect.

"I'll answer that myself: none that I would care to know. Which is why we suggest you leave the room during the examination. It makes it so much easier and less burdensome. For all concerned."

She had no intention of leaving and told him so, taking care to thank him for his thoughtfulness.

He studied her, as if deciding whether to force the issue. After a moment he shrugged.

"Suit yourself. Now please, the boy."

Instead, she reached into her dress and drew out the purse of coins. It was warm from contact with her skin. She offered it to Dr. Valid, who made no move to take it.

"You don't believe me," he said wearily. "They never do."

It was Crisp, eventually, who took it from her. He loosened its strings, peered inside, then passed it on to Valid for his inspection.

"Quite light," the doctor observed, juggling it in his palm. "But I'm sure you don't mean to measure your son's worth in money. Nor do we." He returned the purse to Crisp, who pocketed it. "No more delays now, or I'll get cross. If you please, the boy."

"Take me instead," she said.

"Excuse me?"

"I'll be a subject for your experiments."

He raised an eyebrow. "Mine?"

"The ones they do in Rampart."

He considered for a moment. "Come here. Let me look at you."

Steeling herself, she went to him, and he perused her. He had her lift her arms, turn, bend at the waist, straighten. At his command she took down her hair, exposing the raised hump of her skull. He eyed this without comment, then questioned her.

"Do you know how unlikely it is your son will pass the test? How minimal the chances are he has the gift?"

"He doesn't," she told him bluntly.

"Then you have nothing to worry about."

"You took my first."

"Even less likely then."

This wasn't true, but even if it were, any likelihood at all was too much of one. "Did I pass your test? That's all I need to know. Can I assume we have a deal?"

"It makes no sense. Why leave him without his mother? Why abandon him when you yourself say there's no need?"

"Do you have children, Doctor?"

That, he said, was immaterial.

She thought not. "I don't want him subjected to this procedure. This test. I don't want him humiliated in any way."

He frowned, then shook his head, looking disappointed. "You people baffle me. Do you have any idea of a healer's worth? How much good they do? How essential they are? In Gode the gift means nothing and never will, but in the world outside it's one of the most precious things there is."

"And the Drain?"

"Enough," said Valid. "Bring the boy to me."

She eyed him and then the Enforcer, who in turn was eying her, ready, she was sure, to intervene at a moment's notice. She could beg them but sensed that that would only make things worse. Other, more extreme measures crossed her mind, but wisely, she rejected them. She hated these people but had no choice. She would have to trust the odds, along with what she and her husband had done to influence them.

She called her son. Almost instantly he appeared, followed by his father, who towered over him. To his mother's eye Payne seemed not quite there. His father bent down and whispered something in his ear, then straightened up and with a hand planted on his shoulder, guided him across the room.

Valid watched impassively, observing the boy. When he halted an arm's length away, he bid him come nearer. But before Payne could obey, his father stepped in front of him. Reaching in a pocket, he announced he had a business proposition.

Instantly, Lieutenant Crisp was on him. He grabbed his hand and twisted it behind his back. Then he patted him down for a weapon. What he found instead was a pouch of precious and semiprecious stones.

Valid was impressed. "Such largesse. And they say Grotesques do not know how to treat their guests. Stand back, Lieutenant. Give the man room to breathe."

Crisp did as he was told, allowing Payne's father to empty out the pouch. The stones, for which he'd pawned his wedding ring and everything else remotely of value to him, filled the broad cup of his hand. He offered them to Valid in exchange for the life of his son.

Valid scowled. "His life? I don't traffic in life. Human, tesque or otherwise. You offend me."

"His freedom then."

"Now that's different. Freedom, sadly, can be bought and sold. Bribery, however, is unlawful." He made a motion with his hand. "Put away your jewels. Buy something for your wife. And take heart. As I explained to her, the odds are with you. Decidedly."

So saying, he returned his attention to Payne. "Now, young man. You see how much your parents love you. I'm sure you're worth every ounce. Come closer so that I may judge for myself."

Payne did as he was told, maintaining his composure as best he could. The thorns that his father had collected and methodically pricked him with that morning helped. In addition to further muting whatever incipient healing power he might possess, they had a distancing effect on his mind. Everything that was happening to him seemed faraway, as if it were happening to someone else.

Valid looked into his face, noting that his pupils, despite the room's dimness, were constricted, then felt his pulse and scowled. To Payne's father he said, "Why do this thing? Did you think I wouldn't notice? Do I look like a novice to you?"

From a pocket he produced a small dark vial, stoppered with a bulb-topped dropper. Unscrewing it, he sucked up a dropper full of the vial's amber liquid, which he squirted beneath Payne's tongue.

A minute later, the drug began to take effect, counteracting the one his father had administered. Payne felt his heart speed up. The room brightened, as his pupils ballooned. The sense that he was elsewhere, in a muffled and protected world, disappeared. The skin of his back began to tingle where his father had pricked him with the thorns. He felt warm, then cold, and broke into a sweat.

Valid seemed to take his reaction for fear, which was a common, if not universal, response to the examination, and he had ready words of reassurance. They were not there to hurt him or anyone. If he'd heard that, then what he'd heard was wrong. The test was quick and it was painless. Many, in fact, found it pleasurable.

Payne glanced at his father, whose face was stony and controlled, then back at Valid. He was frightened, but truth be told, a little curious about this test. He didn't want to pass, of course, but he also didn't want to fail.

"Anything else?" Valid asked impatiently, addressing Payne's parents. "No? Then with your permission we'll proceed."

Rising from his chair, he extended a hand to Unerrant Sorly and helped her to her feet. She was very old, and once she pushed back her cowl to reveal her face, it was clear that she was also very ill. Her eyes were dull and sunken. Her skin was gray and her lips were cracked. Her tired hair lay like pale threads across the mottled cap of her scalp.

Using Valid's arm for support, she slowly shuffled forward, until she stood in front of Payne. She touched his face, felt the sheen of sweat across his protuberant forehead, peered into his eyes.

"Don't be afraid," she whispered, her voice as dry as leaves, her breath sour. "It's just a test. A little probe. Nothing deep or harmful. We would never hurt a child."

She smiled a toothless smile, which did little to allay Payne's apprehension. He'd been told by his parents what to expect, but nothing had quite prepared him for this woman.

She was an Unerrant, and she looked to be dying because, in fact, she was. Perennially dying, poised forever on the brink. All her systems were in a state of failure, which made her the perfect tool for the examiners, the supreme diagnostician. She was a magnet for healing energy, drawn to it like north to south, like full to empty, like yes to no. It was said that Unerrants recognized immediately when someone had the power to heal, overt or covert or incipient, for they were attracted to its merest whisper, awake to its most subtle, hidden nuance, often long before the one who was gifted knew.

Hunched at the waist, she stood arm to arm beside Payne and laced her fingers into his, pressing their palms together with surprising tenacity and strength. Valid then wrapped a broad cloth around their forearms. Payne felt a little tingle in his skin but nothing more. His os melior, notably, felt as lifeless and inert as stone.

He threw a glance at his father, then his mother. Their faces were drawn and tense, and to their palpable relief he shook his head.

Valid saw the exchange and shrugged. He was a philosophic man. The world needed healers, but he did not relish tearing children from their families. It was grim work, and he looked forward to the day when their research bore fruit, for then there would be a far greater supply of what was now a rare and precious commodity. There would be no need to steal an apple when the trees were everywhere, and every tree was ripe with fruit.

He unwrapped the cloth, folded it and put it away. He helped himself to one last piece of cake, then made his way to the door.

Where he paused. Unerrant Sorly had not followed him. Unerrant Sorly, in fact, had not let go of Payne.

Her eyes were gleaming. Her face had taken on a blissful, rapturous look.

Valid chided himself for being hasty. Normally, she was quicker to let him know. Then again, normally she did not get quite so swept away as, clearly, she was now.

He had trouble unpeeling her fingers. She swatted at him with her free hand, which was also unusual behavior, and in sympathy he gave her a few minutes more. At length, though, it was time to end the liaison, and he was forced to separate her from the boy. He handed her to Crisp, who, against her wishes, escorted her to the door.

Payne was confused and frightened. He had felt something he had never felt before. From a distance he heard the doctor tell him to pack his things and hug his parents and say good-bye. His father's face was ashen. His mother had crumpled into tears. He was going on a journey, the doctor said, a lifelong journey, full of deeds of healing and service.

PANNUS

ONE

ive years later, long on lessons but short on experience, he
received his first assignment, the Pannus Mining Company,
which shipped him immediately to its Great North Mine. Remote and
isolated, the mine had been in continuous operation for more than a
hundred years. It was legendary for its wealth of ore, having yielded
trainload upon trainload of high-grade copper and of late, other, more
exotic minerals. Legendary, too, for the breed of miner it attracted:
hard-bitten, self-sufficient, able to withstand the long, harsh winters,
the lack of amenities, the isolation. Taciturn men who favored the
company of other men or no one. Payne's job was to keep them healthy
enough to work. In its wisdom the Pannus Corporation kept the healer
tours of duty brief. His was slated for three years.

The trip to the mine took a week by rail. He was the sole tesque
in a four-car passenger train filled with miners. It was summer, and
traffic to and from the mine was at its peak. The rails were clear, the

days were long, and miners, being miners, were on the move. There was not a lot of talk among the men; it was a point of pride to look and act reserved. But beneath the surface there was an undercurrent of excitement. A new mine, whatever its record or reputation, always conjured the hope of being better than the last.

For the first few days they traveled through a prairie with tall grass as thick as fur, bleached pale yellow by the sun and swept by gusts of wind. Payne had never seen such grass before, nor such a plain. There seemed no end to it, no limit; it stretched as far as the eye could see in all directions. Overhead, the summer sun seemed suspended in an equally vast sky. It hovered up above like a kiting bird, and when it neared the horizon, it hovered there as well, as though afraid to set and put an end to the day. And it rarely did set, and rarely rose: as they drew farther and farther north, the days grew longer and longer. Nights were brief and never fully dark. Payne found it hard to sleep in the insubstantial, gauzy light.

One day passed, and then another, and another. The landscape didn't vary, mile after mile of the same pan-flat prairie and cloudless sky. Before long, he lost track of time and distance. In dreams and half-dreams he imagined that he would never reach his destination, that the longer he traveled, the longer he would have to travel. When he searched the faces of his fellow passengers for someone who might share this peculiar and troubling thought, all he saw is what he usually saw when their eyes happened to meet: indifference.

They weren't interested in him and kept their distance, which was a human habit when it came to tesques. It was a pity, he thought, and a wasted opportunity, for humans were notoriously ignorant of his kind. They were also, it was said (and he was taught), notoriously fragile creatures, at heart soft but on the surface guarded and hard to get to know. Which was also a pity, because he was interested in learning more about them. And he could have used the company, for it was a long journey to endure alone.

Then one day there was a break in the monotony. Something new on the horizon, a line of darker color set off against the flaxen pallor of the grass. It stretched north to south a great distance, and steadily widened, like ink spreading through cotton, broadening from a narrow stripe into a band and then a sheet. The color of the plain seemed to change before he saw what caused the change, before he even could discern movement. Ort, someone said, and then the train's brakes squealed, and everyone in the car lurched forward, then back against their seats. The herd was still a quarter mile away when the train ground to a halt. Payne pressed his face against the glass in great excitement as the tide of near-legendary animals approached.

Ochre-colored and glossy-skinned, with shaggy hair, blunt noses and rounded heads, ort walked on two stout legs, with a third, thinner and more agile limb behind them. They were only slightly taller than the tallest grass, and like a flock of birds or school of fish seemed to travel as a single entity, veering one way then the next for no discernible reason but always in the same general direction. They reached the train, engulfed it, and with no more sound than that of bodies brushing grass, moved on. There were thousands of them, hundreds of thousands; Payne tried to keep his eye on one, any one, to study it, but couldn't. They were so similar to one another and so numerous, his eye kept flicking from one to the next, and it occurred to him that this might be a survival mechanism, that a predator, if there were such a thing for ort, might have the same difficulty singling one out. Indeed, there was no word in the language for a single ort, no distinction made between one and many. As far as anyone had observed, the animals did everything together, moved and ate and bathed and slept and mated in large, often enormous, throngs. They lived together and they also died together, a fact that the Pannus Corporation had been quick to notice but slow to absorb, slow to assimilate and fully comprehend. The early trains, on encountering a herd, plowed right through it, the soft, pliant creatures no match for the impatient wheels and hard, pointed prows of the locomotives. The conductors might have stopped had there not been a timetable to keep and ore to deliver. Besides, an animal with any brain at all should have known the meaning of danger or at least known enough to learn from its mistakes. It was a pity, but not to be helped, for industry required a wide berth, and progress, as everybody agreed, had a mind of its own.

Thing was, when one ort died, others came forward. If blood happened to be spilled, and blood was, much blood, many ort came to investigate. More of them died, which in turn drew still more, until the tracks were covered with the creatures, sometimes for a mile ahead, milling, cooing, lowing, and doing that strange thing that ort did with their third appendage.

Blocked and surrounded, the trains could not proceed. Victims of their very speed and doggedness, they foundered.

It was a scary business, for conductors, engineers and passengers alike. Here they were, awash in a sea of animals with globelike, rather human-looking faces, that had every reason to be peeved and out of sorts, every reason, if so inclined, to seek revenge. But ort were not vengeful creatures, or if they were, it took a form beyond what humans understood. All they wanted, it seemed, was to stand with their dead, mingle with them and perhaps prevent further killing. At any rate, the trains could not move until they dispersed. Later trains carried bounty hunters to shoot the animals, which they did by the hundreds, by the thousands. But this did nothing to diminish the herds; in fact it seemed to have the opposite effect of increasing them, exponentially, until the plains—and, more to the point, the railroad cutting through them—were literally overrun with ort. It seemed that the death of even a modest number of animals had a profound effect on the entire herd, far and near, transforming all save a tiny portion into breeding females. Simultaneously, it shortened the gestation period and dramatically increased the number of offspring, sending the birth rate soaring. The hunters could not keep up. The hunters, it turned out, were their own worst enemies.

So now there were no hunters. There was no killing, no carnage, no barreling of train through flesh. The conductors, upon sight of a herd of ort, would instantly cut back the throttle and apply the brakes, giving the animals room to breathe and time to pass. If it took hours (and it never took less), then it took hours. An entire day, then it took a day. Going faster only slowed things down.

The last ort crossed the tracks at dawn, and the train resumed its run. Later that day Payne caught sight of a line of hills in the distance, blue and hazy, and beyond them, higher hills. They wavered and bent in the waves of heat radiating off the grass, and when the train tracks took a lazy turn and he lost sight of them, he thought that maybe he'd been dreaming. But then he noticed a subtle change in the cadence of the wheels as they ticked along the rails—a slowing, as if they'd begun to climb a gentle grade. Trees appeared, scattered broadbeams with enormous horizontal branches, bronze-skinned arbitis, fat-trunked puzzlewoods with jigsaw bark. The land began to rise, inconspicuously at first, but soon audaciously. Hills swept up on either side of them, rolling into one another like waves of water, like muscles. Some were cut by dried-up, jagged creek beds, some were smooth, some topped by rocks that looked like fists. Payne had never seen such land before. Desert born and bred, schooled like a monk, he had rarely seen a tree.

All day long they climbed, and all through the brief and ersatz night, and for once Payne was happy with the partial darkness, the ever-present twilight glow. Too excited to sleep, and too enchanted, he stared out the window, watching the land soar up around him and the trees multiply.

By dawn they were encased in a forest, stands of fir and pine so dense they kept the ground perennially in shade. Paralleling the tracks was a river, another miracle that Payne had never seen. Such an extravagance of water. In Gode the only riverbeds were dry ones and the only water at the bottom of deep wells.

After a while, the train began to labor as the grade steepened. The river dropped away into a slotted canyon, and the trees all at once seemed to be leaning forward, as if into a stiff wind.

Without warning the car was plunged into a thick and total darkness. It was a shock, and at first Payne thought that something dreadful had gone wrong. He was frightened, and apparently some of the other men were, too. But then he heard the word "tunnel," and shortly after that, they emerged to light and level ground.

Now the train seemed bent on reaching its destination without delay. It surged forward, and the stout trees that lined the tracks whipped past. Some of the miners began to gather their belongings. Payne had only one small bag, and he took it down from the overhead rack and held it in his lap.

An hour later the train slowed and with a long, tired squeal of its brakes, accompanied by the shifting creak of heavy metal, came to a grinding halt. On one side of them stood a weathered wooden platform, and beyond it, a wide expanse of flat, cleared land. Here, enormous trucks were busy digging, scooping, pushing, scraping and loading. Some had big buckets in their fronts; some, thick steel plates; some, massive jaws; some, interlocking tusklike pincers. They moved on gigantic spiked metal wheels or on equally gigantic treads. Mounds of rock, some the size of small hills, were being bullied into shape. A pair of cranes, looming over these hills hungrily, like their namesakes, were simultaneously disassembling them, bucketful by huge bucketful, transferring the rock to empty hopper cars. Other, fully laden cars were being coupled to an engine. The yard was the source of a symphony of blaring, belching, rasping, thunderous noise. The air above it was smeared with smoke and dust. For a hundred yards in every direction the ground trembled.

One by one the miners exited, congregating loosely on the platform. A man appeared and led them down a broad dirt road that gradually climbed and circled above the yard, then disappeared behind a hill. Payne followed, keeping to the rear of the group. After a week of travel he was happy to be outside, and he slowed, enjoying the freshness of the air. The sun beat down on him, and he enjoyed this, too. It was a whole new world here, and despite his lowly position, he considered himself a lucky man.

The road wound around the hill, then forked, the right branch leading northward through a copse of fir and spruce, the left leveling off to become the main street of the camp proper. At the fork Payne got his first glimpse of Pannus Mountain. It took his breath away.

It was immense, shoulder after shoulder of bare-knuckled rock sweeping upward to a dome-shaped summit capped with snow. The rock was mostly gray, and it was fissured into enormous slabs and faces, which were separated by vertical chutes and chimneys, some of which looked to be hundreds of feet tall. Cliffs gave way to ledges, which gave way to new and higher cliffs. It seemed, in fact, that this one mountain was made of many mountains. He had never seen a thing so massive or so big.

Or so oddly shaped. One whole face of it looked all wrong—scooped out and craterous and deformed, as though some mythic bird as mighty as the mountain itself had come and taken an enormous bite of it. Or as if the mountain had been eviscerated and then imploded on itself, which, in a sense, is what had happened. It had been mined since ancient times, but in the century since Pannus had lain claim to it, the mining had accelerated: millions upon millions of tons of rock had been excavated from the mountain. Beneath the surface it was honeycombed with tunnels, riddled with them, in some places riddled rotten. In parts of its upper reaches it had been almost entirely hollowed out and allowed to cave in upon itself. Which is why it looked so lopsided and so strange. It was an awesome sight, this vast, transfigured monolith. Payne had never felt so tiny. Or so in the presence of something beyond his powers of expression. He'd seen a forest, he'd seen a river, and now he'd seen a mountain. Life would never be the same.

By the time he started up again, the men were out of sight, and he made his way into the camp alone. The first building that he came to was some kind of storage shed, the next, what appeared to be a bunkhouse. Across from it a man was sitting on a porch, feet resting on a rail, watching him. Payne smiled and crossed the road to introduce himself and ask directions. The man regarded him for quite a while before eventually pointing the way.

Ten minutes later, he stood in front of the mine and camp headquarters, a solid-looking wooden building with painted siding and an overhanging A-frame roof. A black dog lounging in the shadows jumped up and barked as he approached. The door to the building swung open, and a man in overalls came out. He halted when he saw Payne, looked him up and down, spat in the dirt, then motioned with his thumb for him to go in, he was expected.

The door to the building was ajar, but Payne took no liberties; despite what he'd been told, he knocked. A rig nearby was kicking up a racket, and he could barely hear the sound of his own knuckles. He knocked louder, to no response, and after waiting for what seemed a polite amount of time, he entered.

The site boss, a lanky man with short-cropped salt-and-pepper hair, was looking out a window on the far side of the room, his face averted, his back to the door. There were several beat-up chairs on the uneven wooden floor, small casement windows in all the walls, a desk, and an ancient potbellied stove in one corner. Payne couldn't tell if the man knew he was there and cleared his throat to announce his presence.

The boss didn't turn. "Have a seat."

Payne did as he was told.

"Nice trip?"

He nodded, then realized he would have to speak. "Yes. Very interesting."

"Too damn long if you ask me." His attention was fixed on something in the distance. "What the hell?" He leaned forward as if to get a better look, swore, then wheeled around and with a scowl rushed out of the room. Ten minutes later he was back. "Morons. You'd think they see a line go all goofy like that they'd know to cut the switch."

He looked to be about sixty. Gray eyes, lined and weathered face, stubbled chin, with a prominent, beak-shaped gouge in one temple that might have come from a bird of prey but more likely was from a rock.

"Bunch of clowns. I'm too old for this. Tell me you're not a clown."

"No, sir."

"So what's your story?"

"My story?"

The boss grumbled something, evidently still displeased, and continued glaring out the window. At length the tension eased off his face and, satisfied, it seemed, that things were finally under control, or at least as much under control as he could hope for, he took a seat behind his desk and turned his attention to Payne.

"So you're the new healer."

"Yes, sir."

"You look too young to be a healer."

Payne did not reply.

"You ever worked before?"

He shook his head.

The boss shook his. "That's great. And I don't suppose you've ever been in a mine before."

"No, sir. But I've read what I could. I've studied them."

"You've studied them."

"Yes, sir."

His face sagged, as if punctured. "What's your name, son?"

"Payne."

"Well, Payne, let me tell you something. *I've* studied mines, forty years' worth, the last twenty here at Pannus. Inside out, top to bottom, hardrock mining. What you've done, I wouldn't know what to call it, except I wouldn't call it studying. You go down in the hole, that's studying. You set timber and work the face, that's studying. You get trapped behind a wall of rock and wonder if they'll get to you in time, that's some real close studying." He paused, as if remembering something. "Lucky for you, mucking rock's not why you're here. That's the last thing I want you doing. Your job's to keep my men fit to work. You do that, everybody's happy. You don't, we're not."

"I will," said Payne.

"That's good. Then we understand each other."

He lifted a paper from his desk and started reading it. Half a minute later he looked up. "Is there something else?"

Payne was so thirsty for conversation that he wanted there to be, but he couldn't think of anything.

The boss regarded him, not unsympathetically. "Get settled in. I'll send someone to show you around. You start work tomorrow."

Payne nodded, stood, and was halfway out the door when the man's voice stopped him. "They really have books about what we do?"

"A few."

"Any good?"

At this stage Payne had little to compare them to. "Sure. I guess. Kind of dry. But interesting."

"They should talk to me. I've seen things you wouldn't believe."

He made a little noise then shook his head at the wonder of it all, marveling, it seemed, at the breadth and richness of his own experience. In his callused hands and lined, scarred face lay the accumulation of a lifetime's work, the triumphs and the tragedies, the friendships gained and lost, the daily grind along with the crazy, the unheard-of, the un- expected, and the unexplained.

"You say it's dry, but there's nothing dry about it. Mining's wet and dangerous and dirty work. Brings out the worst in some, the best in others. One thing I can tell you though: it's a helluva way to make a living."

Payne found his quarters, which were contiguous to the healing center, a fifteen-minute walk away. Together, they occupied a building near the adit, the main entrance to the mine. The quarters were small, which, given the paucity of his belongings, was not a privation. The healing center was considerably larger. It housed two chairs, a standard examining table, one free-standing metal cabinet, and several shelves of instruments and supplies. At the back of the center behind a narrow door was the disposal chamber, and between it and the main room, separated by a curtain, the healing bed.

It was an old and lumpy bed that had seen a lot of use. The ticking was shiny with wear, and a good part of the stuffing was missing. Most patients, and probably quite a few healers, would have turned their noses up at such a bed. But to Payne it was a thing of beauty. He got a shiver down his spine at the sight of it. A healer healed in many different ways, but never more than when he got to use the bed.

He touched it, tentatively at first, almost tenderly, running his hand along its surface, feeling the worn-out fabric and the dips and crests beneath it, wondering what healer had lain on it before him and whether he would measure up. He sat on it, then gave in and lay completely down. It felt strange. The bed was molded to another body. He shifted around, trying to get comfortable, then closed his eyes. Healing depended on being focused and relaxed, but he felt just the opposite. No matter: for now his mind could race and his heart beat wildly. His imagination could soar a million miles above the ground. There would be plenty of time later to reel it in and do what he was trained to do. The bed was shaped to someone else, but soon it would be shaped to him.

There was a connecting door from the center to his quarters, and he returned, waiting for someone to come and escort him around. An hour passed, then another, and assuming he'd been forgotten, he decided to have a look for himself. The nearest building to his was large and quonset-shaped and sat just outside the adit. It seemed vacant, and quietly, he let himself in.

It was a vast space, with a concrete floor and curving metal walls that seemed to amplify his footsteps. Bolted into the floor were rows and rows of benches. Above the benches, suspended from the ceiling, were wire cages of clothes and equipment. By the door was a large peg-board partially covered with shiny, hanging metal discs, each one embossed with a number. A changing room, he guessed, empty now but probably not for long. The air had the pungent smell of human sweat, male bodies, old socks and underwear.

Payne was male, but here he felt like an intruder. An inner voice warned him to be careful. This place had the feel of hallowed ground.

Humans fascinated him, both men and women; he had no bias when it came to gender—no preference, no prejudice. He would have liked the opportunity to treat both sexes, would have liked the variety, but men alone would do. What worried him a little, and only a little, for he was certain that with time he would adjust, was these particular men, this group of men, these miners. He feared that they were different from other human males. Rougher, tougher, more aggressive. More concentratedly male, if there were such a thing: males distilled. Males, for want of a better word, more masculine. The way they lived and worked—in close, cramped quarters and dangerous conditions far removed from other human beings—had to attract a certain kind of person, independent and able-bodied but also slightly misanthropic, he guessed, short on niceties and long on having things their way. Such a person would not take kindly to authority. As a tesque he had no authority to begin with, but as a healer he could envision a situation where he might. He would have to be very careful how and when he used it.

He lingered in the room for a while, lost in thought, which was a mistake, for he was there when the day shift ended. The first miner who entered caught him by surprise, and in short order, the rest came straggling in. Immediately, he retreated to the door, apologizing for being where he shouldn't be. A few of the men glanced at him, but no one seemed particularly upset, or even very interested. They were too busy with other things, principally being done with work. Relief at that seemed foremost on their minds. They could have been surrounded by a pack of wolves, they wouldn't have cared. They were hungry, they were tired and they were dirty, but more than anything, they were done.

Hard hats were the first things off, then the numbered lamps attached to the hats, then safety belts. Earplugs, safety glasses and gloves came next. Lastly came the steel-toed rubber boots, caked with mud and wet inside with sweat. They stowed the gear in the overhead wire baskets, all the while talking. Conversations were centered on the mine and in particular the shift that had just ended. Water was rising in one of the drifts. A loaded skip had jumped the tracks at Bustem's Curve again—they shook their heads at that, fed up with the company's refusal to correct the obvious problem, and cracked rueful jokes at such shortsightedness, stinginess and stupidity. And the ratty rock on Level 7, and the muck pile waiting down on 8—the swing crew was going to love having to deal with that. And the supe who had caught a bunch of them taking an early break. . . . The stories went on, as individually and in groups they left the building, pausing at the pegboard to brass out and have a word or two with the incoming crew, who to a man did not look happy. There were no illusions about the work. There was camaraderie, but at the start of a shift, going down into the hole, it was always subdued. Coming out eight hours later at shift's end, whether into day or night, sunny skies or storm, it was dependably more lively.

Payne slipped out with the last of the outgoing shift, returning to his quarters where, to his chagrin, he found a man waiting at the door: his escort, he assumed, a huge man, hugely muscled, broad at the shoulders, with a neck like a broadbeam stump. Payne apologized at having kept him waiting and in the same breath defended himself, explaining that he himself had waited for a long time before leaving. And he'd only gone a short distance and seen a little bit, one building to be precise. No harm done.

The man just looked at him, flat-faced and unresponsive, as though he either didn't understand or didn't care, until at length Payne fell silent. In his haste to explain himself he'd failed to notice certain key details about the man. His face was streaked with dirt, which meant he'd probably just come off shift and was therefore unlikely to be the escort he'd been expecting. More to the point, his left pant leg was torn. It was also stained with something dark and shiny.

Payne sucked in his breath, feeling incredibly stupid as it dawned on him what this was.

"You're hurt," he said.

The man would not admit it. Payne offered his shoulder as a crutch to get him into the healing center, but the man refused his help. Stoically, he limped inside under his own power. He had to duck to clear his head.

Payne guided him to the examining table, trying hard not to betray his nervousness and excitement. He'd already made a number of mistakes, and he doubted that the man would tolerate many more.

He began by asking what had happened.

The miner grunted.

"Did you fall?"

"Got slabbed." He had that human way of talking to a tesque: curt, dismissive, as though it were an imposition or, worse, a sign of weakness to have to speak at all.

Gingerly, Payne rolled up his pant cuff to expose the wound. "How exactly? Were you working?"

"How 'bout you just fix it," the miner snapped.

But Payne was in no hurry. The cut had stopped bleeding, and there was no immediate danger. He wanted to savor the moment and, if possible, find out more about what had caused the injury. It was his first case, his very first, and he intended to milk it for everything he could.

Careless boy. How quickly he forgot his resolution of just an hour before to be careful with these men. And his lessons, rule number twelve, for example: be prompt in attention, and in healing, be swift. And rule number thirteen, its corollary: avoid unnecessary conversation. Humans wanted treatment, not friendship. They wanted a quick fix, a shot, an ointment or a pill. If such a remedy existed, no words were necessary. And if it didn't, it was unlikely that words would help.

But Payne thought differently, Payne knew better, Payne the callow and the headstrong had ideas of his own. He liked to hear a human speak, had a weakness for the human voice the way that other people had a weakness for the sound of running water. And along with that, he had this notion—this strange, presumptuous notion—that the more he knew, the more he could help. Starry-eyed, idealistic child, he thought that, given the opportunity, humans—and especially humans in need—would want to talk to him.

"Have you ever hurt yourself before?" he asked.

The man, who'd been looking at his leg, slowly transferred his look to Payne.

Who obliviously pressed on. "You know. Scrapes. Injuries. Broken bones."

The man's eyes narrowed. He could have crushed Payne if he had the notion. Fleetingly, it appeared he did.

"What's your problem?"

"I was just thinking that maybe we can keep this from happening again."

It was a tactless comment. Human or not, the man had cause for offense.

"You afraid of blood, tesque?"

Payne stiffened. "No," he answered softly, registering the threat.

"Good. So how 'bout you shut your mouth and do your job."

Even stones can learn to hear, and obediently, Payne bent to the task at hand. The sight of blood and damaged tissue, and the prospect of healing it, helped to quiet the self-reproval at mishandling his first patient, along with the humiliation of being put in his place. There was beauty in the way the clot had formed, beauty in the scarlet crust and the blush of erythema. The surrounding tissue was already warm with all the fluid flowing in to heal the wound. There was beauty in this too, beauty in each and every aspect of the healing process. Even the most obnoxious human had a beauty when he stood before his healer naked and exposed.

☙☙☙

Payne never got the tour that he was promised, but over time and by necessity he found his own way around the camp. It was more a small town, really, with named streets and numbered houses, a sewage system, a recreation hall, a modest house of worship, two saloons, a playing field, and a basic grocery store. Some of the men liked to cook, and a few hunted. Most, though, ate together in the large, company-sponsored mess hall. On the north side of the mountain, across a broad saddle and reached by rail, was the Two Prime operation, a secondary mine nearly as extensive as the primary one, with its own adit, its own dry, and its own healing center. The miners were split between the two operations and worked around the clock. At any given time there were close to a thousand of them underground. Hoistmen, boilermen, mechanics, skip operators and sorters worked the surface. With more or less proficiency (more, when everything was running smoothly; less, when the inevitable equipment breakdowns and cave-ins interfered) the ore kept moving day and night, a point of pride with the Pannus Corporation. All told, the mine and its ancillary operations fed the mouths of some three thousand men.

In the early days there had been animals in the mine as well as humans. Before the advent of skips and conveyors to transport the rock, donkeys and mules did the job. Initially, they were kept corralled and stabled on the surface, but as the haulage drifts got longer and the mine got deeper, it became more efficient to house some of them underground. Typically, to save time, the animals were trussed and bundled in a canvas sack, then lowered directly down a ventilation shaft to where they were needed. Because it was so much easier lowering them than lifting them, once an animal was down, it was usually down for good. The legendary Bust Your Chops, a sturdy, placid mule known to all as Bustem, had been lowered at the tender age of two, and had spent the remainder of her thirty-odd years beneath the earth, eventually dying as she had lived, hauling ore. She was a much-loved animal and at the time of her death as blind as a bat, which didn't interfere one iota with her abilities because her eyes were in her feet. She knew every inch of every drift, and her body was interred where she had fallen, in a little cul-de-sac that bore her name.

But the mine no longer needed beasts of burden. As far as Payne could tell, the only animals left in the vicinity, not counting birds, which came and went at their own discretion, and head and body lice, which were epidemic, were dogs and rats. The former, except for a few wild escapees, were pets; the latter, to a one, vermin. An occasional bear or moose wandered into camp, and the men who hunted spoke of a variety of smaller game. On many a winter night Payne heard the howling of wolves, but as a rule they kept to the forest. Ort were rarely seen so far north.

☙☙☙

On his first day of work Payne saw no one. On his second he saw a man with an ankle sprain; on his third, one with a twisted knee. Mashed finger, puncture wound, rash—little by little the patients began to trickle in. But it was slow going, especially to someone so eager to get started. Hours and sometimes days went by when he sat in the healing room bored and alone.

And it wasn't as if there was a lack of illness. Respiratory disease was rampant, and there were other maladies less obvious and more poorly defined. But the men didn't like to ask for help. That ran contrary to their nature. And they didn't trust him, or so he imagined, which he felt was unwarranted. True, he was young and lacked experience, but he didn't lack skill, and as for youth, this simply meant he had more energy and passion for his work. Healers aged so quickly that by the time they gained experience, they frequently couldn't use it. It was an ugly and depressing paradox that a seasoned healer was in all likelihood a finished one.

Which made Payne all the more anxious to get going. Still, it was weeks before he got to use his meli. This, the pinnacle of his craft, in a real way its essence. He'd been desperate to do a meli healing since the day that he'd arrived, had thought of it and dreamt of it and had even gone so far as to map it out beforehand in his mind.

At long last, he got the chance. It was a simple problem, a pulmonary illness, First Degree. Not surprisingly, his nervousness and inexperience added layers of complexity to what otherwise would have been straightforward, making it more difficult and challenging to him. He miscalculated several basic steps, misjudged others, and on the whole, made a number of mistakes. Even so it was a thrill beyond compare. Lying down beside the miner on the healing bed, wrapping their arms together, touching skin to skin. It was strange and awkward and incredibly, impossibly, intimate. The miner almost bolted, and Payne himself was as jittery as a jump bug. But somehow he managed to get through it, systematically running through the stages, extracting and extruding and then disposing of what he'd made. Sublime it wasn't, not that first time. But it hinted of sublime. It tasted of it. And afterward he couldn't wait to do another.

The miners felt a little differently. They had an aversion to meli healing that bordered on the pathologic, beginning with the simple fact of having a problem, any problem, that needed such deep, invasive care. Having to appear before a tesque and ask for help was humiliating enough, but then actually having to touch this tesque, be bound arm to arm and skin to skin with him, and further, to then lie back and surrender up control—this was almost too much to bear. Better to suffer and grow strong from suffering than to be put in a compromising position like that.

But sometimes there was nothing to be done for it; there were problems that would not respond to any other treatment. After Payne's first success he had another, and then another. He gained a modest following, not that the miners had much choice. But bit by bit they started coming in.

Nearly every one of them had a cough, and most found a way to tolerate it, but some could not. And some went on to develop trouble deeper in their lungs. These constituted the majority of his patients; there were days when all he saw were pulmonary problems. Before long, he became something of an expert in them.

Coughs, for example. Like shades of the same color, like variations on a song, there was a wide and nuanced variety of them. Some were intermittent and spasmodic; some continuous, around the clock. Some of the coughs were productive of phlegm, which ranged from clear to murky yellow to green, from thin and watery to thick and tinged with blood. Some were moist but nonproductive, some were dry and hacking, some musical, some barking, some booming like a drum. Some men, with great effort, could control their coughs. Others could not stop for anything and would hack away until they literally spit out lung.

Many of the men were short of breath, most with exertion but a few poor souls at rest. The worst ones wheezed and panted day and night. It was hard to listen to this: one person's lack of breath seemed to make everybody breathless. To Payne it served as a reminder that no body part or system could be taken for granted. The simple act of breathing was a miracle; it was perfect, but only until it failed.

Before long, he had his wish: his days were filled with work. And now, sometimes, he questioned the wisdom of that wish. For if sickness was hard to witness, it was worse to bear. It was a curse the way the men struggled to breathe, a plague the way an illness—any illness—sapped one's strength, a scourge the way it hurt and disabled.

He hated to see people suffer and wished they didn't have to. He felt sympathy and compassion for those who did.

And yet he couldn't deny that he was grateful to be working. Nor could he deny the cold, hard fact that while health was ever the goal, illness was more interesting. It was more stimulating and challenging to the mind. It demanded the full use of all the senses. How the body fell apart was a window into how it worked, and for Payne it was also an antidote to boredom.

But antidotes are not panaceas. To the curious and restless mind they only work their magic for so long. After months of dealing with the same patients, the same coughs, the same complaints, Payne began to pray for something different, something new and unexpected, to walk through his door.

TWO

His prayer was answered in the person of a man named Covert. The night before he appeared at the healing center, the camp had been dusted with its first snow. Payne, who had never experienced snow before, was outside admiring it. The way it sparkled in the sunlight and crunched then melted into little footprint puddles beneath his feet seemed quite wonderful and magical to him. It put him in a whimsical, childlike frame of mind, which the miner's arrival quickly banished.

A jackleg driller with the arms and shoulders to prove it, Covert did not look well. He coughed like all the men, but there was something else wrong with him, too. His skin was yellow and pasty. His breath had a fishy, slightly fetid scent. And he had a funny way of walking, climbing the stairs to the healing center with a sort of prancing gait, lifting up his knees much higher than necessary, as if he couldn't trust his feet.

Payne knew enough by now to keep his questions to a minimum. Covert was more polite than most, possibly because he was also sicker. But he didn't mince words, bluntly stating that he had to get back to work as soon as possible. He needed the money. When Payne reminded him that wages lost to sickness were recoverable, and, furthermore, that he might want and even need a day or two to recuperate from the healing, he remained adamant (and to Payne's mind, unreasonable) in his determination to return at once. If he could walk, then he could work. His buddies who were in the same boat as he was did. He had one and only one question for Payne: Did he know what he was doing?

There was a time for modesty and a time for candor. At the risk of sounding boastful, Payne assured him that he did. Then he led him to the healing bed.

The smell of the man's sickness, up close, was quite strong, along with the unmistakable sense that something was seriously wrong. Part of the problem was in his lungs, but the bulk of it turned out to be in his kidneys. Payne had no trouble identifying it, and he proceeded through the subsequent stages of the healing methodically. Every healing had its differences—large or small—from every other, but this one, rooted as it was in an entirely different and more advanced disease than he had yet encountered, was more complex. But not, it turned out, more difficult to cure, not for Payne, who ended up enjoying the experience immensely. As he extruded the Concretion, a waxy chunk of darkly stippled matter, he felt proud of what he'd done. It changed shape briefly as he carried it to the disposal shaft, and he imagined that it would probably change shape again as it fell. None of them ever reappeared; they only lived, if lived was the proper word for it, a few seconds. And the shaft was nearly bottomless and its walls were polished smooth to prevent the Concretions from catching on something and lodging there.

When he returned, he helped Covert into a sitting position. The miner seemed a little dazed. Gradually, he recovered his senses.

"All done?"

Payne nodded.

Covert surprised him by thanking him. "That didn't take long."

"No. Everything went smoothly."

"You sure you did what you were supposed to?"

It was an odd thing to ask. He was a healer. No one had ever questioned him before.

"Yes. I got rid of it. You should be fine."

Covert nodded, then stretched. "I feel pretty good." Suddenly, his eyes narrowed. "You sure you did it right?"

"Yes. Everything's fine. You needn't worry."

Payne had a notion to lead him to the disposal shaft to prove it to him. Some of the Concretions took their time to fall; there was still a chance that he could get a glimpse of it. On the other hand, he hadn't met a miner yet who wanted to.

⊚⊚⊚

There was another healer at the Pannus mine, a tesque named Vecque. She had been originally assigned to care for female miners when, for a brief time, there were such things. Never more than a handful, the women had always been utterly outnumbered by their male counterparts. Shortly after Vecque arrived, there'd been an incident that led to a walkout by the female workers, followed by a week of tense negotiations. On paper they won concessions, but in practice nothing changed. When another incident occurred two months later, they lodged a protest, then departed en masse, leaving the mine in the capable, but forever after bereaved, hands of the men.

Work was never slow for Vecque. She was always busy. She'd been brought to care for women, but it was the men who seemed to most prefer a female's touch. This, despite the fact that Vecque's touch was nothing to write home about. Like her nature it was far from gentle, intentionally so, for she hated her job with a passion. She was brusque and heavy-handed with her patients; much the same, she observed, as they were with her. If she'd had the choice, she would have been anywhere but where she was. And anything but what she was, a healer.

She and Payne were as different as the sun and moon, but they were tesques, which meant they had their similarities. They were also healers, despite Vecque's wishes to the contrary, which was another thing they shared. Under other circumstances they probably never would have been together, but under the present ones they had little choice. Among the miners they would always be outsiders, and if they were to have any companionship at all, it would have to be with one another.

In point of fact, Payne liked Vecque well enough, which, given his nature, was no surprise. He liked most people. He looked up to her, although he also found her difficult. Vecque suffered Payne as she suffered most things. She had little patience with his interest in his job and his desire to do more. She had little patience in general.

"You're an idiot," she told him, not for the first time. They were in the mess hall, a vast rectangular building heated by two enormous cast-iron boilers at either end. They met when their work allowed it, usually over a meal. Vecque always chose a side or corner table if one was available, as far from the men as possible. When the hall was filled, as it was now, she had no choice. Wherever she sat, she felt surrounded.

"Why am I an idiot?" he asked.

"One, for wanting more to do. Two, for telling me."

"There's no one else to talk to."

"Make that no one, period."

Vecque was big around the middle and narrow at the head, as though the contents of her skull had been subjected to a lateral force and squeezed downward. She looked a little like a tick, and when she got in the mood that she was in, she was just as ornery.

"You've got ambition," she said. "Fine. Find something to do with it. Don't tell me. I don't want to hear about it. Frankly, it's insulting."

"How? How is it insulting?"

She went back to her food. "You figure it out."

He was afraid to make things worse, which usually didn't take much, but more afraid to have her finish her meal then walk away, leaving him alone. He was alone enough during the day. So he took a chance.

"Because I should pay more attention to you?"

This stopped her in her tracks. She raised her eyes. "Are you trying to offend me?"

He shook his head. The situation was not improving.

"Well, maybe you should try not to then."

He did. He tried. "I'm sorry for liking what I do. If it'll make a difference, I'll try to feel more like you." More disgruntled, he almost said.

And then it hit him. He felt incredibly dumb.

"The Drain? Is that it?"

She gave a shrug.

He leaned forward, alarmed. "Has it started, Vecque?"

"If it hasn't, it will soon enough."

Most healers had a good ten years, some more. Vecque had completed barely two full years of work. "Soon" seemed unnecessarily pessimistic and bleak.

"Why do you say that?"

"Because it's true."

"But not soon," he argued.

Again she shrugged, and when he asked if she had any of the symptoms, she refused to talk about it any more.

After that they ate in silence, which Payne didn't like, particularly when he felt responsible for it. He searched for something neutral to talk about, something that wouldn't set Vecque off. Sometimes he talked about his cases, and sometimes she would listen. She rarely cared enough to talk about her own.

"I saw a guy the other day. He was coughing so much he couldn't sleep."

Vecque said nothing. She seemed indifferent, but he pressed on.

"It turned out it was his bunk mate who couldn't sleep. How many times have you heard that? He's the one who made him come."

"So?"

"He wanted medicine."

"They all want medicine."

"I told him medicine would hide the cough, but I could heal it."

"I bet he loved that."

"I doubt it, but he let me do it. I convinced him."

He was proud of himself, but she was unimpressed. "You're wasting your time. They all have coughs. You heal them, they'll just get them back again."

"It's the mine," he said. "It makes them sick."

"Of course it does. But it's their choice. They could get a different job."

He conceded this. "But someone has to work the mines. And the conditions could be improved. They could be a lot better than they are."

"Could be. But that's their choice, too."

"How do you mean?"

"You been underground?"

"No. Not yet. But I want to."

"Don't bother. It's a pit. A hole. It's loud and cold and wet, and the air's so thick with dust you can barely see, much less breathe."

"How is that their choice?"

"It doesn't have to be like that. The noise, yes, but not the dust. You know those jackleg drills they use?"

He recalled Covert's massive chest and arms, and how, when he'd wrapped their forearms together on the healing bed, he'd felt puny, like a boy beside a man.

"I haven't seen one, but I know you have to be strong to use them."

"You bet you do," she said. "They're monsters. The drill operators are supposed to drill wet, which keeps the dust and dirt down by their feet where it belongs. But they do it dry. Not everybody, but all it takes is a few."

"Why do they do that?"

"Because they're trying to make themselves sick. They want to breathe that lousy air."

"I doubt that's true."

"It's true all right," said Vecque. "It's money to them. They're as abusive to themselves as they are to us. You'd think they'd be smarter than that, but you'd think wrong. That's a human for you."

"What do you mean 'it's money to them'?"

"I mean they trade their health for cash. It's the free enterprise system, that's what I mean. At our expense."

Payne still didn't understand what she was talking about, but he didn't get the chance to find out. They were interrupted by a commotion at a nearby table, where a fight was breaking out. One of the miners shoved another, the other one shoved back, and suddenly the two of them were squaring off, fists drawn.

Vecque glanced over, then back again, a smug and vindicated expression on her face. At the same time she warned Payne not to stare. If things got out of hand, if the boys actually started throwing punches, the two of them would quickly and quietly leave.

A minute later, it was over, the tension, or at least the threat of physical violence, gone. A peacemaker had emerged, separating the men, both of whose egos and reputations were thus allowed to survive intact. That's the way it usually went, said Vecque, sounding a little disappointed. Lots of posturing but never any blood.

Payne recognized one of the two fighters as his very first patient, the one he'd treated for the leg gash. He'd seen him more recently for a different reason, which he thought Vecque might find amusing. Briefly, he gave her the backstory, explaining how he'd copiously washed the wound but how little bits of rock had gotten stuck inside. Stained the man's skin all up and down the scar, tattooing him.

"Happens all the time," she said.

"He came back a few days ago."

"Sure. Wanting you to get rid of it."

"No. Actually he liked the way it looked. What he wanted was for me to touch it up and do the other leg the same. Said it reminded him of a snake. Wanted me to add a pair of fangs."

"And did you?"

Payne pulled a face. "I did not. I'm a healer, not a cosmetician."

Vecque almost laughed. "I think you lost an opportunity there, boy. I would've cut him good. Biggest, dullest scalpel I could find."

A group of miners fresh from work arrived and passed by their table. Payne got a heady whiff of them and glanced at Vecque, whom he was certain found the smell repugnant. But to him it had a different effect. It reminded him how much he liked to lie beside these men on the bed and do a meli healing, how quickly he became absorbed in the raft of physical sensations, how deeply he felt connected. It was a privilege to be allowed to touch a human, to be mandated to probe beneath their skin. In all other ways he was subordinate to them, and even this was a kind of subordination, but to him it was a rich and even joyful one.

He watched the new arrivals being greeted warmly by their friends. Drinks were passed around, and space was made for them to sit. He envied the camaraderie.

"I don't understand you, Vecque. Why do you hate them so much?"

"They hate us," was her reply. "We're ugly and misshapen and have holes in our sides where no self-respecting hole should ever be. It's unsightly. We're unseemly. I'd hate us too."

He figured this as sarcasm, although with Vecque you never could be sure. Meanwhile, his hand had unaccountably found its way to the frontal boss upside his head, the grapefruit-sized protuberance that marked him unmistakably as tesque. Unconsciously, he raked his hair to try to hide it, as if he ever could.

Watching him, Vecque smiled. "I think the question isn't why I hate them, but why you don't."

"It doesn't help to hate."

She rolled her eyes. "Look at you."

"What?"

"You're embarrassed to be seen in public."

"I'm not."

"Wake up," she said. "They think of us as animals and treat us like indentured servants. Like slaves. How would you suggest I feel?"

It was true, the part about being looked upon as animals, singled out and plucked from their families and trained to heal, then discarded when they dried up and no longer were of use. As for being slaves, there was truth to that as well. Humans had the upper hand in every aspect of healer life. Payne felt intimidated and sometimes frightened of them; at other times he simply seethed. But then there were still other moments, almost always in the healing center, when a fleeting gesture or expression revealed another side to humans, a fragile, vulnerable, approachable one. And in these moments he was drawn to them. He felt a bond. It was true they used him, but the reverse was also true. In some ineffable way the two of them were linked.

"I could help you, Vecque."

"Help me not hate them? I doubt it."

"What I mean is, I could help you feel better."

"I doubt that, too." But she was curious. "How?"

"I healed a man the other day of a kidney problem. It was fairly serious, but it wasn't hard. In fact, it was easy."

"So?"

"I could heal you."

She almost choked.

"I could."

"A meli healing?"

"Yes."

"Are you crazy?"

Strangely, he didn't feel crazy, which, in retrospect, was probably proof he was.

For Vecque it was as though the bad news that seemed constantly to dog her had just, impossibly, gotten worse. The conversation was over for her, right then. When he tried to continue, she stiff-armed him into silence.

"Enough," she said. And then, "I was wrong about you, Payne. You're not an idiot. Or not only an idiot. You're dangerous. And you're out of your mind."

❧❧❧

A few days later, he stood before the mirror in the healing center, staring at himself. He regretted what he'd said to Vecque about healing her. It was boastful and foolish, as she'd so trenchantly pointed out. As much as it upset him not to be taken seriously, she'd been right to snap at him.

What wasn't right, or at least what bothered him more, was what she'd said about his being embarrassed to be seen in public. He didn't like it, and wondered if it was true. Which is why he was looking in the mirror, hoping to find out. Hoping, actually, to convince himself it wasn't true. Out of habit, he compared himself to the men.

They were symmetric—all humans were—their features balanced, their heads and faces proportionate and beautifully arranged. Tesques, by any definition, weren't. His own head was a parody of symmetry, lopsided and ballooned out on one side, nicely smooth and rounded on the other. Vecque claimed that she was ugly. He had never thought so, but if she was, then so was he. Naturally. He was Grotesque.

Except he didn't feel grotesque, not in other ways, not in the ways that he'd been taught as a child were all the most important ones. And as far as that went, humans could sometimes be far uglier than any tesque would ever attempt to be.

It was puzzling, and it made him wonder, and all through that day, and the next one, and the next, he kept coming back to the mirror, and at the same time studying and analyzing the men who came in to be treated, comparing them to himself, himself to them, grappling for some insight, a change of perspective, a way for his eyes to see what his heart believed, that he and they were not as different as everybody claimed.

The breakthrough, when it came, surprised him. It was, in fact, a shock. He'd expected it to come from the mirror, and maybe by some roundabout route it did. But it originated in the men, in their faces and their bodies. That's where it was centered. It was as if a mist had suddenly lifted from his eyes, and he saw what he had never seen, or allowed himself to see, before.

These human beings were not symmetric, not perfectly, not the way he'd always thought they were. It stunned him when he saw it, and at first he thought it couldn't be true. But the closer he looked, the more he discovered that it was. One man had an ear that was set a little lower than the other. Another had an eye that was flecked a slightly different color than its mate. This one's eyebrow was tufted out and upturned, while the eyebrow on the opposite side lay straight and flat. Moles in all the men were scattered about at random, legs were different lengths, veins took different paths on right and left, and the testicles always hung aslant. The more Payne looked, the more a human body announced its side-to-side asymmetry. Cut it down the middle, duplicate each half, then stitch the halves back together, and the two resulting wholes would never look the same.

It was a revelation to him. He had been deceived. He had deceived himself. Was it possible that beauty was a matter of perspective? It was a scandalous idea.

But it gave him insight into a particular way the men acted when they were together, a sort of asymmetry of behavior that he'd always found perplexing. They loved to mock each other and fight each other, put down, humiliate and trick each other, and then in the blink of eye they would turn around and extend a helping hand, pick someone up, even sacrifice themselves in time of need. And considering the pure aggressive force they brought to bear on all the mountain's rock, the joules of energy they unleashed every minute of every working day, true fights were rare. Confrontations were mostly verbal, not physical. The men loved to strut and posture, which, as the one responsible for patching and sometimes sewing those who went too far and came to blows, Payne had thought a fine and useful pastime. Now he was able to see the beauty in it, too. And the verbal abuse, when it came down to it, didn't seem to bother anyone all that much. It seemed, in fact, to do the opposite: forge friendships and create a kind of unity, afford these disparate, thrown-together hardrock tramps and travelers a sense of place and status and belonging. Which is all anybody wanted, tesque or human.

中 中 中

It was summer when he'd arrived, but now the days began to shorten. Autumn came and went so fast he barely noticed, and on its heels the dog of winter settled in. Temperatures fell to levels he had not thought possible. Snow transformed the camp.

Timbers, roofs and ancient headframes, blackened by years of soot and oil, were suddenly whitewashed clean. The sloppy, mud-encrusted streets first froze and then became carpeted in a deep layer of what looked like down. Edges softened, and familiar landmarks took on unfamiliar shapes. Greens and browns and yellows turned to whites and grays. As the snowdrifts rose, buildings seemed to shrink into the ground.

Work in the mine continued unimpeded; aboveground, surface

crews were dispatched to plow the major roads and keep the rail lines clear. Payne did his part by shoveling out a path from the healing center to the street. The physical exertion was a novelty, and he liked it. In a small way the sweat and toil made him feel like the other working men.

But winter had its drawbacks. Daylight was in short supply, while nights dragged on and on. The nighttime sky, when clear, was a wonder; the stars sparkled and the constellations shone. But there was only so much stargazing a man could do before wishing for the sun, and in that far northern reach the winter sun was hardly a wish come true. It was wan and weak, about as warming as a fire of ash. And every day it seemed less willing to appear, and when it finally did, it seemed to sulk and pout instead of shine.

For much of the time there was no sun at all; dense clouds or a thick mist or falling snow obscured the sky. On windless days the snow fell in great silent sheets, as if the sky were quietly shedding its skin. But on stormy days, which were not infrequent, it rode in like a beast, howling, screeching and wailing.

The men dug in. When they weren't at work or at meals or hunkered in their cabins, they hung around the rec hall and the saloons. The playing field was plowed for sports, but as winter deepened, it was rarely used. For the most part, it was too cold to be outside. Frostbite was a constant hazard, and every few weeks it claimed at least one poor and witless soul who spent too many unplanned hours in a snowdrift on his way home from one of the saloons.

But there was a group of miners, about sixty in number, that routinely braved the elements. Once a week they assembled near the mess hall and, bundled in their greatcoats, mittens and wool-lined caps, took off at a bracing jog for parts unknown. Payne sometimes watched them pass, and one day during a lull in work, he decided to follow them.

It was the first clear day after two stormy ones, and bitterly cold. He pulled his hat down and his scarf up until he had only a slit of watery eye exposed. The men were headed out of camp on the road that swung down past the staging yard. He couldn't keep up with them and didn't try, staying out of sight a safe and respectful distance behind them.

Below the yard was the playing field, which seemed their destination. It sat on a sill of roughly level ground under a thick base of old snow and a foot or more of fresh powder. Surrounding it on two sides was forest, and at one end was an equipment shed, where Payne halted. There were long and tapered icicles hanging from the shed's roof that reminded him of canine teeth. He thought of the wolves that he'd been hearing lately and fancied that these were nature's echo of their fangs.

The miners were making their way around the field, kicking up snow. A few jogged briskly, but most plowed slowly and deliberately along, huffing and puffing from the effort. Payne recognized Covert among the front-runners, pleased to see he had his health back. The others seemed to have less energy, and most were strangers to him.

They took another lap around the field, picking up the pace a little; then all at once they stopped. They were close enough for him to hear their panting and to see their breaths condense and cloud the air. Together, as though scripted, each man reached into his pocket and pulled out a clear glass jar and some sort of wooden scraper, comb-shaped but without teeth. The scraper went in the jar, and the jar was then placed upright in the snow. Then, to Payne's astonishment, the men disrobed.

Hats and mittens were followed by coats and shirts. Using these to stand on, boots and socks came next, then pants and long underwear. Some of the men went so far as to remove everything.

Payne pressed himself against the back wall of the shed, quite certain that he shouldn't be seen but equally certain that he wasn't going to miss this. Such tender bodies! Fat and thin, hairy and hairless, all pink and mottled and glistening with sweat from their run. Within a minute the sweat froze, coating their skins in a layer of rime. It had a faintly greenish tint to it, which was odd, for frozen sweat was ice and should have been a frosty white. Or better still, thought Payne, no color at all, no frost to begin with, for to be naked in this cold was madness.

But this madness seemed to have a purpose, for as soon as they were covered in their coats of ice, the men bent down and picked up their toothless combs and began to scrape it off, building up little piles on the edge of the scraper, which they then carefully scraped into the jars. They were thorough and meticulous in their collection: not a single inch of their suits of frost was left untouched. For areas they couldn't reach, a partner helped them.

It was over quickly. The men obviously had done this many times before. And what exactly was it they were doing? Payne wondered. Some sort of bonding ritual? A rite of passage? A bizarre new sport? By now he knew a thing or two about humans, but he'd never seen or heard of this. It was a mystery, as baffling as no doubt it was profound.

Once they had their clothes back on, they slowly left the field, carrying their jars with great care, some in their pockets, some in the crooks of their arms. Most of the jars were about half-filled with the pale green ice. There was no running now, no jostling in the line, no jogging. They were more like weary monks, plodding homeward. At one point the sun happened to strike a number of the jars, kindling them with an emerald glow, and then it seemed that they were carrying lanterns.

Their path from the field took them by the shed, and it didn't take long for Payne to realize his danger. He'd read stories of what happened to people who stumbled onto secret rituals or rites. How they were flayed alive and had their tongues cut out and were hung from trees and disemboweled, and not necessarily in that order.

Unfortunately, there was nowhere to hide, so he did the only thing he could think of, quickly retracing his steps up the snowbound road, then turning around and pretending to be just arriving. Whether it fooled anyone, he never knew. The men didn't seem to care about him one way or the other. All save one.

Covert halted in his tracks when he saw him.

Payne responded with a timid smile. This was a man he liked, more courteous than most, a man whom he'd done well for. His smile, however, was not returned. Covert waited for the other men to pass, then made his way over.

Payne welcomed him. "It's good to see you. You look better."

But Covert's face was dark with anger. He shook his jar in Payne's face. "Look at this! Look at what you done!"

Like the other jars his was half-filled, but the contents, instead of being a pale green, were opalescent. As they should have been, thought Payne.

"I don't understand."

"You said you'd do me right. That's what you said. But look. Look." Covert could barely control himself. "Three years. Three long years, that's what it took me. Now look what you done."

"You were sick," said Payne. "I healed you."

"You took what was mine is what you did. You robbed me." He sounded so distraught. "Never trust a healer. That's what they say, and now I know why."

He held up the jar, gazing at it with a kind of longing, then hurled it against a tree, where it shattered. He started back up the hill, but after a few steps stopped. "I've got a memory, healer. Being ignorant's no excuse. I owe you one."

৯৯৯

That night Payne had a dream. Or part dream, for part of it he was sure had happened. He was back in Gode. His brother Wyn was walking down a dusty road to join up with his friends. It was nighttime, and Payne was tagging along behind him. Wyn kept telling him to get lost, but Payne kept pestering him, until finally Wyn gave up and said fine, do what you want, you will anyway, but don't blame me if something happens, you're on your own, don't look to me for help. Which is how it often went. They rounded a corner and came into an open space, a field outside of town, flat and empty. Wyn's friends were waiting for him, five or six of them, all boys, all dressed in the hooded robes that grown-ups wore on special occasions. The moon was out, and as soon as Wyn joined them, they took off their robes and dropped them on the ground. And then they started dancing in the moonlight, naked.

It was a funny dance, and they were goofing around and clowning it up, but then from somewhere a drum began to beat, and they formed a circle and started twisting their heads and stretching out their necks and presenting them to one another, and darting their tongues in and out and hissing. Payne sat outside the circle, mesmerized and a little frightened. He had never seen this dance before. None of the boys had, though every single one of them had heard of it. The Viper Dance was infamous. More than a century before it had spawned riots and was, some claimed, responsible for the uprising of '09. Ever since that time, it had been banned. This was how the boys imagined it, what they thought it might or should be.

One of them detached himself from the circle and sauntered over to Payne. He was a mean boy, one of Wyn's friends Payne didn't like, a bully. He pulled Payne to his feet, and then he somehow got his clothes off, and before he knew it, Payne was dancing naked like the others. He was scared to death but couldn't stop, and he kept looking to Wyn for help. Wyn glanced at him and made a face as if to say "I told you so," then looked away. The mean boy grinned at this, and at Payne's uneasiness, and he made the hissing sound and flicked out his tongue and thrust his meli closer. Payne danced on helplessly. His throat was choked with dust, and he could barely breathe. And then, in horror, he watched the boy snake out his arm and thrust a finger toward his meli.

Desperately, he tried to wake up, and he did, only to discover that the same thing kept happening, the waking was a dream, too. He tried to cry out but had no voice. Then all at once Wyn was at his side.

He shoved the boy away, and backed him down. Then he helped his little brother get his clothes on. He was gentle and comforting, not gruff as he sometimes could be. He threw an arm around Payne's shoulder, and Payne huddled in its shelter, shaken but safe. He adored his brother. He felt like boasting as they walked away. Who but Wyn could have done this thing? Wyn the protector. Wyn the giant. Payne idolized him.

THREE

Between his own busy work schedule and the site boss's forget-fulness or disinterest Payne had all but given up hope of going underground and seeing the inner workings of the mine. It was a surprise, then, when a miner showed up at his door one day, offering to give him a tour. It was a quiet moment in the healing center, a rarity, and Payne leapt at the chance.

The man's name was Slivey; he'd worked at Pannus for a good ten years. He had fair hair, narrow-set eyes and a broad, spadelike nose that bent across his face at a crooked angle on account of being broken, by his recollection, at least a dozen times. Payne recognized him as one of the men who'd been on the playing field that day. He seemed quite friendly.

He took Payne to the dry and outfitted him with the basic gear. Rubber boots, oilskin coat, safety belt, gloves. There was no hard hat that came close to approximating the shape of Payne's head, and the one they finally settled on was so big it seemed to float above his head rather than fit it. Slivey next chose a lamp for him and tested its battery. It seemed to work fine, the lamplight strong and powerful, but for some reason he decided to replace it with a different one. He showed Payne how to strap it to his belt and then how to clip the lamp on. Its weight pulled the rim of the ill-fitted hat aslant across his forehead, nearly to his eyes, and Slivey laughed. "That looks good," he said. "Shows you got attitude."

As they made their way through the adit, he instructed Payne on procedure and basic safety measures. "You hear a bell, that means a skip's coming, you move to the rib. You hear a siren, that means there's been an accident, you get yourself out as fast as you can. Watch your head. Don't walk into timber sets. Watch your feet. Don't get tangled up in hoses. And be damned careful of the ventilation tubing. You punch a hole in that, you're robbing air from the boys at the face. It's like stepping on their throats. Rails, too. You catch a foot, next thing you twist an ankle. And don't get separated. Rule number one is no man goes down alone. We stick together. Do not forget that. Don't leave your partner and don't let him leave you."

Payne was grateful for the advice, though he didn't understand it all, and of what he did understand, he only absorbed about half. He was too busy adjusting to the strange new environment, which at present involved trying to negotiate the ever-deepening darkness without stumbling, hitting his head, or otherwise injuring himself. The problem with the headlamp was that it only pointed straight ahead. It did little to illuminate objects to the side of him. And there was a rail and ties to watch out for around his feet, and puddles of water whose depth he couldn't judge. It was a tricky business being a miner.

Gradually he got the hang of things and started to feel more comfortable. The adit tunnel was tall and wide and, to his head at least, posed little danger. He still had a tendency to stumble, but if he matched his stride to the distance between ties, he could walk a little faster, which was a timely realization, for he'd fallen behind Slivey and needed to catch up. But then he heard a bell and froze.

He knew it meant something but couldn't remember what. In the distance he saw a single light approach and thought perhaps it was a miner. He stood and waited as the light grew larger and the bell clanged on. He heard a yell, and then in rapid succession had his breath knocked out of him by a blow to his chest, was lifted off his feet, then launched sideways. He ended up sprawled against the rib with Slivey on top of him. A second later, a fully laden skip rumbled past.

Slivey rolled off him and got to his feet, brushing off the dirt. Payne was embarrassed, bruised and shaken.

"Go on, get up," said Slivey.

Payne did as he was told.

Slivey's headlamp shone in his eyes, half-blinding him, then swept across his body as though examining it. He couldn't see the miner's face, but he could imagine its expression.

Seconds later, the light swung away, and in a flat voice Slivey repeated himself. "You hear a bell, you move to the rib. You hear a siren, you get out. Don't get separated. Don't wander off. Now let's get going."

This time Payne stayed as close behind the man as he could without tripping. The shoulder he had landed on throbbed, which seemed to heighten all his other senses. For the first time he heard the drip of water. He smelled the dampness in the air and tasted something faintly acrid and metallic in his throat. He saw shadows dance on walls. In front of him he watched the darkness dissolve and the tunnel unfold as if by magic.

Distance, he found, was hard to judge, and he stayed glued to Slivey, until at length the miner halted. They had reached a wide, low-ceilinged room that was obviously man-made. Lights were affixed to its walls, and in the middle of the floor was a covered metal booth occupied by a man at a control panel. Bolted to the floor outside the booth sat an enormous steel drum wrapped with a thick wire cable. Coming off the drum, the cable line was taut, and Payne followed it to its point of attachment, a metal cage partway across the room. The set of rails that they'd been following disappeared down a haulage drift in the opposite direction.

Slivey spoke to the man in the booth, then ushered Payne into the waiting metal cage. His nerves a bit more settled, Payne snuck a peek over the side of it and had just enough time to feel a draft of air in his face before being unceremoniously yanked back. Slivey muttered something about a death wish. Payne protested. He had nothing of the kind. He was curious, that was all. Slivey growled at him to stay put, and an instant later, with a lurch the cage descended.

Every hoistman, Payne later learned, had his own distinctive way with the levers that controlled the movement of the cage, a sort of signature touch, and this one, he decided, had to have a tremor in his hands the way it jerked and jumped. Either that, or he was doing it intentionally—perhaps every newcomer got hazed this way. Slivey didn't seem to mind, but Payne felt uneasy. It was pitch black, and as they banged and rattled downward, his stomach churned and he had visions of a cable snapping, followed by a long and mortifying fall.

But they reached the bottom without incident. The shaft, Slivey told him, was three thousand feet deep. And that was just the beginning of the mine. The current working levels were several hundred feet deeper and reached by foot. He asked if Payne had had enough.

"Enough?"

"You ready to go back?"

The idea, in fact, had crossed his mind. "Not at all."

"Good," said Slivey. "Excellent. Follow me."

He led Payne down a long and gently sloping decline, his pace steady and sure-footed, the advancing cone of his headlamp pointed straight ahead and never veering. Payne had to walk a little faster than he wanted, and his breath came a little harder, too. The air was not as fresh or wholesome as it was outside, and it stung his lungs to breathe it. According to Slivey, this was due more to the dampness than the cold. It never froze so far beneath the earth, but it never warmed up either. The temperature pretty much stayed the same year round.

"No seasons in the hole," he said. "No hurricanes, no sandstorms, no blizzards. It's a steady place to work with a steady climate. Only thing that changes is the rock. She keeps you on your toes. Keeps things interesting."

For a miner he was talkative, and Payne was grateful. In some real way it made him feel safe. When he stopped talking, the idea of where they were began to weigh on him, how far beneath the ground, how massive the mountain overhead. Massive and oppressive. He trusted Slivey, but his every instinct told him that this was not a place for him to be. His body needed fresh air, sky and natural light. Instead, it felt compressed and trapped. It wanted out, and he had to exercise an iron will to keep going.

It helped somewhat to know they weren't alone. Nearby were hundreds of other men, although you couldn't tell by listening. The drifts were so long and twisting, and the rock between them so thick, and the air so heavy, that sounds were either deadened or entirely absorbed. Once, far-off and muffled, he heard what he assumed was an explosion. Otherwise, save for their muted footsteps, the drip of water and the low sibilance of air flowing through the ventilation tubing, it was quiet. This world did not seem one to suffer noise.

At the foot of the decline was a crossroads, and without hesitating Slivey proceeded to the left. They passed another crossroads and then a fork, and the drift began to narrow. At the same time the air began to thicken with dust. The light shed by their lamps, which had been bright yellow, turned a hazy brown. No more than ten feet ahead of him, Slivey's figure blurred.

Payne hurried to catch up with him, and all at once a bomb seemed to go off inside his head. Next thing he knew, he was flat on his back, seeing stars. Then he felt a hand grip his and pull him to his feet.

"You can do it that way," said Slivey, "but it's better if you duck. You don't want to go and knock your cribbing loose." He searched the ceiling, what he called "the back," with his headlamp. "Stand back a little."

Head pounding, Payne retreated several steps. Slivey pulled a crowbar from his belt and, keeping his distance, poked at the back with the pointed end. Some pebbles fell and he jammed the bar in a little deeper, levering it downward. Suddenly, a chunk of rock half the size of his body came loose and thundered to the ground. It raised a cloud of dust and made Payne jump. Slivey studied the back awhile and poked at it some more, then satisfied, moved on.

The timber sets grew more frequent on account of the testy rock, which, according to Slivey, needed extra bracing. The wood in the sets creaked and moaned, and in his brave but uneasy heart Payne moaned a little, too. Then Slivey halted, announcing that they'd reached the face. Through the haze about fifteen feet away Payne could make out two men. One was bent over a box, fiddling with some wires attached to what looked like sticks. The other held what could have only been a jackleg drill. It was, as Vecque had said, a monstrous thing, with a huge and heavy body and a drill bit not an inch less than six feet long. It looked like a giant, legless mosquito, though surprisingly, the miner wielding it was not a giant at all, but he handled it with ease, as though the trick involved not size or strength so much as leverage and agility. Both men wore ear protectors but only one of them wore a mask. Slivey was also maskless, and Payne made a mental note to talk to him about that. The air in the heading was bad enough as it was, stale and stagnant and oxygen-deprived, without the added dust from drilling. He was happy, though, to see the ear protectors. Without them the noise of the drill would have been deafening.

After a few minutes, Slivey touched his arm and motioned for them to leave. When they were far enough away to hear each other, he explained that the men were getting ready to shoot a round.

"A round of what?" asked Payne.

"Dynamite."

"I'd like to see that."

Slivey shook his head. The rock was pretty ratty, and things sometimes happened. He didn't want someone with no experience to be nearby if something did. Besides, it was time they headed out.

Slivey offered Payne the lead, and flattered, he accepted. By this point he felt more comfortable and self-assured, although that might have simply been the knowledge that soon he would be breathing fresh air and standing upright aboveground. They passed the first fork, and at the crossroads he confidently took the right-hand branch. Then he came to a fork he didn't quite remember. He turned to get Slivey's advice, but Slivey wasn't there. He felt a little stab of apprehension, which he put aside. It was silly: the man was right behind him. Probably had stopped to fix some bit of cribbing. He waited for the reassuring beam of light.

A minute passed and then another. Neither light nor man appeared. Payne refused to worry. Slivey knew what he was doing. But after a bit more time he turned around and headed back.

He retraced his steps to the crossroads, where he paused, trying to remember which way they'd come. There were four drifts fanning out in four directions, and he took a few steps into each one, looking for something that might jar his memory. To this point he'd been too embarrassed to call out, for it would have been an admission that he was lost; but now, his anxiety rising, embarrassment took a back seat to the desire to be found. In a modest voice he said Slivey's name, waited, repeated it a little louder, then cupped his hands and shouted. The sound died almost as soon as it left his mouth. It was as if the mine had opened up its own mouth and swallowed it.

In one of the passages the air seemed just a bit fresher than the others, which gave him hope that it might lead him to other men. But after a hundred yards there was a fork, and he had to choose again, and this time both drifts seemed the same. Or almost the same—on close inspection one was slightly narrower and lower-backed than the other, and, reasoning that a smaller drift was less likely to be a major branch, he took the wider one. But soon this one narrowed, too, and when he had to stoop his head to keep from banging it, he knew that he'd gone wrong. At this point it occurred to him that maybe he should stop moving altogether and wait for them to come to him, that wandering around willy-nilly might make it harder to be found. For surely they were looking for him—any second he expected to hear voices and see a light.

But moving kept him warm, and not moving felt too much like giving up. And in the back of his mind he worried that he'd strayed far away from everybody, into some burnt-out, unused abandoned section of the mine.

So for a second time he turned around and headed back the way he'd come, or at least the way he thought he'd come, following the drift as it took a leftward turn. Half a minute later, he heard a noise ahead, and, heart racing, he rushed forward. But when he rounded the bend, his hopes were dashed. At the center of a cloud of billowing yellow dust lay a pile of newly fallen rock. The sound had come not from any rescuer, but from the mine itself. It was a cruel disappointment. But not as cruel as what came next.

As he stared and cursed his luck, the dust began to flicker, the sort of flicker that a moth made with a candle as it danced back and forth around the flame. But he saw no moth in the light of his headlamp, and in fact could think of no good reason why one would live three thousand feet beneath the ground. For a second the flickering stopped, and he put it out of his mind, for there were other, more pressing things to be concerned with. Then suddenly, his light went out.

To his shame he panicked. And by some miracle tamed the panic. In the darkness he felt for his lamp and then its cord, making sure that they were still connected. He checked the battery connection too, then unclipped the battery from his belt and, reasoning that a heart, which was a sort of battery too, could sometimes, when stalled, be jump-started with a thump to the chest, banged it on the wall. It made a dull thudding sound not so very different from what a chest would make but, sadly, did not spring to life. He went through the motions of doing everything again, to no avail. The battery and lamp were dead.

With his hand against the rib as a guide he inched forward, until he banged his head on a nasty overhang of rock and nearly knocked himself out. After that, he decided to stay put: if he couldn't find his way in the light, what possible chance was there to find it in the pitch black? He had his brass, which at least was something. When the men brassed out and his was found unaccounted for, they would send a party out in search of him. And Slivey, of course, would already be looking. Unless something had happened to him, too. Which is how his mind had started to work, imagining things that in other circumstances he would never have thought of. He couldn't understand how they'd ever gotten separated to begin with. The whole thing beggared reason.

The cold was starting to get to him, and he huddled in a ball against the rib, knees drawn to his chest to conserve heat. His teeth began to chatter, and every now and then he heard the disconcerting moan of shifting rock. It was not hard to imagine that the mine was speaking, and it did not sound happy, seemed in fact displeased. He felt so stupid for getting lost. So cold and frightened.

He had never been in darkness so complete. It seemed like something new on earth, to night as night was to day. It swallowed up his cries for help, making them sound futile and pathetic. How could anything hope to penetrate such blackness? And little by little a new fear arose.

All this noise of his might not be so smart. It might be stirring something up that shouldn't be stirred, waking something that shouldn't be woken. His imagination? Maybe, but maybe not. There were many things that skulked and lurked in darkness.

He began to shiver, small involuntary tremors in his arms and legs and chest. And then he started having trouble breathing. The stale, heavy air offered little in the way of nourishment, but more than that, the mine seemed to be closing in on him. He could feel its imponderable weight of rock, millions upon millions of tons of it, pressing against his ribs, bearing down and constricting him. It was as if the mountain itself sat upon his chest, squeezing out the air, and in a panic he started hyperventilating.

He couldn't understand why they hadn't found him yet. Surely by now the shift was over and they knew that he was lost. But maybe not; maybe the men were still at work. He had no idea how much time had passed, except that it seemed forever.

He was shivering freely now, and his fingers and toes were numb. How much longer would he last? People died like this, and he didn't want to die. He gulped air and took deep breaths, trying to master his fear, forcing himself to calm down and breathe slower.

And now the cold began to get to him. It had seeped deep into his body, and now it started working on his mind. He began to have trouble thinking clearly. A lethargy came over him. He felt more tired than he had reason to be. Tired and sluggish and apathetic. He began having thoughts not of rescue, but of escape and release.

His eyelids drifted slowly downward, then closed. Terrified, he snapped them open, knowing he had to fight the urge to sleep. But seconds later, they closed again, and he promised himself it would only be a minute. Just enough time for a little nap.

It lasted longer than he planned, and would have lasted longer still, too long, had it not been broken by a dream. It was a bothersome, annoying dream: a swarm of insects was buzzing in his ears. He tried in vain to swat them away and stop the buzzing, but the sound persisted, and then they, or something, was jostling him. This was even more annoying, and he shrank from it and tried to get away. All he wanted was to be left alone.

And then a voice was saying, "There you are," and then a light was shining in his face.

"Been wondering where you wandered off to. Guess you forgot rule number one."

It was very real sounding to be a dream, though waking up to it was quite a struggle. He finally got his eyes to open but couldn't get his tongue to work. His lips and jaw were numb.

The voice turned out to be Slivey's; clustered around him were other men, Covert among them. No one looked particularly alarmed or worried about his being lost. If anything, and this was strange, they seemed amused.

"Up you get now," Slivey said, offering his hand. "No more sleeping on the job. Shift's over. Everybody's tired and hungry. Time to brass out."

FOUR

He was having dinner in the mess hall several days later when Vecque entered. They had not spoken since the incident in the mine, although everybody else seemed to know about it, and so he assumed she did. She wound her way past the tables to the serving line, getting teased by the miners in the process. They called her uppity for not joining them, not that they wanted her to or would have known what to do if she had. For one thing, she was tesque, and for another she was their healer, both of which set her well apart. She was also female, which to many of the men was the most alien thing about her.

As a rule, she had the sense to ignore their catcalls. From her point of view, responding only encouraged them and made things worse. Payne was a man, but he was different from the miners. He wasn't hostile and didn't ever laugh at her. If he had a fault (and Vecque was not one to let a fault go unnoticed), it was that he was so damn upbeat.

73

And so fervent sometimes. But she was almost always glad to see him, especially when she compared it to the alternative of eating alone.

After getting herself some food, she joined him at his table, pulling up a chair. "I heard about your little escapade."

"News travels fast."

"Like lightning. How are you? Recovered yet?"

He didn't really want to talk about it, mostly because he didn't want the miners to overhear and get started in on him again. They were ruthless with their hazing. Emotionally, he was still a little raw.

"I'm fine," he said.

She knew he wasn't. "You should have listened to me. I told you not to go."

He shrugged. "Nothing wrong with going. Only with what happened."

"I'll say."

"And nothing even wrong with that. It was a learning experience. No harm done."

"Oh stop."

"It was."

"Admit it. You were scared to death."

"Not really."

"No? I would have been."

This was as close to sympathy as Vecque had ever gotten, and it loosened something up inside of him. All at once he was gushing.

"I was terrified. Beyond reason. And afterward, when we were coming back, they were cracking jokes about it. I felt so embarrassed and so incredibly dumb."

"That's just the way they like it. Makes 'em feel smart."

Heads were turning toward their table, and he lowered his voice and leaned forward. "They are smart, Vecque. Down there at least. They know exactly what they're doing. I'm the one who made the mistake of getting lost."

"Is that what you think?"

"It's what happened. You can't blame them for that." It seemed stupid, but here he was defending them.

Vecque regarded him, wondering how anyone could be so out of touch. Was the point even worth pursuing? She had her doubts.

"I hate to burst your bubble, but you didn't get lost."

"Yes," he answered stubbornly. "I did."

"They ditched you."

"You're wrong."

"I'm not," she said. "They did. Intentionally."

He didn't believe her. "Why do you say that? How do you know?"

"Because I know these men. I know what humans are capable of."

It was just as he thought. This was Vecque speaking; it was prejudice, not fact.

"That's your fantasy. It isn't mine."

"It's no fantasy, Payne. I heard them talking." She hesitated, not thrilled to be the bearer of this news. "Look, I'm sorry, but I heard."

"Heard what?"

"That they let you get lost. That they left you there."

"They said that?"

She nodded.

"Oh," he said, then "oh" again. "So that's why they were laughing."

"I imagine so."

He considered this, and at length he brightened. "It was all a joke."

"Not exactly."

"Sure it was." He had heard of pranks being played on new miners, harmless things like bolting down their lunch pails or serving them grease sandwiches. Humiliating in the moment but not to be taken personally or confused with the intention of doing a person harm. More like rites of passage, required for acceptance in the group. Which had to be what this had been.

He took it as a sign of progress. "They were kidding around. It was a joke. I can take a joke."

"You're not getting it," said Vecque. "It wasn't a joke. They were teaching you a lesson."

"What do you mean? What lesson?"

"For what you did to that miner. The one with the failing kidneys."

"Covert?"

"That sounds right."

"He was sick. I healed him."

"You took away his livelihood."

"No. I did the opposite. He could barely walk and hardly work. Now he can do what he wants. He even runs around with that crazy group of his . . ." He stopped, remembering their confrontation in the snow. "What livelihood?"

"Musk," she said.

"What's musk?"

She shook her head. At what point, she wondered, did innocence become ignorance and something to be disdained? "Musk is what they make when they get sick. They collect it and then they sell it. An ounce is worth a week of wages. More than a week. It's precious stuff."

"So that's what they were doing in the field? Musk is frozen sweat?"

"Sweat plus what their kidneys make. Frozen just because it's easier to collect."

"So all those guys were sick?"

Vecque hadn't seen them but imagined so. "Not everybody gets that far. You have to inhale a lot of dust. And it has to be a certain kind of dust. Not copper, but one of the rarer ores. Rokonite, I think. Or gravellium. And even then, most of them just get the breathing problems. Only a handful get the kidney changes, too. For most of the guys it isn't worth the trouble to find out if it's going to happen the way they want it to. It takes a long time to get sick enough to start producing musk. And it makes them feel awful."

"So why do it?"

"I told you why. The money. It's a business venture. I guess you could call it an investment."

"What do they use it for? The musk."

"Perfume," she said with half a smile. "What else?"

Payne was incredulous. "They make themselves ill so someone else can dab themselves with perfume?"

"No," she said. "You're not listening. They make themselves ill to make money."

"That's just as bad."

"How is it bad?"

"Trading in your health for money? Getting rich by getting ill? It's perverse."

"I doubt they're getting rich. For all we know, they're sending money home to their families. Making life easier for the wife and kids. Raising more snotty humans to lord it over us."

"I'm sorry, but I can't condone that."

"Who cares?" she said, leading Payne to believe that it made no difference either to the miners or to her. "It's their choice. That's the difference between them and us. They get the freedom to be stupid. We get the freedom to do what they say."

"But not that. We don't have to do that."

"Oh yes," she said. "We do. Unless you want to have more adventures like the one you had."

But Payne was not convinced. Healing was a precious thing to him. It was a gift. In a way it was the only one he had. And he would not have it for long. No healer did. Which was all the more reason not to be reckless with it, or to squander it, or to practice it unscrupulously.

"They need us, Vecque. We can use that as leverage. When they come to us, we can talk to them. We can teach them. There have to be other ways to make money. Higher wages, better prices for the ore, I don't know. But I do know that they don't have to walk around half-sick. That's no way to live. It has to take a toll on them. If they stay that way too long, the condition might become permanent. They might not ever be able to be fully healed."

"You're missing the point again. They don't want to be fully healed. And if at some point they change their minds and do, and can't be, well, that's the risk they take. I'm not a teacher, Payne. Even if I thought that what they're doing is wrong, which I'm not sure I do, I wouldn't interfere. It's not my place for one thing, and it's a waste of breath for another. Besides, I'm not interested."

"That's our job," he said. "We have to be interested."

"Not mine," said Vecque.

Payne hated it when she acted like this. She could be such an unreasonable, exasperating, bull-headed person.

Vecque, in turn, hated it when Payne told her who to be and what to do. As far as she was concerned, as soon as he started preaching, that was it for her.

She turned her attention to her food, which in a world where she was either being lectured or being used, was one of the few predictable pleasures. Lately, though, it hadn't been tasting that good. And her appetite, which had always been robust, was slightly off, too. It would help, she supposed, if she weren't so tired all the time. It made eating, as well as nearly every other activity, a chore.

She pushed the food haphazardly around her plate. For the past week, the smell alone was enough to make her stomach turn.

"You know, I didn't ask to be a healer, Payne. I never wanted to be one."

"A part healer, you mean."

"You make it sound so contemptible. But it's not. Think of it as a kind of maintenance therapy. It keeps them going, which is what they want. If it were you, maybe you'd want the same."

He couldn't imagine such a thing. If he were sick, he'd want to be healed completely. And by the same token, if he could heal a human fully, how could he stop at healing only part?

"I doubt it," he replied.

She sighed. Talking to him was like talking to a wall.

"You really don't understand, do you?"

"Oh, yes," he said. "I think I do."

"I'm not just doing it for them."

"Who then?"

"Myself."

"What does that mean?"

"It means it's easier for me."

"What? Healing them partway?"

The boy was relentless. "Yes. It's not such an effort. Such a strain."

"That's a pretty lousy reason not to do what's right."

"Right for you maybe. Not for me."

"It doesn't work like that," said Payne, high atop his horse. "There's right and there's wrong."

She stared at him. "Is that so?"

He stared right back. "Yes. It is."

He was making it personal. Well, she could make it personal, too.

"So," she said. "I'm morally delinquent. I'm glad to have that clarified. It explains so much. But enough about me. Let's train the spotlight on you for a minute. Such a pillar of virtue. I'd love to know more. What goes on inside that brain of yours? What makes Payne the healer tick?"

"I won't heal anybody partway," he said, oblivious to her tone of voice and the daggers flying. "For me that's not an option."

"I understand," she said. "It's too . . . what? Easy? Charitable? Indulgent?"

"It's dishonest," he said. "It's not why I'm here."

"Of course," she said. "Let's talk about that. Why exactly are you here? You're a conscientious boy. Ambitious, one might even say. You're always looking for more work. Harder work, too. Is that intentional? Is that your plan?"

Healers didn't make plans. They went where and when they were told. Personal ambition only hastened the inevitable and was disdained by other healers, few of whom lasted long enough to see the distant future, much less make a plan about it. Taking on added work was like slitting one's own throat. It was a nasty and inflammatory thing for Vecque to say.

But, deaf to insult, Payne took no offense. Instead, he answered her sincerely.

"I'm here to do my job. That's all. To do it as well as I can."

"Which is very well indeed, I'm told."

He looked to see if she was making fun of him, and finding nothing in her face to suggest it, gave a modest little shrug.

"I do my best. It helps, I guess, to like what you're doing."

"You like to heal."

She knew he did. He'd said as much.

At the risk of offending her, he nodded.

Vecque smiled. This was really much too easy. "No you don't."

She glanced around the room as if to make sure nobody was listening, then leaned across the table and cupped her mouth with a hand. She had a secret for him, along with a twinkling eye and an evil grin.

"You *love* it."

It sounded dirty how she said it. Wicked.

"Don't you?"

He didn't answer.

"It's intense, isn't it? You feel attached."

He shrugged.

"Connected," she said, so close that he could smell her breath. "Don't lie. *Connected*, Payne."

It was true, but the way she said it made him feel that it was wrong. Lowering his eyes, he gave a guilty nod.

Satisfied, she sat back in her chair, a look of pity on her face. "So does a prisoner with his guards. And a victim with his torturer."

"It's not like that."

"Oh yes," she said. "It's exactly that."

"I'm not being tortured. And I'm not a prisoner."

"No? You're free to go? You're free to choose what you do? If you wanted to be something else besides a healer, if you wanted, take my tongue, a different life, you could have one?"

The thought had never occurred to him. "I don't."

"You see? You can't even consider the possibility. That's not loving something. That's obedience. That's blind devotion. A dog has that. Are you a dog?"

His face grew hot. "You're cruel."

"It's a cruel world." She pushed her plate away, barely having touched her food, and stood. Payne looked miserable.

"Cheer up," she said. "I'm leaving."

She turned and walked away, but after a few steps stopped. He was such a child. So guileless and innocent. And she . . . so full of bile. Both of them were victims of the human world—how sad that they could find nothing better to do than take it out on one another. She through meanness, he through thoughtlessness and self-absorption.

"Look," she said, more gently. "I was speaking for myself. I'm having trouble here. It's hard for me. I'm tired and worn-out all the time. Anything to make things easier I'm going to try. It's different for you."

"What would make things easier would be if you were nicer."

She felt like shaking him. "Maybe so, but that's not the point. You have a talent, Payne."

"You have a talent, too."

"No," she said. "That's what I'm telling you. I don't."

۞ ۞ ۞

He had ample time to reflect on what Vecque had said—and what he had—in the days that followed. A weather system ushered in a series of storms, one on top of another, that lasted nearly two weeks. The coup de grace was a raging blizzard unlike anything that he had yet seen. It cut off the One and Two Prime sites from each other and suspended all but the most essential services in camp. Crews worked around the clock and still couldn't keep the streets and rail lines open.

The storm finally blew itself out and the sky lifted. Staggering outside, the men emerged into a transformed world. Some of the snowdrifts were as tall as buildings. Many of the buildings, in fact, had all but disappeared. Smoke curled and spewed from hidden chimneys, giving the appearance that the snow itself was smoldering. Pannus Mountain was a dome of solid white.

Payne shoveled out a path, first to the healing center, then to his quarters. He was relieved to get out after being cooped up inside so long. He was anxious to talk to Vecque, for their quarrel had disturbed him. He thought he knew where things had gone wrong.

First off, he had to admit that she was probably right. He did have a talent. Where she was mistaken was in thinking that she did not. Every person had a talent. In some—and maybe he was one of these—it was obvious and accessible. In others it was sleeping, hidden or submerged. His job, he felt, was to coax Vecque's talent to the surface, to make it visible and useful to her. He also wanted to apologize. Whatever the problem was, he was determined to set it right.

He left a note on his door saying where he was going, then made his way to the saddle and the rail line that linked the One and Two Prime operations. The camp looked strange to him, nonsensical—concealed and at the same time enlarged. Like one of the snow geese he'd once seen with its chest ballooned out in courtship: magnificent and half again its normal size, a promise built on puffs of air. Despite the presence of men and plows, there was a stillness that pervaded everything. Sounds were muted, as though this beautifully feathered concoction were too delicate and fragile to be disturbed by noise.

The rail line had been cleared, but not the roads beyond it, and for the final half mile or so, he had to make his way on foot. The snow was not as deep as it was on his side of the mountain, for the northern escarpment had acted as something of a shield against the storm. Still, there was enough of it to make walking a chore, and by the time he reached his destination, he was winded and thus annoyed to see that he had further work to do. There was a chest-high bank of snow that ran a good twenty feet from where he stood to the door of the healing center. Vecque, apparently, had not yet seen fit to shovel out a path.

It was left to him, then, to make his own way in, and by the time he did, he was hot and sweaty. The room, by contrast, was frigid cold. Which was odd, because there should have been a fire going. Vecque, it seemed, was either out or sleeping in.

He pressed his ear to the connecting door to her quarters, listening for signs of life. He heard what sounded like deep breathing, and with apologies for waking her, knocked.

The creak of bedsprings was followed by a groan. And then a tired, slurred voice. "Who is it?"

"It's me," he said.

But Vecque was already struggling to her feet. Even half-asleep she understood that it didn't matter who it was, only that there was someone, and that that someone was waiting for her. Asking who had been a lapse.

"Never mind. I'm coming. Have a seat."

A minute later she appeared. She was wearing her customary outfit, a loose fitting shirt and pants, although the shirt was rumpled and in need of cleaning and the pants seemed a shade too big.

"You," she said.

"Me," he replied with a smile. To his eye it seemed that she'd lost weight.

She yawned, then lost her balance for a second, steadying herself against the door.

Instantly, he was at her side. "Are you all right?"

She mumbled something beneath her breath.

"Vecque?"

"What?"

"I said are you all right."

"Why shouldn't I be?" she snapped.

This, at least, was familiar territory. He allowed himself to relax.

"Hello, Vecque."

"Hello yourself." She rubbed her eyes and then her arms. "It's cold in here."

"There's no fire."

She frowned, glancing at the stove. "Should be. I had one going just a while ago."

Payne went to see if he could stir it back to life. The ashes, though, were cold and gray. There hadn't been a fire for some time.

"It's dead," he said, a little puzzled.

Vecque frowned again, then shrugged it off. "Blankets work."

She went into her room and brought one out, wrapping it around her shoulders. "Guess I've been in bed longer than I thought."

"How long's that?"

She didn't know, nor did she seem to care. "I'll tell you something, this storm's the best thing that could have happened to me."

"How's that?"

"I finally got some rest."

"I'm glad," he said.

"And it kept the wolves away."

"You saw a wolf?"

"Every day," she said. "Lots of them."

He narrowed his eyes. "What wolves?"

"You know. The two-legged ones."

She took a chair but had trouble getting comfortable. She drew her blanket tighter across her chest.

"So, what brings you?"

"I came to apologize."

"For what?" she asked.

He explained as best he could. She listened to him patiently, although he got the sense she didn't know exactly what he was talking about. As if she hadn't thought about it near as much as he had. Maybe not at all. Still, when he was done, she thanked him. She seemed touched by his words.

"You're a good man," she told him, then got a little teary-eyed. Embarrassed, she looked away.

"I haven't been myself lately. As you can see." She wiped her eyes. "It's been rough."

"I'd like to help you."

"I think you just did."

"More," he said.

"That's sweet. Unfortunately, I don't believe it's possible."

"It is," he said. "I can. I know I can. I want to."

He was so earnest and well-meaning, and she, so not herself, that it took a moment for her to grasp what he was saying. And then her hands flew up to ward him off.

"Oh no. No no no. Not that again."

"I don't mean *that*," he said, although, in fact, he had been thinking of the very thing. Healing the miners was so easy for him. He was ready for something harder and more challenging, something new.

But he had to be more clever if he was going to persuade her. Or maybe just more patient, let her come to it on her own.

"What I mean is, I could help you with your own healing. Help you make it easier."

She doubted this. Moreover, he was annoying her. "Do you know what's going on with me? Do you understand what's happening? I'm being drained, Payne."

As soon as she said it, he knew that she was right. She had the symptoms: the lassitude, the fatigue, the weight loss, the malaise. But this didn't stop him from denying it. Nor from trying to talk her out of it.

"Work is an enormous burden. Some of these illnesses are close to Level Three. It's natural to be tired. I'm tired, too."

"No you're not."

"Sure I am. And another thing. You said that it was happening before, and it wasn't. What makes you think that this is any different? It could be another false alarm."

"It's not."

"How do you know?"

She glared at him. "Look. I'm sorry, but it's happening. Please don't argue with me."

Despite everything he knew of the Drain, everything he'd heard and now, through Vecque, was witnessing, Payne believed it could be stopped, or at least slowed down. He was like a man who, never having been sick, does not believe in illness. Instead, he believed in the power of the will, most notably, his own.

"I can still help you."

"You can't."

"I can. But you have to trust me."

"But I don't."

She might as well have slapped him.

"I'm sorry, but you don't understand me, Payne. You don't know what I'm going through. You're different."

"I'm not."

"No? You know what it's like, the way it drags you down and saps your strength? The way that everything's an effort. The way you lose your will? All you want to do is rest, but rest doesn't make you feel any better. Familiar, Payne? Tell me you know how it feels."

"You have to stand up to it," he said. "You have to fight. You can. You have the power to resist."

"Do you?"

"Do I what? Have the power?"

"Do you fight? Do you even know what it means?"

"Sure I do. Sure I fight."

She would have liked this to be true, even if it meant that he, too, was under siege. Just to feel, if only for an instant, that she wasn't all alone.

"Liar. You don't fight. You don't have to." With a sigh she pulled the blanket tighter, huddling in its thin cocoon. "I hate you, Payne."

◈ ◈ ◈

The weeks passed, and he kept at her, not satisfied with no for an answer. She told him to mind his business, called him names, refused to speak to him, but in the end threw up her hands and let him have his way. She couldn't compete with him: he was tireless, and she was not. She needed to preserve her strength for work.

For a while, then, he became her teacher. Which took some getting used to, because it was a reversal of their customary roles. What he lacked in a concrete plan he made up for in gusto. And while Vecque remained skeptical that anything would work, for nothing in the history of healers and healing ever had, she agreed to give it a try.

One by one they went through the steps and then the stages of a healing, comparing notes, discussing styles, dissecting subtle differences between the two of them. The most important one Payne found, the only one that seemed significant, was in their attitude. He enjoyed the work. Vecque despised it.

This, he guessed, made everything more difficult for her, from identification to enhancement, which naturally affected all the other, downstream stages of a healing. She was like a runner throwing obstacles in her own path. Of all things, the Drain did not require such assistance.

But how to change a person's attitude and feelings? Especially a person so committed and attached to them? Vecque was fueled by her anger and hatred the way that other people were fueled by food. They seemed to prop her up and keep her going when little else did. She claimed they gave her bearing and a sense of identity and even comfort, like an old familiar friend.

"But those feelings are hurting you," Payne pointed out.

That, she said, was putting the cart before the horse. "Humans are the thing that's hurting me."

"Don't let them. Don't fight them so hard."

This brought a scowl to her face. "Make up your mind. Before, you said I had to fight. Now you say I shouldn't. Which is it?"

"Don't fight yourself," he said.

"And how exactly do I do that?"

He took a breath. "Don't hate so much."

۞ ۞ ۞

He tried to teach her by example, modeling tolerance and compassion for even the most lowly miner. For him this was a matter of personal integrity, but that, he learned, was not the way to reach Vecque. He tried appealing to her intellect. She was smart, and he sought to reason with her.

"Don't think of them as humans," he suggested.

"No?" This was a novel idea. "What then?"

"Think of them as cousins."

She gave him a look. "In what possible sense?"

"In an evolutionary sense."

"You don't believe that story?"

"It's not a story. We're related, and you know it."

"I'm sorry to disappoint you, but my memory doesn't go back that far."

"You don't have to remember anything. All you have to do is look."

One by one he enumerated all the things they shared, from the structure of their long bones to their skin to their internal organs; their metabolism, too. In almost every respect tesques and humans were alike, and their minds worked more or less alike, as well. Their speech was similar, and all the other sundry sounds they made—from whimpering to laughing to squealing to crying—were virtually the same.

Vecque acknowledged this, while observing that she much preferred to hear a human whimper than a tesque. The sound was almost pleasing to the ear. And it had the ring of justice, for they deserved to be in pain.

Payne gnashed his teeth. Was she trying to make it difficult for him?

"They're the same as us," he snapped, losing his patience. "If they deserve it, we do too."

"Well I am in pain," said Vecque.

"Well you don't deserve to be."

"Well all right."

"So do something about it."

Her eyes flashed. "Are you blaming me?"

Blame was strong, he said, unfair, oversimplified.

"I'm being drained," she reminded him. "If you think it's my fault, I'd say the teacher needs a lesson of his own."

It was a standoff, one of many. Vecque usually outlasted him, but on this occasion it was she, not he, who gave in.

"You say that we're the same," she said, "but you're leaving out the most important part."

"What? This?" He slapped his frontal boss, the swollen hump of skull that set him apart from every human. For Vecque it was the narrowness of her head. For every tesque it was something. It had never before been a subject of conversation between them because it was a given. They lived with it day in and out; it was not worth mentioning. But now, apparently, it was.

"It's not the most important," he said heatedly. "It's superficial. A quirk of nature. Close your eyes, it's gone."

She'd touched a nerve, which had not been her intention. Nor was his head, or hers, or any of theirs, the part she meant. Turning her attention to herself, she placed her hand below and to the side of her right breast, atop her os melior, pressing down as if to blot it out, or at the least to stanch its flow.

"But why?" he asked. "Why is that the most important? Why the one thing that does make us different? Why not all the things that are the same?"

There was something plaintive in his voice, a cry, a plea for under- standing, that gave her pause. It made her feel, strangely, that he was worse off than she was, and her heart went out to him. Her life was destined to be short, but his, she sensed, would be more difficult. He had no shields, and she feared that he would suffer a great deal before he found any.

FIVE

Every day there were accidents in the mine, mostly minor ones. Mashed fingers, bruised muscles, cuts, sprains. Major accidents happened only rarely. The worst that Payne had seen in his brief career was a broken leg. Which is more or less what he expected when the siren started up. When it didn't stop, he began to think he might be in for something more serious, and he dropped what he was doing and raced outside, then to the adit, where he joined a group of anxious, grim-faced men.

There had been an explosion. One of the jackleg operators had inadvertently drilled into a pocket of methane gas. The gas had been ignited by an errant spark from a faulty electrical wire. The force of the explosion had thrown the miner back some twenty feet, which had saved his life, because it landed him on the far side of the resulting fireball. His partner had not been so lucky. Word was that he was severely burned.

Before long a skip appeared, flanked by half a dozen men. Their headlamps bobbed as they trod forward, the lamplights fading as they emerged from the darkness of the adit into the light of day. On the floor of the skip was the injured miner. His hair was singed and his face was burnt. Kneeling beside him, another miner held an oxygen mask to his face.

The driver brought the skip adjacent to the healing center, where the man was lifted out and carried inside by his companions. Not sure yet what he might need, Payne had them lay him on the healing bed. Rapidly, he checked for a pulse and briefly removed the mask to look for signs of breathing. Where the man's skin wasn't charred, it was gray and dusky. His blistered lips were blue.

Payne clamped the mask back over his mouth and hurriedly joined him on the bed. Rapidly, he wrapped their arms together, then lay down, closed his eyes, and commenced a healing. He hadn't time to pull the curtain, but the miners who had carried the man inside knew enough to turn their backs. Outside, as news of the accident spread, a crowd grew.

Payne did absolutely everything he could. He labored for half an hour, and then, exhausted, labored more. He made it through the first three stages before being stymied, then without a break tried again, this time making it only through the first two. The longer he worked the less progress he was able to make. Soon he was making none at all. At length he stopped, for there was nothing more he had to offer. Nothing more to do. The man was dead.

Slowly, he unwrapped their arms. His was hot and sweaty; the man's, clammy and cool. He sat up, and had to brace himself against a wave of dizziness and exhaustion. After it passed, he gave a sigh and stood.

Stirred by the sound of his movement, the two miners who'd remained in the room turned and looked at him. For a second there was hope in their eyes, but rapidly this fled.

"I'm sorry," Payne said softly. "I did everything I could."

The men nodded, and one of them heaved a sigh. "He was pretty far gone when we brought him up." A moment or two passed. "Hell, the man was dead."

Payne bowed his head while the men shifted on their feet. All were at a loss for words.

At length one of the miners said, "I'll go tell the men."

He left. The remaining miner couldn't take his eyes off the dead man. After a while he cleared his throat. "Maybe you should put a sheet on him or something."

Payne had never handled death before and reproached himself for not having thought of this. There were sheets in a cabinet, and he got one out and proceeded to unfold it, beginning at the dead man's feet. When he reached his waist, the miner stopped him.

"Seems like we should say something." He glanced at Payne. "You got any words?"

Again, this was something Payne had not thought of. He was as unprepared for eulogies as he was for death, and to makes matters worse, his mind chose that moment to go blank.

But the miner didn't seem to notice. He had bowed his head, hard hat in hand, and stood beside the bed, waiting patiently.

"What was his name?" asked Payne.

"Rinker."

"What about his first name?"

"Rinker's all I know."

Payne gave a nod and drew a breath. The fragment of a childhood lullaby came to him.

> "Go to sleep, Rinker,
> Find a happy place and slumber.
> No dreams disturb you,
> No worries encumber."

This seemed to satisfy the miner, who whispered a word of his own, then raised his head. "I expect there'll be a service, but that'll do for now. I thank you."

He replaced his hard hat and turned to go, then stopped and

turned back. Reaching underneath the sheet, he removed the dead man's brass, stared at it a moment, then pocketed it.

"They'll want it back," he explained. "Not that anyone's going to use it."

He made his way out, leaving Payne alone. He drew up the sheet until it completely covered the man, then closed the curtain and sat down. He was exhausted, though inside he was shaking like a leaf. It was true what the miner had said, the man had been dead by the time Payne got to him. But this didn't stop him from second-guessing himself. Surely, there was something he could have done to save the man. Something different from what he had. He'd tried his best, but his best obviously wasn't good enough. His best had failed.

The miners felt differently. They felt, in fact, that he had done a hero's work. Word spread that he had almost brought a dead man back to life. That he hadn't was beside the point, or at least it paled before the more important point that he had tried.

After that, their attitude toward him changed. His currency rose, and with it came a measure of respect that previously had been absent. He noticed it in the way the men looked at him and inclined their heads if he happened to catch their eye. And the way they lowered their voices when he was nearby, as though not to sound crass or stupid. They were more polite to him, sometimes even deferential. A few even took to calling him by name.

Payne welcomed the change with open arms. It was a step, he believed, toward being fully accepted by the men. But as time went by, this didn't happen, and gradually he came to understand that being held in high esteem kept him outside the circle of their friendship as surely as being held in low did. In a world where weakness was ridiculed, a special talent or intelligence did its damage, too. As much as ever, the miners kept their distance from him.

As his only friend, Vecque had the job of listening to his troubles and his woes. Normally, she wouldn't have had the patience, but thanks to him, or to something, she'd been feeling better lately, and she felt she owed him at least this much. Like everybody else, she had heard the story of the dead man nearly coming back to life. When he complained that this had done nothing to bring him any closer to being accepted, she surprised him by siding with the men.

"You're a dreamer if you expect their friendship," she told him. "It's like asking a man to consort with a god."

"I'm not a god," he said.

"Of course not. But you have a power they don't, and it scares them."

They were at a table at the periphery of the mess hall, not far from one of the two big drum-shaped wood-burning stoves. Winter was on its way out, but there were still cold days, and this was one of them. The stove was crackling, and Vecque shed her coat and rolled up her sleeves. A month before she would have been chilled to the bone despite this added heat, but now she was getting her own heat back. Her body was able to warm itself. And her plate was full: her appetite was returning, too.

"I don't want to scare them," said Payne.

"Then don't try to heal a dead man."

"I had to try something."

She shrugged at this, prompting him to defend himself.

"The men who brought him, they expected me to act. You should have seen their faces. I couldn't just let him lie there. I had to do something."

"So you lay down beside a dead man. You want the truth, that gives me the creeps. It's bad enough we have to lay beside the living ones."

He had tried so hard. He could still feel the effort in his body, his meli. It was part ache, part longing, a physical sensation, emotional too. How the men would have talked about him if he'd succeeded! How his brother, if he'd been there, would have looked upon him, the praise in his eyes, the admiration.

A voice broke his reverie. He only half heard it.

"Did you say something?" he asked Vecque.

"I said, you thought you could, didn't you?"

"Could what?"

"Bring him back."

He considered what to say and thought it best to say nothing.

She couldn't believe it. "All right. Now I'm scared, too."

"Why? What did I do?" He raised his hands in a gesture of innocence.

"You tell me."

"Nothing. I didn't do anything."

"But you tried. You did. Admit it."

"So? Nothing happened. No one got hurt."

She stared at him. "Who do you think you are? Mobestis? Emm?"

The invocation of the legendary healers, one the father, the other the son, took some of the starch out of his sails. He felt a little sheepish and ducked his head. No, he muttered, he didn't think that he was them.

Vecque was glad to hear it. She liked him, and he had given her good advice. She was definitely better. But as a result, and somewhat to her dismay, she had found herself beginning to depend on him, and she didn't want to find out that she couldn't.

"There's enough craziness around here already. Don't add to it, all right? I want to be able to trust you, Payne."

"You can."

"Then use your head." She brandished her fork at him in mock menace. "I'll be keeping my eye on you."

The hall had filled, and it was a rowdy crowd. Previously, this would have driven Vecque to distraction, but under Payne's tutelage she had found a way to keep the men from getting under her skin and bothering her quite so much. It was a combination of mindfulness and inner strength. She was learning how to be more possessed of herself and less by them. It was remarkable, really, how much they could be tolerated. They still got on her nerves, sometimes deeply, but between love and hate, there did, indeed, seem to be a middle ground.

Not that it was ever easy: occupying this ground required constant vigilance and effort. She had her good days and she had her bad ones. So far today was good. But that, she knew, could change in a heartbeat. She had to continually be on guard. She walked a razor-thin line. Her state of mind and body had improved but remained precarious.

Out of habit she glanced around the room, looking for potential trouble spots, anything that might erupt and spill over to involve her. Or be aimed at her to begin with. Her eye was drawn to a nearby table, where there was some heavy drinking and hazing going on. She only recognized a few of the men. Of the ones she didn't, most were young and had the bewildered and slightly overwhelmed look of new recruits, fresh off the train. One, a pimply boy with sandy hair and eyes a bit too dreamy, she thought, for blasting rock, was being harassed by some of the old-timers. It was in their nature to be drawn to weakness, and they were plying him with drinks and goading him. It was up to the boy to stand up to them and prove himself a man.

At length he took whatever bait it was that they were dangling and got up from the table. Hitching up his pants and puffing out his skinny chest, he sauntered over to the only female in the hall.

"I got a pain," he said.

Vecque had seen him coming and had prepared herself. She pointed out that she was eating. "I'll be happy to take care of you when I'm done."

"Happy" was pressing the point, and she congratulated herself on sounding so convincing and remaining so composed. The boy glanced back at the other men, looking to see if he'd completed what was required of him. Fat chance. They were watching him like hawks. Apparently, he'd just begun.

He turned back to Vecque. "This thing won't wait."

She closed her eyes and counted, praying that when she opened them, he'd be gone. It was such a pleasure to be eating. The food, at long last, tasted good again.

"I'll be finished soon," she said. "Fifteen minutes. Let's do it then."

"It can't wait that long." The drinks had made him unsteady on his feet, and he braced himself against the table edge. "It's urgent."

"Urgent, is it?"

"Yes." His voice had taken on a nasal whine.

She sighed. "I see."

The only area where a healer had any say, the only one where his or her word came close to being law, was in healing. Except in emergencies, patients were not treated outside the healing room. There were good reasons for this, and it was a rule that humans didn't challenge. After looking him up and down, Vecque returned her attention to her plate, where a juicy cutlet sat begging to be eaten. Deftly, she sliced a piece and lifted it to her lips. In her book, initiation into manhood was no emergency. And she hated it when people whined.

"It'll wait," she said.

"It won't."

She placed the slice in her mouth and started chewing. Closed her eyes and savored its rich and aromatic taste. Next to her the boy hovered like a bird afraid to land. Tensions rose.

"She'll see you soon," Payne promised him. "It'll be better if she's not so hungry. Just let her finish eating."

Across the room the miners had started jeering. One was banging his cup, demanding action. Another mocked the poor boy's mother.

"Look," he said. "I'm sorry, but you need to do it."

Vecque ignored him.

He insisted.

"Later," she said.

"No. Now. You need to do it now."

She cut another piece, then stabbed it with her fork and held it up, considering her options. She could go on eating. She could put the food down. Change, she knew, came slowly. Progress didn't happen overnight. Even the best of people had their setbacks.

Raising the fork to eye level, she levered it back with a finger, paused a moment, then let it fly, catapulting the bloody morsel of meat into the young man's face.

For all intents and purposes, this ended the conversation. He was stunned.

Instantly, Payne was on his feet. Reaching for the boy's wrist, he tried to coax him away from Vecque. "I'll do it. Please. I'm done here. I'll heal you now. Let's go."

But the boy wasn't moving. Bloody red juice trickled down his cheek. His face had hardened.

Pulling out the empty chair beside Vecque, he swung into its saddle, straddling it like a horse. He wiped his cheek with the back of his hand, then leaned in close to her and said, loud enough for all to hear, "I got a pain that can't wait. Don't make me ask again."

At his table the men erupted. Drawn by the drama, men at other tables were clamoring for action, too.

Desperately, Payne tried to head things off.

"This isn't necessary. Really. Let me help you. I can take care of this right now."

But Vecque had crossed the line and knew it was up to her. The boy was an annoyance and could be handled, but the other men, who so far were only ugly individually, could, with little further provocation, turn ugly collectively. She didn't fear one man, but she did a mob.

Steeling herself, she rose, prepared to lead the boy to the healing center and do whatever stupid thing he wanted her to do. But the boy did not rise with her.

She felt a momentary panic.

"C'mon," she said. "Let's go."

"Sit down," he commanded, not budging.

When she didn't, when she took a step away, he grabbed her wrist and forced her down into her chair. He had surprising strength, and before she could react, he had taken her hand and interlocked his fingers with hers, then planted his elbow against his side so that their forearms were locked in place and touching.

It was a shocking thing to do, and everyone knew it. Vecque, Payne, the miners, everyone. Even had it been consensual, a meli healing was not an act to perform in public. It was a breach of common decency, a violation of the most basic level of conduct and respect.

Payne was dumbstruck. The miners, to a one, transfixed. Vecque tried in vain to free herself but could already feel the healing process starting. Had she had a few more weeks to strengthen herself and solidify her gains, she might have stopped it. But among its other effects, the Drain removed that option.

෧ ෧ ෧

He was not a bad boy, but insecure and more concerned with what he wasn't than what he was. She identified several problems in the making, one in his liver, one his heart, and two in the small of his back where a joint was out of place. What overshadowed everything, however, was in his dick, or more precisely, in what she had come to identify as the dick brain, which ran roughly from the corpus cavernosum of his penis to his spinal cord and thence to the primitive underbelly of his brain. It was not a problem so much as a condition, a universal one and, as far as she could tell, incurable. She had tried without success to capture and extract it from other of the men.

Still, she toyed with trying again to do something about it, at least that obnoxious part of it that made him, that made all of them, so loathsome. It would serve him right, a fitting climax to this pathetic little show.

Unfortunately, she couldn't get a hold of it, much less wrest it from him. She didn't have it in her; it was unclear if anybody had. She was left with healing him of one ridiculously minor malady, and even that effort, in the wake of everything that had gone before, was enough to nearly do her in.

❧❧❧

When she came out of it and disengaged herself, she felt assaulted. The hall was in an uproar. All around her men were clapping, hooting, making noise. Beside her, the boy had staggered to his feet. She watched him shake his head as if to clear it, then grin and raise a fist in triumph.

A part of her knew that even now, especially now, she must sit tall and not give in to them, not quail or flinch, but she couldn't do it, she lacked the strength. Why her? she asked herself. Why this? A wave of nausea swept through her body and seemed to wash away all the good that she'd accomplished. She felt battered. She wanted to strike out at someone. She wanted to curl in a ball and disappear.

Several minutes later she got a contraction in her side, and shortly after that she extruded a Level One Concretion. Reaching underneath her shirt, she removed it from her meli and placed it on the table beside her plate. It was bean-sized, gray and shriveled. She wasn't even sure what it represented, what she'd cured him of. Dully, she watched it wriggle for a few seconds before becoming still. Coiling her finger against her thumb, she flicked it to the floor in disgust. Then she struggled to her feet.

Immediately, Payne was at her side, reaching out to help.

She shrugged him off. "I'm fine. It's no big deal."

But she wouldn't meet his eyes. Nor would she look at any of the men as she made her way past their tables. What use was it standing up to them anyway? What good did it do her being tolerant and nice? They would have their way regardless. There was no escape, either from humans or the Drain.

❧❧❧

Following this incident, Payne began to see more miners at the healing center. This was due, he subsequently discovered, to a downturn in Vecque's ability to treat the men. He was desperate to talk to her, but she had stopped coming to the mess hall, and work kept him too busy to get away. He was worried about her, and he felt responsible for what had happened, that having raised her hopes, he had somehow primed her for a fall. The look on her face and her body language as she'd left the table haunted him.

A week passed, and he didn't see her once, which was odd though not entirely surprising. Then he heard a rumor that she was actually turning patients away. This sounded ominous and forced him into action. The next time there was a lull in work, he closed the door to the center, left a note, and made the trip to the Two Prime site.

She wasn't in the healing center, but he found her close at hand. She was in her quarters, propped on a pillow in her bed.

Her appearance shocked him. How could a person change so much, so fast? Her cheeks were hollowed out and sunken, her hair disheveled, her eyes as dull as doorknobs. She looked as if she hadn't slept or eaten in a week.

"Hello," she said in a whisper.

He stared at her, barely able to muster a response.

"It's not as bad as all that." She managed a weak smile. "Actually, it's better this way."

"Better? What's better?"

"No more pretense. No more stupid fighting. It is what it is."

"You need to eat," he said.

"Not hungry."

"And you're wrong. It's not what it is. It's not inevitable."

Another wan smile. "It's good to see you, Payne."

"It's what we make of it. It's how we respond. You have to resist this, Vecque."

She sighed, then patted the bed. "Come sit."

He did as she asked, perching on the edge of the mattress, feeling strangely like a suitor, pleading with her not to give up.

"It is better," she insisted. "For both of us."

"It's not."

"Yes. You finally get your wish. You can have all the work you want."

"That's not my wish."

"It is. Don't you remember? You like it. It's what you look forward to most."

"Not like this."

All week long she'd been wondering if he'd come, hoping that he would. In this new and dreary world of hers, ever more difficult and diminished, he was the only light, the only one she cared to see. But now that he was here, she found herself resenting him.

"So next time be more careful what you wish for," she said sharply.

"That's unfair."

"Life's unfair," she snapped.

Payne stiffened but refused to be intimidated. He had come to help, and help he would. For her part, Vecque was surprised and even a little pleased to discover that she still had some bite left. If it was any consolation to him, soon she wouldn't have the strength to be so nasty. She'd be as dumb and docile as a doormat, with no teeth or bite at all.

The Drain was on her, and despite her pose, she was terrified. Already it had robbed her of ability, and soon it would rob her of dignity, too. It was a crippling process. Her senses would eventually falter and then desert her. Her mind and then her spirit would collapse. The Drain was not a death per se, but it was like a death. It was a slow and torturous depletion, a life without a life, humiliating, deadening, and prolonged.

"You want to know what I wish for," said Payne, "I'll tell you."

She saw the look in his eyes and felt a quiver of fear. "I do know," she said, looking away.

"Then say yes. Let me do it. Let me help you."

She needed some kind of help, that was certain, if there were such a thing for her. Either that, or to be left alone. But what he wanted truly frightened her.

"You never stop barking, do you?"

"It's up to you," he said. "You can make me stop."

"And if it's a trap?"

"If what's a trap?" Unlike her, he was not dominated by wariness and suspicion. To his eyes the world was plain to see. All he wanted was a chance to heal her. To use his meli. To bring her some relief.

"Hope," she answered. "Thinking there's nothing to lose."

"It's never wrong to hope. It's never wrong to try. That's the Drain talking. That's not you."

"Is it?" The thought had not occurred to her, or if it had, she'd forgotten. It was hard to tell the difference between the one and the other anymore.

"It's no trap if we go in with our eyes open. If we know what we're doing. If we're prepared."

This made a certain sense to her. She sat up in bed, buoyed by his confidence.

"And the fact that it's never worked before? Not ever. Not once."

"Mobestis healed Emm."

"That's a story."

Payne was not so sure. In his zeal, fact mingled freely with fiction. At this stage it seemed irrelevant to draw too fine a line.

"It's a good one, if it is. And if it isn't . . . well, that's even better, because then it really happened; it's true."

He took her hand, sandwiching it between his own. "How old are you, Vecque?"

She blinked, caught off guard by both the question and the touch. In all their time together, their intimacy had been limited to words. She had never known a person's skin to be so hot. He burned, while she felt deathly cold.

"I'm twenty," she said.

He shook his head. "Too young. Far too young." He being barely nineteen. "I can stop this. With your help I can heal you."

She was frightened; she believed him; her head spun like a top. If only the future weren't opaque. If only the present weren't so awful. She was weary to the point of collapse.

"I have a wish, too," she said, then hesitated, knowing it was a mistake in her condition—in any condition she could presently conceive of—to make wishes. "I want to see the sky again. The one above Gode."

Her voice was so low Payne had to lean in to hear it. Up close her breath had the fruity smell that came of starvation. Her tongue was coated with a sticky paste.

"And the wind. I want to hear it. How it blows and blows in summer. You know. Like someone singing."

He hadn't thought of Gode in a long time, but the wind, and especially the fearsome summer wind, was not a thing he could easily forget. As a child he had lain in bed at night, terrified by the sound of it, imagining that his house had been uprooted and set down in a den of hissing snakes. He had a fear of snakes. And Wyn sometimes had seized on this, hissing at him in the dark, though other times he had been kinder and more comforting.

Boldly, he vowed that she would hear the sound of singing wind again. He promised this to her, feeling whipped by winds himself, winds of recklessness and passion and conviction.

"But I need your help. We need to work together."

He stood, then bent and tried to lift her, but she was heavy and unwieldy, and enfeebled by her days in bed. There was a moment when he thought that she might fall; then all at once she lifted herself, startling both of them. Immediately, she felt light-headed and gripped his arm. Her legs were wobbly and weak.

"Promise that you'll stop at any sign of trouble. For either of us."

"There won't be any trouble," he said, steadying her.

She had barely strength enough to stand, much less argue with him.

"Oh, Payne. Please. Just promise."

⊜⊜⊜

The night before the healing, he had a dream that filled him with a sense of dread. His brother was in the dream, and was besieged by someone or something; then all at once there was a reversal, and it was Payne who was under attack. He woke up in a sweat, but eventually calmed down enough to get back to sleep, and in the morning he felt better.

And better still after healing a miner of a nasty little pleural ailment, extracting and then extruding the Level Two Concretion with ease. Holding life in the balance and then tipping that balance toward life was a feeling unlike all others. It was visceral and it was thrilling, and it gave him confidence. By the time he met with Vecque, the nightmare was forgotten. He was ready, and he was able. The racing of his heart was excitement, not foreboding.

He prepared a little differently than he did for other healings, removing his shirt entirely instead of simply rolling up his sleeve. Like every healer, his dermal recognition follicles ran from wrist to shoulder, but for what he'd had to deal with so far, he'd never had to use more than his forearm. With Vecque he wanted every bit of contact he could get.

He helped her onto the healing bed then joined her, wrapping and binding their arms with care. Her skin was dry, but he was sweating enough for the two of them. Sweat was needed to create an effective neural bridge. She took several deep breaths while staring open-eyed at the ceiling. Then like gates, her eyelids closed.

"Good luck," she whispered.

Payne said nothing. Half-naked, he felt a stirring in his groin.

This sometimes happened, that he became aroused. There was a kinship that he had yet to understand between healing and sexuality, or, virgin that he was, what he imagined sexuality to be. The way his senses came alive. The way his meli throbbed. And the waves of force and energy that ran back and forth between him and the person he was healing.

It was such an intimate connection. It gave rise to such a sense of power and release. Sometimes he wondered if it was normal to feel the way he did. If it was common. If it was somehow wrong. He would have liked to ask Vecque, who lay so unaware and trusting beside him, what her own experiences had been.

Stage One went well enough. It wasn't hard to identify what was everywhere, in every system, every organ, every cellular conglomerate, every cell. The Drain was ubiquitous, a sump of energy with the tenacity of a parasite. It was bland, bottomless, and unyielding. While not contagious per se, it had a quality of contagion. A kind of infectious magnetism. Payne felt attracted to it, or perhaps it was the reverse, it felt attracted to him.

Cautiously, he recruited more neurofibratory bundles up his arm, enhancing the signal, defining it. Oddly, he encountered no resistance. The source of Vecque's deterioration seemed almost cheered by his attention, surrendering to it without opposition.

Stage Three required more effort. The epitopic signature was polymorphic, a fusion of Vecque's native identity with the Drain's wild, multicentric form. In no living creature was health an absolute, but rather a constantly shifting balance between function and dysfunction, efficiency and breakdown. In all bodies, from the simplest to the most complex, there was some degree of illness, some structure that did not perform as optimally as it might, some system in need of repair. In most cases, these would right themselves naturally, in the normal course of a body's self-healing. In a few cases, however, they would not.

These trouble spots were the seeds of future maladies, true illnesses in the making. Distinguishing between the two—between what required intervention and what did not—took time and patience, and the Drain's pervasiveness made this extremely hard. Over and over Payne followed strands of dysfunction that led to knots that led to nowhere. He felt benumbed by choices. Time and again he had to start from scratch.

Finally, though, he had the thing identified in all its manifold dimensions. It was something like a cloud and something like a heavy blanket, and it had a gagging smell and a choking taste, and infiltrated Vecque with a dense, restrictive weight. He surrounded it as he had learned to do, joining with his patient, completing the stage of capture. But when he tried to extract it, it wouldn't budge. This had never happened to him, and he bore down harder, then harder still.

And now it did resist, with a force and tenacity that was new to him. His efforts to dislodge it seemed only to accomplish the reverse. It was like trying to pry a clinging child from its mother; the more he pulled, the more its hold tightened. He wasn't sure that he could, or even should, muster the energy to yank it free.

At length he paused to consider the situation. Healing had always been so easy for him, and this was something new. He had never been pushed to such a limit, never felt so put-upon and opposed. In his mind he returned to the beginning, reexamining the initial stages, looking for flaws in observation and technique. It was tiring work, and puzzling when he could find no errors in anything he'd done. Yet still the thing resisted his extraction. There seemed no choice but to use more force.

Reaching down inside himself for all the strength he had, he tore at it and with a last-ditch effort finally wrenched it free.

But now, as he prepared to shape and then expel it, he found that he had made a few miscalculations. It was larger and more deeply rooted than he had first perceived. And its boundaries were not fixed but shifting, as though it were unstable, and more, still an active, growing thing. He had captured it, but now he couldn't identify it. And without identity, upon which all else depended, he could not extrude it, and it was dangerous to try.

But try he did; he worked his meli feverishly, laboring to turn the thing into something material and substantial, something concrete. It took every bit of skill and talent and resourcefulness he had, and in the end he could not do it. It was like breathing in a vacuum. The strength bled out of him. His mind ebbed, then emptied, and after wavering briefly at the edge of consciousness, he passed out on the bed.

And like an outgoing tide the Drain returned to Vecque. And having passed through Payne, it was transmuted. No longer would it suck the life from its victim, which in other circumstances might have been a victory. But in this case it was the opposite; a chilling, horrific defeat. For now it would neither kill nor be killed. It would live on in Vecque, extending her life, but a life she could never have imagined, much less wished for. A life whose sole intent, she would soon come to believe, was to cause her pain.

SIX

Payne's punishment was swift. He was given twenty years at the Pannus mine, twenty more than the year he'd already served to do what he had long since mastered. Twenty years to hear the same complaints and treat the same old problems, to see the same tired faces day in and out. Twenty years to be excluded by the miners. Twenty years to doubt himself and hate himself, twenty years to take the blame for his mistake.

But healers did not last for twenty years. Most survived for less than ten. For all intents and purposes, then, Payne's sentence was for life.

A harsh punishment, but worse by far was what they meted out to Vecque, which was nothing. They left her as Payne had left her, at the mercy of a thing that gnawed and scraped and clawed inside her, as if it, too, were under sentence and none too happy about it. Vecque was now the bearer of a new condition in the annals of the healing craft, a novelty born of her and Payne's joint and ill-considered effort, an amalgam of their foolishness, a curse.

In a cruel bit of irony, the symptoms of the Drain relented. Vecque's body was no longer ravaged by it, her brain no longer addled, her senses no longer dulled. But beware the treatment that is worse than the disease, for what took its place was far more terrible. She had known one extreme, and now she became acquainted with the other.

Suddenly, she was aware of everything. Sensitive to the faintest whisper, the subtlest smell, the dimmest light. Voices made her cringe. A candle and she recoiled. The smell of food, which had once been her joy, was especially painful, and when the pangs of hunger forced her to eat, the touch of it on her tongue, the taste of it and then, unbearably, the swallowing, were excruciating. It was as if her body had been stripped of its protective coating. As if every nerve were exposed and raw.

She took to her quarters to escape the sensory bombardment, and yet she could not bear to be alone. Nor could she tolerate standing still. She was possessed by an unrelenting restlessness, her arms and especially legs in constant need of motion, as though these nerves, the ones controlling her muscles and her joints, her posture, balance, and position, were firing nonstop, too. So while her room was dark and relatively quiet, she was driven from it to pace the streets and the upper tunnels of the mine, seeking and yet avoiding contact, caught between a desperate longing to connect and a mordant fear of anything that might cause further stimulus and pain.

Payne tried desperately to help her, but what was there for him to do? She could not bear to be touched, even for comfort's sake, and the words he murmured in an effort to soothe her sounded hollow, even to him. Medication sometimes seemed to dull her pain but just as often didn't, and he was left to sit with her, when he had the time, as anyone would sit with someone who was suffering, listening if she chose to speak, which was rare, consoling her in whatever way he could think of, mostly just attending her in the vague and unrequited hope that his being there was better than his not.

A year went by and then another. For reasons Payne could only guess at, Vecque had not been replaced, leaving him as the sole healer for the thousands of workers at the mine. As she had foretold, he had all the work he wanted, but it had ceased to satisfy him. It was so predictable by now, so monotonous, he could do it in his sleep. It was busy work, and it bored and frustrated him. He knew that he had more to offer and to give.

Though maybe not for long, which was another worry, that his skills would atrophy. He feared they already had. Which was the only possible explanation and defense for the idea that kept popping into his head of trying to heal Vecque again. It was pure insanity, he knew, to dare to even think it. But such was his pity for her and his own crying need to fight the tedium and stagnation that he did.

Winters were the worst. They seemed to last forever, cold and dark and dreary, mirroring his own sorry fate and state of mind. The days seemed hardly days at all, but hints of days, terse, foreshortened preambles to the long and cheerless speech of night. Life in camp went on, but it was a pallid life, subdued, attenuated and limited. Outside of work, the men withdrew into themselves. They hunkered down. Or else they turned to drink. It was a time of isolation, a time, for those inclined, to sink into depression. Payne was not the type, but the winters wore him down. They did something similar to Vecque. He hadn't thought it possible, but they seemed to make her even more miserable and anguished than she was.

In winter everyone spent more time sleeping, Payne included, just as in summer he spent less. He had more dreams in winter, too. One night he was dreaming of being asleep in a cave of rock and snow. It was a peaceful dream and a peaceful sleep, but then it became disturbed, and he woke with the sense of something wrong. At first he thought there'd been an accident in the mine, but there was no warning siren. Instead, he heard the howling of wolves, not so rare an occurrence, only this time they sounded close at hand. Curious, he threw on his clothes and went outside to investigate.

The moon was full and low in the sky, half-hidden by the trees. It lit the night with a ghostly, bluish glow and cast pale shadows on the snow. He could hear the pack distinctly, close enough that he could make out different and distinguishing sounds. Some of the wolves were howling, some were barking, while others were growling low in their throats. It sounded almost like a conversation, as if they were discussing something. Maybe, he thought, they had an animal surrounded and were debating how best to bring it down. If so, this was something he wanted to see.

Leaving the relative safety of the main camp, he headed downhill toward the playing field, which seemed the source of the sounds. The streets were empty, and he met no other men. All who were awake, save him, were underground.

As he came in sight of the field, the moon slid behind a cloud. When it reemerged, he was halfway down the slope and got his first glimpse of the pack. There were six or seven of them in a ring, light gray bodies against the pearly opalescence of the snow. In the middle of the ring, gaunt and motionless, stood a person. His heart sank, then started pounding, because he knew at once who it was.

The wolves were circling her, growling, snarling, yipping, all the while closing in. Payne shouted and ran at them, hoping to drive them away, but the snow was deep, and he lost his balance and fell, sprawling. Struggling to his feet and wiping the snow from his face, he yelled at the top of his lungs, then rushed to make a snowball, which he hurled at the pack. It was a futile gesture, for the wolves were a good fifty yards away, well beyond the reach of his arm. Besides, they were not concerned with him. To a one, their eyes were on their prey.

They moved in closer, their teeth gleaming in the moonlight, their circle tightening. One of them, the largest, leapt forward and nipped Vecque's arm.

Payne screamed at them, and as he drew a breath to scream again, he heard another sound, a new one, soft and whispering, like the sigh of wind through leaves, though there was no wind to speak of. Then, from the corner of his eye he detected motion.

From the forest that edged the field, shapes appeared: two-legged, upright shapes, scores of them, moving quickly forward, coalescing. At first Payne thought that they were humans, small humans, a tribe perhaps, but then he saw the third limb at their backs and realized that they were ort. They didn't sink into the snow but somehow glided over it, moving toward the pack as effortlessly as they had moved across the grassy plain. When they reached the wolves, they didn't stop but streamed between and past them until they had Vecque surrounded, with the wolves on the outside of a now much wider circle.

And then the strangest thing occurred. All together, as if on cue, the ort raised their hind limbs, first pointing them as straight as arrows toward the sky then curving them downward and looping them around one another, until, within seconds, the entire drove was linked and intertwined. From a distance it looked like they had formed a knot and been transformed from many separate bodies into a single, indivisible one.

At first the wolves looked baffled and confused. Then they started howling. But they didn't attack the ort. Didn't bite or even nip them. They yipped and growled and stalked about the perimeter of the circle, but the ort just stood their ground until eventually the wolves gave up and padded uneasily away.

Payne watched all this from where he stood above the field, too stunned and mesmerized to move. When at last he roused himself, the ort had started drifting off, and by the time he reached Vecque, they had vanished. All around her the snow was trampled, and here and there he made out tracks. But neither ort not wolf remained. Vecque stood alone in the middle of the field, hugging herself and moaning.

"Why did they do that?" she cried.

"It was a miracle," said Payne. "The wolves were trying to kill you."

"Yes. Why didn't they let them?" Haggard and shivering, she seemed to have lost her mind. Strings of tears had frozen to her cheeks. She looked ravaged. "Kill me, Payne. Please. I beg you. Put me out of this misery."

Instead, he threw his coat around her shoulders and led her back to his quarters. Repeatedly, she pleaded with him to end the torment, until her pleas turned to sobs and then, at length, her sobs to a woeful, haunted silence. Payne put her in his bed and sat up the rest of the night, unable to sleep. Many thoughts went through his head. What was he to do? He couldn't take her life, and he thanked the ort, for, truly, they had saved her. His thanks were followed by another thought, and he hung his head and prayed to be forgiven, because he wished they hadn't.

This happened in the winter of his fourth year at the mine. It was his worst winter yet, one he feared would never end. But eventually it did, and even though his future was the same regardless of the season, he rejoiced to see the days begin to lengthen and the weather thaw. He had not a single reason to be hopeful and every reason not to be, and yet, like every living thing, with spring his spirits rose.

Everybody's did. The camp itself seemed to breathe a sigh of relief when spring arrived. Like an old dog dreaming of its youth, it woke with a sense of purpose, wagging its tail and shaking free of the winter doldrums.

There was plenty of work to do outside the mine, and the men set to it, if not with eagerness then at least with energy. Buildings damaged by the winter storms had to be repaired. Broken windows replaced, roofs and stairs that had buckled under the weight of snow shored up and mended. Iron rails that hard fingers of ice had loosened and in some cases popped free of their ties had to be reattached, and muck heaps impossible to deal with because of snow and freezing temperatures had to be sorted and attended to.

It was a busy time of year. Rail traffic picked up dramatically. Long and fully laden trains left camp once and sometimes twice a week on their way to processing plants in the south. Empty trains returned, some carrying passengers. One of the first that year was an officer of the Pannus Corporation. He was accompanied by an engineer and a team of surveyors. They stayed a week, analyzing rock samples and scouting out a site for a new decline. Along with them came a variety of peddlers and tradesmen, drawn by the scent of unspent winter money. One natty gentleman arrived with money of his own and left with a suitcase full of musk.

There was other traffic, too. The prospect of a better job elsewhere was a constant topic of conversation and source of speculation among the miners, and in spring and summer they had a habit of getting happy feet. Miners were a restless breed to begin with, tempted by dreams of greener pastures, prone to migratory bursts. Early that summer, fed by a rumor of a hot new mine on the jungle island of Sopor, a record number of men tramped out. The camp looked half-deserted. A week later, a record number tramped in to take their place, and the bunkhouses and mess hall were once more filled to overflowing.

When he had the time, Payne liked to watch the trains come in. He played a game with himself, a seemingly harmless game, imagining that one of the passengers carried news for him. Part of the game involved trying to guess which one it might be. That man, with the look of a mine official? That one, with the lined and weathered face? Or was it that one, with the deliberate, premeditated movements of a courier—was he the messenger boy, the bearer of the happy news?

For, of course, the news was happy: he'd been given a reprieve. Here's the letter, the man would say, and here's your ticket out. You've been here long enough; it's time to move on.

Every year he played this game, and every year it backfired. No one ever had a letter for him. No one even knew his name. It was not a harmless game at all, but depressing and self-defeating. If he played it a hundred years, he would have a hundred years of disappointments. Better not to get his hopes up, which is why every year, after a few weeks, he stopped watching incoming trains.

He was not on hand, then, the late summer day a passenger train arrived with but a single car, carrying a mere three passengers. Two of them were human, one male and one female. The male was large and portly. The female, tall and more finely built. The third passenger, a male, was tesque, and he reported immediately to the site boss. The humans went in search of Vecque.

They found her in her quarters, huddled in her bed. She shrank at their arrival, prompting the man to scowl and demand that she stand up and look at him. When this achieved nothing, the woman asked his permission to try a gentler approach. Kneeling beside Vecque, she spoke softly to her, and at length was able to coax her to her feet.

Immediately, Vecque started pacing, head down, arms against her sides, hands clenched. The man found this intolerable and ordered her to stop. When she didn't, he stepped forward and grabbed her by the wrist. His grip was strong, his fingers fat with many rings. With the other hand he pinched her chin and raised her head, forcing her to look at him.

But she couldn't. Her eyes darted this way and that, like flies unable or afraid to land. His voice, his grip, and now this, his look, were all too much for her. She whimpered and pleaded to be left alone. A moment later, grim-faced but apparently satisfied, he released her.

Next they sought out Payne. He had just completed an unremark-able extraction from a miner who'd been coughing blood, forming the Concretion into a gooey red rouleau and dropping it down the disposal shaft, when they appeared in the doorway of the healing center. The man he recognized at once as Valid, Doctor of the Mental Latitudes, and lately, it appeared, of the bulging equatorials as well. Jowly-faced, plethoric, with slicked-backed, scented hair and bloodred lips that gleamed from licking, he had put on weight and girth since Payne had last seen him in the final year of training. What he'd gained in size he seemed also to have gained in vanity. And power, or at least authority. He wore the pin of full Professor now.

The woman was a stranger. She wore loose trousers, a long-sleeved, chambray shirt, and sturdy boots. Unlike Valid's, hers were working clothes, sensible for a visit to a mining camp. Her mass of dark hair was pulled back and gathered behind her ears. High cheekbones, a graceful nose and chin, and pale blue eyes completed her face.

Valid swept into the room, cast a look around, then fixed his attention on Payne. He squinted, as if to draw him into better focus.

"Is it my imagination or have you shrunk?"

Payne, who was shocked enough to see him as it was, had no reply for this.

"Something in the air, you think? The food? The lack of stimulation? Remind me, Payne, how long it's been."

"How long?"

"That you've been here."

He knew to the day. "Four years," he said, rounding off.

Valid looked surprised. "That long? How time flies. I hear that you've been busy."

"It's a busy job."

"Yes. And you've been all alone to do it."

With someone else this might have been a simple observation. Maybe even a compliment. But with Valid there were always double meanings.

"I've managed," he replied.

"No doubt. No doubt. We hear wonderful things about you. The Pannus Corporation feels very lucky to have a healer of your capability. It understands that productivity begins and ends with the health of its workforce. And the Pannus workforce has stayed remarkably fit and productive. Profits, I'm told, are at an all-time high. Congratulations are in order."

Was this a cue? Warily, Payne thanked him.

"Don't thank me. Thank the corporation. It's the one that agreed to keep you on after that debacle of yours." He paused, and this time Payne had no doubt what was expected of him.

"I'm grateful."

"Yes. I'd imagine so. And it has every intention of retaining you. For the duration, I might add."

He paused again, as if to allow this grim reminder ample time to sink in. Pursing his lips, he swept a critical eye about the room and by extension, the entire camp and its surroundings.

"Such a far-flung place. So beyond the gem and jewel of the civilized world. So isolated. Though not without a certain rustic charm. If only there weren't so many trees. And so much . . . how shall I put it? Emptiness. Still, I could imagine worse. I'm sure we all could."

Payne doubted this was meant to cheer him up. More likely it was some sort of threat, though why Valid would care to threaten him he had no idea.

"Speak up," said Valid. "I didn't come all this way to entertain a mute."

"Why did you come?" asked Payne, risking a rebuke for being impertinent.

"To question you. To observe how you respond. To see if you've changed. To judge for myself if you can be trusted."

"Ask the men."

"And what would they say?"

"They'd say yes." With nothing to lose he went further. "I can heal them in my sleep."

Valid raised an eyebrow. "And humble, too. That's good. But what concerns me is that other matter. It concerns all of us. Can we trust you not to go off half-cocked? Can we be assured you'll use your head?"

"Yes," said Payne. "Absolutely."

"You've learned from your mistake?"

"Yes. I have. Believe me."

"Let's hope so. I'd hate to discover that you hadn't."

Valid glanced at the woman as if to share an understanding, perhaps to consummate some prearranged agreement, but her attention was fixed on Payne. He watched her for a moment, hungrily it seemed, then wet his lips and continued.

"We've brought another healer with us. He's getting settled as we speak."

It was not the news Payne would have hoped for if he had been so brazen or so foolish as to hope, but it was good news nonetheless. He sorely needed a companion.

He thanked them.

"You can thank us by your actions," said Valid.

"I understand," said Payne, reiterating that he'd learned his lesson.

"I'm glad to hear it, but you miss the point. We're making a swap, him for you. You're coming with us, Payne."

Nothing could have shocked him more. His heart seemed to stop midbeat. His voice deserted him.

"We leave tonight. Sooner if at all possible."

"I'm coming with you?"

"You are."

"Why?"

"Because we choose to take you," Valid answered flatly.

"You have a gift," the woman said. They were her first words.

"What gift?" asked Payne, shifting his attention.

She started to reply, but Valid cut her off. He had the floor, he seemed to believe, until he chose to relinquish it.

"Perhaps he does; perhaps he doesn't. He's hardly been tested now, has he?" To Payne he said, "If it were up to me, you'd serve your sentence. But better minds than mine think otherwise. They think your talents are wasted here."

Another glance around the healing center, with its muddy wooden floors, shabby furnishings and rudimentary equipment, seemed to convince him that this might well be the case. "There is a world outside, you know. A world beyond this . . . this hovel. In any case, it's best to keep an open mind. Everyone deserves a second chance. And healers are a precious commodity. There are places clamoring for one with experience."

"What places?" asked Payne, hardly daring to imagine such a thing.

"Does it matter?" answered Valid.

No. Of course it didn't. "And Vecque? What about her?"

"Vecque?"

"The other healer," said the woman.

"Ah, yes. Our sad, unfortunate Vecque. What shall we do with her?" Valid pursed his lips in thought. "But of course you knew the consequences. Did you think that somehow you were immune? Or perhaps you blame us for not teaching you properly? For not drilling into your heads what every first-year schoolboy knows?"

"No," said Payne.

"No what?"

"I don't blame you. I blame myself."

"Yes," said Valid. "I'd think you would."

"We knew the risks."

"Did you?" Valid struggled with this for a moment before brightening. "Youthful exuberance then. Not so terrible a crime. But how to deter it? How to prevent such catastrophes in the future?"

Hands clasped behind his back, he took a step or two around the room, head bent in contemplation.

"Thoughts?" he asked.

Payne knew enough not to volunteer.

Valid provided his own. "I've one. We'll take her with us."

Payne's heart leapt. "You can help her?"

Valid snorted. "Help her? Not likely. We'll use her as an example.

An illustration for anyone who thinks he can flout the laws of nature. An object lesson in what? Stupidity? Arrogance? Ambition?" He seemed genuinely perplexed. "Hard to know what you were thinking. If thought, in fact, was involved. The vigor of youth so often resides outside the brain.

"Help her, you say? No, my friend, can't do. So sorry. But she'll help so many others. If you need consolation, and it appears you do, I'd take it in that."

"You can't," said Payne.

A furrow worried Valid's brow. Two furrows, in point of fact, troughs in a glistening and otherwise placid surface. Disturbances in the calm.

"Can't?"

"It's wrong."

"You'd rather she stayed?"

"I'd rather you helped her."

"I?" He placed a hand upon his chest. A preposterous idea.

At which point the woman intervened. Stepping forward, she faced Valid. They were roughly the same height, and she stood eye to eye with him.

"If you could give us a moment, I think that we can settle this."

Valid had his doubts, but her voice and manner brooked no argument. Bowing slightly, he deferred to her good judgment and with a parting glance at Payne left the two of them alone.

Payne was relieved to have him gone, although the residue of his presence, like a vapor, lingered. The woman made him nervous, but in a different way.

"You do have a decision to make," she said. "Your friend's not coming with us. Valid was only goading you with that. And frankly, it's better that she's not."

"I can't leave her here."

"No. That would be a cruel thing to do."

"Then what?"

She didn't answer, but instead invoked a cagey sort of silence that sent the question back to him. But he was out of answers. He didn't know what to do; if he did, he would have long since done it. One thing was certain though: he'd had his fill of guilt and grief and helplessness, standing by while Vecque remained in agony.

"What would you do if the situation were reversed?" she asked at length. "If you were in her place?"

"If I were Vecque? I wouldn't do anything. I wouldn't be able to. If you've seen her, then you know what I mean."

"But what would you want?"

"Help," he said, which was all Vecque ever asked of him. "Relief. An end to the misery."

"Yes. Of course. What anyone would want. So how can you help her? What can you do?"

He was afraid to mention the one thing that had occurred to him. Who was this woman anyway? Why should he confide in her?

"It might help to get it off your chest," she said.

"Get what?"

She assured him that anything he said would be held in the strictest of confidences. Not a word would leave the room. Valid, in particular, would never hear a thing. She didn't answer to him, or, for that matter, to anyone.

Still, he was reluctant to speak openly with her, and she didn't pressure him. She seemed, in fact, familiar with the concept of waiting, with the idea that certain things required time to mature and ripen. Beyond this, she seemed to have a talent for drawing people out.

In the end he told her. It was surprising, really, how quickly he acquiesced. Or not so surprising, considering how long he'd been alone, with no outlet for his thoughts and feelings, how thirsty he was for contact and conversation with someone else.

"I had one idea," he said.

She nodded her encouragement.

"I wouldn't actually do it. It was just a thought."

"I understand."

"I mean, how much worse can things get?"

"I mean."

She seemed to be teasing him in a gentle sort of way. Then all at once she smiled. It was a look that lit the room. Payne caught his breath, amazed at how beautiful a smile could be. And how long it had been since he'd seen one.

After that he wanted to tell her everything.

But he contained himself. This one secret would be enough. Drawing his breath, he confessed to the thought of trying to heal Vecque again, then waited anxiously for her reaction.

She didn't look particularly surprised. In fact, it seemed as if she'd been expecting to hear something along this line.

"I haven't acted on it," he rushed to add. "I wouldn't. It's just a thought. A stupid one."

"Not stupid. No thought is stupid. I'm glad you haven't tried it, though." She seemed so very calm and at the same time keyed in to him. So poised and so astute.

"Any other secrets?" she asked.

It was a huge relief to get this one off his chest. If there were others, he couldn't think of them.

"We were talking about your friend," she prompted him. "Ideas about how to help her."

"It's been three years," he said. "A lot goes through your mind in three years."

"A lot goes through it in a day." She gave another smile, a sadder sort of smile, this one, it seemed, meant for herself. And then it was Payne's turn to wait, as her thoughts turned inward.

At length she asked him if he'd ever owned a pet. He shook his head.

"My family had a dog. He was already old when I was young, and every year he got older and more crippled and uncomfortable. It got to the point that he could barely eat. And he whimpered all the time. Eventually, we had to put him down. It was hard, but it was right. What I mean is, it was the decent and humane thing to do."

"I can't do that to Vecque," said Payne.

"Have you asked her what she wants?"

"I don't have to ask. She's begged me to take her life. A hundred times. But I can't. I won't."

"Why not?"

"I'm a healer, not a killer. I foster life. I don't destroy it."

She took him at his word, despite the irony, given what he'd done. "That's an honorable sentiment, but what exactly in Vecque are you fostering? What kind of life is she living?"

"Two wrongs don't make a right," he said.

"What's wrong is letting someone suffer needlessly. What's wrong is not acting for fear of making another mistake." She spoke forcibly and with authority, as if she had firsthand knowledge of this. "There's killing and there's mercy killing. The first is a crime. The second is an act of charity. It's a generosity. A blessing."

"By whose authority?"

"The heart's authority," she said. "By order of the laws of kindness and compassion and basic human decency."

Payne felt obliged to point out that he wasn't human.

A look of impatience crossed her face. "Stop it. You're not ignorant, so don't act it. Tesque, human, what's the difference? Mercy's mercy. And as for you and your so-called mistake, a healer's job is to intervene. The outcome of what you do is not always what you planned or hoped for, but that doesn't mean it was wrong to act."

He appreciated her support, though he was a little taken aback by the heat of its delivery. It was also slightly strange: was she condoning what he'd done? Whatever she meant, it didn't change his mind. The idea of helping Vecque by intentionally taking her life was an oxy-moron.

"The poor thing's begged you to put her out of her misery," she said. "She's pleaded. She wants to die. For both of you, in the deepest and maybe truest and most abiding sense, her death would be a healing."

"You're telling me to kill her then? Is that the cost of my train trip out? Is that the price of my ticket?"

"No," she said. "There is no price. We're leaving and you're coming with us, and I doubt that you'll ever be coming back. As for Vecque, you're free to do as you please. You can leave her as she is or you can help her find some peace. It's a difficult decision, but it's the only one you get to make."

She headed for the door, then stopped for a final word. "It's an unfair world, Payne, and not just here. There're problems everywhere. Solutions, too. That's the good news. The bad news is, there are no per-fect ones."

AKSAGETTA

ONE

The man had silver hair and a ruddy, intemperate face. His eyes were bloodshot and wild. In front of him lay a dwindled pile of checkered chips; ahead of him, if his luck didn't turn, a cold tomorrow. But he had a hunch, which came to him in the form of a voice that seemed to originate outside his body but to be lodged in the very center of his being, and clutching his remaining chips, he reached across the felted table to place his bet on Number Five. Five fingers in a hand, five prayers, five combos to the Big Money, five paths to glory. But suddenly, the hand seized up, became a fist, a knot of clenched and trembling muscle. It was the right hand, the hand farthest from the heart but closest to the avid, thinking brain. In the gaming halls of Aksagetta, where thought was captive to desire and cupidity ran rampant, this rebellion of the distal forelimb happened frequently enough that it had a name, the Claw, sometimes also called the Tetany. To this some people tacked on Greed, the Tetany of Greed, as greed was felt by many to be the cause behind the reflex, rooted as it was in the fear of letting go. But when the spasm moved from the puzzled man's hand to his forearm and then to his shoulder, someone suggested that perhaps this was a different sort of tetany, and when it moved to his face and jaw, an aisle was cleared in the clamorous hall and he was wheeled out on a serving cart swept clear of drinks and condiments and rushed by elevator to a room thirty floors below. Where a healer waited.

The aisle closed up in seconds. No holding back the press of humans, surging through the doors, streaming in from all directions to fill the gaps and take their places, to feel the heat and play the games. The plushly carpeted floor, the dim, forgiving light, the vast pavilion and hundreds like it in dozens of buildings crowded side by side like stacks of chips—all this and more defined the city, beckoning any and all to take a chance, have a little fun, loosen up the joints, live a little beyond your means for once in your penny-pinching lives, share the wealth, dig deep, buy in.

Aksagetta, poco loco, diablo puro, paradise for games and gambling of every sort. Aksagetta, caterer to the wanton best of human nature, the optimus eternus, the pleasure-loving, self-indulgent creature unwilling to be tamed or denied. Aksagetta, where avarice was not a naughty word. Aksagetta, where fun was the ripe fruit and conscience, podrido, rotten. Aksagetta, spun of gold. Aksagetta, built on promise. Aksagetta, shameless, brash and fine.

The city had it all: the tables and the tracks, the hippodromes and elevated circuit jumps, the faux dirt fighting pits, the bandstand relays, the filamented bowling greens. And more: the crap-shoots, the funnel races, the futures toss, the psychic lift, the winking jacks of opportunity, the betting parlors, the chambers of hyperbole and accident. And more still: the six-two montes, the pea and princess games, restitution bingo, extreme assault and sanction, the pools of exactitude, the final lottery, the roving pony shows. There was a game, a shuck, a fantasy for everyone, and the people came in droves, young and old alike, filing into the vast halls and casinos like ants to sugar, hungry for the sweetnesses of life, liking their chances, ready for a roll, and for the most part orderly, like the good citizens they were. Although sometimes a wave of panic would come from nowhere and sweep the lines, causing a frantic rush to get at things that were never in short supply on Aksagetta, as though implicit in plenty lay the fear of scarcity, and elbows would be thrown and bodies pushed and shoved, and people would get hurt. Which was one reason to have healers in the buildings, to tend to the fallen.

There was another reason, slightly more sobering: of the humans who came to Aksagetta a fair number were elderly, enjoying an extended vacation, perhaps one last final fling. Of these, some would fall ill, or be ill on arrival but not know it, or know it but be in denial, hiding it from their loved ones or themselves. And, as was often the case with old and worn-out flesh, these illnesses were sometimes grave and advanced. Healers were needed to combat them, healers of something more than modest skill, to ensure that these holidays were not beset by misery, or worse, demise.

Payne was one such healer, and nothing he had seen since his arrival had caused him undue trouble or alarm. Healing was his element, and the conditions under which he worked were much better than at the Pannus mine. The hours were long but not interminable; a part of every day was his to do with as he pleased. And the equipment at his disposal was new and up-to-date. Principally, this was for the benefit of his clientele, who demanded it, although there were advantages that accrued to him as well.

The healing bed, for one, was downy soft and heated. Far more comfortable than the worn and lumpy bed he'd known at Pannus, especially if a session lasted long. The walls and ceiling of the healing chamber were backlit with retinal-harmonic light that had a mild, analgesic effect on patients in pain. Similarly, there was a Boomine synthesizer to soften or disguise the healers' voices, as certain humans could not relax in the presence of the gamey diction and rhythm of unmodified tesque speech. Every room was stocked with an epidermal barrier spray for those who on principle decried skin-to-skin contact with a tesque (and were willing to accept the decreased efficacy that accompanied its use). And for those too squeamish or genteel to lay eyes on their own concreted illnesses (which applied to virtually all humans), there was an entirely separate extrusion room.

These amenities made the work go smoothly, as innovations, in health as elsewhere, often did. Of course, with improved technology went heightened expectations, the paradox being that the patients of Aksagetta, on the whole, were less satisfied than the Pannus miners had ever been. For after all was said and done, the act of healing fell to the healer. And healers—their patients' wishes, desires, demands and presumptions notwithstanding—were the flesh, bone and brain they'd always been.

When Payne first laid eyes on the stricken gamer from the casino, the man was stiff as a board, though anything but still. Underneath the thin blanket of his skin his muscles twitched and popped like static. From his throat came a panoply of grunts and gasps as he tried in vain to move air in and out of his lungs. In one respect his condition was a blessing, for rigid bodies were much easier to move than limp ones. With the help of the floor manager who'd brought him, Payne had little trouble transferring him from the makeshift gurney to the healing bed.

His larynx incapacitated, the man could not express himself in words, but the pupils of his eyes, spared the paralytic tetany, spoke volumes. He was terrified, not merely, Payne surmised, by the sensate imminence of death, but by the closeness of the tesque who hovered over him. Without time to activate the Boomine synthesizer or coat him with the barrier spray, Payne uttered a word of encouragement, tied him down to avoid being flattened by an errant, spastic limb, then joined him posthaste on the healing bed.

It was hard at first to relax, for the man himself was so tense, his body wound so tight it seemed about to snap. This worried Payne. The stress of muscles contracting all at once, agonists against antagonists, flexors against extensors, could fracture bone. Not to mention what it did to breathing, which was to make it simply impossible. The man was turning blue for lack of air. Fortunately, he was also sweating, providing the crucial electrolytic bridge for Payne to start his work. Quickly, he wrapped their arms together, lay back and began.

It didn't take long to identify the problem. It was coil-shaped and finely toothed and sat astride the hypothalamus with trailing fibers that stretched into the nearby mammillary bodies and beyond. When he enhanced the signal by increasing the area of neuroepidermal contact (thereby recruiting additional recognitive buds), he found a similar lesion in the man's premotor cortex and a third one in his pons.

In an orderly, stepwise fashion he defined the epitopes, synchronized himself harmonically and began the process of capture and exchange. Extraction followed, and abruptly, as if a rigid pike had been removed from him, the man went limp. He sagged into the bed as if deflated and drew a gasping breath, and then another and another. The chips that he was clutching in his palm fell clattering to the floor.

Remodeling and concentration could take from hours to a day, depending on the level and complexity of the Concretion. Payne completed his in thirty minutes, then went into the inner room to extrude.

Each stage of healing had its pleasures, but to him the last stage, extrusion, was the best. He got to see the fruit of his labor. He got to make a thing, an entity, that was singular and had not been made before. Best of all, for however long it took, his meli was alive, and the feeling that that gave him was like no other. Visceral, and utterly sublime.

What came out was long and thin and straight, like fishing line. It had a liquid coating, a sheen that dried upon exposure to the air. And as it dried, the Concretion slowly twisted on itself, until it resembled on a larger scale what he had visualized inside the man.

For most healers, this similarity in appearance was uncommon, for while Concretions in theory derived equally from both parties, in practice, because of the effort put into extraction and extrusion, they typically bore the imprint of the healer more than the healed. But Payne was not like most healers. He found it better not to force the issue, preferring to allow his Concretions to take their natural forms, shaping them only subtly, with a deft, almost feathery touch. He teased his creations but did not coerce them, and the results he found more beautiful and striking for such restraint.

By the time the Concretion had reified and he'd disposed of it, the man he'd saved from death was gone. He'd left a chip behind him, a tip, it seemed. Being relatively new to Aksagetta, it was the first one Payne had received.

He eyed it with uncertainty. Was it ethical, he wondered, to accept a gratuity for services that, for the pure pleasure of it, he would have done for free? Was it honorable, or principled, to be paid for one's enjoyment? Was this a form of bribery? In the future would the man expect a favor and would he, Payne, feel obliged to bestow it? Would he feel pressed to cater to him in lieu of someone else who was in greater need?

In fact, they never saw each other again, for after returning to the hall from whence he came, the man put all his chips on chance, and when he lost, he moved to restitution bingo, where, deeming it most unlikely that fate would curse him twice in a single day, he wrote a promissory note for all his worldly goods and savings, and was a heartbeat away from realizing his wildest dreams when the same inner voice that had previously whispered to him spoke again, this time with a force that seemed to shake the hall, causing the bingo ball to pop improvidently from one slot to the next, so that instead of winning, he came in second, which is to say, he bought the farm. Scarcely two hours after being pulled from the brink of death, he was faced with death again, this time self-appointed, as he balanced on a ledge thirty floors above the teeming street and contemplated suicide, while below him Payne finished his shift and left the building, unaware of the danger of falling objects, tired but satisfied with another day's work.

There were places where a healer could blow off steam, basement joints and backroom parlors off the beaten path for those with energy to burn. Principally, these were newcomers who, not yet affected by the Drain, were in the market for short-term situations, personal but fluid, friendly but not too involved. Given a healer's future, there was much to recommend a relaxed, low-maintenance level of commitment, and, freed from the straitjacketed world of Pannus, Payne initially had been an avid participant. But after several months he tired of the life, which, for all its pleasures, left him feeling hollow.

Now after work he went directly home to his apartment, which was small and austere. He ate alone and had begun to wonder if solitude might not be best for him, might, in fact, not be his natural state. He'd heard the rumors circulating among the healers about him. That he was a lone wolf, a recluse, that he set himself apart. That he didn't like the company of others. That he thought that he was better.

And more, that he was different from the rest of them. Invulnerable, they said. Immune to the Drain. An aberration among healers, an anomaly, a Grotesque among Grotesques. He would raise the humans' expectations and make all of them have to work that much harder. He was a threat to their already abbreviated lives. He was a menace.

And other rumors, too, contradictory ones, that, in fact, he was no different than the rest of them, only treated differently, which was why he didn't get drained. He was someone's favorite, it was whispered, someone's pet, and not required to work so hard. His quota was lower. He saw less, they said, than half his fair share. No wonder he kept to himself. Who under such circumstances would dare to show his face? And it was just as well because he couldn't be trusted. He had a temper. He'd killed another healer. And not just one.

All of which explained why the other healers, on the whole, kept their distance from him, and why he, in turn, kept his from them. They had a low opinion of him, which mirrored his opinion of himself. They rarely approached him, and never outside of work. Which made it all the more remarkable when one of them came knocking at his door.

Her name was Nome. Petite, dark-haired and micrognathic, she stood a safe distance away, looking unsure of herself and ill-at-ease. She lived across the street, she said. Could she bother him for just a minute of his time?

Payne was curious but guarded. Given his reputation, he was suspicious of anyone showing an interest in him. He cracked the door enough to listen but not so much that she could possibly mistake it for an invitation to come in.

"I need advice," she said.

"I don't give advice." And then, "Why me?"

"They said."

"Who said?"

"A lot of people."

"Who?"

She scuffed at the floor with the toe of her shoe. "I need help."

"I don't give that either."

"They said you can."

"They're wrong."

She raised her eyes, braving a look at him. "They said you did before."

This was the rumor he hated most of all.

"At the Pannus mine," she said, but that was it. Before she had time for another word, he cut her off, shutting the door in her face.

He paced the room, then went and stood by the window. Across the street was the building where she claimed to live, a boxy piece of work, hatched, it seemed, of someone's dead imagination, gray and flat and drab, like his. A minute later he saw her on the street. She paused, then turned and raised her face in his direction. He stepped away from the window. A moment later he crept back and peeked out, but she was gone.

TWO

There was another section of Aksagetta, less frequented than the gambling halls but just as noble, just as fine. It lay across an ancient bridge that spanned a slotted gorge that cut the city in two. Through an arch and down a broad, marble-tiled boulevard, this was the city's spiritual heart, its second kingdom.

Here, like sphinxes, sat the bastions of religion, huge elaborate complexes of breathtaking proportion and imagination, as well as more modest structures of a simpler, but no less celestial, design. There were pointed pyramids and lofty steepled cathedrals, dome-shaped temples, flying tabernacles, marble-pillared citadels with ramparts and chiseled battlements, minarets, mosques and mausoleums. There was a hilly park with a granite dolmen at its crest and a wetland park with a lacquered wooden shrine. There were chapels that catered to the well-to-do and chapels that catered to the indigent. Corner churches, storefront churches, missions for the meek and ministries for the mighty. There was something for everyone, a smorgasbord of offerings for those with a spiritual hunger and a taste for religion.

And were these havens utilized? Were they ever. While nothing could approach the verve and volume of people parting with their money, the traffic in the Aksa half of Aksagetta was never less than brisk. Faithlessness, once rife, had fallen out of fashion. The gamers and the gamblers, the pleasure seekers and the sybarites, the true believers and the agnostics flocked like geese to these holy houses. Pilgrims from afar and city-folk alike. With such a feast there was simply no reason for belief and honest prayer to go begging.

In a sense it was an extension of the laws of gambling. The odds of anything were mathematical and could be calculated, and any decent gambler would know them cold. But beyond the odds or apart from them was something else, luck or chance or accident, something that could not be predicted or foreseen. And while over time the odds—and the gamblers using them—would have their way, any single moment was a moment unto itself, a chance for something wholly unexpected and extraordinary to occur. Beginner's luck. Dumb luck. The hand of fortune. Blind chance. It happened in cards and dice and bones and the desiccated eyeball games that the fabulously wealthy played behind closed doors. And it happened in the field of faith. Experience showed that the laws of mathematics and science couldn't explain everything. It was only logical to realize that logic wasn't all there was. Miracles did happen.

Payne didn't expect one, but he was curious what drew people to the Aksa districts. He had never been a religious man, but he was not on principle opposed to religion, particularly if it did what it seemed to do: bring people together, create a sense of community and belonging, fill a void, light a path. He was in a muddled state of mind and could use some light.

He took to crossing the Bridge whenever he had the time, exploring the different faiths, sampling whichever ones would let him in. For a tesque this typically meant those that were beset by one misfortune or another, that were foundering, as it were, and needed new blood in order to survive. In the course of history, tolerance had been known to flourish under such conditions, and so it was that Payne, a tesque, was welcomed into a number of sanctuaries.

In every one he listened diligently to what was said. There was much to understand and decipher, points of fact as well as metaphor, historical references, homilies and parables, calls for mercy and calls for action, rhetoric, litanies, pleas for strength and pleas for help, and always, prayers that pleas be heard. Each house of worship had its message and its messenger, chosen by virtue of talent or calling or, in some cases, it appeared, by default. Quite a few knew how to wake the spirit and stir it up, but only a handful seemed to have the gift of actually lifting it.

It was on one of these journeys that Payne got his first glimpse of a healer fully drained. The man lay at the foot of the statue of St. Pitay—a grim-faced, solemn saint—in the Plaza Gorga, a stone's throw from the doors of the fabled Cathedral Abolique. He had seen the cathedral on other occasions; it was hard to miss. No other structure in either half of Aksagetta was so magnificent or intricate or beautiful, with flying buttresses and steeples topped by dove-shaped finials and stained-glass windows and pointed spires and doors the size of castle gates. He had never known that human beings were capable of such craftsmanship, or such dedication and devotion to a piece of work. Or such whimsy: there were statues and pillars of humans in every pose and with every manner of expression. And other creatures too, imaginary ones, fashioned from a hodgepodge of wings and snouts and tails and claws. Some resembled tesques, or caricatures of tesques, and Payne's blood rose, until he saw that some were caricatures of humans, too. The Cathedral Abolique, at least at the time of its construction, seemed to have been egalitarian about whom it mocked. He'd thought, perhaps, this might extend to whom it admitted, but when he'd tried to enter it, he was turned away.

Tesques aside, it was a popular destination for tourists, as was the Plaza Gorga, and even, to a certain extent, the statue of St. Pitay. The drained healer was only one of many visitors, but to Payne at least, he was by far the most conspicuous. His hair was all but gone, revealing the wing-shaped contour of his exposed parietal skull. His skin was a sallow gray. He wore no shoes, and his toenails were thick and yellow, curling over the tips of his toes like horns. His pants were put on backward, and his shirt was tattered and torn.

Payne's first impulse was to stare; his second, to help the man; his third and possibly strongest, to pretend he hadn't seen him and hurry past. A group of humans came out of the cathedral and crossed the plaza, passing the fallen healer as if he didn't exist. He held a hand out to them, but they ignored it, and he let it drop. After that, he seemed to lose interest in begging. His head drooped to his chest, his eyes closed, and he began to snore.

Payne felt a welter of emotions—indignity, disgust, pity, sympathy, shame. Minutes later, when a second group of humans paused near the statue and stared, first at the prostrate healer and then at Payne himself, he felt mortification as well. Could they possibly believe that the two of them were in any way connected? The one able-bodied and productive, the other fallen and expended. Couldn't they see the difference?

He fled the plaza, putting as much distance between himself and the downed man as speedily as possible. But for days afterward he was troubled, and when he finally got the chance, he returned. The healer was gone, which was no surprise, nor was it likely that he could have prevented this. But he felt guilty for his behavior and, leaning against the pedestal of the statue of St. Pitay, he hung his head and closed his eyes, unintentionally mimicking the posture of the bronzed saint. His thoughts spiraled downward. Half a minute later, something like a prayer rose inside of him, and he asked forgiveness of the poor depleted healer he had spurned.

After that he left the plaza, wandering the streets and alleyways of

Aksa, continuing his search for meaning, feeling somber and morose. It was an aimless sort of search, and depended, it seemed, as much on him and his state of mind as on anything he might find. A major drawback was that he wasn't sure what he was looking for. He wasn't sure in general, didn't trust himself the way he once had. He should have helped the downed healer. He shouldn't have tried to help Vecque. He was making one mistake after another.

The morning wore on. He dragged himself halfway around the city, it seemed, ending up not far from where he'd started, in a small park of unkempt bushes and dried-up grass. He was exhausted, and he hadn't eaten all day, which was another mistake, and sagging to the ground, he promptly fell into a swoonlike sleep. When he woke from it, he was hungrier than ever, and sitting up, he rubbed his eyes, then blinked them in astonishment. Across the street was an old building that looked to be a church of some sort, with wooden stairs leading to a porch and a set of arching black doors. On a small table beside the doors, plain as day, was a tray with a glass of water and half a loaf of bread. He did not recall having seen the tray (or the church, for that matter) prior to falling asleep; they seemed to have popped out of thin air. Was he still asleep? He rubbed his eyes again and looked around.

Beyond the park was a quiet, little-used street. There was no one else in sight. Some weeds, some garbage, some poorly kept-up homes, some nicer ones. It didn't look particularly dreamlike. It seemed, in fact, quite real. He stood and made his way across the street.

The bread was a little hard, and there was a small, drowned gnat floating in the water. This, too, seemed quite real. Before helping himself, he looked around to make sure he wasn't the object of some antitesque prank, then tried the doors to the building, which were locked. He knocked, but no one came. On a whitewashed wooden plaque beside the doors was written, in faded letters, "The Church For Giveness," and beneath it, in an equally faded hand, "The Reverend I. F. Banisher Presiding."

Payne decided to take the offering. If it was meant for him, then he was meant to have it. If not, it would be easy to replace. And he would certainly apologize. Food and water were the two things he needed most right then, and that alone seemed reason enough to have them.

He tore the bread into chunks, chewed and swallowed them ravenously. The water he drained, all but a mouthful, in a single gulp. He saved that mouthful, as well as a small piece of bread, in the event that another starving, parch-tongued supplicant happened by. Then he left.

But returned, drawn first by the mystery of the manna and later, by the purveyor of that mystery, not the Reverend I. F. Banisher, as the plaque announced, but the Reverend C. L. Meeks, who for various reasons had decided not to place his name on the church.

But he had brought his message, and it was an ancient one, Payne came to learn, of an ancient faith that had spawned hundreds of other faiths in its time. The church itself was ancient, or relatively so. It was the first built in all of Aksa, and in its heyday one of the finest, attended by the finest people, a source of neighborhood and civic pride. In those days the neighborhood had been the seat of the city's aristocracy, a realm of palatial homes, tree-lined streets and fancy gardens. It had sported a watercourse, a weather-making tower, a zoologic park and a xenofloric arboretum. The first mayor of Aksagetta had lived in the neighborhood. His grandfather had been one of the founders of the church.

As the city grew, the neighborhood changed. More homes were built, not quite so elegant and grand. Trees were cut to make room for them. Other trees succumbed to diseases. To supply the growing population, the watercourse was tapped for water. The weather tower malfunctioned one time too many and was finally disassembled. The zoologic park became a dusty barnyard petting zoo.

The old and moneyed families began to drift away, and with the coming-of-age of Aksagetta as a tourist attraction, the drift became a full-fledged flight. Their homes were broken up into apartments, and businesses that reflected the city's new, pervasive theme park mentality cropped up on once strictly residential streets. The neighborhood pulsed with life, a different sort of life than before, and then in time it changed again.

Driven from the city center in Getta, a poor and disenfranchised element began to trickle in. Beggars and bagmen appeared on corners. Squatters took up residence in doorways and abandoned buildings. Muckers high on muck, or running low, prowled the nighttime streets.

Metal bars began appearing on store windows and locked gates in front of residential doors. Garbage, along with human waste, became a common sight on the streets. The first mayor's mansion, which had long been vacant, was converted into a treatment center for muckheads and the like. Another mansion became a halfway house and thrift store. The Church For Giveness, which had survived primarily through the continued patronage of its loyal core of now absentee (and dwindling) first families, entered a period of accelerated decline.

Once the jewel of the neighborhood, it was now an eyesore. Its roof looked like a swaybacked old horse, its siding was loose, its paint all cracked and peeling. It leaked when it rained, it was drafty in a wind, and its plumbing dripped continually. All of this would have been tolerable had its members not been in a similar state of disrepair. When the Reverend Meeks arrived, membership was at its lowest point ever. He was not the man to turn it around either; probably no single man could have. Fortunately, this was not what was asked of him. If it had been, he would never have applied for the job.

As a young man the Reverend Meeks had been exceptional. At home and at school he had excelled. He had chosen the ministry over a promising career in the arts, and had risen rapidly in the ranks, out-distancing many older colleagues and all of his peers. At the age of twenty-three he'd been awarded his first position, and at the age of twenty-seven had been lured from it by an offer to assist the Pompossus Jocoband himself, who had tutored him in the more advanced, refined and political aspects of the profession. Three years later, he was rewarded with a large and influential congregation of some thousand members, which he'd led until an ill-conceived decision lost him its support. It was the first in a string of ill-conceived decisions, and in the span of ten years the Reverend Meeks saw his fortunes plummet. He lost his confidence, and eventually he lost the will to lead. By the time he made his way to the Church For Giveness, he had ceased to hope that he would find either.

He was now in his late fifties, but he looked like an older man. His face was deeply lined, his eyes tired, his shoulders slumped and drawn. He looked sad, though not incapable of warmth. Despite his misfortunes, he had managed to save some money, and this job, he promised himself, would be his last. He had no business—no right and no desire—to work longer.

He was one of only two applicants for the position and the third minister to be hired in as many years. The church's Council of Deacons was tired of the turnover. They were tired of just about everything in connection with the church: how it looked, the people it attracted, the money it was hemorrhaging, the neighborhood. They needed someone to shepherd it for a year or two while they solidified their plans for its demolition.

The Reverend's life experience had taught him lessons that would help, the council believed, with this transition. He knew firsthand, for example, how it felt to be on the losing end of things. He could communicate with people who expected to be deprived, uprooted and displaced, people like the current members of his congregation. He had been all these things himself, and he knew about resignation. These people would understand another loss. They were malleable, if for no other reason than they had to be.

The Reverend understood his role. If any in the congregation happened to have forgotten that the world was unfair, he would remind them. He would do so gently, of course. He would be gentle in every way possible. Until the day the church was razed, if that day did truly come, whatever small amount of comfort and solace he could offer would be theirs.

It was in this spirit that he welcomed Payne into the fold. He welcomed everyone and made a point of saying so from the pulpit every week. Initially, Payne got some narrow looks from people who weren't crazy to be sharing their church with a tesque. There was a pecking order, and he was at the bottom. But once that was settled, he was accepted well enough. In truth, most of the motley group that made up the congregation had enough to worry about without worrying about him.

They were poor (all of them materially, and many, spiritually as well) and they were downtrodden. A large portion complained about their fate and their lot. Some were ungrateful, but others gave thanks for what little they had, including their church.

It had seen better days without a doubt, but the Church For Giveness still retained a vestige of its glory. In a certain light, and with a certain generosity of spirit, one could not help but glimpse its grandeur. It was there in the lovely vaulted ceiling (now waterstained). It was there in what remained of the triptych of stained glass. The church boasted two dozen painstakingly hand-carved wooden pews. And a dais made of marble. And a pulpit that, while a handsome piece of furniture in its own right, was elevated to another level entirely by its striking face.

From top to bottom it was covered by a thick sheet of burnished copper, embossed on which were various religious figures and symbols of the faith. The metal, Payne learned, came from the early days of the Pannus lode, when the ore was rich and plentiful. It had a natural resistance to verdigris, but even so, received a weekly polish. This was a task reserved for the Reverend, one of the few he took to with zeal and delight.

Opposite the pulpit, high in the wall above the entrance to the church, was an oval window, and for a few minutes every day the sun and the pulpit would be in line. And then the sunbeams would reflect off the pulpit's polished surface, filling the sanctuary with a fierce, coppery light. A clever orator could time his sermon to coincide with this moment, and further, that point in it that deserved illumination, for it created a wonderfully theatrical effect. The Reverend Meeks had been schooled in theatrics and at one time was a great practitioner of the art, but he had lost his penchant and his taste for it. Now, as often as not, he missed the sun completely, or else it arrived unexpectedly, at an inopportune time. This seemed in keeping with his character, for in some ways he was a man at odds with himself, both craving the spotlight but also wary of it, or of what it might reveal. Or maybe, Payne sometimes thought, it was the message he was at odds with, which was in itself odd, for it was a plain and time-honored one.

Work hard, it went. Show mercy. Practice forgiveness. For temptation was inherent in life. Temptation was ubiquitous. The Creator and Supreme Authority, whom the Reverend called the Author, had created it as surely as he had created redemption. No man or woman was beyond its reach.

No one in the congregation doubted this, and they were happy to have a man who knew his doctrine. The Reverend had clearly lived a life with firsthand knowledge of what he preached. He spoke of it sometimes, his life, mostly in metaphor, in the form of parables and stories (which, he was fond of observing, the Author was perpetually in the process of writing). One of his favorites was from a section of the Song of Stilton, which charted the Rebellion of the Angels and the Sundering of the Palace, and the fall from grace of the Highest Angel, and the creation of the Abyss. The lesson revolved around the sin of pride, and the terrible cost of becoming a slave to it.

The sermons were announced a week ahead of time, and for this particular one, rumored to be among his best, Payne made sure he had a front-row seat. The Reverend entered from the wing, took his place behind the pulpit, then waited for the coughs and murmurs and shuffling feet to die down. Bowing his head and clasping his hands, he opened the service with an unaccompanied prayer, then led the congregation in another. A hymn followed, anchored by the Reverend's solid baritone, another prayer and finally, the sermon.

It was a powerful and moving story, and in the end Payne was surprised to find himself feeling sympathy and compassion for the Fallen Angel. His transgression, to challenge the will of the Author and the unity of His palace and His vision, seemed incommensurate with his punishment and fate. He sensed that the Reverend felt the same, or at least questioned the finality of the Author's sentence. Pride indeed was a heinous sin and could lead to much suffering, but what of mercy? What of forgiveness? The Reverend posed these questions rather casually, but then he paused, and his voice rose, which happened rarely, and which caused Payne to sit up in his seat. If there was no room in a person's heart for grace, he asked, what chance was there for any decent kind of life? What chance for peace? What chance for salvation?

"Amen," came a voice, and other amens followed. The Reverend concluded the lesson with an amen of his own, then led the congregation in a prayer of worship, then ended the service with a benediction. As was his habit, he made his way down the central aisle to the church's front door, which he opened, receiving his flock, such as it was, as it filed out. Payne hung back, waiting until the last of them had gone, then approached the Reverend and asked to have a word with him.

The Reverend looked tired. The sermon, which he'd probably given a hundred times, was one, it seemed, that wearied him. But this was his job, and he rose to the occasion.

"Yes, my son? What is it you wish to talk about?"

Faced with his moment of truth, Payne suddenly got cold feet. He dropped his voice and eyes, mumbled something beneath his breath, then apologized and asked to be excused.

Had Payne been a human, the Reverend might have allowed this, for human confidences and confessions were nothing new to him, were, in fact, as plentiful as they were predictable. A human he could trust to come back later. But this was a tesque, and in all his travels the Reverend Meeks had known only a few of them, and none well. So he prodded this one a little.

"We haven't spoken privately yet. I blame myself. But you'll find I have an avid ear. You were right to take the initiative and come to me."

"I've done wrong, Reverend."

"So have we all," he answered kindly. Then, more probing, "What exactly have you done?"

"What you talked about in your sermon? That."

"What? You've committed the sin of pride?"

"Yes."

"It's a common one."

"Mine was very bad."

The Reverend had heard this many times from humans, how bad they'd behaved, and had often wondered at their eagerness not only to proclaim but to exaggerate their failings. It was a way, he supposed, to feel self-important. He wasn't particularly surprised to hear the same thing from a tesque.

"Shall we sit, my son?"

Payne was willing and followed the Reverend to a rear pew, where they sat facing forward. The Reverend bowed his head and turned it slightly to the side, for which Payne was grateful, for it meant he would not have to meet the Reverend's eyes. It freed his tongue to sit beside a man who seemed to understand the importance of this small accommodation.

After another false start he told his story. All of it. He opened up his heart completely for the first time. The Reverend listened solemnly without interrupting, and when Payne was done, but before the silence grew uncomfortable, he responded.

"A horrible series of events. And you were punished?"

"Yes," said Payne.

"And then absolved. Released."

"Yes."

"But still, you punish yourself." The Reverend turned to him. "Have you asked for forgiveness?"

"Asked who? Vecque? Yes. I did. A thousand times."

The Reverend allowed himself a small smile. "The Supreme One. The Author of the world and everything in it. Every thought and every soul and every substance. Every sin and every act of grace. Every horror and every delight. Have you asked forgiveness of Him?"

"I will," said Payne. "Gladly. But how should I ask? What words should I use?"

"Humble ones," suggested the Reverend. He paused a moment, then added, "We all have our weaknesses. Sometimes they strike us without warning. Sometimes we nurture them, and then they strike us all the harder. My advice, don't nurture them. Let them out before they fester and grow."

It was solid advice, and gravely spoken. And enough, he seemed to feel, for the present. Standing and gathering his robe, he thanked Payne for opening his heart and mind. It was a virtue, he observed, that balanced many sins.

He slid out of the pew, then paused in the aisle, as if forgetting something. "Oh yes," he said at length. "While you're asking Him for forgiveness, you might ask yourself as well. It can be painful, but that, I believe, is the point. Pain teaches us to avoid those things that hurt."

THREE

Few among the current congregation had much of value to part with when the plate was passed, and in lieu of this, some volunteered to work and do chores. There was sweeping and there was mopping, there was dusting and there was scrubbing, there was trapping vermin and fixing pipes and repairing broken furniture. Payne took on the job of putting out the bread and water, which he did first thing every morning, legging it to church and back before work.

One drizzly morning, he arrived to find a bedraggled man beside the table, his hands about to clutch the day-old, stale loaf. At the sight of Payne he snatched them back and declared his innocence. Payne assured him there was nothing wrong. The bread was meant to be eaten, and as proof, he tore off a piece of the fresh loaf he'd brought and offered it to him. The man eyed it suspiciously but at length accepted it and put it in his pocket. Payne pressed the rest of the loaf into his arms and invited him to come back for that week's service.

The man shrank at this and retreated down the stairs. A few days later he was back for bread again, and a couple of weeks after that Payne noticed him at church. He was sitting all alone in the rearmost pew, doing his best to pay attention, nervously shifting his eyes between his lap, the pulpit, and the door.

After the service Payne shared a word with him and in time made other friends, people who greeted him when he came to church. He had learned that the quickest way to make a friend was to listen when that person talked, and since many, if not most, of the people who made their way to the Church For Giveness seemed to prefer talking to listening, he had ample opportunity to practice. There were tales of misfortune he could scarcely believe, and no lack of storytellers to spin them. When someone arrived with a willing ear, they exploited that ear, and as a healer, Payne's ear was trained to be open. The only person who rivaled him as a listener was Reverend Meeks, who, despite a growing indifference, could still be moved to curiosity when it came to matters of the psyche and the soul. Payne could talk to him, and the two of them spoke at least briefly every week.

It was a time of reflection for Payne, a healing time, and gradually, he mended. He stopped beating himself up so much about Vecque and slowly came out of his shell. He didn't know how thick the shell had been until he saw how different everything began to look and feel. His depression and self-recrimination had colored the world, and now that same world was altered.

He noticed the change in every facet of his life, from work to leisure, from healing to simply being out in the city. Before, he'd often found the street experience jarring and oppressive: the crowds of tourists, the crush of bodies, the stares, the veiled and unveiled scorn. But there was another way to take it, another world alongside the one that assaulted him. It was a matter, he discovered, of perspective. The streets around the gaming houses, where he lived and worked, were packed and noisy, yes, and the people on them were in the grip of a barely suppressed hysteria, yes, that too. But they were also festive, the press of bodies heady, the atmosphere dynamic and exciting. And the gambling, which often seemed so horribly obsessive to him, had another, carefree quality to it. A kind of goofy optimism. The people were hungry, some of them desperate, and for something they would never have; this was undeniable. But they were also having bales of fun.

He brought this new perspective to work. Healing was dependably a source of pleasure to him, but there was always room to make it better. There were tools like the Boomine synthesizer he had yet to fully take advantage of. And nuances of diseases and their treatment to explore and understand, marvels of the body and its remarkable pliancy and adaptability—unlooked-for, unexpected, astounding things.

There was the man he saw, for example, who spoke solely in epithets. A high-placed spokesman for the Authorities, a master of the euphemism and the fib, his brain had been damaged in an accident. And there was a woman who gave birth to triplets, only two of whom had normal skin. The third, fully human in every other respect, bore a coat of feathers. And another woman who died, clearly died, after winning at the winking jacks of opportunity, then snapped back to life an hour later. Her brain, remarkably, was undamaged, save for the loss of a depressive streak that had dogged her for years. And a man who became infected by a mutant strain of the bald soprano virus that made his hair fall out. When it grew back, it came in willy-nilly, in tufts and whorls and tangled patches, and three months later, and then every three months after that like clockwork, it fell out again.

Miracles of science, miracles of life: Payne was inspired even as he grappled to understand. He felt tremendous gratitude to be who he was, a healer, for what passed through his door was truly a feast. It fed him mentally and materially, and the trust that people put in him, people who under other circumstances would not have given him the time of day, this fed him, too. He worked hard, and was rewarded with a measure of success. He gained something of a reputation, although not everybody came to him. Unlike Pannus not everybody had to. There were other healers in Aksagetta, which was fortunate, for between the city's permanent residents and its many visitors there was a steady flow of humans looking to be healed of one thing or another. Some of these other healers also had reputations; a few of them Payne knew by sight. He often wished he knew them better—wished, that is, that he wasn't so outside the healer group. He was as much to blame for this as anyone. Initially, he'd kept his distance, and now, with his newfound family at church, he had the friends he wanted. Still, there could be no harm in having more.

❧❧❧

One of the pleasures of going to church was crossing the bridge that knit the two halves of the city. It was an ancient structure, built at a time when labor was cheap and materials like the milk-white marble of which its walkway was constructed were plentiful. It was the first bridge built in Aksagetta and had a proper name, but no one used it. It was simply called First Bridge, or, more commonly, the Bridge. Up and down the gorge there were other bridges, imitators, originals, beauties of form and function, but none that rivaled the first.

It was cantilevered below and open to the air above, with an arch at either end. The arches were tall, perhaps forty feet high, and half again as thick. They spanned the width of the Bridge and were held aloft on the heads and uplifted palms of two pairs of epicene statues. Each pair was joined at the back, one facing inward, the other outward. The spandrels of the arches were inscribed with tributes and encomiums to the Bridge's builders and the city's early luminaries, although few now could read them, for the language was a cryptic one and also dead. In the rainy season, which in Aksagetta was a brief period between the end of winter and the middle of spring, the arches provided shelter from unexpected cloudbursts. In the height of summer they offered shade. In fall they were often shrouded by fog. At other times of the year they most approached what the builders intended: something simply to look at and pass through, monuments, memorials.

Payne had arrived in Aksagetta in summer, and now it was early spring. The weather was predictably unpredictable, cloudy, rainy days alternating with cloudy, dry ones. The sun was creeping north and had reached that point in the year when its trajectory paralleled the gorge. At dawn, when Payne was usually on the Bridge, its long, slanting light painted the sheer rock cliffs a brilliant orange. If it had rained, and it often had, and the air was crisp and clear, a person could see deep into the canyon. Payne liked to stop at the midpoint of the Bridge and peer over the chest-high wall that ran its length on either side, and one morning on his way to church he did just that. The air was cool on his face, the bread of charity warm in his arms. At his back the low sun was fat and yolky. The upper reaches of the gorge were bathed in light, but farther down remained dark and murky. Payne had a vision of the Angel's Fall into the Abyss. The gorge was said to be four miles deep, though no one knew exactly. Even when the sun was directly overhead, Payne had never been able to see the bottom. But he'd heard stories about it, and he became aware that he was hearing one now. A family on its way to worship had stopped within earshot to admire the view, and the father was speaking to the son. He held him up to look over the side, then put him down and told him how the Devil lived in a pit of icy fire at the very bottom. And he was always looking upward toward the sky, longing for the home he'd lost. He could see who crossed the Bridge, and if he happened to catch a glimpse of someone, a boy for example, who'd done something naughty, he would spread his wings and flex his talons, then fly up and snatch that boy away. And what happened after that, in his pit, well, one hated to imagine. The father made a scary face, and his son's eyes widened. Then the father smiled to show it was just a joke, and reached out to comfort his son. But the boy, his lower lip now quivering, backed away from him into the arms of his waiting mother.

158 | THE HEALER

All at once, it started raining. In drips and drabs at first, but rapidly the drips became fat droplets. There was a thick black cloud above the Bridge. There was lightning, then thunder, and then the drops became a downpour.

Payne pulled his coat around the loaf of bread and hurried to the arch. He was joined there by others, including the mother, son and father. The boy was now crying, and on impulse Payne offered him a piece of bread. The boy shrank back at the strange man but stopped his whimpering. His mother refused on his behalf and gently scolded him for not using his words.

The cloudburst lasted twenty minutes, and as a result Payne was late for church. People were already in their seats when he arrived, several of whom were new to him. There was a well-dressed man and woman in one of the middle pews. The man was cleanly shaven, and the woman wore a picture hat and earrings. There was another similarly well-groomed woman sitting near the back. There was an empty seat beside her, and Payne took it, sliding noiselessly in.

The reading that week was from the Book of Moh and told the story of the outcast brother, who for various offenses, some real but most imagined, was exiled by his family and his tribe. Years later, now a wealthy and powerful potentate, he returned to find the tribe enslaved and persecuted. Shamelessly, they begged his help, and putting the past aside, he granted it, using his wealth and influence to buy them their freedom.

Part of the lesson was, of course, about forgiveness. But another part, and the one the Reverend chose to focus on, was about tolerance. The tribe was punished for its treatment of the brother, and even though the story ended well, many suffered gravely—and needlessly—before it did. This was what came of intolerance; it was the Author's hand at work. For in His eyes every man and woman was precious. Rich or poor, saintly or fallen, He loved them all. And so, therefore, should they love each other.

As the Reverend pursued his exegesis, the woman beside Payne cleared her throat with a little cough and tugged down the hem of her skirt, which remained well below her knee. She threw a furtive glance at Payne, then took another moment to rearrange herself, subtly increasing the distance between her thigh and his.

Payne saw the woman again the following week, and this time she had a man and a young boy with her. He introduced himself, discovered the man's name was Trotter, Elv Trotter, hers was Elsa, and the boy's was El. This was all he discovered, as the two males were disinclined to speak, and the woman, inclined to speak to them alone. They had a haughty air about them, and their presence, along with the other couple, who had also returned, changed the atmosphere in the church. It stifled it a little, making some of the regulars self-conscious. After the service a few of them dropped hints that these newcomers weren't welcome, prompting Payne to rise to their defense. Tolerance meant tolerance for everyone. It was not an arrow to be aimed. How many of them, for example, had been driven out of one place or another because of prejudice? It was just this sort of thing, this fear, that stood in the way of harmony and progress.

There was a nod or two of agreement, but then someone said that it was just the opposite, that it was progress that led to fear. Progress as in the city changing. Progress as in being thrown out on the street because you couldn't pay the rent. Progress as in being told you couldn't beg anymore, or being rousted out of your bed in the park, right there across the street. There was a lot of progress in the city and now the neighborhood, good for some folk maybe, but for a lot of folk not so good.

There were nods of agreement at this, murmurs of support and calls for action. Eventually, the group dispersed, and Payne, whose knowledge of the neighborhood was limited, decided to have a look around and see for himself what they meant.

The street the church was on was residential, as were the cross-streets at either end. Some of the homes were tidy, but a greater number were dilapidated and run-down. This was pretty much as he remembered it from the last time he'd thought to look, but a block or two farther on, he came across some newly painted homes. Several more were under construction. One old rambling place, half a block long, was getting a complete face-lift. Soon it seemed that wherever he turned there were signs of development. Roofs were being replaced, entryways rebuilt, walls defaced by time and streetwise artistry scrubbed clean. Trees and beds of flowers were being planted. On a commercial block he counted six new businesses, which he could tell by the way they contrasted with their neighbors. There was a bakery, two restaurants and three boutiques. There were people shopping and eating, affluent people, many of whom resembled the newcomers to church.

The following week he spoke to Reverend Meeks, mentioning what he'd observed along with the concerns that his friends had raised. It was after the service, and the two of them were alone.

The Reverend, of course, had noticed the new faces in the congregation. He had met most of them and found them friendly. He was surprised to hear that others regarded them as a threat. In any case, it made little difference. The Church For Giveness was not long for the world. It had had a rich and illustrious life, but sadly, that life was about to come to an end. There were plans in the works to tear it down.

Payne felt like he'd been punched. "Why? I don't understand."

"Because it's an eyesore," said the Reverend. "Because it's bleeding money. Because the membership, the community, the support . . . it isn't there."

Payne contested this. "It is. People come. As many as ever."

The Reverend cast a doleful look overhead at the once-fine vaulted ceiling, then followed the open beams down to the chancel, then turned and gazed upon the modest nave. "There was a time, I'm told, when it was filled to the rafters with churchgoers every week. When it took the minister till noon to work his way through the receiving line.

When members who couldn't get seats stood two and three deep against the walls to hear the sermon."

"Do you need that many people?"

"Do I? No. I had that many once. Twice that many. That time for me is past."

"It could come again."

"Yes. And the world might swallow itself. Neither one, though, is likely to happen."

"But there must be something we can do."

The Reverend spread his hands in a gesture of sympathy and helplessness. He had not meant to speak of this yet, not until the plans were finalized. He apologized for having done so, knowing in his heart that he would be better able to brave the inevitable outcry if there was nothing to be done, and attempted to move on.

But Payne was not about to give up so easily. This was a home for people. It was his home. He had not entered it as a religious man in the beginning, but he was changing. At church he experienced things he had known only rarely before, and then only in the act of healing. The sense of something greater than himself. The comfort and wonder of being in that something's presence. The certain, sublime knowledge of the interconnectedness of all things.

"It's a sanctuary," he told the Reverend. "No one cares how it looks or how run-down it is. What's important is what happens here, on the inside." He pressed a fist to his chest. "In the heart and the spirit and the soul. That's what matters most."

The Reverend did not disagree. Indeed, it was a consolation to know that men of faith could live without a roof or walls. And for those who needed them, who needed a house to worship in, there were other sanctuaries. Other churches that carried the message and spread the word.

"But not other ministers," said Payne.

"Yes. Those, too."

"But none like you."

"You flatter me."

"I don't. It's true," said Payne, and went on to raise more objections, until at length the Reverend asked him to stop.

"This is painful. I know. I shouldn't have burdened you. Forgive me. It was a mistake."

But Payne would not be silenced. "When were you going to burden us? When they locked the doors? When the wrecking ball struck?"

The Reverend winced. He'd been hired to be the bearer of this news but clearly did not relish the job.

"I have to ask you not to speak of this to others."

"Why? Because they'll object, too?"

"The plan is not finalized. Nothing's been decided for certain yet."

"Meaning what? We could change their minds?"

The Reverend sighed, then bowed his head, as if praying for guidance. He was not a man who liked to lie.

Payne took his reticence as a sign of hope. "If it's a question of people, there are new people coming. If it's a question of money, they have money, too."

"Perhaps so. But the real question is one of influence."

"You have influence."

"With the Deacon's Council? No. Not an ounce."

"But these new people might. You could talk to them. Let them know what's happening. I'm sure they'll want to help." Without thinking, he grabbed the Reverend's hand, pressing it between his own. "Please. Don't give up. The church is worth saving. Our church."

Payne's earnest and heartfelt supplication moved the Reverend Meeks more than he wished, and it woke something dormant in his heart and mind. He recalled an earlier time in his life, when every day brought a new idea into his head and every morning he greeted with joy. It was an exciting time, when he aspired to great things and strove to make a difference, when he did not fear failure, and failure, if it came, did not cripple him.

"You understand there's little hope," he said. "The outcome is unlikely to change, regardless of what I do."

Payne felt a wave of gratitude. From where he stood, there was little the Reverend could not accomplish if he put his mind to it, and he told him so, flat out.

The Reverend could not suppress a smile. "You are the Devil, my friend. The snake. You strike me where I'm weakest. Now go, and leave me in peace. I need to think."

⊚⊚⊚

A month went by, and then another. When Payne asked the Reverend what was happening, the Reverend said he had his feelers out. The issue of preservation had been raised, and there was interest, to the point that a meeting was planned. That said, he cautioned Payne not to get his hopes up, and above all, urged him to be patient. These things took time.

Payne was heartened to hear this news, and he was further encouraged by the continued appearance of new faces at church. Every week it seemed there were one or two more. Young families like the Trotters, and also single men and women. Many of them seemed to know each other or be connected in some way. They seemed to bring their own sense of community to the church, along with their own ideas about what a church should be. These were not very different from Payne's ideas, from anyone's, although in practice the newcomers and the old-timers tended not to mingle. As time passed, some of Payne's friends deliberately stopped coming, while others seemed to simply drift away.

He was thinking about how things were changing on his way to church one morning, and how a person had to be flexible and spread his blanket on the ground that he was given. For a tesque especially this was true. At the same time, he missed his friends who had left. He was looking forward to the service and the sermon that day, which promised to address this very topic. It was titled "Charity in a Time of Transition: Rising to the Challenge," and he knew the Reverend would have something wise and useful to say.

He crossed the Bridge and passed beneath the arch, which someone had defaced with the words "Who Heals the Healers?" painted in bright red. Payne had seen this scrawled on one of the apartment buildings near where he lived, and hadn't give it much thought at the time, but here on the stately monument it seemed profane. He hurried past it, arriving at church with the daily loaf of bread still warm and fragrant. But when he mounted the stairs and went to the table to replace the old loaf, he found that this had already been done. And the glass had been refilled, too: he could tell by the level of the water. Puzzled, he went inside to talk to Reverend Meeks, whom he found at the pulpit, polishing its face. He was dressed in his deep blue cleric's robe and seemed preoccupied, which he often was while polishing. It was a ritual he performed every week, a time to gather his thoughts, the simple and repetitive work a meditation. He barely noticed Payne, and after a moment's hesitation, Payne chose not to interfere, resolving to speak to him after the service.

Over the next hour the church gradually filled, and at the appointed time Reverend Meeks entered and began. He was more spirited than usual, and had been for several weeks. He led the congregation in prayer; then one of the new members, a stout woman with a rich contralto voice, joined him at the altar to lead them all in a hymn. After that, Elv Trotter came up to give the reading. The sermon followed, but Payne had trouble concentrating. He kept thinking about the bread.

After the service the members of the congregation gathered near the door, chatting with each other while waiting to greet the Reverend, who stood outside on the porch, shaking and pressing hands. Payne made sure that he was last in line, for what he had to say he didn't want overheard. Finally, it was his turn, and as always, he thanked the Reverend for the service and the sermon. Then he asked if there was any word.

"Word?"

Payne dropped his voice. "About the church. The plans." He reminded the Reverend that there was going to be a meeting.

"Ah. Yes. The meeting. There was one, and a committee's been set up. It appears that our church is a historic landmark."

"Does that mean it can't be torn down?"

"No, not absolutely, but it does give us another argument to preserve it."

Payne was delighted.

"It would have to be restored. Which takes money. Lots of money."

"Isn't there always money? If you want a thing enough?"

"There is," replied the Reverend, "though it has a habit of coming with strings attached. In any case, we're not at that stage. We're taking it one step at a time. We'll just have to wait and see what happens."

Their conversation was interrupted by laughter that came from a knot of churchgoers who had gathered at the bottom of the stairs. The Trotter family was at the center of the group, and Payne waited for the laughter to die down.

"Something strange happened to me today."

The Reverend was enjoying the scene below and responded with an absentminded nod. "Did it? What?"

"When I came to put out the offering, someone already had."

"That is strange."

"Do you happen to know who?"

The Reverend turned to face him, looking a little lost. "I'm sorry, but I've been very busy lately. Preoccupied with all these new developments. You'll have to excuse me if I don't keep track of every little thing. We're talking about what now? The water? The bread?"

"Both," said Payne, feeling petty.

The Reverend knit his brows and put his mind to it, and Payne hap-

pened to catch a glimpse of Elsa Trotter. She was watching the two of
them, trying to catch the Reverend's eye. And eventually she did, and
flashed him an ingratiating little smile, which appeared to jog his memory.

"El," he said.

"El?"

"Yes. The Trotters' son. His mother wanted him to do something.
Something to contribute to the church."

"But that's my job," said Payne.

The Reverend lowered his eyes, then drew a breath and slowly let
it out, then pinched the bridge of his nose, then finally raised his eyes
and looked Payne squarely in the face.

"It's my fault," he said. "I should have asked. Forgive me."

Payne was speechless.

"I've been trying to juggle a great many things." He sighed again,
and then, uncharacteristically, his face brightened. "Perhaps we can
work something out."

"Like what?"

"There're other ways to help. Other duties. We've lost our mopper,
for example. The man just up and left. We could use someone to
replace him."

"I don't want to mop. I'd rather do what I was doing."

"Yes. Well." The Reverend glanced at Elsa Trotter, then back at
Payne. "Perhaps you and the boy can share."

"Share?"

"Yes. You bring the bread, he the water. Or vice versa. I'm sure his
mother would be more than happy to supply the bread."

Payne didn't want to share. He wanted to grab the bread and
throw it. He wanted to toss the water on the ground.

"All right," he said. "I'll share."

It didn't last. Payne's pride got the better of him, and at length he
gave up and relinquished his job to the usurper. A week after that, he

missed his first service ever. Then he missed another. Three full weeks went by before he could bring himself to return.

It was late summer. The day was already hot (though not as hot as it had been a month before), and waves of heat had begun to radiate off the sunlit cliffs at the top of the gorge. They distorted the air, creating an illusion of softness to the sharp rock, an inviting mirage that put Payne in mind of the story that the father had told his son about the Devil and his deceit. He wondered if he'd been wrong to act the way he had, spurning the church. Certainly pride had been involved, and he wondered if it was justified—if pride was ever justified—or if it was the Devil's voice. Reverend Meeks spoke about the Fallen Angel, and he spoke about temptation, but he rarely spoke directly about the Devil, and when he did, he never depicted him as a monster but more a creature, like every man, of faults, who often took the guise of an extremely persuasive and untrustworthy friend. After being slighted, Payne had concluded that the Devil had taken up residence in Reverend Meeks, but since then he'd been thinking. It did no good to bear a grudge, and he'd been practicing tolerance, which came naturally, and forgiveness, which did not, and had made sufficient progress that he felt safe—safe enough, at any rate—in returning.

The reading that day was from the Song of Stilton again. This time it concerned the snake. It came in many forms and disguises, the snake, and how was one to know its faces, and to recognize which were true and which were false? Sometimes it was hideous and frightening, sometimes so beautiful the heart ached. Was one to shun the beauty? Fight one's fear and embrace the ugliness? How was one to choose between right and wrong?

The answer, the lesson, was to look into one's heart and soul, because that is where the Author lived. There, and in every corpuscle, and in every mote and every atom. He lived in every mystery and every hope, everything contained in the world and everything beyond it, seen and unseen and unimagined. And He was speaking all the time, preaching as it were, from the book that ran forward and backward, to the end and to the beginning of time, a book that was ever deepening. Sometimes His voice arrived in the form of a question, sometimes a commandment, sometimes a compliment, sometimes a rebuke. In His wisdom He sometimes asked for a sacrifice, but often He asked for nothing. One had to listen carefully to hear His words, and this took practice, for His voice was faint and whispery. Only rarely did it trumpet forth, just as only rarely could one ever hope to glimpse the living fire that was His face.

The Reverend paused, and the sun chose that moment to pierce the oval window high in the wall opposite the altar, sending its shafts of light in a slanting path downward. The beams struck the pulpit, reflecting off its burnished copper surface as though it were the sun itself, filling the church with a blinding, refulgent light. Payne had to shield his eyes, as did others. It took some minutes for the sun to move, and when it did, it shifted upward, so that now it was the Reverend who was blinded. For a second he didn't know what to do, except to shade his eyes, but then he seemed to come to some new understanding of the light and the moment, for he dropped his hands and raised his chin. The sun fell fully on him, and a look of pleasure, then wonder, slowly spread across his face. The lines of worry and failure that he'd worn so long seemed to melt away. He looked radiant, lit from outside and from within. A hush fell over the congregation. No one so much as breathed, bearing witness to the Reverend's rapture.

Somehow he concluded the service and afterward received the congregation in his altered state. Gradually, drawn by the flesh-and-blood handshakes and hearty congratulations of the flesh-and-blood people in the line, he returned to earth, so that by the time Payne reached him, he seemed more or less himself. Still, Payne felt at a loss for words. He wanted to ask the Reverend where he'd gone and what he'd seen and heard, but ended up simply thanking him. The Reverend accepted this modestly, replying (as he had already many times) that it was he who had cause for thanks. But then he paused, and his expression changed, as though Payne had triggered something, and dropping his voice, he asked if he would mind staying.

When the church had emptied, the Reverend took a seat in a pew and invited Payne to join him. For a while he sat without speaking, head slightly bowed, hands folded in his lap. At length he cleared his throat.

"I have news. There's been an offer to restore the church. And not simply to restore it, but to revive it."

"That's wonderful," said Payne.

"There're several stipulations. A portion of the money is to go to cleaning up the neighborhood. Another portion, to security." He paused. "A number of people mentioned that, security."

"The money's coming from a group?"

"The money's being raised, but yes, a group is at the center. Some of our newer members have formed a steering committee. A few of the old guard have combined with them to make a generous pledge. There's been some spirited debate about the direction the church should take. And, I should add, whether I'm capable of leading it in that direction."

"What direction is that?" asked Payne.

"As I said, our goal is to revitalize the church. To resurrect it, if you will. We want to give our membership the sense that when they step through our doors, they've stepped into a pertinent and useful conversation. Steeped in tradition, but also relevant to today. Timeless and at the same time timely. Physically, we intend to make the church a jewel again, as it was in its heyday, a focal point of both neighborhood and civic pride. We're not looking to be envied by anyone, but neither do we intend to give quarter to anyone either, be it a person or another house of worship. Not the Temple of the Elations, not the Dome Pechone, not the Cathedral Ablique. In the loyalty of our membership, in our appeal, and eventually in the influence we command, we intend to rival any and all."

It was an impressive vision, although something in it, or in the Reverend's depiction of it, made Payne uneasy. In his own experience, principally with his brother Wyn, nothing good came of rivalries.

"It's an opportunity for you," he told the Reverend, who acknowledged this. "As for being capable, I'm sure you are."

"Yes. I believe I am. More importantly, they believe it, too." He paused, drew a breath, then turned his attention from himself and his church to Payne. "Let me ask you a question. As a healer. Have you ever saved a life?"

Payne nodded.

"Have you ever lost one?"

He thought of the burned miner. The Reverend and the church had helped him see that he was not to blame for the man's death. "No. Not yet."

"What would you do if you had to? If to save a hundred lives you were forced to lose one?"

He had never been faced with this and had therefore never asked himself the question. "I don't know."

"Say there was some sort of epidemic, and there was a novel treatment that might effect a cure. But it needed testing first, and you knew ahead of time that the test would damage the person you tried it on. But you also knew that, with what you learned, you'd be able to halt the epidemic. Would you do it? Would you sacrifice a single person to save a hundred lives?"

"I'd try to save them all," said Payne.

"Yes. Of course. I try to save each and every one I can, too. But that's not the question I'm asking. I'm asking is there any condition, any situation, where it's defensible to sacrifice the good of one for the good of many? And not just defensible, but justifiable, from a moral point of view?"

Payne wondered why the Reverend was asking him this question, when it was the Reverend himself to whom he looked for answers about right and wrong.

"I suppose you'd have to ask the one who's going to be sacrificed. At the very least, you'd have to get his permission."

The Reverend mulled this over. "I don't think that would be quite sufficient. I think we'd want something more."

"Like what?"

"I think he'd have to volunteer."

Yes. That sounded right. Payne waited for the punch line, but the Reverend didn't deliver one. Instead, he fell silent.

They sat for a while without speaking. Payne grew restless. Something the Reverend had said gnawed at him.

"What do you mean, security?" he asked.

The Reverend nodded, as though he'd been waiting for this. Still, he took time to choose his words.

"Security means different things to different people. It's a delicate issue. In this case, unfortunately, it's one that involves you."

"How? In what way?"

"Some of our members have expressed a certain tension, an uneasiness let's say, around you."

"Who?" he asked.

The Reverend refused to say, except that it was not confined to one or two people.

This infuriated Payne. "What? I make them nervous? I frighten them?"

The Reverend sighed. "Both, I'm sad to say."

"Why? On what basis?"

"You mean what do they say? Or what do I believe is really at issue?"

"What do they say?"

"There's a radical group that's been in the news lately."

"What group?"

"A tesque group," said the Reverend. "I don't recall the name, but they've made some charges and declarations that make people nervous. Some people, anyway."

"But I'm not part of that group. I'm not part of any group. This is my group. This. The church."

"Yes. It has been. As anyone who knows you knows. But these are people who haven't known that many tesques. Some of them have not known any. They tend to lump them all together. They jump to conclusions."

"It's absurd to link me to some group I've never even heard of."

"Of course it is. These people are unschooled and ignorant. In some ways they're like children."

"They don't want me here?"

The Reverend sighed.

"It's me? I'm the one to be condemned?"

"It's shameful, I know. They need to be taught, which I fully intend to do."

Payne was stunned. "Teach them by standing up for me. Tell them it's wrong, that you support me. Tell them you're my friend."

"I am your friend. And as a friend, I'm telling you you won't be happy here. You won't be comfortable. Not right now. As a minister, a messenger, I promise to do all I can to work to change that. To engage these people's minds and consciences and souls. To teach them tolerance, which is what I've always taught. To dedicate myself to making this church all-inclusive, merciful and strong."

"And then you'll take me back? Is that it?"

"Yes. I won't stop until that day comes."

"Don't waste your breath," said Payne. "I won't be coming back."

The Reverend gave him a long look, then bowed his head. "As you wish."

Several moments passed, and then the Reverend lifted his face, so full of sorrow and regret, and touched Payne's sleeve.

"I'm sorry. So very sorry. This is not what I foresaw or intended."

"No?"

"No. Never."

"I don't believe you."

The Reverend sighed. "I'll keep you in my heart and in my prayers."

Payne looked at him with daggers in his eyes. "Don't bother."

☙☙☙

It was the last he saw of the Reverend Meeks, though not of the Church For Giveness. In the following weeks he returned several times, drawn by a perverse need to add salt to the wound. Twice he crept by under cloak of darkness. Once he hid in the park across the street in broad daylight, watching with a knot in his stomach as scaffolding was raised around the church in preparation for its restoration. His final visit came on a day of worship. It was a deliberately reckless decision, and he was spotted almost instantly. It was the Trotter boy, the one who'd stolen his job. He pointed out the tesque who was hiding in the bushes to his mother. The news spread rapidly, and soon there was a small crowd of humans eying him from across the street. Heart pounding, he stepped out of the bushes so that they could see him clearly. He felt righteous, scared to death, defiant. One of the men took a step toward him, but Payne stood his ground, refusing to move. Seconds later, a woman took the man by the arm and pulled him away, and after that, the crowd gradually lost interest. He watched them mount the stairs and file into church, and when the last of them had disappeared inside, and the doors had closed, only then did he let his guard down. He felt close to tears. A sparrow poked its head out of the bush, looked around, then hopped onto a branch and started singing sweetly. Payne did not hear it. Nor did he hear, when it arrived, the answering song.

FOUR

P ayne did not return to the Aksa side of the city. The closest
he came was halfway across the Bridge. The gorge was like a
void, and he felt suspended in it, poised between two worlds, the sec-
ular and the spiritual, the crass and the crasser, caught between the
light above and the dark below. Staring down into the canyon's depths,
he could lose himself. Others stared too, and some sad few, called or
driven, chose to leap to their deaths from the Bridge. Payne was drawn
to the Abyss—he had no choice; it seemed he had to look—but he
would never allow himself to become one with it. He was depressed,
angry, and hurt, but he wasn't suicidal.

He was on the Bridge one evening after work when he became
aware that he was being watched. There was a figure on the other side
and down from him a little. Fall had come to Aksagetta, and along
with lower temperatures there were fogs that often hung above the
gorge. There was one now: earlier in the day it had been wispy, but

with the loss of the sun's heat it had condensed. The nearby Getta gaming halls suffused it with a garish purple light. Visibility was almost nonexistent, save for every few minutes when a gust of wind from below would swirl the fog and briefly lift it. It was during one of these gusts that Payne recognized the figure as a woman. She stood on tiptoe, hands braced against the wall, peering over the side, where there was nothing to see. He watched her from the corner of an eye, wondering if she was thinking of jumping and what he should do. She looked familiar, and when she turned her head and glanced at him, he recognized the face. It was Nome, the girl who had come to him for help. He'd seen her a number of times since that day, but they hadn't spoken. She would avert her eyes when she saw him coming and either speak to someone else or pretend to be preoccupied. He might smile as a courtesy, but more likely would do as she did. But every so often he'd catch her staring at him from a distance. Or from his front room window he'd see her pause at the entrance to her building and glance up in his direction, chewing on her recessed lower lip as if trying to decide if what she wanted was worth facing him again. He wondered if she had followed him to the Bridge. It occurred to him that he could ask. But then the fog settled back down, hiding her and everything else, and he decided he preferred to be alone.

When it lifted again, she was gone, which suited him, but only until he remembered what he'd been thinking about her harming herself. Then he rushed across the Bridge to where she'd been standing and peered over the side, which was useless. Frantically, he searched the wall and walkway for a note or some other evidence she might have left. He found nothing and feared the worst. Recalling that she'd asked his help, he blamed himself. Would it have hurt him so much to listen to her? Would a kind word have been so hard?

He left the Bridge in a state of shock. He needed to talk to someone, someone like the Reverend, and he almost turned around. Back in his apartment he found no peace, pacing it as though it were a cage. He didn't know who to tell or what to do and kept glancing out the window, as if by sheer repetition he could bring the girl back to life. At one point he saw someone who looked like her. She was walking briskly down the street, head bowed as if to keep from being seen. Near his building she slowed and stole a glance upward, toward him. It was dark outside, but not too dark to recognize the face. It was her, Nome, and he let out a cry, then rushed downstairs, flooded with relief. But when he arrived, she was nowhere in sight, which was a disappointment and a loss, though not, as before, a mortal one. He felt giddy, and before he knew it, he was laughing. The laughter bubbled out of him, as though he himself had been snatched from the brink of death. Passersby narrowed their eyes, shook their heads and gave him a wide berth. For once, their scorn didn't matter.

Without the Church For Giveness work became the center of his life. Healing was one of the few areas, perhaps the only one, where he retained his dignity and self-respect. Remarkably, he continued to find things about humans that he liked, although it took more effort than it had before. His mind tended to drift, and sometimes he imagined getting away from them, completely away. Was that even possible? he wondered. Was there any place where humans didn't live and breathe and dominate? If there was, it was somewhere far away and undiscovered. Though not necessarily uninhabited. No, it could be a land of tesques, and why stop there? It could be an entire country of tesques, where he was not just one, but one of many, one among his own, and welcome.

Not that tesques were faultless. Or didn't have their prejudices. Or do wicked things. Still, the idea of a place like that: city after city of tesques, with not a human in sight. It was strange to think of it. A little spooky too. And wonderful.

What he missed, he came to realize, was not the religion or the humans so much, or the human friendship, as the friendship in general, the sense of shared purpose and understanding, of community. This more than anything was what he'd lost, what hurt, and even now—now more than ever—what he longed to have again.

There was a community of healers, but it was loose-knit, and he'd never felt particularly a part of it or that he belonged. There was another group of healers, not loose-knit at all. It was small and clandestine, had a slogan and an agenda. And a name: A New Day. It had made the news with a series of pronouncements espousing healers' rights, a heretical idea. Beyond that, no one seemed to know much of anything about the group, which only fueled speculation. Who were its members? Where did they meet? Did they have anything further planned? As for their stated goals, opinions ranged from agreement to indifference to outright disdain.

Payne felt in no position to disdain anything. He was curious about this group, and he asked around until he found a healer who knew another healer who, it was rumored, had some concrete information. The name of this healer, as it happened, was Nome.

Payne found out where and when she worked, but the day before he planned to drop by he saw her from his window and rushed downstairs, intercepting her just as she was about to slide her card into the slot of her apartment building's door. She took a step backward and raised her hands in self-defense at the sudden onrush of a strange man, then relaxed a little when she saw who it was.

He was panting, and she asked if something was the matter. She glanced across the street, then up and down the block, then back at him.

"Are you being chased? Is someone after you?"

He shook his head and got his breath. "I want to talk to you."

"About what?"

"A New Day."

She gave him a blank look. "They're all new. Every one."

"The group."

"I don't know what you mean."

"You don't?"

She shook her head, then paused, then seemed to change her mind. She admitted to having heard of them.

"Do you know where they meet?" he asked.

"I might."

"Will you tell me?"

"It's a party," she said.

That didn't sound right. "What kind of party?"

"A revolutionary one. And it's closed. Membership's by invitation only."

"How do you get invited?"

She mulled this over for a moment. "Why do you want to be?"

He didn't know that he did, which wasn't much of an answer. He did know, though, that he wasn't prepared to open up to her. Not with his wounds still fresh.

"It's complicated," he said.

She seemed to accept this, although not without amusement.

"What?" he asked.

She slid her card into the door and invited him inside. "Isn't everything?"

He followed her through a deserted lobby and up a flight of stairs, then down a long dim hall of many numbered doors that smelled of must and was eerily quiet. Near the end of it she stopped, flipped her entry card around and let him in the door marked 67.

"My place," she said, turning on the light.

The room was much the same as his—same size, same square shape, same spartan furnishings—but more chaotic. There were clothes piled on the standard-issue couch and two allotted chairs, and dirty dishes stacked on a counter.

"Have a seat," she said, rounding up the garments and tossing them into the bedroom. "Excuse the mess."

He remained standing. "You said you'd tell me where they meet."

"A New Day?" She frowned. "Did I? I don't think so. It's secret. They're very careful who they tell."

"I have to be invited first."

"That's right."

"Will you invite me?"

"That wouldn't help much. I'm not a member."

"But you know who is. Couldn't you arrange something?"

"I don't associate with them anymore."

"Why's that?"

"We had a falling out."

This piqued his interest, but she seemed just as guarded about her past as he was.

He tried a different tack. "That day you came to me. What was it you wanted?"

Months had passed, but she had no trouble remembering. "I told you what. Advice. Which you don't give. You made that very clear."

"What kind of advice?"

"Professional," she said.

"About what, specifically?"

She crossed her arms and gave him a look. "It doesn't really matter now, does it?"

Payne took a moment to think about what he might be getting into. Considering the shambles he had made of Vecque's life, professional advice was the last thing in the world he felt qualified to give. At the same time, his profession was the thing he knew best. Moreover, in a funny way he felt linked to this woman, as though he had, in fact, witnessed her death and now, days later, her rebirth. It wasn't true but it felt true; between his fear that she'd jumped and the fact that she hadn't lay some sort of obligation.

"I'll make a deal with you," he said.

"What sort of deal?"

"I'll help you if you help me." He paused, then added, "I promise to be careful."

"What does that mean?"

It means, he thought, I won't do anything stupid. I won't fall prey to arrogance and put your life at risk.

"We'll talk," he said. "If I have something useful to say, I'll say it. But only that, only words, nothing more."

A moment passed, and then she nodded. "All right. I'll agree to that."

But he wasn't done. "I want to be crystal clear about this. Any advice I give is purely advice. It's your decision, completely yours, whether or not to take it."

And so a deal was struck. She wouldn't tell him where to find the group, but she did agree to contact them and convey his interest. Which, she observed, they were probably already aware of. In return, he agreed to be a sounding board for her.

She was having trouble with her healings. The early stages were going fine, but the later ones, especially extrusion, were problematic. She couldn't seem to get Concretions out without hurting herself. Her meli was always sore.

Payne took a moment before responding. There was an axiom in healing, capsulized in rule number forty-one: identity precedes containment. He reminded her of this and in the same breath wondered if she might not be a step or two ahead of herself. In his experience, difficulties in the later stages were often due to difficulties in the earlier ones that had gone unnoticed and therefore unaddressed. He suggested she pay more attention to identification and enhancement, then watched her nod, but dully, as if she weren't listening.

He forged ahead. "You have to order your approach. It's not a random process. Line up the afferents by gradient potential. Adjust them every millisecond, or even more frequently, every twitch."

"Can I ask you something?"

"What?"

"Do you ever get scared?"

"Scared?"

Another nod, this time less self-absorbed, more alert to his response.

"Of what?" he asked.

"Of what you make."

He didn't quite understand.

"They're so beautiful sometimes," she said. "It hurts to look at them. It hurts my eyes."

"Your eyes?"

"Or something. It hurts to watch them die."

"Because you made them?"

She didn't know why, only that it hurt.

"Don't watch," he suggested.

"That doesn't help. I know it's happening, whether I look or not."

This he understood. He was always aware of the extinction of what he made.

"Don't think of it as death then. It's not, not the way it is for us. Concretions don't have consciousness or feelings. They're not flesh and blood or anything like it. They're constructs. We make them."

"They're real to me."

"They are real. But they're objects. They're not alive."

"But they have life. Maybe not like ours. Maybe like a pebble or a stone or water. If not life then spirit. Something."

"Not for long," he said.

"No. Not long."

"Would you rather it were longer? Or maybe you'd prefer they didn't die at all."

He'd meant to say "die on their own," which is how Concretions left the world; they self-extinguished. Nome didn't answer, and so he answered for her.

"They have to die. We need them to. Humans need them to. They depend on it."

"Humans hate to look at them," she said.

"Yes. They do."

"They hate to even acknowledge that they're connected. If they didn't die, they'd find a way to kill them on their own."

Payne suspected she was right, and it gave him insight into what was troubling her, or so he thought. "Would you feel better if you killed them yourself? If you didn't have to wait for them to die? If you were less of a bystander, if you didn't have to be so passive?"

"I don't think that's the problem."

"No?"

She shook her head, then stood and wandered to the window, pressing her forehead against the glass and absentmindedly rubbing her meli. Payne felt that he was seeing something private and was about to say good night when she turned and, apropos of nothing, said, "They're different ones."

"Different?"

"Different levels."

He listened to her count them out, the six distinct levels of Concretions. It was elementary knowledge.

"That's right," he said.

"Fives and Sixes don't die."

"Yes, they do. Eventually."

"Not all of them."

He frowned and asked her if she'd ever seen a Five or Six. Had she ever made one?

"I've heard," she said. "They have a pen for them in Rampart. They live for weeks and weeks. Some of them for months."

"Maybe so," said Payne, who'd never seen or made one either. "But they're there and we're here. It's unlikely that we'll ever meet."

But Nome had heard something else. Something more unsettling.

"They say that some aren't snuffing out the way they're supposed to. Even after months and months. They say there's been some kind of change."

"What change?"

"That they're surviving. On their own. Outside their hosts. That they're really truly alive."

"That's nonsense."

"Why is it nonsense?"

"Because they can't survive on their own. They need a body to live in. You know that. They need a host to feed on."

"They could feed the way we do."

"On what? Fruits and vegetables?"

"You're making fun."

"No, really. What do you think they'd eat?"

"I don't know. Meat?"

He cocked an eye.

The next word was an effort for her. "Us?"

At this he could not contain himself, but stood and placed himself in front of her, hands on her shoulders, forcing her to look him in the face.

"This is a story you're making up. It's a fantasy. It's not real. It's not true."

"It could be true," she said.

"No. It's not."

"You don't think they want revenge?"

"Not revenge, not food, not anything. In whatever sense they are alive, it's only long enough to die. They don't think. They don't have motive or intent. That's you. That's your mind working. It's not theirs."

"But they're a part of me."

"Were," he said. "When you were making them. Once they're out, they're not. They're gone."

"It's hard to separate myself."

"Don't look at them," he said, knowing how tempting it was to pore over one's creations, how hard to turn away. "The beauty is a trick. It's their last defense. Leave the room as soon as you've extruded. Let it go."

"I should," she said.

"You can."

"You think?"

"Yes. I do. Absolutely."

She raised her eyes to meet his, drawing strength from his confidence in her, his self-assurance. Ever so slowly she nodded.

"All right," she said. "I'll try."

FIVE

The meetings of A New Day were held in secret, in a hot bunker of a room buried in the subbasement of the Easytime, the city's largest and most popular gaming establishment. The room sat at the bottom of four steep flights of heavy metal stairs, then through a tunnel and behind a pair of hulking concrete pillars. It was the type of room that in a different age would have served a different purpose: a bombardment shelter, a torture chamber, a banishment cell. In this one it was a storage room. There was a coil of cable in a corner and a stack of rusted transvex brackets in another. Some prismatic quarter panels, a moebic dowel, and a random pile of flanges, nuts and bolts, inverse clamps and beveled harlequin screws. The air inside the room was dank and stale, the walls were stained, the concrete floor hard and cold. There was a pool of standing water in a shallow depression. It was not by any stretch of the imagination a comfortable room, but then revolution was not a comfortable idea. If it could take root here, it could take root anywhere, and in fact, it seemed only fitting that this should be its birthplace.

At Payne's first meeting there were seven cadre present; at his second, twice that number, and at his third, a tidy dozen. They sat on pillows and carpet remnants and sometimes burned a bustion stick to drive away the subterranean smell. The group—or party, as he came to know it—was composed entirely of healers, which was a welcome change for him, although it took some getting used to. At the Church For Giveness he'd been the token tesque, and his opinions had therefore carried a certain weight with the Reverend Meeks and a few others, at least for a certain while. Here what he thought was no more or less important than what anybody else thought. Equality was one of the central tenets of A New Day. In point of fact, he was both less informed and less experienced about politics and related matters than any of the others, so while in theory his ideas were of equal value to theirs, in practice he kept his mouth shut, listening and observing and only rarely speaking up.

A New Day, he learned, was a vanguard party. It was revolutionary, and its decisions, unlike other revolutionary parties before it, were by consensus only. Which meant not only that everybody had a voice but that all voices, eventually, had to be united. Which, in turn, could make decision-making a painfully slow and laborious affair.

The main objectives of A New Day were justice and democracy for healers. As for tesques as a whole (the so-called tesque nation) and other ancillary questions, there was less consensus and more debate. Careful study and analysis of the issue—all issues—was another principle of the group. This was embodied in the maxim "Thought before action" and its offshoot "The present matters, but the future matters more."

A New Day, he further learned, was an egalitarian organization. Everyone received equal treatment and respect. That said, some received more than others. Cadre were well aware of their position in the group, of who sat with whom, who spoke more or less, and more or less eloquently, and who garnered more or less attention. A New

Day had many virtues, not the least its noble purpose and high ideals, but it was a group, and groups by nature were hierarchical, starting with groups of two, and, for certain troubled individuals, groups of one alone. So while in theory everyone stood on equal footing and commanded equal respect, in practice, some commanded more.

The one who regularly commanded the most was the founder of the group, a healer named Brand. Chisel-faced and compactly built, he had a keen and moral intellect, along with a passion for the cause that was balanced by a kindly manner and an even temperament. When he cleared his throat, which he did rarely, for he was more inclined to listen than to speak, the room fell silent. Heads turned and ears were bent to what he had to say.

Over the course of a number of meetings Payne pieced together something of Brand's history. While little more than a child, he had lost his parents. Both had perished on the final day of the Gode uprising of '09 (the Abortive Gode Uprising, as it had come to be known). He was raised by an aunt and grew up on the fringe of other boys and girls, who weren't that attracted to a boy who disguised his wounds by acting angry and aloof. He had radical ideas, even as a child, which didn't help his having friends, and he remained an outsider into the early years of his healer training, when he had something of an epiphany. If he wanted people to listen to him, which he did, or if he simply wanted to be with them sometimes, just hang around and mingle, which he thought he did, he realized that he had to be more appealing than he was. He had to improve his people skills. So this became his plan.

First he learned to listen to other people, at least enough to hear what they wanted. The world ran on fear and desire—this he knew—and what people wanted was to be rid of the one and to realize the other, and so he learned to make promises. He formed a highly secretive radical healer cell, Rising Tide, dedicated to the overthrow of the system. The Tide struck once, and the system did not flinch. It struck a second time, and then a third, each action more provocative than the last. Growing ever bolder, it struck a fourth and, as it turned out, final time, for the cadre of the Tide were captured and jailed. If it had been only one of them, one subversive unit, one radical, he would have been left to rot in jail, to suffer what they called "the living death," a lesson and a reminder to others who might think of trying something similar. But with five healers, five dedicated extremists (which, in terms of membership, was the high-water mark of the group), there could be no thought of prolonged incarceration. The city where they lived was not large, and they would be sorely missed. The humans of that city, humans everywhere, needed their healers.

Consequently, these misguided few were hurried through the penal system. To expedite their release and reentry into the workforce, various reconditioning programs were employed. For the first time Brand experienced what it was like to have his body violated. He was shot up with drugs. Sensory-deprived, then subjected to the Grimlatch Simulator. For the coup de grace, he received a dozen sessions of Accelerated Counseling, known widely—and notoriously—as the "Deep Probe."

He was the last of the group to be released from prison. After three months of treatment he was deemed cured of his rebelliousness and insurrectionist ideas, enough, at any rate, to be reentrusted with his job. Unfortunately, along the way he had developed an appetite for one of the many drugs that were used on him. Contrary to some of the other drugs, which set his nerves on edge and made him rave and rant and tremble, this one brought him peace and tranquility. It was the first time in his life he had ever felt those things.

He got hooked on the drug, but eventually kicked it in favor of a natural approach to serenity. Six months later he relapsed. He started using mist, also known as miss, or, in its most lethal form, muck, a nasty, illicit and highly addictive derivative of musk. Humans put it in their bloodstream; Brand rubbed it in his meli. A year into the habit and he was blissed out to the point of inanition, one day praying for more drug, the next for the Drain to take him first.

But the Drain didn't take him. He reached thirty, then thirty-five, which was getting on in years for a healer, and, despite his habit, or maybe because of it, he was still going strong. Then one day the muck supply bottomed out. Something about the men who made it, the miners, inexplicably not producing like they had before. That was the rumor, but whatever the reason, the drug stopped flowing. Initially, this was Brand's excuse to kick the habit. When flow resumed, he lost that excuse, and hadn't been a user since.

It was seven years now. He was forty-two, which for a healer was positively ancient. He'd founded A New Day in an effort to change the lives of healers. He knew the kind of changes he wanted but wasn't sure of the best method to achieve them. That was one of the main purposes of the group, to arrive at a consensus. The other major purpose was to attract—and gain—a critical mass of members.

Personally, he believed that effective change, by which he meant deep-rooted, lasting change, could only come through nonviolence. This was the lesson he had learned from his life. It was also the lesson he had learned from his study of history. There were other healers before him who had preached a similar message. Mobestis, of course. Emm after him. Jewl the Epicene. Ract, whom they called the Two-Headed.

In the meetings Brand stumped for this position, though he was open and even eager to entertain different points of view. This combination of outspokenness and respect for others was one of the qualities that made him popular. The "people" skills he had taught himself so many years before as a way to manipulate others had undergone a long and sometimes painful transformation into something kinder and more humane.

Brand had a narrow ribbon of bone that extended upward from the dome of his skull and encircled his head. With his hair shorn, which is how he wore it, and with the light just so, it looked like he was wearing a crown. He was a genial man. Many of the things that had once made him angry now made him smile or laugh.

There was another healer in the group opposite to Brand in temperament. His name was Shay, and he had a restless energy, along with a streak of militancy and defiance. He believed in action—confrontational, if necessary—and often grew impatient with the lengthy political discussions and consensus-building. He, too, had a following, smaller than Brand's, and reminded Payne a little of his brother Wyn. There were times he was wholly likable and times he was not. Certainly, he was not a man to be overlooked. A burly healer with a hyperteloric face, his eyes were widely spaced, to the point that they were almost on opposite sides of his head. It was the feature that marked him Grotesque. No matter where a person looked and how he fixed his gaze, he could only meet one of Shay's eyes at a time. The other, like a hawk's, was always aimed elsewhere.

One evening, after a particularly spirited meeting, Brand invited Payne to join him for a walk. In the month or two that Payne had been attending, they had never spoken privately, and he was flattered. They left their hiding place and climbed to street level, exiting the Easytime into the alley around the corner from the building's main entrance. Brand went first, and after a suitable interval Payne followed him, standard procedure to avoid cadre being seen together and inadvertently linked. They reunited several blocks away.

It was a warm night, and Brand was talkative, parsing what had happened in the meeting, soliciting Payne's opinions, reexamining the various issues and points of view. He seemed concerned whether his message was getting across. Payne, who had become something of a devotee, assured him that it was.

"I hope you're right," said Brand. "In the long run it's our only chance."

"Do you think we really have a chance?" It was a credit to the kind of man Brand was that Payne would even think of asking such a question.

"Oh yes. And not just a chance. Change, I would say, is inevitable."

"But we're so small. So secretive. No one even knows what we stand for."

"Growth will come in time. Maybe not in our lives. But eventually. All things start small. What's important is that they start properly. That even in the smallest form—especially the smallest form—we create and practice the qualities we would want in the largest. That's why it's so critical for us to listen to each other. To talk things out. To show respect. To feel that we've given voice to what we truly believe and want.

"And not just that, but to study too. We need to understand the present—certainly the present—but also the past. Economics, demographics, geography, philosophy, religion, science—we need to study all these things. We need to learn what constitutes change. And what doesn't, what masquerades as change but is false.

"All this takes time. And effort. And trust. And patience. If we try to run before we walk, we'll fall, I promise you. I've fallen enough that I should know."

"I've fallen, too," said Payne.

"Yes," said Brand. "I've heard. With that healer at the Pannus mine. Trying to make your own little revolution."

"I'd hardly call it that."

"No, I'm sure you wouldn't. Mobestis probably didn't think that he was doing anything unusual by curing Emm. And he wouldn't be who he is if he'd failed. I offer it merely as another way of looking at things. A slightly different and perhaps more benevolent interpretation of what happened."

Payne was not surprised that Brand knew about his debacle with Vecque. Many healers seemed to know. What did surprise him—and again he felt flattered—was that Brand had taken time to give it thought.

"I wasn't trying to change the world. The idea never occurred to me."

"Of course not. And to me it did, when I made my own little

attempt. The lesson being what? There are limits to a person's powers of perception? One cannot swim in the river and simultaneously see where the river is going? Certainly, I think we'd have to say that from different starting points we achieved more or less the same result. Mine will be at most a footnote in history. Yours: who can say? I doubt Mobestis or Jewl ever thought of themselves as revolutionaries. Or Ract, who failed. Or Soo, who failed miserably. Now they're legends."

"I'm not sure I want to be a legend."

Brand laughed. "It does have a grisly connotation, doesn't it? As if you have to endure horrid things in order to achieve such a lofty status. Better, I think, if we concentrate on what's in front of us. Enjoy the time we have. Try not to see so far into the future that we lose our motivation and sense of purpose. But far enough that we don't do something brash now that will only make things worse in the days to come."

Their walk had taken them away from the city center to a weathered road that paralleled the gorge, six or seven meters from its lip. On one side of them were scattered warehouses and empty lots; on the other, a tall barrier fence to keep the unwary and unmindful from stepping off the edge and falling in. It was a breezy part of town, and bits of garbage and debris had lodged against the fence. There was a breeze now, a gusty one, stirring up the dust and papers. It triggered a memory in Payne: he was back on Gode, in the midst of a sandstorm. It was summer, the season of such storms, which could blow for days at a time, driving sand into every crack and cranny, piling it into drifts against the walls of buildings, sending paper, clothes, trash—anything not tied down—flying. This particular storm had struck so fast and unexpectedly that he had been caught outside and within minutes had been engulfed. It was a frightening thing to be lost in a sandstorm, and he was duly frightened, until Wyn somehow had found him and led him home.

In some ways it was Brand more than Shay who reminded him of his brother.

"Do you remember the day that you were chosen to be a healer?" Payne asked the older man.

"Chosen? I don't think there was choice involved."

"Identified, I mean."

"Yes. That I do remember. Vividly."

"Were you frightened?"

"I think we all were frightened."

Payne nodded, glad to know he wasn't alone. "It was the first time I ever touched a human. It was a woman. She clung to me like she would die if she let go. They had to peel her off."

"It wasn't quite like that for me," said Brand. "Nothing so dramatic."

"I liked it," Payne confessed. "I liked the feeling I got inside, and I liked the power. And the touch. I wanted to be a healer. To be close to humans. Is that wrong?"

"In what way?"

"I'm not sure. It seems wrong."

Brand shrugged. "I wanted to be a healer, too. For different reasons than yours. For me it was a way out of Gode. Out of my life. I never worried about the Drain. That was for other people. Older and weaker and more susceptible." He paused, then gave a wry smile. "Life does catch up with you, doesn't it? I'm those people now."

"What about a revolutionary? Did you always want to be one of those?"

"Ah. That. A fine word, 'revolutionary.' Though misunderstood. By everyone, myself included. As soon as you think you have a grasp of what it means, it changes."

There was another gust of wind, and Brand lifted the hood on his jacket. Payne, who had trouble fitting into hoods, raised his collar.

"Did I always want to be a revolutionary? The answer, I think, is yes. Perhaps because I was deprived of my parents at so early an age. I was raised on stories about them, and wanted to make a story for myself. Something worth hearing. Worth telling. Sometimes now, when I think back on the days of the Rising Tide—that's what we called ourselves, we were ready to drown the world—I see them as my attempt to relive my parents' lives. To somehow join them."

"They were executed," said Payne.

"Not join them like that." He paused. "Well, maybe a little like that: I was so angry then. So self-destructive. What I meant, though, was to join them as in to love them and bring them back. And since I couldn't—and can't—bring them back physically, I do it through their ideas and what they stood for. I honor them by honoring their principles. When I try to understand who we are and where we're headed and how to get there, I try to remember our history. Which was what my parents believed, that you couldn't go anywhere without knowing where you'd been. The Gode Uprising was a product of the times. So was the Rising Tide, my own personal rebellion. And ever since, or maybe all along, the Authorities have been tightening their grip. Appealing to every imaginable fear. Spreading misinformation. My mother and father believed in fighting fear. They believed in building community and nurturing tolerance. It was one of their most cherished beliefs. And how do you nurture tolerance? By being tolerant yourself. Which is the answer to your other question."

"What question?"

"Why I'm willing to listen to Shay. Why I have such patience with him."

Payne had not asked this question, but he did wonder about it. More than wonder. Shay could be so disruptive sometimes, so antagonistic, and it sometimes bothered him that Brand did not do more about it.

But Brand was a teacher, not a disciplinarian, and now he was in the teaching mode. "We have to model what we want from humans. It starts with us. Shay is speaking the truth as he sees it. He's not lying when he says he favors confrontation. He's an angry man. I was an angry man myself. I understand the temptation to act through anger. I understand the impulse for violence and retaliation."

"He watches you," said Payne.

"Yes. I know. He's waiting. And while he is, I'm working on him. Showing him another way. He doesn't know it though." He grinned. "Devious, aren't I?"

❮❮❮

After that, Payne and Brand took frequent walks together when they had the time, ranging all around the city. Brand was a sturdy walker and a good companion. He had stamina and endurance that belied his years.

At one point Payne remarked on this. How was it that he managed to stay in such good health when other healers his age were long since drained? Brand's reply was typically humble. He didn't deserve it. He was fortunate. Considering the havoc he had wreaked on his body, he should have been dead years before.

Which brought up the topic of drugs. Muck, in particular, which Brand new intimately. Was it as bad, Payne wondered, as everyone said?

"Muck? Oh no. Muck is good. It's wonderful. What's bad is that it's hard to get. What's bad is being forced to be a criminal. Don't ever put yourself in a position of depending on something beyond your control. A drug, a political movement, or a person."

"But it made you sick."

"It did do that. But I got well. So you could also say it made me strong. Sometimes, in fact, I think that it's the source of my longevity."

"What? The drug?"

"Maybe the drug. Maybe the struggle. Maybe both."

If it was the drug, Payne thought, maybe more healers should be using it. "I worked at Pannus."

"Yes," said Brand. "I know."

"The men claimed they were making a perfume."

"They were," said Brand. "It is. Sweet and fragrant and deadly. Isn't that the way things are? Poison's only poison if you take too much of it, or in the wrong way. Take just a small amount and it's a remedy, or a potion. Take it with care and it can be a blissful and sublime experience. It can be a journey."

"They called it musk."

"Yes. The source. And you helped them make it?"

"I wouldn't. Not at first. There was another healer who did. But then she couldn't, and I was the only one left." His voice trailed off, and the silence grew.

At length Brand said, "And this bothers you."

"It made them sick. I was being asked to sanction that. To collude in it. And this was before I even knew about muck."

"What would have happened if you hadn't helped?"

"I wanted them to understand the consequences of what they were doing. I was hoping they would stop."

"You wanted to teach them a lesson."

"Yes."

"And the only way you could think of was not to help. To let them stay sick. Or possibly get worse."

"Talk didn't work. They wouldn't listen."

"I understand. But you couldn't do it."

Payne shook his head, remembering how bad he felt the first time he half healed a miner, how compromised. But then, after a while, how he gave in and stopped fighting each and every time they came to him, how he allowed his resolve—his morals—to weaken.

"Was I wrong?"

In reply, Brand told the story of two different healers he had known, each of whom, on the pretext of being drained, had refused to heal a human. In both cases the humans were quite ill. The first healer felt no compunctions whatsoever; the second was plagued by guilt for years afterward.

"I think I would have been the second one," said Payne.

"Then that's your answer. Sometimes the only choice is the lesser of two evils."

"It would be a lot easier to be the first."

"Amoral?" Brand gave a rueful nod. "Wouldn't it."

They were nearing the end of their walk. Brand's building, an older and less institutional version of Payne's, was within sight. Beside it was the polyhedral Crimson Crag, a nouveau gaming house and the site of the elevated circuit jumps and funnel races. Its angular and slightly concave glass facade reflected the nearby city landscape, bizarrely distorting it, making random human passersby appear grotesque.

Brand slowed. He had something on his mind.

"I have a confession to make," he said. "I'm not quite as healthy as I look."

"Don't say that."

"It's coming. After all this time. I can feel it. Its fingers, its evil little rootlets, they're working their way in. Up to now I've had the strength to stave it off. But I don't know that I will for that much longer. There's something I want to show you while I still can."

Payne did not want to hear this. "Do the others know?"

Brand waited for a twist of eager circuit jumpers, already roped together and glossed in crylic, to pass before responding. "Maybe one or two. The more perceptive ones. I haven't spoken openly of it. I haven't wanted to cause undue alarm."

"Shay?"

"No. Shay certainly not. But please, let's not talk politics. That's not why I brought this up. I want to teach you something."

Already Payne could feel himself withdrawing. He felt wounded, the all-too-familiar sense of losing something that he loved.

"Don't be angry," Brand said gently. He laid a hand on Payne's shoulder and gestured toward his building. "Come inside instead."

SIX

It was a dance. That's what Brand wanted to show him and, moreover, to teach him, and Payne was annoyed. This was no time for dancing. It was a time for talk and planning for the future, and if there was any time left, for kind, courageous words. But Brand refused to be drawn in by this, and before Payne knew it, the healer had removed his shoes and coat, pushed the furniture against the walls to clear the floor, and started dancing.

He began by swaying side to side, dipping his shoulders and gently rotating his hips and torso. After a while he lifted his arms above his head, twined them together and began to weave them in and out of one another. With his squat body, he looked a little like a stubby blade of grass, waving in the breeze. He raised his chin, exposing his neck, and slowly started turning.

He was not without a certain grace, though it was strange to see a grown man dance, and stranger still to see him dance in silence. When he closed his eyes and let his tongue slide out and in as though he were a snake, it was the strangest thing of all. This was not just any dance. It was the Viper Dance, and Payne remembered it.

Brand invited him to join in, but he could not do it. His body, suddenly, felt cold.

"Close your eyes," said Brand. "Pretend I'm not here."

Out of respect for him Payne tried this, taking a few tentative and uneasy steps before stopping. "I'm sorry. I'm not a dancer."

"But you are," said Brand. "This is your legacy." And he proceeded to explain what he meant.

The Viper Dance that Payne remembered, beyond being an adolescent fantasy and satire, was based on a bastardized version to begin with. The version that his parents knew, and his parents' parents, and his parents' parents' parents, was only the most recent incarnation of a much more ancient rite. It was a dance, Brand said, that Mobestis had brought to them in his first and elemental form, the snake. He had taught it to his enemies to turn their minds from thoughts of violence. It had the power to heal. It could transport a person into an ecstatic state.

Brand had learned the dance from an unlikely source, a human, an anthropologist interested in tesque and healer culture. Her name was Matai; he remembered her clear as day. She had come to him because she was unable to conceive. He had found a blockage in her body and removed it (it was a globe-shaped, membranous Concretion covered with thin sharp spines—he remembered that, too), and in her gratitude, she had taught him a piece of his own history. He remembered watching her dance, how enchanted and entranced he'd been, and how close he had come to violating his personal code of ethics and making a fool of himself in the process.

"She was a human who liked tesques," he said. "A remarkable and determined woman. She gave me another gift. I should have thought of it before."

He left the room for a minute, returning with what looked to be a thimble. "I don't need this anymore; for me there's music in the silence. But you'll do better with a rhythm. It'll be easier for you."

He offered it to Payne, inviting him to give it a try.

Payne was skeptical. "Whatever it is, I don't think it will help."

"You know what it is."

He frowned, looking closer. "It's not an ortine."

Brand smiled.

"But they're not real. They're make-believe. You only hear about them in stories."

"Some people say that ort are make-believe. That any animal so peaceable could never survive. And being no such thing as ort, there obviously can't be an ortine." Grasping the thimble between his thumb and forefinger, he held it in front of Payne's lips. "It's always a challenge to know who to believe. Very softly now. Like a thrown kiss. Blow."

Payne held his breath, afraid to injure the delicate instrument, to rupture the fragile and fabled tympanic head. Then, ever so slowly and carefully, he let his breath out. If he'd been an ant, or smaller, a microbe, he might have had the eyes to see the drumhead bulge.

A minute went by. At the very periphery of sound he sensed a vibration. Gradually it gathered energy and grew louder, until it was easily audible: a deep, repetitive and pleasing thrum.

Brand began to dance again. At first he held his arms overhead and intertwined like before, but then he dropped them to shoulder level, stretched out his neck and threw back his head. "Like this," he said, and starting turning, revolving slowly with his elbows bent and his palms uplifted. "It takes practice. You can do it." Pumping off the ball of one foot, he picked up speed and began to spin.

Payne did his best to copy him. At first he felt self-conscious and ill-at-ease, and the turning made him dizzy. When he spread his arms and threw back his head, strangely, the dizziness lessened. The longer he danced the better he felt, and when he finally gave himself up to the drumbeat, surrendered to it completely (which wasn't that hard, after all, for this was an ortine), the dizziness vanished and his head cleared.

He closed his eyes. The drumbeat heaved and throbbed. It was, he discovered, his own internal beat, the pulse of his own body and of the forces that held him together, that heated him and nourished him and gave him life. It was a deeply personal, intimate and pleasurable sensation. He and the beat were synchronized; they were one and the same. This was the ortine's gift and its magic.

Sometime later, he stopped. His heart was beating like a bird's. His cheeks were flushed. He felt radiant and happy.

Gradually, the drumbeat faded, leaving in its wake an afterglow of sound.

Brand, who had also stopped, was smiling. "That didn't take long to learn. I've shown others. Few take to it so quickly."

Payne pressed his hands to his chest in astonishment. "I feel so . . . good."

Brand's smile deepened. "Do it longer and who knows what might happen."

"I want to."

"You will."

"Now," said Payne. "Let's do it now."

Brand laughed. "Don't tempt me. In my younger days I could spin for hours. Even a year ago an hour or two was not hard. But these days I tire much faster. I have to make do with less. If I were to dance too long, I'd exhaust myself, and I can't afford that. I've learned to concentrate my energy. Half an hour, or less, a quarter, is enough to get what I need."

To spin for an hour, thought Payne. He could scarcely imagine it.

Brand seemed pleased. "It does feel good, doesn't it? I'm glad that I could show you. It's not a meli healing—nothing so fine and noble as that—but it does work its magic. Sometimes I think this, more than anything, is the secret to my longevity. Wishful thinking maybe, but I know it doesn't hurt."

The following week Payne danced again with Brand, and this time two other cadre joined them. It was another exhilarating experience, though not quite as profound and euphoric as the first. For one thing, he was self-conscious having other people besides Brand in the room. For another, the ortine was set in rhythm by someone else's breath, and he found it difficult to let himself go. Brand explained that this took practice. It was a question of learning—despite many perfectly good reasons not to—how to surrender.

They danced again the next week, but the week after that Brand was too tired. This kept him from dancing the following week as well, and Payne danced alone, but it wasn't the same. Thereafter, the dancing became sporadic. There were days Brand had the energy for it and days that he did not. The Drain had him in its grasp. His condition deteriorated slowly until it reached a certain point, after which it entered a much more rapid and precipitous decline.

This was evident at work, where he struggled to do his job. (He would have struggled far more had not Payne secretly arranged to cover for him, working longer hours, taking on a greater load.) It was evident at meetings, where he was less alert and less engaged. At first, the very fact that he kept coming despite his obvious ill health was a source of inspiration to the group. But after a while, like a guest who'd overstayed his welcome, it became awkward. It was distressing for the others to watch someone, especially someone they admired, deteriorate. It was discouraging, too, and led to a feeling of resignation that they could ill afford. Moreover, it distracted them from their work, which was to make a revolution. Brand could not help but agree.

Out of respect, then, for both the cadre and the cause, he stopped attending meetings. Physically, it had gotten to the point that he had trouble going up and down the steep flights of stairs. His time for leisurely walks was over too, and after work he now went directly home to rest. Payne visited him when he could, once a week at the very least. He'd started taking notes at meetings, and if Brand was able, they'd discuss how things were going in the group, especially how its direction was changing now that he was gone.

In his absence Shay had asserted himself. Payne had feared that this would happen, but to his surprise and relief Shay was showing a gentler, more appealing side. It was as though, no longer having to stand up to Brand, he was freed to be less aggressive and contentious. He was solicitous of others. He listened as much as he spoke. It was a difficult time for A New Day, a time of transition, and he, more than anyone, was rising to the challenge.

Brand was glad to hear it. The tesque had many admirable qualities and deserved the opportunity to be heard. As always, Brand counseled consensus-building and nonviolence. And patience, for if Shay had a weakness, it was to see things one-dimensionally and then go off half-cocked. The revolution Brand foresaw would not happen overnight. Society was too complex and its habits too ingrained to change any way but slowly.

But his patience with Shay was not inexhaustible. Some of what the healer said (and what Payne had dutifully written down) disturbed him. This, for example, which revealed, he maintained, Shay's tendency to minimize complexities:

"The world is not that complicated. The world, in fact, is easy to understand. There are those who act and those who are acted upon. For us no other distinctions matter. When we heal, we are both these people. Thus the confusion over whom we properly serve."

And this:

"Humans have the seven apertures. Grotesques the eight. To say that we are lesser for it is to say that living in a higher dimension is inferior to living in a lower one. For the meli is a higher dimension. Through healing we know the innermost secrets of life. We know what holds it together and we know what pulls it apart. We know these humans intimately, but they do not know us."

Brand found this divisive, but Payne, who usually deferred to him, disagreed. It mirrored his own experience with humans, and he thought it not only astute but shrewd.

⊲⊲⊲

Winter came to Aksagetta, which, after the winters at the Pannus mine, seemed drab and changeless. It never snowed and didn't start to rain till season's end. Nights were cool and days were mild. Skies were typically cloudless.

There was a monotony to the weather, just as there was a monotony to the city, which was what made it a favorite destination for tourists. It was a dependable place to visit and to play. Every day was pretty much the same as every other, regardless of the season. And nights were pretty much the same as days.

This was especially true for healers, most of whom worked in windowless rooms, which was supposed to keep distractions down. By the end of his shift, Payne was always happy to get outside. When he had the time, he still took walks, although it wasn't the same without his friend. Brand had been urging him to ask others in the group to join him, and once or twice, with mixed success, he had.

He arrived at a party meeting one night to find a candle burning. It sat atop the coil of unused cable in the corner of the room. Shay often used the image of fire when he spoke, alluding to its bright and cleansing power, but the candle was something new. When everyone had assembled and settled down, he lit two more. The first, he explained, stood for justice. The second for democracy. The third for steadfastness and strength. He had them all link hands and form a circle. This, to show their unity. After that, the meeting formally got under way.

One of the cadre presented an analysis of the current political situation in Aksagetta, which, he believed, was unstable. Economically, the city was teetering on the brink of ruin. Its leaders, of course, corrupt to the core, denied this, but the fact was, even some of the humans were clamoring for a change. It was a time for action, a time for A New Day to move from theory to practice, from talk to making concrete plans. He proposed that they do so, and do so soon. He made a fist to emphasize this point, then with a glance at Shay, who nodded his approval, sat down.

Thereafter, the discussion centered on what action to take. One member suggested leafleting to publicize their plight. Another, a work stoppage. There was debate over how confrontational to be. Most of the cadre favored passive resistance and remained opposed to violence.

Shay allowed the discussion to continue for a while before offering his own opinion. Quietly, he pointed out that passive resistance had been tried. He paused, then added that perhaps it should be tried again.

"Conditions change. History teaches us that. What doesn't work at one point may possibly work at a later time. Unfortunately, what hasn't changed is us. Our condition and our servitude. We give our lives to humans. When will we take back these lives? We heal them, but who heals us? Who heals the healers?"

Brand had coined this phrase, and it had become something of a party slogan, though Brand had always been quick to deflect credit for it. In the history of healers it was certainly not the first time that the question had been asked. He had used it as a teaching tool, a way to stimulate discussion. Shay seemed to be using it somewhat differently. On the one hand, to pay homage to Brand's contribution to the party. On another, to be recognized as his successor. And yet another, as a call to action.

He turned to Payne.

"Brother Payne, stop scribbling for a moment and talk to us. Tell us what you think."

Payne put down his pencil. "I think it's a good question. Who does heal us?"

"No one," someone said.

"We heal ourselves," said someone else.

Shay quieted them. "Let the brother speak."

"I'm not sure," said Payne. "I don't really have an answer. What do you think?"

"I think," Shay said pointedly, "that you do have an answer. Why not share it with us?" He waited half a second, then added, "Come now. If you have special knowledge, let us in on it. Secrets don't serve anyone."

There was silence in the room. Payne became aware that everyone was watching him. He wasn't sure what Shay wanted of him, but he didn't like being put on the spot.

"I don't keep secrets. Are you saying that I do?"

Shay regarded him, as though judging just how far he could push. In a flash of recognition, Payne saw his brother Wyn. This was just the sort of thing he would do: push and prod and poke until he provoked a reaction. He'd had a habit of measuring himself by the level of the competition. Shay seemed to have the same habit, but apparently he decided that the time was not ripe, or the competition perhaps too stiff, for he backed off.

"No," he said. "I'm not. We'll take it as a good and honest lesson. Trust must be earned. Anything not freely given is not worth the price."

For Payne the remainder of the meeting was a blur, and after it ended, he was the first one out the door. But before he reached the tunnel, a hand stopped him.

"Don't run away," said Shay.

"I'm not."

"Just walking fast. I know the feeling." Holding out the olive branch. "I'm sorry for singling you out like that. If you have the time, I'd like a word with you." He lowered his voice. "In private."

It was an invitation Payne, at that moment, would have liked to skip, but he saw no way to do so gracefully. When the room had emptied and the cadre all had disappeared into the tunnel, Shay steered him back inside.

His first words were aimed at Brand. He asked how he was. Payne replied, as he had in the past, that he wasn't doing well.

"I'm sorry to hear that. How long do you think he has left?"

"I don't know. But I doubt very long."

"I'll miss him," said Shay, then turned to snuff out the candles. Over his back and in a deceptively casual voice he asked, "And what does he have to say about us?"

This was a subject, Payne thought, that was best left alone. "To me? Not much."

"Come now. You scribble everything down. I know you talk to him. What does he think?"

Payne professed ignorance, but Shay kept at him, until at length he relented. "I expect you know."

"Yes. Go slow. Be patient. Don't do anything that might actually lead to change." He gave a snort. "You're right. I expect I do."

"Actually, the last thing he said was that you deserve a chance. That I . . . that we should listen to you."

Shay was not expecting this. Spear raised but shield down, he was caught unaware.

"You could visit him," said Payne.

He wanted to. Payne could see it in his face. But his pride wouldn't allow it, and with a sigh he shook his head.

"That, I think, would be a mistake. But please, give him my regards. Tell him that when he's gone, we won't forget him. Tell him we'll make sure that the humans won't forget him either."

"I don't think that's his main concern."

"No. Of course not. He wouldn't be Brand if it were. But it could be ours. We could make a statement. Send a message. Light a torch."

"A torch? What do you mean?"

Shay was lost a moment in thought. Then he got excited. "A funeral pyre. We could build one for him. Right here, above us. In front of the Easytime. Light the fire and let the good citizens of Aksagetta and all the tourists watch him burn."

Payne was appalled. "That's horrible. It's a gruesome idea."

"Not while he's alive," protested Shay; then seeing Payne's face, he laughed and clapped him on the shoulder, as though it were all a joke and Payne naive for taking it seriously.

"I'm glad to have you with us. I know it's hard with your mentor gone, but it's healers like you who make us strong."

"Strength comes from all of us together," Payne replied, echoing Shay's own words. And while "mentor" was accurate enough, he didn't appreciate the way Shay used it.

"Yes. It does. Though some are naturally stronger than others."

Shay was a tall, broad-chested man, and he had yet to release his grip on Payne's shoulder. Physically, if he chose, he could be intimidating.

"It's the responsibility of the strong to help the weak. That's what I was getting at, or trying to, in the meeting. If you, or anyone, has a gift, they have a duty to share it. That's what I want to convey by forming a circle in the beginning of our meetings. The idea that we're connected, we depend on one another. If one person breaks the circle by holding back, it's a threat to us all."

He clasped Payne now with both his hands, face to face with him, as if to prove, indeed, that two were stronger than one, although for Payne the discomfort of being so tightly held had something of the opposite effect.

"Without trust," he said, "we're nothing."

Payne agreed.

"So tell me then, are the rumors true?"

"What rumors?"

"That you healed a healer."

"No," said Payne. "That isn't true. I didn't."

"Did you try?"

"Yes."

"You failed?"

"Yes."

"Did it hurt?"

He had never been asked this question before. "Yes. As a matter of fact it did. A lot."

Shay's eyes bore into him. One, at least. The other pointed elsewhere.

"Would you ever try again?"

"Never," he said, shocked that Shay would even think to ask. Then shocked again when he understood the real question, or thought he did. He broke out of Shay's grasp.

"Is that what you were asking in the meeting? Is that what you want from me?"

"I want your allegiance," said Shay. "I want what's best for us. We're entering a new stage in the struggle. We need to stick together and help each other. Unity, Payne. That's the meaning of the circle. I want you in it, not somewhere else."

"Healers don't heal healers."

"Yes. That's what they say."

Shay studied him a moment, then let the matter drop, turning his attention to the room, stowing the candles, along with the pillows and scraps of carpet, underneath a tarpaulin, then checking for anything that might have been left behind.

"We can't be too careful. Up to now we haven't attracted attention. But soon, I think, we will."

"But we're still so small," said Payne, relieved to change the topic of conversation.

"Don't mistake lack of size for lack of impact. A single stone can fell a giant. A single match can start a blaze."

Satisfied with the room, he closed the door and started down the tunnel, Payne at his side. "It's true that not every healer is with us, not right now. Despite what they know will happen to them, despite the inevitability of it, they're afraid of change. I understand this fear. They need a spark. A catalyst. They need to know what's possible. We can be that spark. We can ignite them."

His words echoed in the tunnel and, dying, gave way to the sound and echo of their footsteps, two lone soldiers marching toward the battlefront, one eagerly, the other haltingly, with profound reservations. To Payne it seemed a vast and unbridgeable distance from where they were to what Shay spoke of. But Shay was not concerned with distances. Sparks bridged distances. Given enough juice, they leapt them.

"It's time for action. Time for A New Day to step forward and put its theories into practice." He paused, and a light came into his eyes. "We could start by giving ourselves a new name. More appropriate to this point in the struggle. The Spark . . . How does that sound? Sweeping Fire? Burning Fist? Or maybe simply Ignition."

"We have a name," Payne pointed out.

"Brand's name. It's time for a change."

"Aren't you rushing things a little? People move slowly. They don't like to change. You yourself said that. It takes time."

"Our lives are short," said Shay. "We don't have time."

He stopped at the end of the tunnel and faced Payne. The air vibrated with the hum of generators. His presence seemed to vibrate too, charged with the force of his conviction.

"Come out from Brand's shadow, Payne. Open your eyes. Look around. The Drain is killing us. It's killing him. How can you say it isn't time?"

"I can slow it down."

"What? By doing Brand's dance?" He gave a laugh.

"No," said Payne. "There're things that we can do. Pay closer attention to the details of healing, for one. Shift our focus in the early stages. Change our technique. Little things, but they help."

Shay looked at him with interest. "I've heard something about this."

"I can teach them. The skills aren't hard to learn."

"And we'd be grateful to you. All healers would." He paused, then frowned, as though bothered by something, a fly in the ointment, an incipient snafu. "Though maybe not. More healers lasting longer means what? More time to serve humans. More time to give everything we have and not get anything in return. That would certainly make the humans happy. Perhaps it's them, not us, who'd be grateful to you."

"You misunderstand me."

"Do I? Forgive me then. It's a common error among the oppressed to mistake the oppressor's good for his own."

Payne felt the bite of sarcasm, and encased within it, as was often true with Shay, the kernel of intelligence and truth.

"There's something else I've heard," said Shay.

"What's that?"

"That you're unaffected by the Drain."

"That's not true."

"They say that you're immune."

"I'm not. I feel it like everybody else."

"Do you?"

"Yes," he lied. He felt he had to lie. "Of course I do."

◈ ◈ ◈

By the end of the following week A New Day had A New Agenda. Stage One called for nonviolent action. A work stoppage was organized, which was joined by a handful of other healers and broken by the Authorities within a day. A month later, another one was staged, which evoked a similar, though more aggressive, response. Healer conditions did not improve and in some ways worsened. Still, Shay judged the action a success, as it drew attention to their plight, and furthermore, it exposed the brutal, authoritarian and vindictive nature of the system.

That accomplished, Stage Two of the New Agenda was implemented. This involved setting fires. In back alleys and untrafficked streets, storerooms and the occasional store, always under cover of darkness. Random acts designed to foment fear and shake the pillars of the state and therefore directed at property, which was the linchpin of these pillars. Care was taken not to injure human beings, who were expressedly not to be targeted in these attacks, although on one occasion—a small blaze that was started in a Musque boutique—a late-night janitor was inadvertently exposed to a lungful of smoke, and in a bit of irony ended up on the healing bed beside Shay, who himself had set the blaze and was now called upon to undo its damage, which he did professionally and without a word.

These blows against the system did not change the system, but they did evince a predictable response. Healers (and a small number of humans) were rounded up, detained and questioned. Security was tightened. Guards and Enforcers were given free rein in patrolling the streets. There was not exactly panic in the city, but there was fear and consternation. The populace was on alert, which was the perfect time, as any revolutionary—any pedagogue of any merit—knew, to be heard.

SEVEN

Between his own work, what he was doing for Brand, and his increasingly demanding job as a revolutionary, Payne was running himself into the ground. He was getting by on half the sleep he needed, and the deprivation was beginning to take its toll. When a slight miscalculation in a healing turned a routine Level Three into a nightmare Level Four, replete with auditory hemorrhage, cochlear infarcts and a cerebrospinal leak, he knew he had to get some rest. But when he arrived home from work, Nome was waiting at his door.

"I've been trying what you told me," she said.

It had been a long time since he'd seen her, and he didn't remember what that was, nor at the moment did he especially care. "I'm exhausted. Can this wait?"

She frowned and pressed her lips together. "It wasn't easy getting past the guard. I had to sneak in." She lowered her eyes, then lifted them, searching his. "I guess if you want I could try to sneak in again."

It was a canny way to phrase it, putting the onus on him, but he was too tired to argue, and instead took the path of least resistance and let her in. Immediately, he sank into a chair.

She glanced around the room. "It's so neat. Mine's a mess." She gave a nervous little laugh. "Like me."

"Clean it up," he said.

"You're supposed to disagree."

He looked at her, his mind half-asleep, and stifled a yawn.

"It's all right," she said. "Actually, it's true. I am."

"You look fine," he said.

"Do I?"

"Yes."

"I doubt it," she replied.

He couldn't manage any further reassurance and fell silent. A moment later he was nodding off. She shifted on her feet. He jerked awake.

She was looking at him, a warm expression on her face. "Wish I could do that."

"What? Fall asleep when you're tired?"

"I should put you to bed."

He almost asked her to leave at that point, but something in her offer disarmed him. When he was a boy and had nightmares, his mother would let him sleep in her bed. Nome was being nice. She was being motherly. And she was right about how she looked. Not a mess but not entirely put together. Eyes a little bloodshot, bags under the eyes. It occurred to him that she was short on sleep herself.

"Are you still having nightmares?" he asked.

Instantly, she came to full alert. "What nightmares?"

He recalled her having said something about them. "Weren't you worried about being attacked?"

"Attacked?"

He remembered. "Eaten, about being eaten."

"Oh, that."

"No?"

"It hasn't happened yet."

This sounded ominous, and he was about to say something when she rolled her eyes and told him not to take everything so seriously.

Meaning her, he could only suppose.

"It's a joke," she said.

Somehow it didn't seem funny, but then he wasn't in the mood for laughs. He was exhausted and at the same time all wound up, and it wasn't just from lack of sleep. The struggle for political hegemony, a term that Shay had taught him, was heating up. The city was tense and seemed about to explode. According to Shay, this was inevitable. And welcome. Explosion was a necessary step toward resolution.

"Hey, look," said Nome. "You helped. No kidding. You really did."

"Some people say it's wrong to help."

"That's stupid."

"They say it's counterproductive. That slowing the Drain only prolongs the agony."

"Who says that?"

"You don't believe it?"

"Shay," she said.

He didn't reply. Instead he asked her why she left A New Day.

"Him," she answered, "mostly."

"What about him?"

"He wasn't nice to me. I didn't like some of the things he said."

"What things?"

"Like what you just said. That it doesn't help to help. That it's somehow wrong. I don't believe that. Do you?"

He didn't, not really; he'd never fully bought Shay's argument. But that was water under the bridge. A New Day had moved on.

"He's responsible for these fires, isn't he?" said Nome.

"I wouldn't know."

"He is. And this crackdown by the Authorities. What else is he planning? What's next?"

It was time to change the subject. "Do you want to tell me why you're here?"

She gave him a long look, as though she were having second thoughts. Moments later, she started picking at her blouse in the area of her meli. Half a minute passed before she became aware that he was watching her, at which point she glanced down at her hand and forced herself to stop.

"After what you just said, I'm not sure I do."

He gestured toward the remaining chair. "Have a seat. Tell me."

She took the invitation and in response to further encouragement confessed that her meli was still sore. It embarrassed her to admit it, and she started rubbing and picking at her blouse again, whose fabric, Payne noted, was worn.

"Don't do that," he said, reaching for her hand, taking it in his and stilling it. "It takes time to heal. Playing with it only makes it worse."

"How much time?"

"How long has it been hurting?"

"A while."

"A while then."

"Actually, it never stopped." She glanced at him, then quickly looked away. "I didn't do what you told me to." Gulping down the words as if afraid to say them.

"Why not?" he asked.

She shrugged, conveying many things at once: ignorance of how to answer, helplessness before powerful and unnamed forces, shame, guilt, defiance.

He pondered this, this nuanced, multileveled shrug. "What exactly did I tell you?"

"You don't remember?"

"Not every little thing."

She brightened. "Really?"

"I'm sure we talked about technique."

"Yes. Vary the signal, you said. Focus the pulse. Pay more attention to Stages One and Two."

He nodded, feeling the specter of Shay's opposition, which was rendered somewhat moot by the fact that she, like so many seeking advice, hadn't listened.

"Why didn't you try it? What stopped you?"

Another shrug, but this time she graced it with an explanation. "It's not technique."

"No?"

She shook her head.

"How do you know if you didn't try?"

In response, she drew her knees to her chest and hugged herself into a ball, clearly afraid to say more. Payne found this disturbing, on the one hand, that she felt that way, and on the other, that he, the least intimidating person he knew, could be the reason. With a sigh and a silent wish that this would soon be over so that he could get some sleep, he leaned forward, placed a hand on her knee and gently asked her what was wrong.

Miraculously, this was all it took. Whatever was responsible for her resistance seemed to melt away. Slowly she uncoiled until she was sitting upright. She glanced at him, then, taking her blouse by the hem, folded it back to reveal her bare and naked meli.

He stared, then averted his eyes.

"No," she said. "I want you to look. Please. I want you to see."

More than any other part, a healer's gland was private. It was a breach of etiquette, and deeply embarrassing to him, that she would expose herself this way.

"Look how red it is," she said. "Look how sore. It used to be so pretty. Now look at it."

"Nome. Please. Cover yourself."

But she was in another world. "Ugly little thing."

She fingered it and winced, not surprising considering how red and swollen it was. Tiny scratches and ridges of dried blood crisscrossed its lips. She spoke to it as if it were a pet.

"You used to be so pink and blossomy. Like a flower. Now look at you. So sad. So hurt. And still you make such wonderful things."

With a sigh she dropped her blouse, covering the wounded organ. "It's my fault. I'm the one to blame."

Payne didn't know what to say. It was a truly alarming display. All he could think of was to reiterate that she might benefit from some help in technique.

"That's not the problem."

"No? What then?"

"Work."

"Work," he said, nonplussed.

She nodded. "I'm busy."

Every healer was busy. "How busy?"

"Very." Her tongue was looser now but still tied up. It needed help to get it working right; it needed Payne.

He obliged. "How many healings a week?"

"I don't keep track."

"Okay. A day. How many a day?"

"As many as I can."

"What? Seven? Eight?"

She wouldn't look at him. "I don't feel right when I'm not healing. You know? I don't feel good."

He did know, but he also knew to rest. Which at that moment is what he needed and desperately wanted. He yawned and asked again how many.

She mumbled something. Ten, it sounded like.

"Ten's too many."

Her voice subdued, almost a whisper. "Sometimes more."

This was a troubling admission. "What level?"

"Since when do we get to choose?"

This was true, although the higher the level, the longer a healing generally took and, consequently, the fewer they were expected to perform.

"I take it you know a Two from a Three," he said.

She glowered at him.

"And a Three from a Four?"

"I'm not dumb," she snapped.

"Then why are you doing so many?"

"Because I want to. I like it."

"It's hurting you."

"I know it is."

"Then stop."

"Oh, good advice," she said. "Really good. Why don't we talk about technique? You can lecture me about affinities and plasma nets and how to keep my focus and concentration when I'm doing whatever walks through the door." She let that bit of information sink in. "That's right. Anyone who wants it. All comers. As many as I can get."

Eyes flashing, lips compressed, daring him to do something about it.

"That's suicide," said Payne.

"Is it?" Mock surprise. "How horrible."

"Why?" he asked. "What does it get you?"

"I told you why. I like it. I get pleasure, same as you."

He did get pleasure, it was true. He had the healing love but not the craving, not to her degree. And he didn't hurt himself. He didn't inflict himself with pain.

"I take it you're not impressed," she said.

"No. Why would I be?"

Another wordless shrug. She picked at her meli. "I need someone to heal. Someone to take my mind off this."

"You need to rest," said Payne.

"That, too."

If he had been on the job and she were human, he would have helped her then and there. He would have healed her. In lieu of that, he got her up and coaxed her to his bedroom. His bed was not a healing bed, but it was not without its magic. The mattress was firm, the covers thick and warm. It was the sole luxury afforded healers, and he was grateful for it. The way he felt he could have slept a night and day and possibly another night on top of that, but she needed it more. He got her settled down, and on a whim, he tucked her in. Stationing himself outside the door in the event she got it in her mind to up and leave, he said good night. If life were a bed, he thought, sinking to the floor, nearly asleep himself, it could be made just the way a person wanted it. And if a meli were a flower, it could be allowed to go to seed, and the seeds could then be planted, until there were a field of melis, a hundred fields, a million melis, all pink and beautiful and fine.

EIGHT

B rand's door was unlocked when Payne arrived several days later, and Brand was slumped in a chair, staring into space. "Resting," he announced, as he struggled to his feet, fighting gravity, torpor and indifference to welcome his friend.

His condition had deteriorated. He was now completing only a third of his scheduled healings each day. And these were laborious affairs; each one taxed him more than the one before it. And his patients were filing complaints: he was taking too long; he was sweating too much; he was grunting beside them when he should have been quiet; he didn't jump up quickly enough to dispose of the Concretions; he smelled bad; he was old. All of which were true, and he had no defense. It wouldn't be long before his days as a healer were over, his healing bed given to another, his apartment taken away. After that, if he somehow slipped through the cracks, he might end up on the streets, at least for a while. But sooner or later he'd be sent back to

Gode, to his family, if one remained. If not, he'd be placed in the
Facility until his death. Or taken to the Building of Investigation in
Rampart. Either way his prospects were not good.

"I want to thank you," he told Payne, "for helping me these last
few months. For coming to visit. For covering for me."

To Payne, who had not once heard him complain, this sounded
disturbingly like a farewell speech. He didn't want to hear it.

"Thank me again in a year."

"It won't be a year. It won't be a month. I'll miss you, Payne. But
if it's possible to be happy, I'll be happy knowing that you won't be
working so hard. You've been doing two jobs, yours in addition to
mine, and you're not even sure it's the right thing to do."

Payne protested, but Brand quieted him.

"I'm familiar with Shay's argument. Anything we do to put off the
Drain is playing into enemy hands. It's a counterrevolutionary act. I
know the line."

"I don't agree with it," said Payne.

"I'm glad. Perhaps you'll have a better chance than I did convincing
Shay that there's no shame in compromise. Catastrophes happen quickly,
but progress takes time. But perhaps he's changed. We haven't talked
politics in quite a while. What's the party up to these days?"

Payne pulled out his notebook, cheered by Brand's interest.
Despite appearances, he was more alert than he had been in a while.
He seemed to be having one of his better days.

He flipped past a recent page, which contained a diagram of a
building that was being considered as a target, along with some notes
on the properties of various combustible materials. Guessing Brand
would not approve, he found a more suitable entry.

"Here's a poem. Did you know that Shay's a poet?"

Brand raised an eyebrow. "Is he? How interesting. What does Shay
the poet have to say?"

Payne cleared his throat.

"'The os melior is the Mouth of the Creator.
The os melior is the Gate.
The os melior is the Flower that Wilts.
The os melior is the Organ of the State.'"

Brand listened thoughtfully, digesting the words, then narrowing his eyes. "The rhyming of that poem's off. And the meter's all wrong. The words stick in your mouth like glue. They don't flow. And what does it mean anyway, the meli is the gate? How pretentious."

Payne was not expecting such a negative response. He felt defensive, not only on behalf of the verse but on behalf of Shay, the man who wrote it.

"It's not pretentious. It's true. The meli is a gate."

"We need to make it one," said Brand. "Two-way. Because right now it's one-directional."

"What do you mean?"

"Who heals the healers?" he said cryptically. And then, "So you like the poem? It speaks to you? It strikes a chord?"

"Yes. I do. It does."

"I suppose I should be pleased: it's my own poem. I wrote it years ago. Did Shay by any chance mention that?"

Abashed, Payne shook his head.

"Then I owe him," said Brand. "It's doggerel. Pure pap. He can have it. Let him claim it for his own."

Daunted, Payne found something in his notebook he was sure was Shay's, a quote he thought that Brand would like.

"'The humans turn to us for help,'" he read. "'We must learn from this. No change will come if we think and act as individuals. No bread will rise if the flour is not mixed. We must help each other out and work together. In unity alone are we strong.'"

Brand was impressed. "Shay said that?"

Payne nodded, not mentioning that the quote was several months old. "Every meeting we form a circle of unity."

"Do you?"

"Yes. And we light candles. One to justice, one to democracy, one to steadfastness." Knowing Brand would like this, too.

Instead, Brand asked, "And these fires? What do you know of them?"

"Fires?" asked Payne.

Brand suffered him a look. "I set fires when I was young. They're what landed me in prison. Is that where you want to be? Think about it. You could be locked up, maybe tortured, certainly mentally tortured, or you could be outside, spreading the word. You've a gift. Don't squander it."

He paused, and his voice changed, becoming more passionate and urgent.

"Listen. There was a time before the os melior existed. Before Mobestis. I believe there'll be another time, when it's no longer needed. When healing is a universal gift. When everything that separates people reaches an end. Once upon a time, tesques and humans were the same. There was no difference. We diverged, but divergence doesn't last forever. Like the worm that swallows its tail, like light, sooner or later it loops back on itself and reconverges."

He left the room and returned a minute later with the ortine. Attached to it was a thin chain, a necklace of tiny silver scales.

"One last dance," he said, "and then I want you to have it."

Before Payne could reply, Brand breathed on it, setting the tiny drum in motion, its rhythm matched to his own internal rhythm. Then he hung it around Payne's neck. "It's said that the Viper Dance, when performed to its conclusion, takes a person's life. Mobestis only resorted to that extreme with his enemies when he had no other choice. I do have choices, but none, I think, as good as this one. Let's pray that death is like the dance, ecstatic."

He began to dance, and before long, driven by the throbbing rhythm of the drum, Payne joined him. The sound was deep and plangent, sometimes like a wave, sometimes a lonely ululation. It was earth-bound and it also rose above the earth. It was simple and it was rich. It was Brand's sound and rhythm, but Payne felt embraced by it. He felt happy and he felt sad, comforted and on the verge of tears, liberated and about to have his poor heart broken.

An hour passed, and then another. He grew weary, but Brand, head thrown back, arms uplifted, seemed, if anything, to gain in strength. He spun like a man from a world of spinners, never tiring and never losing his step. He spun like a master, like a being at the peak of his powers. He spun as though possessed.

In the third hour the ortine began to beat faster. Titter-tat, the heartbeat of a rabbit. T-t-t, of a restless little bird. And faster still, until each beat fused with the one before it and the one after, and the drumming became indistinguishable from a single warbling polyphonic note.

And then, abruptly, it stopped.

Brand spun for half a minute more, then staggered backward. He clutched his heart and then his meli, then stumbled to his knees. He wore a puzzled expression, as if he'd been in some other world and rudely snatched away from it and now didn't know quite where he was. He blinked, as if to clear his vision, and then his eyes met Payne's. Half a second passed, and then he smiled, a broad, luminous, transcendent smile. And then he died.

᠗᠗᠗

Payne missed the next meeting of From the Ashes, which was what A New Day had become, and several after it as well. His thoughts were not on party politics but elsewhere. He was taking walks—through the sprawl of Getta, along the cliffs, even over the Bridge to Aksa— retracing steps that he and Brand had taken, remembering his friend and mentor, mourning him, trying to come to terms with the loss. Through the grapevine he heard rumors of a crisis in the party. Several cadre had left or been expelled. One of Shay's principal supporters had fallen victim to the Drain, and another had been arrested. Security in the group had been tightened and direct action curtailed. There'd been no arson now for several weeks, but there was talk of a major offensive being planned. They wanted him back. They needed everyone.

He felt torn. In his current state of mind he had no stomach for the rhetoric of battle, for any rhetoric, or, for that matter, any battle. The group seemed far away, like a place he'd visited, its concerns and now its urgency alien to him. And yet it had given him a home and a purpose when he needed one, and he felt loyal to it. He could imagine how besieged they were feeling, Shay especially, how desperate and backed into a corner. Now was not the time to abandon them, much as he would have liked to. He knew how it felt to be abandoned, and likewise, he knew how it felt to be supported. If there was a battle looming, or the potential for one, the best thing he could do was to go armed with Brand's message of nonviolence.

❧❧❧

The crowds around the gaming houses were thick as flies on the night that he returned. Restless too. Something seemed to be in the air. He took great care not to be followed, circling back on himself several times. At the head of the alley next to the Easytime he paused, then again at the underground entrance, making sure he was alone. Slipping silently inside the building, he hurried down the metal stairs.

When he reached the meeting room, the door was locked. For a moment he thought he'd gotten the day wrong. Then he heard voices inside, and he knocked. Instantly, the voices ceased. He knocked again and in a loud whisper announced himself.

Half a minute later, the door cracked open and an eye peered out. The crack widened.

"Payne." It was one of the younger cadre. "Where have you been?"

"Will you let me in?"

A look of uncertainty crossed her face, and she closed the door. He heard muffled voices, an argument perhaps, and then the door opened and Shay appeared. He was dressed in a heavy black robe and wore a stern expression.

"You've been absent."

"Brand's dead," said Payne.

Shay's eyes narrowed. Several seconds passed; then he drew Payne aside and whispered to him.

"We need you, my friend. Now more than ever."

"I have to talk to you. To everyone. I have something to say."

"Yes. We will talk. But come in, come in. Join us."

Throwing open the door, he publicly welcomed Payne back. The room was dark, save for a single candle. Five solemn-faced cadre stood in a circle. There was fear and excitement in the air.

"Open the circle," said Shay. "Let Payne in."

This was done, and Shay struck a match and lit the second candle, then raised a glass goblet that Payne had never seen. It was filled to the brim with a clear liquid.

"To democracy," he intoned.

He drank from the glass, then passed it to the healer on his left, who also drank, then passed it on. As it made the rounds, Payne was reminded of the glass for thirsty travelers outside the Church For Giveness, which was the first thing that had caught his eye about the church and whose simple message of generosity had so enchanted and misguided him. When the goblet came around, he hesitated to drink from it, but under the pressure of the group he relented, tipping the glass up and filling his mouth. The liquid had a fruity foretaste that promised something sweet, but its aftertaste was bitter.

Shay lit the final candle, the one that stood for strength. The goblet was returned to him, still half-full, and he raised it. His face danced in the candlelight. His voice was confident and strong.

"One heart, one mind, one will. The future is in our hands. Loyalty connects us. Unity of purpose binds us. Tonight we take back our lives and gain our freedom. Tonight we rise from the ashes. Tonight a new day dawns."

He tipped the goblet back and filled his mouth a second time, then passed it around the circle until it was fully drained. Then he handed out a hooded robe to each of them, similar to the one he was wearing. Payne found his heavy and a little stiff, and it gave off a pungent, almost oily, smell. He felt uneasy and decided it was time to speak up.

But before he could, the circle reconvened, the cadre joining hands and breathing, simply breathing, to ground themselves and cement their purpose and resolve. Payne had always enjoyed this part of the meetings, and despite his misgivings, he enjoyed it now. The energy in the group was very strong. He could feel it moving around the circle, gathering power and momentum, rising. Something told him that he should resist it; another voice, that he shouldn't. Soon he had no choice, because he was literally swept away.

It was an extraordinary feeling. Never had he felt so much in common with his friends and comrades. Never so interconnected, unified and intertwined. One heart, yes, they did possess a single heart as Shay had said, a single circulation, and yes, yes, a single body, too. He imagined that he was hearing with his comrades' ears and seeing with their eyes, and then, miraculously, he was. And thinking their thoughts, too. And feeling their feelings. They were not connected— no, connection implied separation, and they were not separated; they were one. One cell of many parts. One people of many strengths. One single, blissful, inviolate organism.

Shay uttered a word, and they raised their hoods, gathered by the door, then followed him out single-file. Like monks they passed through the tunnel. Payne felt that he was floating on air. The vast pylons and concrete pillars on which the building rested seemed made of liquid. All around him the air crackled with energy and life. Soon, he discovered that he could discern individual molecules, which pulsed and gave off waves of greenish light. The surfaces of objects, of his hands, of the hooded figures in front of him, of the soaring columns, throbbed and melted. The resonating hum of the generators was a hymn that glowed.

Everything had meaning, and meaning was in everything. Their footsteps on the metal staircase were a fanfare and a promise. Shay was a prophet, his wide-set, burning eyes beacons in the night. The other cadre were products of Payne's love and desire. Their ascent from the depths was oracular, ecstatic and preordained.

They reached the surface and assembled in the alley. Then Shay led them around the corner and down the block to the entrance of the Easytime. There they formed a circle, linking arms.

Humans continued to enter and exit the gaming house, but their way was now obstructed, and soon there was an angry crowd. They jeered and hurled insults. Before long, the insults turned to threats.

For Payne, who favored almost anything to confrontation, this ugly turn had a negative effect. The ecstasy that had so bedazzled and enthralled him began to wane. The crowd's rage was disorienting. His fingers, which had been quivering with the blissful force of life, began to quiver with apprehension. His heart pounded in alarm.

He felt assaulted. These were beasts, not human beings. Their snarling, raging faces were a mockery of humanity. And the buildings that they swarmed from, that towered over him and his friends and blotted out the sky, were equally menacing. He felt their weight and their desire to crush him. Like the beasts they were full of malice, and they were alive.

His circle, which only moments before had been a source of strength and power, now seemed on the verge of being overwhelmed. Whatever it was they had hoped to achieve was clearly hopeless. While they still had the chance, they should break ranks and run.

Into this tremor of fear and doubt stepped Shay. From underneath his robe he produced a torch, which he lit and held aloft. The crowd edged back, and in a booming voice he declared the party's creed.

"Justice! Democracy! Steadfastness and Strength!"

In response to his words, the circle tightened. Drawing courage from him, the cadre repeated his cry.

"No more slavery! No more subjugation! We reclaim our bodies! Freedom now and forever. The world is ours! From the ashes a new day dawns!"

All this Shay proclaimed to the now five-deep throng of humans. To his own people he dropped his voice and looked them each in the eye. Eyes, to a one, that were fixed and dilated, as fat as moons and as black as olives. Longing, trusting eyes.

"Strength now, comrades. Who heals us? we ask. Now we answer. We heal ourselves. Our bodies are our own. That is our message, and it will never be forgotten. Never. Be at peace."

Then one by one, true to the principles of the party, he went around the circle, asking each of them a final time if they consented, and one by one they answered, "Yes, I do." All save Payne, who asked what he was consenting to. But his voice was drowned out by the crowd; either that, or he was misunderstood. For Shay proceeded with the ceremony, handing each of them in turn the torch, and one by one they lit themselves; and their robes, which had been soaked beforehand, ignited instantly into blue and yellow flame.

The mob erupted, shouting, screaming, but no one stopped the healers; no one intervened. Payne was stricken with his own paralysis, watching in horror as his friends went up in flame.

He was the last one to be offered the torch. Shay faced him, holding it out. "Quickly now. We have little time."

Payne stared at him, eyes wide, lips frozen. The comrade closest to him had started tottering, and without thinking, he reached out to steady him, a senseless reflex, then quickly drew his hand back but too late, for a tongue of flame leapt out and licked his sleeve. His robe guttered for a second, then burst aflame.

With a cry he broke ranks, stumbling backward and tearing at his garment until he got it off. Shay, who had already ignited himself, seemed to mistake his horror for a loss of nerve and went after him.

"Be strong, my friend. Don't fear. Come, lean on me."

Grabbing Payne under the arm, he tried to help him back into the fold. Payne resisted, but Shay's grip was like a vice. Payne begged him to stop the conflagration.

"Stop? We cannot stop. Be with us now. Be brave."

"No," cried Payne. "No. This is wrong. Let me go."

Shay looked at him strangely, and for a second his face clouded. He was in his own world, deep into it, and it took a monumental effort to tear himself free.

"Go? You wish to go?"

"Yes," Payne pleaded.

By now the other cadre were losing consciousness but fighting to hold onto one another, to keep what remained of their circle intact. Shay looked at them, then looked at Payne, then, relaxing his grip, released him. Quickly, he rejoined his comrades, completing and then closing the circle just as he became engulfed in flame. For a moment, then, they were united. In spirit and in flesh A New Day, as Payne would ever think of them, burned. It was almost glorious. Their ring of fire, like a flaming crown, like a promise, lit the sky.

NINE

Payne was charged with sedition, endangering human lives directly, endangering human lives indirectly, destruction of property (principally, chattel property), unlawful assembly, felonious use of fire, and other crimes too numerous to mention. He was thrown in jail, in a dark and solitary cell, which is where he sat, hungry, alone and nibbled on by vermin, for days and days on end. He was allowed no visitors and had no contact with the outside world. His human guards kept their distance from him, avoiding conversation beyond assuring him that he would never leave that place, never in a thousand years. His fate was sealed by the cruel, self-serving, heinous nature of his crime. Outside, people were clamoring for his death, and the only thing standing in their way were the bars of his cell. That, and the fact that he was valuable as a living lesson.

Deprived of tesque or human contact, and any semblance of a normal life, Payne filled his time with thought, and when thought became too tiresome or painful, with delusion. He imagined he was back at the Pannus mine, huddled in a tunnel, lost but not abandoned, the object of a furious, round-the-clock search. Any moment they would break through the walls, and someone, Vecque maybe, rejuvenated, reborn, would rescue him.

He imagined he was sleeping and any moment would wake up to the world he knew before.

He imagined a plate of food to fill his empty belly.

He imagined sunlight, warmth, a bed that wasn't made of stone.

He imagined he was innocent, and not just that but a hero, that he had saved his friends, not watched them blacken and die.

He imagined that his brother Wyn was alive and would rescue him, and he imagined, too, that Wyn, in fact, did visit, cherished and exalted brother Wyn who could do no wrong. But far from helping him, his brother ridiculed him for making one bad choice after another, for being hopelessly naive, a disgrace to the family, a burden.

He imagined he was not a disgrace. And his tears were not wet. And his fate was not sealed.

He imagined he could walk away and start over.

Strictly speaking, he was not entirely alone. Sharing his body and his cell was an assortment of fleas and lice and spiders. He spoke to them on occasion but found little in the way of common ground. Their thoughts and desires, compared to the labyrinthine twists and turns of his fevered brain, were of a primitive nature. More promising was a rat that scurried out from time to time in search of food. He fed it crumbs, and soon it was eating out of his hand. His burns had mostly healed, and he liked the feel of its tiny feet on his fresh new skin. He liked the tickle of its whiskers and the way its cold nose nuzzled up against his palm.

By placing bits of food in the hollow of his clavicle, he trained it to trot up and down his arm. This he liked most of all. Without realizing it, he had taught his newfound friend to simulate the first stage of a healing.

One day the animal did not appear. When it returned the next day, Payne asked it where it had been.

The rat seemed sullen and did not answer. Payne fed it a crumb and asked again.

Still, the rat offered no explanation, and fearing it had sustained some sort of injury, he examined it. Its beady eyes seemed clear enough, its arms and legs intact. Its tail had not been bitten off, and its coat of fur looked fine. Suspecting trouble of a deeper sort, Payne stroked its back and tried to coax out information. He reminded it that friends did not hold out on friends. He promised to be discreet.

The rat remained close-lipped. Clearly, it wasn't happy to be the object of such intense scrutiny and attention. It seemed about to bolt.

On impulse, Payne lifted it by the scruff of its neck and pressed its belly against his healing arm. Immediately, his neuroepidermal buds began to tingle. The rat nipped at him and tried to claw its way free, but Payne would not let go. When eventually it accepted its fate and stilled, he proceeded with the healing.

After that the rat did not resist him. Every day it came and promptly planted itself belly-down on his arm. Sometimes it rubbed against him as if to copulate. Sometimes it nibbled on his skin and nuzzled him.

There was, in fact, no illness in its body, but Payne had cured it anyway, cured it of its wanderlust and absenteeism. In the guise of freedom he had given it a maze of choices, each of which ended up with him. The rat seemed quite content with this, much as humans were with false appearances. It seemed, in fact, quite human in its motives and its needs.

This was the first time Payne had ever used his talents on his own behalf, selfishly, without regard for what was right or best for the one he healed. That the one in this case was a rat did not relieve him of the pangs of guilt at overstepping his mandate and authority. But in the face of such intense and numbing isolation, he could not help himself. He needed contact with the living. Had there been no rat (and at times he thought there wasn't, imagining that this being was something else; a pixie, a fairy princess, a messenger cloaked in a ball of fur, a superior intelligence in disguise), he would have turned to the lice and fleas and spiders for comfort. How they would have responded to a healing was anybody's guess, but he would have found out, because he would have tried.

The days wore on, one after another, monotonous despite the richness of his inner life, dead and dreary despite his hallucinations. He lost track of time and on occasion would get the nerve up to speak to the guards and brave their scorn. What day was it? he'd ask. What week? What month? What of the world outside? What was going on? Did anyone remember him?

Their answers were the same, regardless of the question, and delivered with the same impenetrability. It made no difference what day it was. It made no difference what was happening in the world. He was living in his world. Prison would always be his world. Now and forever. He might as well get used to it.

Then one day, suddenly, he was free. Without comment or explanation the guards unlocked the door to his cell, hauled him out, threw him under a shower, then gave him a fresh set of clothes and transported him under cover of darkness to the basement of the Crimson Crag. From there, by elevator, they took him to a suite of rooms.

The senior guard knocked on the door, then disappeared inside. A minute later he reappeared and warned Payne not to try anything funny. Then he pushed him in.

She was standing beside an upholstered sofa, one hand resting on its quilted arm, the other dangling loosely at her side, a casual, inviting, homey, and possibly prearranged pose. Her name, he'd learned, was Meera. Her father was a Senator, her mother a distinguished social scientist. The family name of Libretain was widely known.

"Hello," she said. "We meet again."

Payne swallowed. "Hello."

She smiled, he managed to smile back, and after that they lapsed into a silence that she seemed more than happy to inhabit, taking time to look at him and wait to see what he would say or do. He felt horribly self-conscious and was glad at least to have showered and be wearing clean clothes. He would have scrubbed himself a good deal more if he had known his destination, though no amount of scrubbing or fine clothes would have ever made him feel on a level with her.

He tried to think of something to say, something smart, at least not dumb. The room was warm and seemed to dull his senses. The floor was carpeted. He wasn't used to carpets. The room was bright, and he wasn't used to light. After months of isolation he wasn't used to speech. And there was a smell—a dry, sweet smell—a perfumed, human smell that made him woozy. He felt light-headed and worried that he might faint. How embarrassing, he thought, to faint in front of her.

"Please," she said, gesturing to a chair. "Sit down."

He did, gratefully.

"Something to drink?"

There was a tray with bottles of different colors, shapes and sizes. There was a bowl with twists of fruit, a long glass swizzling stick, a bucket.

He felt illiterate. "Whatever you are."

"I'm not," she said.

"That's fine."

"You're not in jail anymore. Feel free."

He didn't, which is to say he felt about as free as he'd felt before, except that now everything was magnificently plush and beautiful.

"How about a glass of water?" she said.

"Water's fine."

She wore silk trousers and a short-sleeved blouse, stud earrings and a thin gold chain necklace. She poured the water from a pitcher into a long, tall glass. After serving him, she settled on the sofa and folded her hands in her lap. She sat as if suspended from a string, straight-backed, elegant and poised.

"You've been busy since I last saw you."

Had he? Was rotting away in prison being busy? "Are you the one who got me out?"

"Yes. I helped arrange it."

"Why?"

"It wasn't right. You were there unjustly." Spoken as if justice were an expectation, not a pipe dream.

"No one else seemed to mind," he said.

"That's not exactly true. But it's immaterial. The point is you're out."

Yes. He had to agree. If this wasn't another of his hallucinations. "I'm grateful."

"There's a string attached," she said.

"What sort of string?"

"I vouched for you. I promised you wouldn't do anything to land yourself in jail again."

"I didn't do anything this time."

She gave him a look. "Really. What an interesting thing to say."

"I wasn't responsible for what happened."

"The immolation? No, I don't believe you were. The rest? I'd say that's using the term 'responsible' rather loosely. At any rate, I managed to convince some people, the right people, you weren't the ringleader. A pawn, I said, although I suspect that you were more. Not innocent . . . who could believe that? But misled and certainly naive."

He had accused himself of this very thing, and would continue to, but he hated hearing it from her.

"Your release is provisional on your future conduct," she said.

"I'm on probation?"

"Yes. Absolutely. They'll be watching every move you make. My advice is, don't make any wrong ones. Do your job. Keep out of trouble. Don't join any crazy groups. Any groups, period."

"They weren't crazy," he said.

She raised an eyebrow. "That, I'd have to say, is a bad start."

"Not in what they wanted. Maybe in how they went about it."

"And which do you think people will remember?"

"I know what humans will," he said. Then fearing that he'd said too much, he said more. "They were desperate. People do extreme things out of desperation. They think differently. They see things differently. They act in ways that might look crazy but to them make sense. To them it might be the only thing that does make sense. It's another world."

He had thought long and hard on this in prison. How events had taken such a turn. What his role had been, what he did and didn't do, what he could have done differently. Loyalty was an admirable quality, perhaps the most admirable, but to cling to it dogmatically was to turn a virtue to a vice. Somewhere, somehow, something had gone wrong. He felt guilty to be the sole survivor and guilty now to distance himself, talking about "them," not "us."

"I'm all for change," she said, "but it's irresponsible to take an action when there's not a chance of its succeeding. You didn't have the numbers or the slightest notion of how to follow through. The fires and then that horrible burning were shock tactics, and shock wears off. It's childish. Brutally childish. It accomplishes nothing."

From the angry way she spoke one might have thought that she, not he, had been the one to lose her friends. "What you did just frightens people. It makes them turn away. Or worse, it makes them retaliate. The world needs messengers, not martyrs. Less violence, not more."

"Retaliation?" He almost laughed. "What worse can you do than drain us?"

"Oh," she said. "Much worse. Much much worse. We humans have a remarkable capacity for cruelty and revenge."

"We're not responsible for that," said Payne.

"We? We? There is no we." Her voice rose in frustration. "Your group is gone, Payne. Get it through your head. No one talks about it anymore. I'd be surprised if anyone remembers. That squalid little room you met in? It's bricked up. The sidewalk where you made your mark? It was scrubbed clean the next day. The only thing that matters from here on out is you. How you act. What you do and, more importantly, what you don't."

"I don't intend to set myself on fire, if that's what you want to know."

Her eyes flashed. "Is that supposed to be a joke?"

He wasn't sure what it was, or why they seemed to be arguing. He much preferred it when she smiled.

"I'm not looking to make trouble," he assured her, "but I don't understand, why take the chance? Why not leave me where I was as a lesson? Why set me free?"

"Six healers went up in smoke. The city can't absorb that loss. The ones who are left are working round the clock—that's their reward for having better sense than you. And they're suffering: you know what it does to a healer to work so hard. No one should have to pay that price."

He hadn't thought of this. It was a new reason for self-reproach.

"No offense intended," she added, "but you're a precious commodity."

"If we're so precious, why do you treat us so badly?"

"That's a good question. Why do people bite the hands that feed them? Why do we hurt the ones we love? Because we don't love ourselves? Because we love ourselves too much? I don't know why. Because you let us? Because we can?"

For the first time she appeared less than fully in command of herself, as though he'd touched a nerve. She fingered her necklace, then rose and fixed herself a drink, which she carried across the room to a steamy, mullioned window. Crimson light spilled in from the building's thousand-bulbed facade, giving her face a harsh, inhuman look.

"Do they hate me?" Payne asked.

"Do who?"

"The other healers."

She stared out the window for a while before answering. "I expect some do. You're an easy target for hate, and the Authorities are more than happy to keep it that way. They're very good at nursing grievances, creating smoke screens and misdirection. Lies and propaganda run in their blood. They love it when people are up in arms about something, as long as it's not them. Which is not to say that I agree with what you did. It's caused a tremendous amount of suffering. But very few are pointing the finger where it belongs."

"Where's that?"

"At us. At humans. We're the ones to blame for this. We use you mercilessly. We take and take until you've no more to give. We're the ones who drive you to extremes, because we're the ones who drain you."

"You have no choice," he said.

"But we do. We could use you less. Let you rest more. Give you time to recover."

"That would be better, but it wouldn't stop it." He thought of Vecque, who was stricken after a mere two years of service. "There're some whom even rest won't help."

"There're other things we could do."

"What things?"

She hesitated, as though reluctant to speak of them.

He asked again.

"We could find a way to make more healers."

"More? How?" Then he remembered the experiments that humans were so fond of doing.

"Valid thinks we can," she said. "Others, too. I don't agree with them. I don't agree with their experiments."

"Why not?"

"They're cruel, that's why. Barbaric. And no one's ever shown they help."

Suddenly, without warning, a human figure plummeted past the window. It was followed by several more, all roped together and shrieking. Payne leapt up and rushed to the window, prepared to race outside to help if he was needed. He saw some people dangling by a rope, and then with a jerk they vanished.

"Circuit jumpers," Meera muttered. "What a waste. Sometimes I think that humans have a death wish."

"It's supposed to be fun," he said, which is what he'd heard. "It's not?"

"One or two die every year."

"But that can't be what they wish for."

"No. Probably not. Probably they expect to live forever."

"Have you ever tried it?"

She shook her head, staring out the window. "No. When I was young, I took other risks. Just as stupid."

He longed to ask her what they were. They were standing near each other, and he longed to stand closer.

"Now I try to be more careful," she said. "Life, I've discovered, has plenty of thrills without manufacturing them."

She turned from the window, and in the process their eyes met for just a second. She seemed surprised to see him there so close and gave a self-conscious little smile, as though she'd been caught at something. But she quickly recovered her composure, crossing the room and distancing herself from him.

"So," she said. "Do we have a deal?"

"A deal?"

"You agree to stay out of trouble. To avoid confrontation. To avoid controversy of any kind. You keep a low profile. The lower the better."

"And in return I go free."

She nodded. "Do you need another incentive? I have one, if you do."

"No. Freedom's plenty."

"That's good, but I have one anyway. What Levels do you see here, Payne? Threes? Fours?"

It took a second for him to understand what she was talking about. It had been so long since he'd done a healing, save with his friend the rat, and those had not involved his meli.

"Some Fours. Mostly Threes."

"And it's easy for you, isn't it?"

"Easy?"

"Let me put it this way. Do you feel challenged?"

It was an opportunity to show her what he'd learned. Choosing tact over truth, he replied, "Humans are always challenging."

She gave a little smile. "Bravo. Very good. But Threes are hardly worth the effort—not for someone like you. Wouldn't you like to work with something more demanding? A Level Five, say? A Six?"

"Sixes don't come here," he said.

"I know that. But you could go to them."

"Rampart?"

"Why not?"

He wondered if she made a habit of this, of tempting people, enticing them with daring invitations, luring them to greater heights. He felt similar to how he'd felt at Pannus when she and Valid had commuted his sentence: the same flutter in the chest, the same sense of being swept away, the same thrilling, vertiginous feeling of his world expanding.

"You'll need to practice," she said. "Hone your skills. Improve your talent. And of course you'll have to stay out of trouble. You'll have to prove you can be trusted. That will take some time."

"Why?" he asked.

"Why? Because trust's a fragile thing. Once lost, it takes time to earn it back."

"No. Why me?"

"You? Because you have a gift. I told you that before. No sense to waste it here." She stopped, then corrected herself. "I don't mean that. Healing's never wasted. But sometimes people use it frivolously."

"Frivolously?"

"Yes. Haven't you seen it? People who come to you on a whim. Who use you capriciously." She gestured toward the window. "Like them. Young people. Thrill seekers. Daredevils."

There was a note of contempt in her voice, and Payne sensed that not all of it was directed outward.

"People who don't know any better," she said.

TEN

In the weeks that followed Payne threw himself into his work. The need was there, and he was willing, even grateful, to oblige. But he was weak from prison, and it took some time for him to regain his strength. Healing was demanding work; both physically and mentally, it required stamina, endurance and concentration.

He had to focus in a way he never did in other circumstances. First on himself, and then he had to lose himself and center on his patient. Empathy was implicit in the act of healing. In a way it was its core. It generated the power for the first three stages of a healing, and lesson number two spoke of it directly. Payne remembered all his lessons, and some that he had once thought puerile he had since learned to see in a different light. The second lesson taught that to identify one must first show interest, and to capture one must first release. As his strength returned and he practiced this, he found his empathic powers heightened. Perhaps he had matured; certainly, having been imprisoned for so long and confined solely to himself, he was grateful for any contact he could get, be it glancing or that most intimate kind that came on the healing bed.

Sometimes what afflicted a person was not restricted to that individual but symptomatic of a more general condition. Something that affected others, an epidemic of some sort. A single human, like a single tree infested with disease, could be saved, but it helped to know about the state of other humans; it helped to keep an eye on the forest. The narrow field of vision required in the healing chamber was often best understood in the context of the larger view.

In the world of disease, as in the worlds of music and art and other disciplines, there was always the element of fashion. Interest in pathologies (as well as pathologies themselves) waxed and waned from public consciousness. What was in vogue one year was out of vogue the next. In part, this was determined by what was actually out and about in the world, what nasty germs (and usually it was germs) posed a threat to life and limb. But beyond this, there was an interest and a buzz that had less to do with the prevalence of an illness than the perception of the prevalence. And perception, as a product of the imagination, could be manipulated. This was not something that was taught to healers, but every one of them experienced it. How humans could be swayed by fear and fantasy and fashion. For more than anything they seemed to love a story, and the ones they loved best seemed to be of threats that didn't materialize, imminent disasters narrowly averted, as well as illnesses that had some glamour to them and epidemics that turned out to be false alarms. Sometimes it seemed to Payne that the people he treated lived expressedly to be saved.

Currently in vogue was a nebulous affliction, purportedly of the central nervous system, that went by a variety of names, the most common of which, Impaired Cognitive Excitation, had found favor less for the aptness of its description than for its acronym. Symptoms ranged from a buzzing in the ears to a tingling in the skin to a nocturnal twitching of the muscles of the trunk. Some complained of a dry mouth and metallic taste on the tongue; others swore the taste was sweet and their salivation profuse and frothy. Commonly, there was a sense of bloatedness and abdominal fullness, but just as commonly a sense of being empty and needing to be filled. Mentally, many described amnesia for unpleasant occurrences and events, while others, remarkably, were quite capable of recalling even the most trivial, glancing and ancient wounds. There was insomnia and there was polysomnia. Lassitude and fixation. Sloth, mania, ennui, obsession, lackadaisy and a kind of hypervigilance that suggested paranoia.

From an epidemiologic standpoint, the most consistent thing about ICE was its inconsistency. That, and the paucity of physical findings. In many ways it resembled the notorious Cryptogenic Protein scare of several decades earlier, which itself resembled the so-called Laughing Man Disease of a century before that. Certain maladies seemed to reside in the human psyche, if not in the actual spongy matter of the brain, and had a habit of resurfacing. Like styles of hair and clothes and speech, they had a way of coming back.

Curiously, Payne found the Boomine synthesizer quite useful in the treatment of the syndrome. Apart from its intended purpose of making him more palatable to his clientele, there was something in the way it seemed to penetrate and ease the human brain. By adjusting its intensity, he could override almost any interference. By adjusting its pitch and timbre, he could simulate virtually any sound.

Different patients responded to different auditory input. Some did well with bird sounds, some with the wind, some the sea. Some liked to hear a soothing voice, reminiscent, perhaps, of a loved one. Some preferred a loud and harsh reproach. The range of sounds able to affect a beneficial outcome seemed, indeed, as limitless as the range of people to receive them.

Payne was called upon to disguise himself so frequently that whole days could pass without his hearing his own voice. And then when he did, it was apt to stop him in his tracks, as though he were someone else. It took time to get the other voices out of his head, and until he did, he always felt slightly apprehensive, worrying that one or two of these impersonations, these false identities, might decide to stay.

Fortunately, not everyone who came to him had ICE, and not all of those with ICE required the synthesizer. A fair number of his patients suffered the misfortune of a more prosaic ill. But all were in the throes of one thing or another, and humans in the throes of one thing or another were not happy humans. They were often cross and grumpy, having neither time nor patience nor tolerance for being ill.

Nor for waiting, and since the New Day debacle and subsequent reduction in the healer population, waiting had become a fact of life. Before his incarceration Payne had been busy. That was the nature of the job. Following his release, he was swamped.

He hated it, hated always being behind. His patients were testy enough without being told they had to wait. Their constant carping and the neverending rush and pressure to please them wore on him, even after he'd recovered his strength. He needed help, and since he couldn't turn to any of the other healers, all of whom were wearing down at least as fast as he was, he turned to the only other place that he could think of: his clientele.

The idea of asking patients to assist in their own healing wasn't new. It was as old as healing was, as old as wisdom. It was logical that people learn to take care of themselves. It was good medicine, and it was also common sense. The incentive was obvious (health), the methods practical, the lessons simple and easy to learn. His patients, on the whole, were all for it. He gave advice, and dutifully, diligently, they listened.

Where they had more trouble, where in fact they continually faltered, was in putting what he said (or what they heard of what he said) into practice. This they simply couldn't seem to do.

The problem was that healing oneself was work. Hard work. It took time and effort and energy. It took commitment. Most challenging of all, it usually required change.

His patients, despite their best intentions, fought change tooth and nail. They fought it nodding yes to him and nodding no. They fought it knowing full well they shouldn't be fighting. It was remarkable how they fought it, but more remarkable still, how much discomfort and suffering they were willing to put up with to avoid having to do anything about it, to avoid having to change.

They resisted out of laziness. They resisted out of inertia. They resisted out of fear. His patients—patients everywhere—clung to pain and suffering because, quite simply, the alternative looked worse. And when they'd had enough, when they couldn't stand it anymore, even then they tried to negotiate and compromise and gain concessions. It was just too damn hard and inconvenient and bothersome to change.

Still, some patients tried, and Payne never stopped encouraging them. It was personally rewarding when someone actually listened to him, then did what he suggested and got better. For others it was a hopeless undertaking, but even these he tried to reach. Like the woman with the pimple on her chin. A single pimple, small and white and fluctuant, ready to burst any day. He reassured her that before she knew it, the blemish would be gone, but she could not wait. Frantically, she begged him to get rid of it. It was her honeymoon. She feared the groom, who only days before had betrothed himself to her body and soul, in sickness and in health and in every other state, would be displeased.

Or the man who was losing his hair. Not much of it to be sure, a few strands on the pillow and in the teeth of his comb, hardly more than a minor, transitory shed. But his hairline, he was convinced, was receding. It made his forehead stand out unattractively. When Payne pointed out that this particular form of baldness was a manly attribute and thus a manly virtue, he scoffed. It was grotesque, he said, without apologies to a man whose head defined grotesque. It made him look top-heavy, like a breaching whale.

But for all of this, the small and large, the trivial and the conse-
quential, Payne felt a fondness for these humans. Even after everything
they'd done to him. He sympathized with their anxieties. He felt a
kinship with their strengths and weaknesses. Their vanities, petty as
they were, he found endearing, and their pains, whether rooted in the
body or the mind, he understood.

Between work and sleep he had little time for other activities,
which suited him, for he had little interest in them. The city had lost
much of its fascination for him. He was weary of the crowds and of the
gaming houses, and the houses of religion were better left alone. Sometimes he took walks, which were bittersweet, for they reminded him
of Brand. He kept his distance from the other healers, who, with one
exception, did the same with him.

Nome was overjoyed at his release from prison. She insisted on
personally nursing him back to health, which principally required that
he eat more to put back on the pounds he had lost, a feat that he was
quite capable of doing on his own. But he allowed her solicitude
because it seemed to make her happy, or at least it made her feel useful,
which in her case amounted to the same.

She took to staying with him, in violation of a law against cohabi-
tation among healers. The law, in actuality, was against impregnation,
which in a female interfered with healing. In the same way that tesques
could not be trusted to govern themselves, healers could not be trusted
to live with one another, as it led (by all accounts) to uncontrolled for-
nication. To head off any possible misunderstanding, Payne made it
clear from the beginning that they would sleep in separate rooms. In
the event he left Aksagetta, a hope he nurtured in private, he didn't
want her any more attached to him than she already was. As for sex, she
did not attract him physically. He had yet to meet a tesque who did.

The weeks passed, and one day there came a knock at his door.
Nome was sleeping in the bedroom. Fearing the Authorities, Payne

didn't answer, hoping they would go away. But the knocking persisted, and then he heard her voice.

His heart raced as he unlocked the door.

She wore a sleeveless dress this time, a pale blue that matched her eyes. Her hair was loose, not pulled back as before, and it brushed her shoulders.

Politely, she asked if he was busy. She didn't want to intrude.

No, he said. Not busy. Come in, come in.

She had some business to discuss with him. But first she asked how he'd been doing. How he was. Any backlash from his patients? From other healers? Any visits from the Authorities? Any word?

Everything was fine, he said (expecting she would have known if it hadn't been). He was keeping the lowest possible profile. Working hard and staying out of trouble. In many ways, most ways, it was a relief.

She was glad to hear it. And glad, too, that he seemed to have recovered his health. He looked well, she said. More rested.

He thanked her.

She went further. He looked almost happy. Thriving, anyway. No?

He followed where she seemed to want to lead him, replying that he couldn't complain.

"And not everyone can say that, can they?" she answered. "Certainly not every healer."

"Every healer's different, if you're talking about the Drain."

She took a few steps around the room, inspecting this and that in a casual, offhanded way. "The girl at Pannus. The one you tried to heal. What was her name?"

She asked it nonchalantly, as if the question had just occurred to her, which Payne doubted. Nonchalance was certainly not his response.

"Vecque," he said.

"Vecque. Yes. What made you decide to do it? To try?"

"Stupidity," he answered curtly.

"Of course. But at the time. What were you thinking at the time?"

"I was bored. I wasn't thinking."

"I doubt that's true."

He shrugged. "I don't know. I don't remember."

She glanced at him, caught, it seemed, between the impulse to prod and the impulse to let him be. "Is this too hard for you?"

Her solicitude annoyed him. "No. It isn't hard at all. I just don't see what difference it makes."

"You don't think that understanding the past makes a difference?"

"I understand it well enough."

"Did you love her?"

"Love her?" The question shocked him.

"Yes. Did you love Vecque?"

"She was being drained."

"I understand. Would you have tried with anyone, is what I'm asking. Anyone who was being drained?"

"No," he said, then, "Yes." Then frustrated, he threw up his hands. "I can't answer that. What's the point? I don't know."

"There is a point, but we don't have to talk about it, since it obviously upsets you."

"I'm not upset."

She raised an eyebrow. "No? Then I have another question. Do you know why there's a law against what you did? Why it's prohibited for a tesque to heal a tesque?"

Yes. Of course he knew. And she knew he knew. And still, she insisted on telling him.

"Because you die when you try it. One or the other of you; usually both. And from what they say, it's not a pretty death." She paused, then added pointedly, "The thing is, you didn't. Neither one of you did."

"Vecque would have been better off if she had."

"Do you think so?" Another pause, followed by a shudder. "It would have been a horrible thing to witness."

"It was a horrible thing to watch her being drained."

"Yes. You've had your share of horrors."

He had, it was true, and he hoped that they were over. "I would have taken her place if I could have."

At this her whole body seemed to come to attention. "Really? Do you mean that?"

"Yes," he said, because it was true, or it had been. He also said it because he guessed that she would like to hear it, would like the sort of man that it conveyed, someone not above self-sacrifice. And by the look that she was giving him it seemed she did, and he wondered, was it a dishonor to Vecque, or to Vecque's memory, that now, now that he had something to live for, or at least to hope for, however brashly, now perhaps it wasn't true, that faced again with such a choice he might feel less inclined to take her place?

"You know, you needn't hide your face," she said.

"Excuse me?"

"Your forehead. With your hair. You have a habit of trying to cover it."

There was a softness to her voice, a tenderness, but for Payne it was simply too embarrassing. He turned away, cheeks burning.

"Can we talk about something else?"

"I thought men liked to talk about themselves. Most of the ones I know do." She was teasing him, but seeing his discomfort, stopped. "Of course we can. What would you like to talk about?"

"My reassignment."

"Ah. Yes. Good. Let's talk about that."

Sadly, he didn't get the chance, as Nome chose that moment to wake up. Tousle-haired and sleepy-eyed, she appeared in the bedroom doorway. Seeing Payne, she smiled and started to recount a dream she'd had that he was in. Then her eyes fell on Meera.

Who, after a start, quickly regained her composure. "Hello. I'm Meera. And your name is?"

Nome looked to Payne for help, but he was as mortified as she was. "Nome," she mumbled.

"Nome. How nice. Don't mind me. Please, go ahead and finish what you were saying."

Nome paled.

"The dream," Meera prompted.

Nome took a half-step back and shook her head.

"No? I suppose you're right. Keep it to yourself. Dreams are meant to stay private."

At which point Payne found his voice. "She's just visiting."

It took Meera a second or two to understand what he meant by this. Meanwhile, Nome's face had darkened.

"Who are you? Who is she, Payne?"

He had the strongest urge to lie to her. To tell her who she was, her name and such, but not what she represented.

Both women waited for his response.

"Meera," he said at length, which Nome, if she had listened, already knew.

Meera herself was only marginally more helpful. "I'm a friend."

Nome crossed her arms and jutted out her less-than-mighty chin. "Payne's telling you the truth. I was only resting. I don't live here."

Meera dismissed her concern with a wave of her hand. "It doesn't matter to me. It's not a law I care about. Although I'd hardly call it keeping a low profile. Or staying out of trouble."

She directed this at Payne, who, in fact, already felt in trouble. With Nome on the one hand. With Meera on the other. Mostly, he worried about Meera—that he'd somehow blown his chance to leave. He was also absurdly afraid that she'd assume he was taken.

Eyes blazing, Nome came roaring to his defense. "He hasn't done anything wrong. Neither of us has." She stormed over to her man and in support and solidarity with him (as well as to punctuate her claim) laced an arm through his.

"Go away," she told Meera. "Pick on someone else. Leave us alone."

Payne shifted uneasily in her embrace and tried to calm her down. "She doesn't want to hurt us. That's not why she's here."

"No? Why then?"

"We were talking. That's all."

Gently, he freed himself of her, leaving her hands to dangle help-lessly, one of which started picking at her meli. "About what?"

"His gift," said Meera.

"What gift?"

"Of healing."

"It's not a gift," said Payne, tired of hearing this. "Every healer has it. It's a given."

But Nome had brightened. "Oh yes it is. It's a wonderful gift. He's a wonderful man. I don't know where I'd be without him."

"He's helped you?"

"Yes, he's helped. In every way." Revitalized now, hands working the air, eager to sing his praises. "You should have seen me before. I was a wreck. Payne took me in and taught me. He showed me what to do."

Meera raised her eyebrows and glanced at him.

"A teacher, too?"

He was irritated with the both of them, but Nome especially. "No. Not that either."

"Oh yes he is. And more than that."

"Even more?" Eyes laughing now, enjoying Payne's discomfort.

Nome, too, was enjoying herself. Mending the wounds of rejection by getting back at him.

"He's the best there is. The kindest, nicest, smartest . . ."

"Stop it," said Payne.

"The absolute best. Who else could have healed me?"

"He healed you?"

"Of course. I wouldn't be here if he hadn't."

And just like that the fun and games were over. The air grew still, as if a spell had been cast.

"You healed her, Payne?"

"No. Not like that."

"He did," insisted Nome. "He helped a lot."

"That's not what she means." He was angry with her now, angry with the both of them. "She means a meli healing."

Nome frowned and glanced at Meera. Then at Payne. Foundering.

"He could if he wanted to. I bet he could. You could," she told him. "I know you could."

"That's enough."

"Do you want to try? I'll let you. I will."

She grabbed his hand and tried to tug him toward the bedroom, but he shook her off, causing her to stumble. Humiliated, she let out a little choked cry. Her eyes darted between the two of them, and then she attacked.

"She wants you for herself. That's what this is all about. She wants you to heal her."

"That's ridiculous," said Meera.

"Ask her, Payne. Ask her if she doesn't."

Payne stared at Nome. "Maybe you should come back another time," he told Meera.

She didn't answer him. She too was looking at Nome, shaken, it seemed, by what she had said.

"I'm sorry," she said at length. "I truly am. I wish things were different. You deserve better. All of you do."

She turned to Payne. "I appreciate your offer, but coming back won't be necessary. That is, unless you plan to stay."

RAMPART

ONE

The priapic Tower. The Building of Investigation. The sun-washed, treeless streets. The wall. The road to Gode. The guarded gates. The other road. The Pen.

Rampart was not a city so much as a destination. For some it was the final destination. Healers, for example, would never leave, not with their faculties intact. Once assigned to it, they stayed until they were fully drained. Nor did every human who made their way into the Tower make their way out again. Not alive. Some could not be salvaged or saved. On the whole, though, success rates were respectable; by many measures, they were commendable. Considering the protoplasm that the healers had to work with, success in any form at all was cause for cheer.

Of the three main elements of the healing triad, two were represented here. The third, instruction, took place elsewhere. Research, which centered on ways to activate inactive melis (for the nine in ten

263

in whom this was the natural state), and, alternatively, to generate arti-
ficial ones, was carried out in a low-slung, branching barrack of a
building where scientists practiced science and subjects were housed.
Healing itself took place in the Tower, a tall, austere, parabolic-shaped
monolith that dominated the landscape, rising like a magic bullet
above the plain.

The Tower was known by other names as well. Some called it the
Citadel, some the House of Hope, some the Temple, some the Tomb. It
was all of those, but more than anything it was a last resort, a magnet
for those who, by virtue of circumstance or habit or simply time, were
afflicted with the worst diseases of the human body and the human
mind, the gravest and the most recalcitrant, the most embedded and
advanced. Some who came were crippled beyond endurance, some
demented, some hideously cachectic, some incapacitated by intractable
pain. A fair number were on the verge of death. Whatever the prove-
nance, all came by way of desperation, out of options, almost out of
hope, their one unanimous request, simple and straightforward: heal me.

For healers, being summoned to Rampart was the ultimate recognition, and it required, on a daily basis, the greatest performance of
their lives. Of all healings these were the most demanding, the most
exacting and also the most exciting, the most intense and the most
extreme. They were also the most debilitating, which had prompted
an enlightened Board of Regulators to institute a rather liberal policy
of rest and recuperation. For these were the finest healers of their kind,
the most talented and skilled and practiced, and the hardest to replace.
They were as precious, literally, as life itself. The Drain would take
them all in due course, but there was no need to hurry it along.

☙☙☙

She waited as long as she could wait, as long as she could stand it, as
long as anyone in her position could possibly stand it, and then she

waited longer. He needed time to learn that Sixes were within his power, well within it, time to prove himself but not so much time that he became too tired, that he lost, if it was possible, his edge. Fortunately, she had other things to occupy her time. There was the house to care for. There was Bolt to keep in touch with. There was the Oversight Committee on Research and Experimentation. There were her parents, who were getting on in years. There was Wyn.

But Payne was preeminent in her thoughts and in her plans. She needed him, and while she had made her peace with this, she still on occasion felt it as a weakness, for she was not the sort of person who liked to be in need. She preferred to handle things herself. This gave her both the pleasure of accomplishment and the certainty of a job done the way she wanted it. Not that she was unwilling to delegate authority, only that she was careful how and to whom she did. She lived a careful life. This, in contrast to the high-spirited, daring, and, in at least one respect, reckless days of her youth. Now, in sustained reaction to those days, she played it closer to the vest. Politically, she remained outspoken, but personally, she kept to herself. This had gained her a reputation for being aloof, which, like most reputations, had its germ of truth while missing much of the underpinning and substance of that truth, but this did not concern her. Solitude at one time would have seemed a sentence to her, but now she welcomed it, or at least had grown accustomed to it. She wore it as a sort of cloak, likening it in her mind to a vow of abstinence, self-imposed and just.

But being private did not mean that she was out of touch. She had many sources of information, and it was a point of pride with her and in some cases of necessity to stay on top of things. Change was in the air: with the Committee; with her aging parents; with the guards at the Pen, who were getting antsy; with Payne. After years of shepherding him behind the scenes, she was about to set him loose, and as she contemplated this, she considered what her responsibility was to him. That she had deliberately kept her distance from him had not prevented her from having feelings for him, nor had she deluded herself into thinking it would. What surprised her, though, was how strong her feelings were. She liked him, more than liked him, and wanted him to like her. Short of that, she hoped he wouldn't end up despising her. But he deserved to make his mind up for himself, which was to say he deserved to know the facts. He had to know them, and she was about to lay them out for him, even to the point of baring her heart if it came to that, although she hoped it wouldn't. But maybe this was wrong. Maybe the best and most responsible thing—responsible in the sense of considerate, decent and kind—was not to tell him anything, to keep him in the dark. Knowledge was a snake, and ignorance could protect him from its bite. She could orchestrate this as she had orchestrated so much already in his life. Take the high road and bear the burden by herself, suffer nobly, silently and alone.

Except she wasn't alone. Wyn was suffering, too. Which was why she needed Payne.

Accordingly, she made plans to visit him in his apartment, which was in the Tower, near his healing room. But as the date approached, she had second thoughts, wondering if this, in fact, was the best place to break the news to him. As a rule, she liked to visit people more than to receive them. It gave her the opportunity to gather information on how they lived— their tastes, their sense of order (or disorder), their means, their private worlds—and it came at little expense to herself. It was a way of seeing into someone else's mind, which was more than an amusement to her. She was never bored by other people's minds. Disappointed sometimes, disgusted, but never bored. Visiting a person at home, or at work for that matter, had the added advantage that she could leave when she wanted. It was the optimal situation, one over which she had the most control.

But she had seen how Payne lived. Moreover, she knew his mind, maybe better than he knew it himself. It was time to open hers to him, time for him to learn something about her own life, since, if all went as planned, he would soon be inextricably bound up in it.

Her house then. She would open her doors to him. It was a relief to come to this decision, and it made her glad. She had not had a visitor in oh so long a time. Change was coming to her, too. The ice of her long wait was breaking.

Hers was a handsome house—thick-walled, whitewashed, haciendalike—with picture windows and flowering vines and palms for shade. It lay several kilometers from the Tower, on a bluff above the Lac du Lac, what some called the Lacrimal Sea. There were other, more ostentatious homes nearby, trophy homes that sat unoccupied for the majority of the year. There were also several rooming houses for temporary visitors to the Rampart hub, most of whom were patients on their way to treatment, who afterward needed a place to recuperate. Frequently, they had their families with them, and at times the small seaside community had the feeling of a resort. At other times, it seemed more like a sanatorium. Some used the sea for its purported healing properties. Its waters had a high mineral content and, to the degree they puckered the skin and kept a body afloat, were said to be restorative. Others took walks, though now that it was summer, only at the margins of the day. The noonday sun brought reptiles out, but the sensible human stayed inside. Dawn and dusk and balmy night were the hours for mammals.

Meera had an old-fashioned broadbeam desk with inlaid wood and carved clawfoot legs that had been in the family for generations. She had an old-fashioned pen, too, and heavy vellum stationery that welcomed ink and absorbed a little of a person's scent. The desk was in a study with a lazy ceiling fan and a window on the Lac du Lac, where she liked to gaze while gathering her thoughts. It was midmorning, and the sea was smooth, in contrast to her state of mind, which was excited. She thought a minute what to say, and when she had the tone just right set pen to paper and composed her invitation. "Dear Payne," she wrote, "I have news to share with you. Please come and join me at my home for a visit." Short and simple, it struck the proper balance, she thought, between formality and friendliness. She added a day and a time, then considered how best to sign it, settling on her full name, which seemed businesslike. She slid the invitation into an envelope, which she sealed and put aside, then, with a glance out the window, turned her attention to the Oversight Committee.

Valid had a new proposal on the table. It was worded in a way that made it sound pressing, almost dire. He, along with a sizable faction of the committee, wanted more tesques for their experiments, many more, and he wanted more liberties and less restrictions on what they were allowed to do. More funding too, all of which she was stridently opposed to. Years before, she and Valid had been allies, committed to a better system of health, which at that time meant to them improving the working conditions of healers. That remained her goal, but his had shifted: he now favored medical research and breeding trials, the former to discover a way to activate inactive melis, the latter to generate new and better healers—healers, that is, less inclined to be drained. He himself was engaged in this very research and was convinced that it would bear fruit, despite the fact that in the long history of human-healer relations, it never had, and not for lack of trying. Scientific research and investigation had been the source of many miracles and wonders, but sadly, a longer-lasting healer was not one of them. Nor had anyone ever found a way to create a greater number of healers. The experiments had been abandoned, not once but many times. Now they had been resurrected, along with the same old hollow claims. In Meera's eyes Valid and his cronies had fallen victim to amnesia.

In drafting a response to the proposal, she considered another fact that might explain the urgent tone of it. Valid, she had heard, was ill. Seriously ill. He had no offspring and if and when he died would leave no legacy but his ideas, his work. This measure, were it to pass, would not go unnoticed. It would change the landscape of tesque and human relations and quite likely lead to protests and counterprotests and possibly even another uprising, one to rival that of '09. She doubted this was his intent, although with men like Valid, one could never be sure. The proximity of death did funny things to people, and she wondered if he feared being forgotten.

This suggested, along with a formal response, a more personal note, wishing Valid well and expressing hopes for a recovery. She did this first, while the thought was fresh, reminding him of their past friendship. He was a man of conviction, she wrote, not to mention a formidable opponent, and, despite their differences, she held him in high regard. She was careful not to go overboard with her praise, for he had a keen and discerning ear when it came to flattery. Too much kindness from a woman who through the years had steadfastly refused his advances would instantly raise his suspicions.

Satisfied with the effort, she turned her attention to the proposal itself. It was many pages long, but soon she had outlined a response. She had a facile mind and a way with words, and the language of opposition, honed by many years of practice, came easily to her.

TWO

Payne was chagrined. Despite his reverent care, the invitation was showing signs of wear and overhandling. Two of its corners were dog-eared, and there was a smudge along its lower edge. Worse, from taking it out of its envelope several times a day and pressing it against his nose and cheek, its scent, her scent, was disappearing. Fortunately, he would soon get to experience that scent in the flesh. He had worked overtime to be in a position to see her at the time she requested. He had one more patient for the day, and then he would be free.

Leaving the invitation within sight on his desk, he called that patient in. It was a woman, a large and overweight one, with pale eyes, swollen, encumbered joints, and thickened skin. At first glance her illness seemed of her own making, a result of gluttony and its handmaiden, shame. This, however, was not the case. She turned out to be suffering from an inner metabolic process, an infiltrative disease where normal tissue was replaced by a fibrous protein. In response, her body had stiffened and her skin and joints had turned into a kind of stubborn paste. It was difficult for her to walk and nearly impossible to get herself on the healing bed. Payne administered a potent anodynic sporophyte to kill her pain, which would help in moving her. While he waited for it to take effect, he indulged in thoughts and fantasies of his upcoming visit to Meera's.

His reveries were interrupted by a knocking at the door. He asked the woman if she was expecting company. She said no and mentioned that the medicine was working, the pain was less, perhaps it was time that they get started. Payne agreed and, putting the knocking, which had momentarily stopped, from his mind, helped her to the bed.

It was a large and comfortable bed. The room itself was large and comfortable, and it contained all the various equipment that a human making his way to the Tower, the pinnacle of the craft, would expect. The Boomine synthesizer, the retinal harmonic generator, the tantalus olfactus, the transdermal euphoid pump, as well as other, more trendy devices. Though here, more than anywhere else, it was the healer who was central to the healing process, a fact that most of the patients who made their way to the Tower seemed implicitly to understand, for in the end these gadgets, more often than not, went unused.

As Payne prepared to lie beside the woman and wrap their arms together, the knocking started up again. He heard raised voices: there seemed to be some sort of commotion in the waiting room. Before long, the knocking became a pounding, and seconds later, the door burst open.

In stumbled a wild-eyed and haggard Dr. Valid, looking like something the cat had dragged in.

"Who are those people?" he snarled, gesturing behind him with a trembling, bony finger. "Has reason deserted us completely? Don't they know what Diplomate means?"

He fixed a jaundiced eye on Payne. "Never mind. It's you I want. It pains me to say it, but I need your help."

He paused as he became aware that Payne was not alone. There was a woman on the healing bed. Half-dazed, she was struggling to sit up.

Valid apologized for the interruption. "You'll have to excuse me, but this is an urgent matter. If you'd be so kind, please wait outside."

Payne was shocked, both by Valid's rudeness and by how he looked, how much he'd changed. His face was drawn, his cheeks hollow, his skin etched and pale. His thick and wavy hair, such a source of pride to him, had been reduced to scattered clumps. The cane he'd carried for effect was now a necessity, for he'd lost both weight and strength and depended on it for support. His voice alone remained unchanged, as sharp, imperious and demanding as ever.

"I'm sick," he said to Payne. "Come look at me."

Instead, Payne looked at the woman, who was now sitting. Their eyes met.

Valid scowled. "You think I'm lying?" He tugged at the skin of his face, then held out a trembling hand. "He'll do you next," he told the woman. "After me."

There was no doubting that Valid told the truth. He was most certainly ill, but Payne refused to jump at his command. The man was overstepping his authority. Furthermore, he could have—and clearly should have—come in sooner.

"This didn't happen overnight. Why did you wait so long?"

"What does it matter? I'm here now."

Both of them knew that it did matter, or that it could. But that was business better left for later.

"Let me heal the lady first," said Payne.

"No. First me."

"Yours might take some time."

"I'm not an idiot," replied Valid, eyes flashing. Then he grimaced. "This is Sixth Degree. I know what Sixes need."

Payne's mind was on his date. He was determined not to miss a minute of it.

"I should rest first, Professor."

"Diplomate," interjected Valid.

"Diplomate. The healing would go much better if I did."

"How long a rest?"

"A few hours at the least. Why don't you come back first thing tomorrow morning?"

"Tomorrow? Me? You put me off?" Outraged, Valid clutched Payne's hand as if he were a hawk and Payne, a rabbit. "There's no rest for me. Why should there be for you? No, my friend, not tomorrow. Now. We'll do it now."

The woman was by this time standing. Payne looked to her for help, but she seemed reluctant to intervene. Standing up to Valid took an effort that she did not have, and she was not alone. Sick or well, this was a man adept at bullying.

On her behalf then, and on his (mostly his), Payne objected to Valid's interference. He had no right to take her place. It was unnecessary, unethical, improper and just plain wrong.

Valid couldn't believe his ears. He sent a look to Payne that had turned other men to stone. Payne braved the look, but then his heart betrayed him. Without thinking, he stole a glance at the invitation.

Whatever his weaknesses, current or past, Valid knew how to read a glance, and he knew about hunger and longing. He followed the upstart healer's darting eyes, and before Payne could stop him, had seized the envelope and withdrawn the invitation. He read it rapidly, eyes dancing.

"Ah. I see. Meera desires an audience with you. The great Meera Libretain. What, I wonder, does she want?"

Payne tried to snatch the invitation back, but Valid held it out of his reach. "She writes of news. What news?"

"I don't know."

"Is she the precious rest you need? Is she the reason you put me and this good woman off? That you delay us?" Valid scanned the note again, an old desire flickering in his leaden eyes, then surrendered it to

Payne. "She's not worth it, my friend. Believe me. She's crafty. Whatever she says, it's herself that she's serving."

"And who are you serving?" asked Payne.

Valid gave him a look. "Fair enough. Myself as well. I said that in
the beginning. I need your help, Payne. I say it again now, plainly.
And what has Meera said? Has she been equally frank with you?"

A cough arrested him, rattling through his chest and dislodging
phlegm, which he lacked the strength to expectorate. When he recovered from it and caught his breath, he took a more conciliatory tone.

"I have no personal quarrel with her. She's a smart and determined
woman. Her faults we needn't dwell on. But have you ever wondered
why she engineered your release from prison? And why she arranged
to have you brought here?"

He had wondered, and she had explained it to his satisfaction.
"They needed healers in Aksagetta. And here, they need healers here.
Healers who can handle Fives and Sixes."

"Yes," said Valid. "And you have that talent. You've developed it.
What did Meera say? You have a gift? Perhaps she's right; perhaps you
do. Did it ever occur to you that she wants that gift? That the lovely
Meera has a use for you?"

"What do you mean?"

"I mean that Meera Libretain does not act idly. For every word she
speaks, every action she undertakes, she puts in hours of thought and
planning. Her mind is a web. She loves to spin her thread. She's cun-
ning. Devious sometimes. She learned it from her father, the Senator.
A master of manipulation."

"She's not manipulating me."

"No?"

"Why would she? For what reason?"

"Who can say? Heal me, then ask her."

"She didn't arrange to have me brought here. I came freely, of my
own accord. I chose to come."

"Did you? A healer? Choose freely? You're naive, my friend. No one, least of all a healer, is free. We're all slaves to one thing or another. I'm a slave to my passions. A slave to doing good. A slave to progress. And now, it seems, for better or worse, a slave to you. How ironic."

"I don't have to be the one to heal you. You could choose someone else. There're other healers with equal talent."

Valid shook his head. "Not for me."

"Why not?"

"I have my reasons." Using his cane, he dragged himself across the room, halting at the healing bed, where he tried to hoist himself without success. His weight was but a fraction of what it had been, but along with fat he'd also lost muscle. His arms were too weak to lift his body. His face turned flushed and plethoric.

The woman, still harboring hope that she might be next, had not left, but retreated to the background. Valid's performance brought her forward, and at first Payne thought that she was going to lend a hand and try to help him, despite being in no condition to. The analgesic had worn off, and her movements were slow and obviously painful. But she made her way to Valid nonetheless, halting perhaps a tad too close for his comfort, and proceeded to upbraid him.

"You're sick, yes, but I'm sick, too. There's a waiting room full of sick people. Why should you go first?" She wagged a finger in his face. "You should be ashamed of yourself. I say you should wait your turn."

Her audacity took Valid by surprise, and for a moment he lost his voice, but the finger in the face revived it. "My turn? My turn? It is my turn. Can't you see, old woman? My time is up. Smell my breath. Listen to it rattle in my chest. I'm dying. I'm rotting from within." He turned to Payne, pleading. "Help me. I'll be gone before tomorrow. What do you think will happen if they hear you turned me away? If they find me dead?"

"Dead?" The woman's eyes narrowed, and she looked to Payne for confirmation of this dire prognostication.

Valid did look ravaged. Payne had seen few who looked so bad. But as a healer he was unwilling to predict the future, not to so fine a point as death by the morrow. It was a fool's game and doubly so with a man like Valid.

"It's possible," was all he could bring himself to say.

But possible was enough for the woman. She would not have this man's death on her head.

"Take him then. I'll wait." Slowly, she made her way to the door, where she paused. "You're a bully," she told Valid. "You need to learn some manners. Still, I wish you luck."

She wished the same to Payne, then added, "Don't use it all up, if you please. I may need some too, and I'm next."

Once she was gone, Payne hurried to Valid's side. He was determined to make this quick and did not even try to conceal his impatience and frustration.

"Easy now," said Valid, wincing as Payne half helped, half hoisted him onto the bed. "I know where you want to be. I know where I want to be, too. We'll both of us be happy when this is over with, but for now I need you here. Don't rush this, Payne. It requires your full attention."

Payne replied that he didn't need a lesson in how to heal. Not from Valid.

Valid shot him a look. "Watch yourself."

But Payne was angry. "There're people who say that death brings peace. That it's better than life. How can you can be sure you wouldn't prefer it?"

This time Valid merely snorted, occasioning another paroxysm of coughing, which left him gasping and in pain.

"Peace is for the peacemakers. I'm not the type. Does that make me any less worth saving?" He paused for breath. "You don't like me, Payne. You never have. I accept that. Sometimes I don't like myself. But that has no bearing on this. You're a healer. Likes and dislikes are irrelevant."

There was no pleading in his voice now, no condescension. It was simply a reminder, a reiteration of the oldest and perhaps most basic precept of healing. And an indication of how well he knew Payne. It didn't matter how selfish, wicked or cruel a person was. It didn't matter what they had done, or what they might do. Healing had the power to change a person, but that didn't matter either. All that mattered was that this was what Payne did. It was what he was. Healing was more than a canon, more than a creed. It was visceral. It was something that belonged to his spirit if he had a spirit, and to his soul if he had one of those. In a dream he might deny a man in need, he might refuse to heal a person for crimes committed, but in reality, in practice, every fiber of whatever he was made of would rebel against turning that person away.

"Close your eyes," said Payne. "Stop talking."

Valid did as he was told while Payne prepared himself. He asked if Valid wanted the epidermal barrier spray, and Valid said no. He was not afraid of contact with a healer. He was not afraid of death, when it came down to it, if only it didn't involve so much agony.

Payne joined him on the bed. He could tell that Valid was nervous, because he couldn't stop talking.

"Is she right?" he asked Payne.

"Is who?"

"Do you have a gift?"

"Be quiet now. Try to relax."

"I hope you do. I know you have a talent. I wouldn't be here otherwise. I wouldn't put myself in just anybody's hands."

Praise, like chatter, was a common reaction before a healing; partly, it was meant to inspire a healer's confidence, partly, to bolster the confidence of the person being healed. Valid was uneasy—more, it seemed, than he should have been.

He opened his eyes. "Be careful, Payne."

"I'm always careful."

"Yes. But be extra careful. . . ."

He seemed about to say more, but didn't. Instead, he closed his eyes and fell silent. Grateful to get started, Payne wrapped their arms together and did not inquire further. He had a date to keep, and he was in a hurry.

For a man of his stature and position, whose word carried the weight of law and whose pronouncements sent men scurrying, Valid's affliction was prosaic. A cancer of the pulmonic infundibulum that had spread to bone and brain and belly. His body was riddled with it, like a bird with buckshot, like a cheese with mold.

Payne was unimpressed.

He'd seen this particular affliction and worse dozens of times, men and women with double cancers, triple ones, and with inborn errors of metabolism, xenotropic malformations, neuropathic fistulae, bizarre reposit fibrillations, and the like. Valid's Concretion would, as he had predicted, turn out to be Sixth Degree, but it wouldn't be the gravest or the most recalcitrant he'd seen. He was in his element, and human beings, at least their pains and sufferings, had ceased to be a mystery to him. He was fully confident he could handle this one.

Identification, recruitment and enhancement went smoothly, and by the second hour he was into capture and moving right along. But then he hit a snag. The Concretion, which had firmed up, suddenly changed shape. And then it fell apart.

Valid, who lay half-conscious on the healing bed, moaned. Payne, who lay beside him, felt a momentary panic. Not all patients who needed healing recovered, nor were all expected to, but neither were they expected to die during the attempt. He redoubled his efforts, raising the level of his attack, trying by dint of force and will to capture what he'd lost.

The problem was he couldn't very well capture a Concretion that didn't exist. Valid's life was ebbing out; in a few more hours he could well be dead. Payne had erred, and with a shock it came to him that he was making the same mistake he'd made with Vecque. He was being too casual, too smug, too arrogant. It was a mistake, he feared, that ran in his blood. Would he never be rid of it?

There was nothing to be done but start over. From the beginning. It was grueling and painstaking, but it was the only way.

For neophytes, the first stage, identification, was largely a process of trial and error, trying to match real-life information with what they'd learned in school. The more seasoned healers relied on the subtler signs provided by experience. But experience could backfire. Even the finest, most perceptive minds, when presented with the same condition over and over, could nod off.

It was shocking when he saw it. A single signature he'd missed. A single one of thousands, which in most cases would have made little, if any, difference. But this particular signature was not like other human signatures. It was not, in fact, a human signature at all.

Payne tried to disengage but couldn't. With a struggle Valid opened his eyes.

"Yes," he whispered hoarsely. "You see it. Good. That's why I came to you. Now do it, Payne. Recruit, enhance and capture. Get rid of this monstrosity. You have the gift. Let's see you use it."

◈◈◈

He was three hours late for his date with Meera. Three interminable hours. It was midafternoon by the time he left the Tower, and the sun was blistering. The sky was white as bone, the air so hot and dry it burned his throat and eyes. He reached the bluff, then found her house, grateful for its shelter.

She was asleep when he arrived and woke to the sound of his knocking. She often napped midday, although this one had not been planned. She had nodded off while waiting for him and now took a moment to collect herself before answering the door.

At first glance she mistook him for a stranger.

He wore an embroidered shirt with polished buttons. A thin, chain-link necklace. Boots with heels that made him as tall as she was. He wore cologne, too; the perfumed scent of Musque was unmistakable. And he'd slicked his hair with grease and combed it off his forehead. His hump of skull stood out as plain as day.

He looked, she thought, like a man trying to be another man. Like a dandy, which was not what he was. It made her uneasy.

"Get lost?" she asked.

He apologized profusely and told her what had happened. With heart in hand he offered to come back another time.

The news of Valid took her by surprise. She wondered what he was up to.

"It's not your fault," she said. "You had no choice. Come in."

She led him to the living room, a large, bright space with two floor-to-ceiling picture windows overlooking the sea. The walls of the room were taken up by abstract paintings, save for one that depicted a group of children. Standing in a corner of the room was a chest-high statue made of dark and shiny wood. It seemed to be a tesque, or someone's idea of a tesque. It had a big head, bulging eyes and a wide, almost demonic, grin. Its arms were raised; one hand held a spear, the other a serpent.

Meera saw Payne staring at it. "You like it?"

"Who is it?"

She wasn't sure. Some sort of deity, she thought. "My mother gave it to me. I like to think of him as the guardian of the house."

She steered him outside to a tiled patio, which was sheltered from the sun by a canvas awning. Below it, a quarter mile from the foot of the bluff, lay the Lac du Lac, slate blue and glassy. Payne had never seen a body of water of any size before. He'd grown up a scant thirty miles away, and he'd never seen this sea.

"Pretty, isn't it?"

Pretty was not was he was thinking. It was awe-inspiring. He was overwhelmed.

"So much water."

"Yes. But shrinking. When I first came, the shoreline was much higher. Every year I've watched it recede."

"How many years is that?"

"Six," she said, and could have told him to the day.

"Why is it receding?"

"You want the story or the truth?"

"What's the story?"

"A very thirsty monster is swallowing the water. The truth is no one knows. Would you like a closer look? We could take a quick walk down."

The idea frightened him a little. The sea was so huge.

"Maybe later."

"That's fine."

They went inside. She offered him food, but he was too nervous to eat. He didn't trust his stomach or, for that matter, his tongue, but fortunately he'd rehearsed some things to say.

He made a comment about the weather, then another about her house, how beautiful it was, thinking that's how they did it, her people, that's how conversations were supposed to be conducted, with compliments and idle observations. He asked her if she lived in the house, then paused. That didn't sound right.

"Permanently, I mean."

"I'm here often."

"What do you do?"

It was an opportunity to tell him what she planned to tell him, but the time, she felt, was not quite right. "I work. I take walks. Sometimes I just sit and watch the waves."

"What kind of work?"

"Now? Now I have a battle on my hands." She told him briefly about the Oversight Committee and the proposal that was on the table, then questioned him about Valid. "Did he happen to mention it when he saw you? Did he say anything?"

"About that? No. Nothing."

"Was he very sick?"

"Yes."

"And you healed him?"

"Yes." He didn't tell her what he'd found in Valid, nor of the heartrending shriek the Concretion had made when he extruded it. Nor, for that matter, how much the sound had rattled him.

"So he's recuperating now?"

"I expect so."

She nodded thoughtfully. Maybe now that death was not breathing down his neck, he'd be more reasonable.

"Did he talk to you about his experiments?"

"No. He didn't."

"Has anyone?"

"One person came by. An Investigator. He wants to study me."

This was no surprise to her. They wanted to study everyone.

"I told him I wasn't interested. I don't want to be studied."

"What was his name?"

Payne told her. She knew the man, and in fact supported his particular line of research. It could be useful, she believed, and it wasn't harmful or cruel.

"Useful to whom?" he asked.

"To you. To healers. He's working on a way to lessen the effect of the Drain. Trying to blunt its impact."

"He won't find one," said Payne.

"Why's that?"

"How long have they been trying? Fifty years? A hundred?"

"More," she said, admitting that success had been elusive.

"It's because of how they work," said Payne. "What they look for and the way that they look. I know about their science. They like to sample things, break them down and cut them up, but I'm not cut-table. If they try, if they take a piece, that's all they'll have. A piece. They won't have me."

"Maybe a piece is all they need."

"I don't think so. That's not how a healing works. It's everything together. It's like an intricate design, like a knot. You don't learn any-thing by studying a single thread. Besides, I don't want to be sampled. I don't want to be cut. It might interfere with what I can do. It might damage me."

The specter of that was enough to shut her up. She didn't know why she was advocating that he be studied in the first place. It cer-tainly was not in her personal interest. Some sort of reflex, she guessed, born of years of working on behalf of healers, trying to better their lot, years of hanging around too many scientific thinkers.

She offered to arrange to have him left alone.

He considered for a moment. "In return for what?"

This stung her, although she had to admire his instincts. He was not the innocent boy he'd been, a sad but inevitable and necessary loss.

"No strings attached. Though you're right to ask. Accepting gifts can be a costly proposition."

"Turning them down can be costly, too."

She assumed he was talking about bribery, which was as endemic to the business of healing in Rampart as it was to human commerce everywhere, as it was, indeed, to human nature. Refusing to engage in it could have nasty repercussions for a healer.

She asked point-blank if he'd ever been bribed, and he had an urge to turn the question back on her, to ask if she had ever bribed someone, or more to the point, if she was bribing him. What Valid had said about her using people had unfortunately struck a nerve.

"I've accepted gifts," he said. "But never before a healing, only after. And only so as not to cause offense."

"Is that what those are?" Meera asked, gesturing at his clothes. "Gifts?"

"These? No. I bought them. Why? Don't you like them?"

"I do," she said without missing a beat. "They're very nice. They're distinctive."

He hesitated, then said, "I bought them for you."

"For me?"

"You said I shouldn't hide. You said I should be proud of who I am."

She remembered this. "Yes. That's true. I did."

Payne glanced at her, then lowered his eyes. An awkward silence followed, too awkward for him. He started playing with his hair, that old habit of his, which he caught and stopped, but a moment later his fingers broke free and started fidgeting with his necklace. He had no idea what to say.

Nor, for the longest time, did Meera. She was not blind to her effect on him; how could she be, faced with such a painfully boyish display? It nearly broke her heart, and she did what she could to comfort him.

"You look very nice. Very handsome. Really. You do."

She did not mention the Musque he'd slathered on himself to extravagance, a scent she'd recognized immediately. On his budget it had to have been a gift, from a lady, she assumed. Had she known the moral quandary he'd gone through before allowing himself to wear it, she would have told him not to bother.

"I like what you're wearing. And I like your hair that way. I like that you're not afraid to show your face. And you're not afraid to wear jewelry."

"Jewelry?"

She gestured. "Your necklace. It's becoming to you."

He'd forgotten about it, hadn't even known that he was playing with it, and at her mention of it he became self-conscious and dropped his hand, paradoxically affording her a better view.

"I don't think I've ever seen a charm like that before."

He was about to tuck it back inside his shirt when he had a sudden notion, a wild and crazy idea.

"It's an ortine," he said.

Her eyes widened, and she leaned in close while he held it up for her to see.

"They're very rare," she said, amazed at how small and delicate it looked. "Where did you get it?"

"A friend gave it to me." He paused. "Before he died."

"A human friend?"

"No. A tesque. Another healer."

It had to be unusual, she thought, for a healer to possess such a precious treasure. "My mother had an ortine once. Before I was born. She gave it away. She used to say she traded it for me."

"What did she mean?"

"She wanted a child. She would have traded anything for one. It was a gift to the healer who helped her conceive."

"What's your mother's name?"

"Matai."

"Does she like to dance?"

She gave him a look. "She used to. Why do you ask?"

He was astonished but not surprised at this, and he felt a wave of gratitude toward Brand for putting the ortine into his hands, for making this moment possible. He had not danced since Brand had died, had not wanted to, but now, suddenly, he did. It would be a fitting tribute, he thought, to dance again, not alone but with the daughter of the woman who had taught the man who had taught him.

He unhooked the necklace, then pinched the ortine between his thumb and forefinger. "I asked because that's what it's made for. Have you ever heard an ortine?"

She shook her head.

"It's hard to resist." He held it up to her mouth. "Very softly. All it takes is the tiniest breath. Purse your lips."

She did, and oh, how he would have liked to steal a kiss. "Gently now," he whispered. "Blow."

It was almost imperceptible to her, the breath, but the drum received it like a mighty wind. Its head bowed inward, snapped back, and then began to oscillate, setting up a wave of low-pitched sound. It was inaudible to her at first, although a fly that had been buzzing lazy circles in the room stopped midflight, then spiraled downward. Seconds later she heard the drumbeat faintly, as though it were coming from outside. It was dull, like someone thumping on the sand. Slowly it grew louder and took on overtones.

She glanced at Payne and saw the way his eyes were glued to her. She knew and feared that look, but the sound and rhythm of the drum swept away her misgivings. She began to sway from side to side. It felt good to move, it felt right, and she closed her eyes. Her feet took up the rhythm, and then her knees and hips. Soon she was rolling her shoulders, and the wave of this motion rippled down her arms into her wrists and hands. She felt a loosening inside and couldn't keep from smiling.

Payne watched, enraptured. He had never seen a sight so beautiful as Meera dancing. If there were such a thing as goddesses, surely she was one. Her face, her hair, the color of her cheeks, her perfect ears, the smoothness of her chin and throat. And the sound that filled the room—lilting, warm, inviting: her sound—that was perfect too.

Before he knew it, he was swaying with her. He felt clumsy at first, an ox beside a willow, but then he closed his eyes and let the rhythm take him. The fly, recovered from its fall but now in danger of being flattened, took refuge on a windowpane.

The drumbeat rose and fell; the air trembled with its music. Payne and Meera danced, swept up in the sound and the rhythm. Once, they brushed against each other, prompting Meera to open her eyes. She was surprised to see whose touch it was and heard an inner voice of caution. But it was a small voice, easily ignored and quickly swallowed by the drum.

The air in the room grew thick. Their bodies radiated heat and were drenched with sweat. Their breathing was rapid. Meera finally stopped and fell into a chair, heart pounding. Her cheeks were flushed;

her toes and fingertips tingled. Her mind for once was free of worries, free of cares. She felt inordinately happy.

She turned to Payne, who had also stopped, prepared to thank him for this gift, this wonder, but when she saw his face, her heart sank. She had hoped to spare his feelings, but what was one to do with idolatry and blind adoration? She shouldn't have danced. It was a thoughtless thing to do. She had only managed to encourage him.

Gathering herself and choosing her words with care, she did her best not to encourage him further. "There's something I have to tell you. It will probably come as a shock."

Payne nodded dreamily. There was something he had to tell her, too.

"I want to take you somewhere," she said. "There's someone you need to see."

This was not what he expected. "Who?"

The sun had dipped below the edge of the roof and was pouring waves of heat into the room. Meera rose to pull the blinds, trapping the fly against the window.

"Your brother," she said, turning.

"My brother's gone."

"Yes. But not forgotten. I've seen him."

"Wyn? You've seen Wyn?"

"Yes."

He stared at her, scarcely believing this. The fly was buzzing wildly, thwarted in its effort to get free.

"He's here?"

"Not far from here," she said.

"Where?"

"He needs your help."

"Where?" he demanded, his blood rising.

"The Snuff Box, Payne. The Pen. He's there."

THREE

Left to their own devices, First- and Second-Degree Concretions lived a minute at most; Third and Fourths, an hour, maybe two. For convenience's sake, Fourths were electively exterminated before their natural expiration, conventionally through large-bore cautery, toxic insufflation, interstitial-clysis and the like. Fifth-Degree Concretions usually responded to these same treatments, but Sixth Degrees were unpredictable. Some actually grew more resistant to degradation when meddled with.

But all Concretions, from First to Sixth, responded to neglect.

Which is how the Pen, aka the Dying Ground, the Cemetery of Joyful Disappearance, the Snuff Box, came to be.

It lay an hour's drive northeast of Rampart on a hard and crusted pan of desert surrounded by a tall and sturdy fence, the posts of which were sunk four feet into the underlying rock and the woven links of which were made of hardened steel and covered by a translucent, small-pore mesh.

There was one and only one way in, through a reinforced and closely guarded gate. Standard issue for the guards included thick metallic-backed gloves, body suits and helmets. Once extruded, a Concretion could not reenter its host, but a Sixth Degree could and would attack a person physically. Hence the need for armor. Hence the fence and guarded gate.

It was late afternoon when they set out, but the temperature had yet to drop. The heat hit Payne as he exited the Tower, along with a gusty, desiccating wind out of the east. This was typical of summer, this afternoon blow as the plain out-heated the hills and sent drafts of hot air swirling upward. The convoy of trucks was already assembled, and the drivers were impatient to get under way. It was a long haul to the Pen, and no one cared to be there after dark.

Their driver's name was Bolt. He had the exaggerated occiput common among a certain class of tesques, along with the thick and narrow forehead, steeply shelved above the eyebrows. A pale vertical scar ran from one corner of his mouth, elevating it slightly. From the side this gave the impression, usually false, that he was amused.

He had just finished securing the rear compartment of his truck when Meera and Payne arrived. She introduced the two of them, then took Bolt aside. A week or two before, she had mentioned that someone might be joining them. Bolt was on her payroll in addition to his regular job as a driver, and she wanted to make sure he understood how important this someone was to her.

He did understand, then took her completely by surprise by refusing to take him.

"You have to," she said.

He shook his head. "No room for passengers."

"He's a healer," she explained.

"I know what he is. Like I said, no room."

The cab of the truck was broad and wide. There was ample room for three.

"Why not?" she asked.

"It's dangerous. My neck if something happens."

"Nothing's going to happen."

The trucks were rocking slightly in the wind, which was gusting. But even when it wasn't, when it momentarily stopped, many of them remained in motion. And there were noises from inside.

"I take full responsibility," Meera said.

Bolt grunted. Like most Grotesques he was profoundly ambivalent toward healers. As for Meera, like the other drivers he thought that she was crazy the way she kept at this thing of hers, the way she wouldn't let it go. By the same token, he respected her grit and determination. And truth be told, he felt protective, too. She was an odd creation. Humans, being humans, could be that way; they had the leeway to be odd and even crazy, where tesques did not.

Abruptly, the lead truck pulled out, and one by one, like ducks, the others shifted into gear and followed. With no desire to be left behind, or worse, to arrive too late, Bolt relented and hurried around the cab to let them in.

Meera sat in the middle. Bolt, who'd ferried her to and from the Pen countless times but had always been careful not to touch her except to help her in or out of the cab, made sure he didn't touch her now. He sat as far away from her as possible to still be in a position to drive. But even that was too close for comfort. He grunted at Payne to give him more room.

Payne, who was engaged in his own debate on the closeness issue, did as he was told, moving closer to the door, then attempting to affect nonchalance as Meera, in turn, slid next to him. His act was successful in every way but one: for fear of breaking the spell of her proximity, he held his breath, and in half a minute, now in dire need of air, he cracked open the window.

Bolt barked at him to close it. "And stay put. Don't for a second think of getting out. Unless I tell you different."

Again Payne did as he was told, cowed by the driver's vehemence and temper.

"You may get it into your mind to do otherwise. Don't."

"He won't," said Meera. "Stop worrying."

From the rear compartment of the truck came a cry. A squeal of sorts, like failing brakes; shrill, metallic, grating.

Reflexively, Payne covered his ears.

Bolt glanced at Meera with a self-satisfied, told-you-so look, then reached into a compartment under the dashboard and pulled out a small box. He handed it to Payne.

"Open it."

The box was full of earplugs. Payne picked a pair out, then offered the box to Meera.

"That's all right," she said. "I'm used to it."

"You go ahead," said Bolt, but Payne was not about to be the only one to wear them. He dropped them back into the box, then closed the lid and said that he'd be fine.

A few minutes later their cargo made another noise, this time one that sounded less like metal and more like a cat in heat. A mutant cat, engineered to torment.

Payne grimaced but kept his hands in his lap. Even Meera made a face. Bolt alone seemed unaffected.

"Not all their calls are that bad," he observed when it was over. He waited a beat, then glanced at Payne and added, "Some are worse."

Satisfied that he'd staked out his territory, he gave an honest grin, and after that eased up on the healer a little. It helped his mood that they were under way.

"You get used to it after a while. Or think you do. And then they come at you with something new, something different. Puts your hair on end. Makes you do something you wish you hadn't."

"Like run away," said Payne half to himself, recalling his impulse on hearing Valid's banshee-mouthed Concretion.

But Bolt shook his head. "No. The opposite. You go to them. Or you want to." He motioned at the box of earplugs. "That's what those are for. So you don't."

The chances of his voluntarily approaching what he'd just heard, of his wanting anything at all to do with it, were, Payne assured him, remote. He wasn't tempted in the slightest.

"Not now," said Bolt. "Maybe not today. But someday you'll hear a call you can't resist. You work with Conks long enough I guarantee it'll happen. Then you'll find out what it is to do something against your will, something stupid."

Payne had done his share of stupid things in his life. More than his share. He was willing to rest on his laurels.

"Has there been a call like that for you?"

Bolt glanced at him. "There's one for everybody. At least one."

Payne asked Meera the same question.

Several seconds passed, and then she nodded.

"What did you do?"

"Like Bolt said, something stupid."

Bolt rubbed his scar. "You never heard a sound like that? You? A healer? You never heard a call?"

Payne never had. Since arriving in Rampart and working on Fifth- and Sixth-Degree Concretions, he'd experienced a number of nerve-rattling sounds, but not a call, not the way that they were talking about it. Frankly, most of the time he didn't hear much of anything. When he got done with extrusion, the Concretions were usually in a state of shock. They didn't make much noise. And then the guards took them away soon afterward.

"We'd do it sooner if we could," said Bolt. "The less awake they are, the better. But awake or not, you stay prepared. You wear your gloves. You get your sleep. You keep your head, and you do it by the book. This ain't no job for those can't follow rules."

Swaggering a little now, flexing his muscle, he threw a glance at Payne. "You ever seen a Six?"

"Oh, stop it, Bolt. He makes them."

The driver reddened.

"But I don't have to handle them," said Payne, who had no desire to see the man embarrassed, or worse, antagonized. "That takes a different kind of talent."

"There is a skill to it," said a grateful and now more circumspect Bolt. "They're crafty things. And some of them are strong. They don't like what you do to them. I'll tell you that. They don't like being forced out."

Payne was well aware of this. Concretions clung to hosts like leeches to warm bodies, like frightened children to their parents, like failing breath to life. They fought his efforts to extract them in every way imaginable, despite the fact their days were numbered whether inside or outside their hosts. In the former state they would die a little later, in the latter a little sooner, but in both they were doomed to expire. Still, it never struck him strange that they preferred to stay where they were. Concretions, like the humans that were their source, resisted change.

"Sometimes I wonder that you don't leave them in," said Bolt. "The trouble that they cause."

"They cause a lot more in than out," said Meera.

"Not to me they don't. And even if I did have the bad luck to carry something like that inside, I'd find a way to bear it. I'm not the kind to spread my troubles around."

"You've never been sick?" asked Payne.

"Not so much that I was willing to put other people in danger by my getting well."

"Humans aren't trying to endanger you," said Meera. "You're the farthest thing from their minds. The ones who come here, they're only thinking of how to get rid of what they have. How to get well."

"I've said this before," he told her, "and no offense intended, but that's a narrow way of thinking."

This was true, thought Payne, but that's what sickness did to people. Although there were some, and maybe Bolt was one of these, for whom it did the opposite, expanding consciousness, opening avenues of compassion and goodwill that were never there before.

"What kind of danger are you in?" he asked. The Authorities, of course, insisted that there wasn't any danger, but like every healer, he'd heard rumors, and this was a chance to find out firsthand.

"He's exaggerating," said Meera.

But Payne was asking Bolt. "Other than the calls. Once they're in the Pen, they can't hurt anybody. They're done with, right?"

"Supposed to be," said Bolt.

"They're not?"

"Pen's a big place. We're running thirty trucks a day. Can't keep track of every single Conk."

"Don't need to," Meera said.

"Not until a human gets it," muttered Bolt. He glanced at her. "Pardon me for saying so, but that's the truth."

"No one's going to get it."

Rampart was now many miles behind them, and they were beginning to leave the seabed flatness of the Godian Plain. Ahead of them were the mountains, hazy blue in the distance, their long-tongued ridges descending to the desert floor and puckering it like old and wrinkled skin. They were entering an area of gulches and gullies, and higher up, of canyons, carved by water, scoured by wind and sand, baked by the sun. It was a vast stretch of country, and to the untrained eye, austere. Many found it numbing.

They climbed a hump of land, then dropped into a sink. A blast of wind kicked up sand and threatened to push them sideways, but Bolt held the truck to the road. It was sweltering in the cab and, leaning forward, he wiped his neck with a rag, then settled back into the scooped-out headrest that was specially shaped to accommodate his head. The sky was losing light, but the sun had yet to set. Meera fanned herself and stared ahead.

Beside her, thigh to thigh, sat Payne. He could smell the sweet, clean scent of her, now mingled with the warm and penetrating odor of her sweat. Had they been alone, there's no telling what he might have done. He loved her and had been on the verge of telling her, but the news about his brother had struck him dumb. Wyn here? In the Pen? It was hard to imagine, much less absorb.

According to Meera, he had gotten caught in the final stage of a healing and now existed in some sort of limbo, half himself, half not, stuck with something he could not fully extrude, in suspension between two states. It sounded horrible and also strange that Wyn would fail in something that Payne could do with relative ease. In the history of their lives together, it had always been the reverse.

Up ahead something caught his eye, the glint of water, or possibly a bit of metal. He leaned forward.

"Is that it?"

"Is what?"

It disappeared behind an outcropping of rock. "The Pen."

"You'll know it when you see it. No mistake."

"I saw something."

Bolt held the wheel against another gust of wind and squinted, scanning the landscape with alert and watchful eyes. The truck ahead of them shimmered in the heat, its linear geometry melting in the thick waves radiating off the road. A brambly ball of tumbleweed blew past.

They rounded a thumb of sandstone and came into the mouth of a broad, sandy wash, when all at once the convoy slowed. To the right, up the wash that they were crossing, was a transport truck, partly hidden by a large creosote bush a month or two past its bloom. Both the front and rear tires of the truck were beached in sand. Its rear door was closed, but the driver door hung open, lolling on its hinges like a tongue. Its chrome handle was the source of the reflection Payne had seen.

"That's it then," said Bolt.

Meera audibly exhaled.

Payne rolled down his window to get a better look, but Bolt snapped at him to put it up.

"What is it? What's wrong?"

"What's wrong is you don't know what you're doing. You're disobeying orders. You don't know what's out there. You don't know what you might be letting in."

"Easy, Bolt," said Meera.

"Easy nothing. Wouldn't be no Conks if no one made 'em. Wouldn't be none of this if it weren't for him."

"It's not his fault. You know it isn't. It's not any of theirs."

"Tell Gird that."

"Who's Gird?" asked Payne.

"The driver of that truck," answered Meera.

"Where is he? What happened to him?"

Bolt gripped the wheel. "You got eyes. You tell me."

It seemed plain that he'd driven off the road and up into the canyon. Why he had wasn't clear.

Payne suggested they take a closer look.

The convoy was moving out again. Bolt gestured to the door. "Be my guest."

"Stop it," Meera ordered, then grabbed Payne by the arm. "You stay right here."

From the rear compartment came a tooth-rattling groan.

"Calling to its master," muttered Bolt, throwing the truck in gear and falling in line.

"What's that mean?" asked Payne.

Meera took the liberty of answering. "They think there's something out there. Something different. Something new."

"Don't think," Bolt said darkly. "Know."

Tactfully, she disagreed. "There've been rumors ever since there's been a Pen. Ever since there've been Concretions. Superstitions. Humans have them, too. No one's ever seen a thing."

"Gird did," said Bolt. "Or heard. More likely that. He was right behind me, bringing up the rear last night. I heard something, too."

"What?" asked Payne.

"I don't believe I could describe it."

"The wind," suggested Meera.

He gave her a look. "You want to think that, you go ahead. And while you're at it, you can tell your friend here how the wind took the others. And why you wouldn't let him go and look for Gird."

"Because you would have left him."

Bolt grunted.

"Why did Gird stop and you didn't?" asked Payne. "Last night. The sound you heard. Were you tempted to stop? Was it a call?"

"Tempted to get the trip over with is what I was. And yes, it was a call. But it wasn't meant for me."

"For Gird?"

Bolt shrugged.

"He can't have gone that far."

"Far enough."

"In a day? We could at least look for him."

Despite himself, Bolt was moved. This healer, for all his foolishness, had a good heart.

"It won't help. Besides, you've got business elsewhere. Save your strength." He shifted gear and picked up speed, heading east along the lip of a wide canyon. After three or four miles, the road turned abruptly north. The sun was on their right now, fat and yolky, and the mountains, hardly closer than when they'd set out, had taken on an amber glow. The wind was dying off. The sky was filled with golden particles of dust.

They switchbacked up a steep escarpment that crested on a rock-strewn ledge. Several hundred feet below, the dirt and gravel road petered out at the head of a long, gently upsloping canyon. At its head was a barrackslike building, and beyond it, teardrop-shaped and at least half a mile in length, the Pen.

Inside it were a myriad of shapes and forms, some moving slowly but most fixed and still. Payne searched for his brother, not knowing where or what to look for. It was too far away to make out details. But not too far to make out sounds.

There were a plethora of them, and the canyon walls echoed them back and forth, doubling and tripling their number. Some were sweet, but most were not. In the van of their truck their cargo answered with a wail.

Bolt now did avail himself of the earplugs, and Meera did the same. But Payne chose not to, demanding of himself the full experience. The sounds might hurt his ears, but he didn't believe that they would hurt his person. These were his creations, after all, his and his fellow healers. In a way he couldn't express, he felt in tune with them.

They reached the canyon floor, then waited their turn to be unloaded. Two helmeted, gloved and armored guards worked the job. Usually, Concretions came out as soon as the rear doors of the van were opened, tumbling down a slanted chute into the Pen. Occasionally, they remained inside, or else, because of something on their undersurface that interfered with motility (tentacles, claws, a sticky or gooey secretion), they got stuck on the chute, and then they had to be coaxed and prodded down. This explained the long and pointed pikes the guards carried, although it didn't explain the pleasure they sometimes took in using them.

At the end of the chute the day's deliveries huddled in a sort of pack, which grew as each truck discharged its load. Payne had never seen such a concentration of Concretions. Few tesques, and fewer humans, had.

There was a fleshy-looking cylinder that had invaginated into itself, like a telescope in reverse, and was writhing on the ground; a two-foot-wide corpuscle whose oozing surface popped and bubbled; a pint-sized, vaguely human-looking pod; a larger pod, shaped like a human torso and covered with lips; a delicately veined purple vapor that flickered with light; a ball of greenish pinlike projections; a branching fan of multijointed filaments that moved across the ground spasmodically, in fits and starts; a brain-shaped bit of protoplasm that quivered like a bowl of jelly as it gradually disintegrated.

And more. Many more. There was a staggering variety of shapes and forms, a bounty of the most deadly Concretions known to man. It was a testament to the creative breadth of the healing art. By giving form to illness, a healer could neutralize the most dreadful threats to human life, restoring health to that noble, but imperiled organism. Here, before Payne's eyes, was object proof of the majesty and greatness of his profession, and he felt honored to be a part of its tradition. Indebted, too, to all the healers who had gone before him and done their deeds of healing. They had paved the way, though few had lived to see what he was seeing now. And none had ever been able to help their own kind. On their behalf, and on his own, he felt cheated.

The truck in the front of them dispatched its cargo, a long and wriggling iteration of interdigitated, mandible-shaped joints that shrieked as soon as it hit the chute, undulating down it like a spastic worm. Payne broke out in a sweat, unaccountably seized with a desire to run after it. He grabbed the door handle, and Meera, in turn, grabbed a pair of earplugs from the box on the seat and jammed them in his ears.

"I know that one," he gasped.

She unpeeled his fingers from the handle, locked the door and told him not to look, but he did anyway.

He'd extruded it that very morning. The woman had been crippled by arthritis and was now walking somewhere on her own, free of her debilitating disease. Likewise, her disease was now free of her, but judging by its cries of woe, none too happy about it. It joined the other Concretions, some of which had begun to wander off. Payne breathed easier. Was that a call? he wondered.

The truck in front of them pulled away, and theirs took its place.

Bolt backed up to the chute and rolled down his window. The symphony of sound grew louder.

"Got a visitor," he called to one of the guards.

Meera was bending over Payne. "You okay?"

He gave a nod, but she was not so sure and glanced at Bolt. "What do you think?"

Bolt shrugged. "You do what you want. You know my opinion."

"Thanks. I appreciate the vote of confidence." She turned to Payne. "Listen closely. I'm going to get out. You stay here and wait until I come back to get you. After that, stay next to me. Don't go wandering off. And don't do anything without asking."

He promised this, and she had him open the door, climbing swiftly over him and out of the cab, then shutting the door behind her. Walking to the rear of the truck, she greeted each of the guards by name. Like every other guard and every driver, they were spooked by the recent disappearances. While neither of them had ever had a problem with the lady, both were happy, once she had the information she wanted, to be rid of her.

Fetching Payne, she headed for the perimeter trail around the Pen, which followed the line of the fence. From up-canyon came the whisper of a breeze, soft and dry in their faces. The sun was close to setting, its line of shadow creeping steadily across the ground, and she set a brisk pace, for they didn't have time to dawdle. The drivers were always impatient to get back, and with what had happened the night before, they wouldn't wait a second longer than they had to.

They passed a mound of sand and dirt inside the Pen, as if some large animal had recently been burrowing. And then a section of the fence that had been freshly repaired. Meera noted this while stubbornly resisting the rumors. Wyn was troublesome, and he was changing, but not the way they said.

After years of relative stasis, during which he had, remarkably, kept the thing, or the process, or whatever it was, at bay, the balance seemed to be shifting against him. Her hope was, at the very least, to shift the balance back. She worried she had waited too long.

They reached a pocket in the canyon wall where the trail curved away from the fence, skirting a clump of cacti. Meera halted just beyond this spot. Inside the Pen, less than ten feet away from them, was a crystalline Concretion in the process of sublimation. It was polyhedric; its prismlike facets, once sharp, were now mostly melted. A dying ray of sunlight caught one of its remaining edges and broke into a rainbow on the ground. Nearby sat a shaggy-headed, dark-skinned creation. It was crouched on its haunches and seemed frozen in place.

No matter how she prepared herself, how much she screwed up her courage and steeled her nerves, the first glimpse was always an ordeal for her. Payne was studying the crystalline Concretion, his expression one of interest, when she said, "That's him."

He followed her finger, then took a step forward, but she put a hand on his arm.

"Be patient. He'll come. He knows I'm here. He smells me."

As if on cue, the creature raised its nose. It sniffed the air around it, quickly honing in on the source of the scent. Rising, it approached them.

"Hello, Wyn," Meera said evenly. "I've brought someone to see you."

Payne gaped. Wyn? In what way, what possible way, could this be his brother?

The creature looked more beast than tesque. It was wiry and lean. Its ribs poked through its skin in the way of an animal living in the wild, existing at the edge of survival. Its body was coated in a layer of dust and grime. There were scrapes and scratches on its arms and legs, and its hair was knotted in long and ropy cords.

It made no sound, and Payne wondered if it had lost the capacity to speak. It stood erect, chin slightly raised, nostrils flared, sniffing in their direction.

This was not his brother. It couldn't be. And yet it was, or at least some semblance of him. It had his mouth and lips. It had his bulging forehead. It stood in a vaguely familiar pose.

It also had a pale blue knob projecting from its side, its meli, like the tip of some appendage, or something grafted on. And it had the strangest colored eyes. His brother's had been as black as coal, but these were a cold, dull blue. And their aim was slightly off, as if the creature couldn't see or focus.

"He's blind," said Meera. "I talk to him, but I'm sure he's deaf, too. He's losing his senses. It's taking them over one by one."

"Wyn," Payne whispered, and then again, a little louder. He took a step forward. His heart was in throat. Another step, and then another, until he was up against the fence.

Dimly, he heard Meera urging him not to get so close. But he wanted to get close; he had questions for this thing, his brother, questions best asked face to face.

He started climbing the fence. Got all of two feet off the ground before his progress was abruptly halted. Meera had him by the legs, and eventually she managed to coax him down and away from the fence. But half a minute later, like a sleepwalker or a bloodhound, he tried again, lunging forward. This time she was prepared, planting her body squarely in front of his, blocking his way.

"I told you it's not safe to get close. He's unpredictable."

Gently, she steered him away and started talking to him, telling him a story to get his mind off what he was seeing, to soften the blow. Bit by bit he came around. It was her voice that did it, that brought him back. The story turned out to be about her father, who'd been sick and had come to Rampart in search of a cure. He tried one healer, then another, but both had failed to help him.

"He was very ill," she said. "He was close to dying. Your brother had only been in Rampart for a little while. He was young to be assigned to the Tower. Too young, I think. But he was confident—he was brimming with confidence—and that convinced people that he was able. At any rate, my father had nothing to lose, and he put himself in your brother's hands. The healing took two days and a night. It was grueling, Payne. By the end he could barely move."

"Who? Your father?"

"No. My father was healed. Wyn had cured him."

Payne tried to digest this. Two days and a night were scarcely imaginable. "Why did it take so long?"

Down by the gate the trucks were lined up to depart. Above the cacophony of the Pen a horn sounded.

"It was Sixth Degree," said Meera. "Embedded Sixth. It was all over his body. Locked in and advanced."

"Still," said Payne, for he himself had never needed more than half a day. And there was nothing in his and his brother's all-too-brief life together, no game or activity or relationship, in which Wyn, his chief competitor and idol, had not bested him.

"He was new to Rampart," said Meera. "He hadn't done that many Sixes."

The creature, his brother, made a noise—part mewl, part growl—then thrust his chin forward and stuffed his fingers into his mouth in mimicry of being fed, of eating.

The horn sounded a second time.

"That's Bolt," said Meera. "We have to go."

Reluctantly, Payne let himself be led away. The shock and horror of seeing his brother were beginning to wear off, or rather, in self-defense he was walling them off. Reason was a refuge, or had been in the past, but when he tried to understand what he'd seen and heard, he couldn't. Meera's explanation seemed inadequate. Knowing Wyn, or having known him, he suspected there was more to it than what she'd said. Then again, he wasn't thinking very clearly. More than anything, he felt numb.

Meera had her own walls when it came to Wyn, and in contrast to

Payne's, hers were coming down. For the first time in years she felt vulnerable. She kept waiting for Payne to say the words she wanted to hear but that she didn't want to have to drag from him. With every step his silence became more worrisome and oppressive to her. The Pen was full of noise, but the only sound from him was the crunch of sand and pebbles beneath his feet. It was strange, she thought, how a person could learn and practice patience, could weave and watch and wait for years, only in the end to lose that patience in a heartbeat. It was a sign, she felt, of something flawed inside her.

She held out to the last second. The trucks were rumbling out, and Bolt was frantically motioning for them to get inside the cab. She turned and faced her only hope.

"Please, Payne. Help him."

FOUR

wo days later, a storm blew in from the south; a storm of
wind, striking like a fist, stirring up the earth and flinging it
into the sky. It was as if the world had been turned upside down. Sand
filled the air in great sheets and billows, blotting out the sun, making
breath itself a hazard. People shuttered up their doors and windows
and huddled in their homes. Commerce ground to a halt. City life,
such as it was, came to a standstill.

The storm raged for three full days before exhausting itself. When
it finally did, and the people of Rampart ventured out, they found the
city's pristine streets a waste of sand dunes overrun by rats, whose nests
and tunnels had been destroyed by the storm. And these rats, deposed
of hearth and home, were in no mood for play. They were angry rats,
disoriented and snappish rats, and they bit whatever flesh happened to
come their way. And in their mouths, their bites, there lived a quiet
and unassuming little microbe, content to coexist in harmony with its

host, but which on contact with the blood of humans multiplied and turned offensive. As if, like the rats themselves, it was not happy being evicted from its natural home, as if, in fact, it bore a grudge. So that just as the good people of Rampart were digging out and cleaning up from the storm, they were forced back inside, for the epidemic of rats and their fellow travelers was not a trifling matter.

And then a strange thing happened. Snakes appeared. Adders mostly, chestnut-backed and stout, themselves dislodged by the storm. But also tempted out by the patter of little feet, by the heat of mammalian blood and the promise of a tasty meal. Wave upon wave of them materialized, swarming across the dunes, twitching their brightly colored tails to lure their prey. In the history of Rampart no one had ever seen so many snakes.

They had a field day with the rats. A bona fide, down-home feast. And when they had gorged themselves, and sunned themselves, and mated if so inclined, they crawled back underground. Or else they left the city completely, for like a flock of migratory birds, they disappeared from sight. It happened overnight. One day they were everywhere; the next, nowhere to be found.

At last, after being trapped inside for days on end, the people of Rampart were able to leave their homes. They could go outside without being pummeled by wind and sand, gnawed upon by a rat, or bitten by a snake. The sun was as fierce as ever, the heat as relentless, but those were everyday occurrences; they were predictable, not fickle like the minds of reptiles and mammals.

No one was more relieved to get out than Meera, who'd been steadily going mad cooped up inside her house, thwarted by the elements. She had to talk to Payne, but first she had to substantiate a disturbing new rumor. But before either of these, before anything, she simply had to get outside and breathe.

A thick layer of sand covered the tiles of her patio. The beach below the bluff was altered by the storm, flattened, as if it had been scoured. The Lac du Lac alone was unchanged; it shone like a medallion. She could see for miles and miles, as if the air itself had been scrubbed clean.

There was one other thing that needed doing before she left, and she went inside to change her clothes, then hurried to the water's edge to have a swim. She swam often, and always before important business. It was a release for her, the sea a calming influence. It put her in the proper frame of mind. Her habit was to swim for a while, then turn and float on her back. She did this, but sadly, it didn't bring the peace she wanted. She was too nervous; she couldn't relax. Had she been a fish, perhaps, with a fish's deep and timeless mind. But hers was human and excited.

☙☙☙

She had not been inside the Tower since accompanying her father years before. She'd had no reason or interest in returning. But as soon as she set foot inside, it was as though she'd never left. The long, forbidding corridors, the echoing footsteps, the lines of patients waiting to be healed: all came back to her in a rush. She heard their hushed voices and remembered her own hushed voice. She saw their weary, shuffling gaits and remembered her father's walk. She half expected to see him shuffling by her side, reaching out to steady himself on her arm.

Wyn's healing chamber had been on the fourth floor; Payne's was three flights higher, on the seventh. His waiting room was furnished in the standard way, with comfortable chairs, a couch and a pair of beds. It was large as waiting rooms went, consistent with the fact that he was in demand. Wyn's, she recalled, was smaller.

Nearly every chair was occupied when she arrived, and there was a woman in one of the beds, tended by a man. All save the bed-bound woman, who seemed to be asleep, glanced up and eyed her as she entered.

Getting seen by a healer of the Tower was a matter, first, of getting to the Tower, the admission to which, provided that a number of fairly easily obtainable documents were in order, was open to any human. After that it was a matter of waiting. Patients were taken in turn, except for those rare few in whom a delay might prove fatal. The people in the waiting room were sizing her up to see if she was one of these, which clearly she was not. Relieved, they returned to the business of waiting.

All save the man beside the bed, who cleared his throat and introduced himself. He also introduced his wife, the bed-bound woman. They'd been waiting since the night before to see the healer. They were second in line, he made a point of saying. There was one other woman ahead of them. She'd just stepped out to take a shower.

Meera had forgotten that there were baths and showers, as well as food and kitchens. It came back to her how long the waits could be.

"She showers every hour," the man added.

"Oh," she said, not so very interested in the bathing habits of a woman she had never met. But he seemed to want to talk.

"Every hour on the hour. That's thirteen since we've been here. Just when she dries out, she gets up and showers again." He shook his head. "Never seen anything like it."

"She must be very clean by now."

He looked to see if she was joking, but her mind was elsewhere. She was trying to think of a way to jump the line.

"It's been packed since we got here," said the man. "He's a very busy guy."

"Every healer's busy," she pointed out.

"Sure. That's their job. But this one . . ." He wagged his thumb at the door to the healing room. "He's something else."

"I have to talk to him."

"Sure you do. So does everybody."

"It's not about me," she said, as though this would make a difference. "It's about a friend."

"You're here to help a friend?"

"Yes," she said, brightening. "That's right."

Clearly, he didn't believe her. "That's good of you. It really is. Me, I'm here to help my wife. Everybody's here for help. So you might as well do like the rest of us, sit back and wait your turn."

But Meera had had enough of waiting, and half an hour later, when the door to the healing room opened, she was prepared to make her presence known. Every eye snapped to the healer who emerged, hers included, and all talk and activity in the waiting room ceased.

This was a part of the job that Payne hated, the one that was hardest to bear. The imploring looks, the tense silence, the never-ending well of want and need. Apologizing for the wait was by now routine, and he always felt he should do more: work harder, work faster, work more efficiently. He was sorry, so very sorry, that they needed him so much, that they were all so sick.

"Who's next?" he asked wearily. He was in his eighteenth straight hour of work. The storm had closed the Tower, and in its aftermath patients were arriving in droves.

The cleanest woman in the city stood up and claimed that right. The man caring for his wife announced that they were after her.

Meera leapt up. "I need to talk to you."

The man shot her a withering look. "She's last. She's not even sick."

The sight of her was a jolt to Payne. His heart began to race. He scanned the room to be sure that there was nothing that couldn't wait and promised to be brief. The man, whose wife had yet to stir, was visibly upset. The woman of the showers left the room. Payne stood away from the door and ushered Meera in.

She apologized for arriving unannounced. She had news for him. They didn't have much time.

Payne told her not to worry. "They can wait a little."

"That's not what I mean. They're after him, Payne."

"Who?"

"Your brother."

"Who is?"

"The guards. The drivers. They've formed some kind of vigilante committee. They think it's him."

"Him? What do you mean?"

"The drivers who've disappeared. They're blaming Wyn."

"But he's locked up."

"They think he has some way out. That he escapes."

"And does what?"

"I don't know. Calls them. Traps them. Kills them."

"Wyn wouldn't do that."

"No. Wyn wouldn't. But that thing, it's growing all the time. In the beginning you couldn't see it. If you didn't know firsthand, you could barely tell there was anything wrong. But lately . . . the last few months . . . it's taking over. Every day there's more of it and less of him."

Payne could remember roughhousing with Wyn as a boy, how sometimes Wyn would fly off the handle and strike out at him. He had a streak of anger, or of something, but it was impulsive, not premeditated or cruel. It was inconceivable to him that his brother would trap and kill.

"If he escapes, then why go back? Why voluntarily let himself be caged? It doesn't make sense."

"For food," said Meera.

"Food?" He didn't understand.

"He has to eat. That's why he comes back. They feed him. I pay them to. Sometimes I do it myself. He comes for food."

"You feed him?"

She nodded.

He was very tired, and his mind was not sharp. Something about this bothered him; he couldn't exactly put his finger on it, and it was strange, because he should have been happy that she was caring for his brother. And he was. But at the same time he had a premonition of danger, as if her kindness were a threat or a warning.

"How long have you been doing that?"

"A long time."

"How long?" he repeated. It seemed important.

"Since I put him there," she said.

Half a minute passed. Noises filtered in from the waiting room. She ignored them. "There's more to the story than I told you."

This did not come as a huge surprise. A healing, even a difficult one, should not have turned his brother into a beast. It made no sense.

She leaned against the healing bed, which was still warm from its previous occupant, and with a sigh unburdened herself.

"After my father was healed, he felt indebted to your brother, and he offered him a gift. A present for what he'd done. Your brother had the audacity to ask for me. This made my father quite angry. It made me angry, too.

"But I was also curious, and, I confess, a little flattered. Or maybe titillated is a better word. And for saving my father's life, I felt indebted to your brother, too.

"So without my father's knowledge, I went to him and asked what he had in mind. What did he want with me?

"He said he only wanted to talk to me, and for me to talk to him. He'd never known a human outside the healing chamber. He was curious about us. Wasn't I curious about him?

"We talked all night, and when morning came, it was time for me to go, but he wouldn't let me leave. He threatened to tell my father that I'd disobeyed him. Then he bragged that he would make it worth my while to stay."

"How?" asked Payne.

"I'm coming to that."

"Why didn't you tell me this before?"

"It seemed enough for you to see him. To absorb one thing at a time."

"Did you think I wouldn't have agreed to help him? If I knew he treated you like that? Do you think it would have mattered?"

"I don't know," she said. "Would it have?"

"He's my brother," said Payne, which to him said it all.

It was what she wanted to hear. "I never had a brother or sister, but if I did, I hope I'd say the same."

"I wish you wouldn't hide things from me. I wish you'd trust me."

She was quiet for a moment. "What he did—what we did—it's not something I'm proud of. I'm sorry I didn't tell you, but that's why."

"Tell me the rest."

"I was intrigued by what he said. What did he mean 'worth my while'? I had everything I wanted, and I wondered what he thought that he could bribe me with." She paused. "You can probably guess."

"I don't want to guess."

She glanced at him, then looked away. "He offered to heal me. 'But I'm not sick,' I told him. He replied that everyone was sick with something. It didn't have to be big; what I had probably wasn't. He dared me to let him try to do it. He was so full of himself. So cocky. I told myself he needed to be taught a lesson. He needed to be brought down a notch. So I let him."

Payne waited for her to say more, but that didn't happen. She fell silent instead.

"What did he heal you of?" he finally asked.

"Nothing."

"Nothing?"

"Nothing important. A little spasm in a muscle, but that's not the point."

"Why don't you tell me the point?" He was exhausted, and this conversation, this confession, was the last thing he wanted to hear.

"I am telling you. Don't you understand? I'm the reason he's the way he is. I'm responsible for that thing inside him. Not my father, but me."

FIVE

Bolt had misgivings, grave misgivings, but for the most part he kept them to himself. With Payne he was out of his element, and as for Meera, it wasn't his place to meddle in her affairs. Still, he insisted on a few basic precautions. For their own safety, they had to wear protective clothing and arm themselves. And for the safety of everybody else, they had to do what they had come to do within the confines of the Pen.

He drove them out in the daily convoy. Meera brought food and water in a satchel. Payne slept virtually the entire way.

"He's gonna do a lot of good like that," Bolt observed at one point.

"He's exhausted. He can use the rest. He'll be okay." She hoped that this was true, but something else was bothering her. "It's not like we had a choice."

"Who does?"

She gave Bolt a look. "We might if you called off your thugs."

"I don't know what you mean."

"I think you do."

He shrugged and wiped the sweat off his neck. "Can't stop you thinking."

Sometimes talking to him was like talking to a sponge. Her words just disappeared, as if they'd never been spoken.

"Then tell me I have time to wait," she said.

A fly was crawling up the windshield. Bolt swatted it away, and it circled the cab before landing precisely at the spot where it had started. Bolt flicked it off again, and the same thing happened.

"Now there's a homing creature if ever I saw one. Got an instinct sure as it's got a wing."

"The Pen's the home I gave him," said Meera, taking his meaning, or what she assumed his meaning, at once. "He doesn't have a choice."

Bolt said nothing.

"He's sick," she reminded him, a position she had maintained for years. It was safer ground with the superstitious drivers and guards than saying what she sometimes thought, which was that Wyn was possessed. Being sick was blameless and demanded patience, whereas possession demanded action.

"No one's planning anything," he said at length. "There's only talk so far."

"And what's the talk consist of?"

"I expect you know."

"Enlighten me," said Meera.

He shrugged. "Self-protection. Watching our backs. No one else is going to do it for us. We need to organize our own defense."

"In other words, you're taking matters into your own hands."

Bolt liked her, he truly did, but there were times she acted so stupid, so out of touch with how things were.

"With all respect," he said, "our own hands are all we got."

From the rear their Conk let loose a peal of almost human-sounding laughter. Unbroken by the need to take a breath, the sound went on and on without pause, its pitch steadily ascending.

Meera got out the box of earplugs, but abruptly, the noise ended.

"I don't envy him," said Bolt. "Or any of them. Having to lie down next to all those sick people. Get mixed up with all that nastiness. Then having to spit it out of their own selves." He gave a shudder. "Makes me ill just to think of it."

"He likes it, Bolt."

"That's not normal."

"He's a healer."

"Like I said."

Payne had settled against the door, his eyes closed, his face upturned. He looked so innocent, too innocent she thought, to be woken up, much less woken up to risk his life. She took heart in what he'd told her about Valid, that pompous, dangerous man. How a part of him, a tiny part, was tesque. It gave her hope that Payne would be able to heal his brother. Unconsciously, she rubbed the scar beneath her ribs where Wyn had bitten her.

"He told me once that what he makes is beautiful to him. Not all of them feel that way. It's one of the things that makes him special."

Bolt cocked an eye at her. "Special?"

"Yes."

"The other one, he's special to you, too."

"That's different."

"None of my business, but you get in trouble having more than one."

"I don't," she said.

"Even one can be a handful."

"Thank you, Bolt. I'll remember that."

"Especially how it is. You and him."

This was as close as he ever came to commenting on her relation-ship with Wyn. He was not an advocate of tesque and human inter-mixing, and he was not alone. Few tesques, and fewer humans, were.

"You came from us," she reminded him. "We're mixed up from the very beginning."

"That was a long time ago. And you got it backward. It's you who came from us."

It was an old argument of theirs. Typically, she invoked the scientific point of view, which prevailed among humans; he, the ancient stories and beliefs of his own race.

But she was in no mood to argue today. "However it began, we're mixed up now."

Bolt had no quarrel with that, except to repeat his earlier observation that Payne, who was now soundly snoring, seemed an unlikely candidate to get anyone unmixed.

They arrived at the Pen without incident, rumbling down in a cloud of dust, then waiting their turn to unload. Afterward, Bolt led them to the guardhouse, a stone-walled building dug into the ground to insulate against the heat. Stairs led down to a thick, tight-fitting wooden door. Several of the drivers sat inside, cooling their heels before heading back. One of them was smoking something pungent. He offered it to Bolt, who took a drag, then passed it on.

Beyond this common room was a smaller room where a guard was cooking. Meera led Payne past this to yet another room, where the equipment was stored.

Here were the pikes, the gloves, the meshwork vests, the helmets that every guard wore. The helmets were constructed of a variety of metal plates that were fastened together. In order to accommodate the motley topography of the tesque skull, these plates were made of different sizes and curvatures. No two helmets were exactly the same, just as no two tesques were. The final product resembled the cranium of a newborn, with its floating continents of bone not yet fully joined or fused. Needless to say, the helmets were not nearly so soft or penetrable.

Meera divided up the food, leaving a portion behind. From a guard she found out where Wyn had last been sighted, then, shouldering the pole she used for feeding him, she left Payne inside to get what final rest he could and headed out to bait the trap.

He was standing in a pool of dust about a hundred yards up-canyon, arms at his sides, jaw set, staring down the sun. He had taken to doing this often, further proof to her of his deterioration. In the desert—even to a blind man—the sun was not a friend.

The pole was long and had a wire basket on one end, which she filled with the food she'd brought. Stepping back, she levered the shaft atop the fence, then twisted it, dumping the offering on the ground. Wyn turned his head, sniffing the air. Enjoy, she told him silently, hurrying back to pick up Payne. Next time at the table.

Bolt was talking to the two gate guards when she returned, and they were looking none too pleased with what they were hearing. They had their own plan for Wyn, and it wasn't the one that Bolt, on her behalf, was laying out. One of them offered to drive a pike through his midsection. The other suggested a lethal blow to the head.

They quieted down when she arrived, scuffing their boots in the dirt and looking merely surly. A few minutes later, Payne joined them. The sun had reached the canyon rim, and the day's Concretions were dispersing.

Meera pulled Bolt aside. "What did you tell them?"

"What you told me to."

"What else?"

"To not let things get out of hand."

"Meaning what?"

He ran his thumb down his scar, considering. "I told them that if your harebrained idea doesn't work, they were on their own."

She nodded, satisfied at least to know where things stood. "That's what I thought you said."

There was a bucket beside the gate containing a grayish, viscous substance, and the guards dipped their pike tips into it before setting out. Meera did the same with hers, and Payne, bringing up the rear, did likewise. The guard in front stopped and told him to grab the bucket.

"What is it?" he asked.

The guard shook his head and turned away, as though offended by his ignorance.

"Conk juice. Wha'dya think?" the other guard said brusquely.

Rather than take the shortest path, which would have led them through the heart of the Pen, they took a more circuitous but safer route around the periphery. All of them wore earplugs to muffle sound. They passed a low mound of dug-up sand similar to the one Payne and Meera had seen before. Beside it was a shallow hole. A grave? he wondered. A hiding place? The beginnings of a tunnel? In the hole lay a glistening substance that looked like hardened sap. From nowhere came a curdling screech, bone-chilling even through the plugs. Payne froze and blindly groped behind him for the fence.

The lead guard halted and with a curse came back. "Don't stop. Keep moving. If you act scared, they'll come after you."

Payne tried but couldn't get his legs to work. "Go on. I'll catch up."

"Not likely." Wedging his shoulder under Payne's arm, the smaller but stronger man got him off the fence and moving. "We should be going the other direction."

Payne twisted out of his grip. "You want to go back, feel free."

The guard snorted.

"I mean it." He was tired of their contempt.

"You can't even walk."

"I'm walking now."

The guard grumbled something under his breath, but in the end wouldn't leave. "She's a witch. She'd have my head."

They reached Wyn without further incident, stopping downwind of him, a safe distance away. He was stuffing food by the handful into his mouth and took no note of their arrival. There were several Concretions in various stages of dissolution in his vicinity, and, pikes drawn, the guards cleared the area of them. Then they sprinkled Conk juice in a wide semicircle around Wyn, beginning and ending at the fence.

The sun by now had set; the first star was not yet out. In the twilight the four of them positioned themselves at equal distances along the circumference of the semicircle. Wyn glanced up, then seemingly unconcerned, went back to eating. A moment later, Meera gave the signal, and stealthily, like bandits, they moved in.

It was over almost before it started. Wyn put up a fight, but he was no match for the four of them. Each attacker took a single limb, pulling it out straight and locking the joint, then sitting on it to guarantee it wouldn't move. Slapping leather thongs around his wrists and ankles, then driving spikes through loops in the thongs, they staked him out spread-eagled on the ground.

"Now there's a pretty picture," remarked the lead guard, standing back to admire their work.

"Not so tough," said the other one.

Tough enough, thought Payne, who until now had never been a match for his brother. He would have liked to see how any one of them, any two for that matter, would have stood up to him in a fair fight. Even now he half expected Wyn to break loose and overpower them.

Removing his gloves, he unbuckled his chin strap, then worked his helmet over his forehead until he got it off.

The lead guard eyed him. "Wouldn't do that, if I was you. There's plenty here'd have your head without sending an invitation."

"But here's the prime suspect," said the other, prodding Wyn with the blunt end of his pike. "And here we are, standing around nattering."

"Get away from him," Meera warned him, and when he hesitated, she took a swift step forward and kicked his pike away.

He responded by turning on her, prepared to fight. "C'mon. You want me, too?"

"I don't want anybody."

"Tell Gird that."

Gird, the lost driver, was this man's son. Upon hearing of his disappearance, Meera had immediately offered a reward for any relevant information. She reminded him of that and repeated the offer now.

The lead guard tried to get his mate to drop the matter. The light was bleeding from the sky, and he wanted to get back. But Gird's father was not appeased.

"She talks all nice, but she don't care. She's more interested in this." He kicked dirt at Wyn. "But me, I'm more interested in her."

He took a step toward her. "It's you that's fed him. You that's kept him alive. Why, I wonder? What's your plan?"

"You know the plan," she said.

"Humans lie."

"Then stay. Make sure we don't."

"Let's go," said his companion.

But he had a better idea. "We got a golden opportunity here. I say we kill him."

At the mention of "kill," Meera raised her lance, leveling it at his chest. In response he strained forward, as though daring her to be the first to draw blood.

At which point Payne intervened. Pushing Meera's spear aside, he placed himself between the two of them.

"You're not enemies. Stop acting like you are. Look."

They followed his finger to where it pointed, at his brother, whose head was thrashing side to side. His arms and legs were straining at the thongs, every muscle taut and ridged with tension. At first it seemed that he was trying to free himself of his bonds, but this was not the case. Rather, it was the thing inside that was trying to free itself of him.

The blue appendage was mushrooming out of his meli and at the same time spreading over his skin. He, in turn, was struggling to contain it. He'd pull it back and for a moment seem to have the upper hand, only for it to spill out of him a second later even more.

Both guards backed away in fear and horror. Meera sucked in her breath and looked to Payne. He was tearing off his clothes, first his vest and then his shirt. Bare-chested, he threw himself on the ground, head to toe beside his brother as planned.

"Stake me, too," he told them. "But first free his arm and wrap us tight. Quick. No time to lose."

Meera jumped at his command but couldn't get Wyn's arm free, and in trying, accidentally touched the blue excrescence. A lancinating pain shot up her arm, and with a cry she fell back. Gasping, she crawled forward to try again.

One of the guards rushed in to help, and together they got the stake out. With a knee he pinned Wyn's hand against the ground while she wrapped his and Payne's arms together. Payne ordered her to make it tighter. When she had done this, he had her anchor the two arms down with a double pair of spikes.

"Now stake the rest of me."

She did, working fast, then knelt beside him. His chest was pale in the twilight, his meli dark red.

"What else?" she asked.

Already he could feel the impulses prickling up his arm, the rising heat, as though he were edging closer to an open flame. He could see that she was worried and tried to cheer her up.

"It's going to be fine. This is how we planned it." He paused, then grinned. "Wyn and I haven't been this close for years."

She managed a smile, then touched his hand and whispered luck. It seemed a small thing to offer him, insufficient for the magnitude of the moment, but it was all she could bring herself to say.

Payne closed his eyes, hiding his disappointment. He needed luck; luck was welcome. But he wanted love, and that, it seemed, he'd have to earn.

SIX

For those of a certain disposition, a certain morbid curiosity, the Pen by day had its rewards. By night, though, it was an altogether different proposition.

Meera set her watch at the midpoint of the semicircle they had lain out, just inside the dribbled line of juice, whose dark viscosity remained visible against the milky brown of the canyon floor. She had her lance, and she had her satchel of food and water. She had some extra clothing and a knife, as well. The guards had gone.

Unlike the flesh and blood from which they sprang, Concretions made no distinction between day and night. They existed and ceased to exist equally by sun and moon, whether the sky was blazing bright or dotted with stars, pink with dawn or black and blue with night. Likewise, they produced their raft of sounds regardless of the hour.

Meera had prepared herself for this, but there was really no preparing. The nighttime noises were simply too spooky and unnerving, especially the more human ones. Some of the cries and laughs and rambling colloquies came so close to human speech that with half an effort she could almost hear words. It came as something of a shock to realize early in her watch that she was trying to.

It was an attempt, she guessed, to tame her fear of the unknown, by making the strange less threatening, by taking something beastly and turning it into something familiar. The trick worked too, after a fashion, which is to say her fear of imminent assault and injury diminished (although, as a body was not designed to sustain such a heightened state of fear for very long, it might have been that she simply exhausted her stores). It was less successful when the sounds were particularly loud or close, for then her heart would race and she would jump to her feet in a panic, or if she was on her feet already, pacing back and forth as she did throughout the night, she would freeze and turn, widening her eyes and brandishing her pike.

Which is how the first hour passed.

Meera hypervigilant and jumpy. Conks whooping like demented peacocks, echoing hysterically off the canyon walls. Payne and Wyn staked out head to toe like pieces of a puzzle. The stars above like pinholes. Twilight giving way to night.

Gradually, the temperature fell. There was heat in the ground, but that, too, slowly dissipated. She would have liked a fire but didn't want to call attention to herself. She spread a blanket, put on a jacket and had a bite of food.

A nearby sound, a crunch of rock, brought her to her feet. Heart thumping, she peered into the darkness, spear in hand. The noise recurred; it seemed behind her. Whirling around, she rushed to Payne and Wyn.

They had not moved or been disturbed that she could see, though because of their peculiar orientation she had to circle them to get a proper look. Payne had insisted on the head-to-toe position so that their left arms, their healing arms, could be in contact, hoping that this would optimize at least the first two stages of the healing. As a result, no matter where she stood, one of their bodies was upside down.

Payne looked the same as he had from the beginning, and at first glance so did Wyn. His face was taut, his jaw clenched, his eyelids half-closed and fluttering. But he wasn't thrashing around quite so much, nor straining at the stakes, and his breathing was less harsh. The blue excrescence, pallid as a ghost, still pulsed in and out of him. It seemed to have neither shrunk nor grown.

She heard the noise again, this time sounding something like a footfall, but heavier and more menacing, and closer, much closer than before. She had the urge to scream at it, but couldn't find her voice. Which angered her.

The sound drew nearer.

Leveling her lance, she cried out. "Go away. Whatever you are. Leave us alone."

More crunching, near the fence. Something shadowy skulking toward her.

"I said go away. You're not wanted here."

An indistinct and gravelly voice answered her, sort of human, sort of not.

She barked at it, "I said be gone!"

The dark shape halted, looking squat and not quite so menacing. "If that's the way you want it. But if it was me, I'd be grateful for a little company."

"Bolt!" she cried.

"Come or go?" he asked soldierly.

"Oh, come," she said. "Please. Come."

He was carrying a small pack, as well as a pike, which he purposefully drove into the ground with each step. Crunch, it went, crunch, crunch.

"You scared me." She was trembling.

"That's good. Worse thing for both of us is sneaking up unannounced." He eyed the prostrate men, keeping a safe distance. "Now that's a pretty sight."

To Meera it was he who was pretty. She was amazed he had come. It was so far beyond the call of duty, an act of almost unparalleled bravery and courage to be inside the Pen at night, especially with a creature on the loose that had him terrorized, him and all the others, drivers and guards alike. But here he was, saying how it only seemed fair that she had company. With a gruff humility he confessed his fear was much abated by the sight of Wyn, its principal source, staked out like the animal he was and immobilized on the ground. The other creatures in the Pen did not worry him near so much, and as for the darkness, he turned out to be no stranger to it, having frequently spent nights alone under the desert sky outside Gode.

He knew the stars, and after he had settled down and they had shared some food, he told her stories to pass the time. One, about the coming of the People, was similar to one she knew. These were pre-tesque, pre-human people, the ancestors of them all. In her story they originated from a string of pearls that fell from the heavens and burst open upon hitting the ground. In his they sprang from the eggs of a serpent. He pointed it out to her, the serpent, a zigzag chain of stars, some faint, some bright, that stretched across the northern horizon. Mobestis, he called it, although it also went by other names. It had lived in the Great Sea in the Great Beginning, before swallowing all the water, which is how the deserts were born. After that, deprived of its home, it was miserable, but being a serpent could not weep, and the Creator, taking pity, had raised it to the sky, where it could live again in the sea, the Sea of Night. And it could drink all the water it wanted (and here Bolt pointed to the dark material, the infinite blackness, between the stars); and it did, it drank to its heart's content. And in gratitude it gave a gift to the Creator. It laid a clutch of eggs, which fell to the earth, then hatched and brought the People to the land. The white of the eggs was the source of the People's mind and spirit; the shell, of their physical strength and endurance; the yolk, when mixed with the mud of earth, of their breath and blood. And the People grew strong and multiplied. And they were One People, for this was long before the rift, the Great Split, occurred.

Here the story ended, and before long the moon appeared, which evoked a new round of stories, until, at last, neither of them had any more to tell. They fell silent, and for an instant the Conks did, too. The sudden stillness was startling, almost deafening, as only the stillness of the desert could be. The night seemed to swell around them.

Meera stood and wandered over to the brothers, who by the wan moonlight looked ghostly and pale. In their splayed-out, topsy-turvy symmetry they could have been the imprint of a new species, a new People, come to haunt the old ones. Or replace them, or maybe just remind them how it was before they had become sundered, when the two races were still one.

Up-canyon a Conk broke the silence with a plaintive cry.

Bolt joined her. "How long you expect it'll be?"

"This? I have no idea."

"What's usual?"

"For a meli healing? There's no such thing. Two, six, twelve hours. More." Her own healing, if she could call it that, had seemed to go on forever. This, she suspected, would take longer.

Bolt gestured at the one who had given them such grief. "You think he's hurting?"

"Wyn?" She almost laughed. "Oh yes. I can pretty much guarantee it. And I think the more he comes back from wherever he is, the more he regains himself, if he does, the more it's going to hurt. That thing is so much a part of him. Getting rid of it might feel like getting rid of a part of himself. It's a ploy they use, making you think it'd be worse without them, worse without the pain."

The blue thing, the spillage, seemed to have grown more opaque. And slightly smaller and more compact, although possibly it was

merely less blurry and more distinct. Taking no chances, Bolt kept his
lance poised.

"What do you think it is?"

The question took her by surprise. "Oh, Bolt. You don't know?"

"Well, it's a Conk. Least it wants to be. Wish it would make up its
mind and get it over with. Then at least we can settle this thing."

She had a sudden vision of bloodshed. "No. Please. Give them
time."

"We got all night."

"It may take longer."

"Twelve hours is what you said." He pointed his pike at Payne.
"You think he's even working at it? Looks to me like he's asleep.
Maybe we ought to wake him up and remind him why he's here."

"He doesn't need reminding." She tugged on Bolt's arm until he
turned away and left the two of them in peace. "I've got another story.
This one's true. It's about me."

☙☙☙

Bolt stayed until daybreak, then left to get some sleep. Meera had packed
an open-sided tent for protection against the sun, and she set it up, cen-
tering the canopy on Wyn and Payne. She was careful not to touch the
blue Concretion, which was smaller now, or at least smaller outside
Wyn's body, and thus easier to avoid. How big it was on the inside, and
what, in fact, its character had become, she could only imagine.

Wyn had to be exhausted. He continued to strain against the stakes,
but with less and less frequency and but a fraction of his previous
strength. His breathing had become more shallow, and his pulse, visible
between the cords of his neck, was as rapid as a sparrow's. His eyes, to
her relief, were finally closed, but his eyelids continued to tremble.

Sometimes a patient had to be brought to the very brink of death
before he could be brought back, before he could be healed. It required

the deepest kind of faith and trust and, ultimately, surrender. Payne had spoken to her of this, and she herself remembered lying on the healing bed with Wyn. She had loved him very much, or what she had felt was love back then. Otherwise, she would never have consented. Theirs had not been a one-night stand as she had told Payne, but a longer and deeper affair, lasting several months. Wyn had never threatened her. For all his swagger he had a streak of insecurity when it came to women, or at least when it came to her. He needed proof of her affection, and by the same token, he had to prove that he was worthy of it. Which is why he had insisted on the healing, despite knowing of her bloodline and the risk it posed to both of them.

She'd been so young. So full of romantic ideas and so vulnerable to words. Flattered into thinking she had the power to relieve him of his insecurity, she had agreed to do what he asked. Undeniably, she'd been swayed by his entreaties, but she was not coerced, as she had laid it out to Payne. She had gone ahead not against her will, but willingly. With trepidation, to be sure, but with excitement, too, with daring and with passion. He had bound their arms together, hers to his, his to hers, and she had surrendered to him.

Now she knelt beside him and whispered for him to do the same. Surrender to his brother. Have faith in him.

Through the morning she stayed beside them, sharing the cover of the tent. She felt sleepy but forced herself by various means to stay awake. She sang songs. She recited fragments of poetry. Near her boot she found an anthill, and for a while she counted ants. In the absence of food it seemed odd that they would take up residence inside the Pen. She searched the ground for carrion, following the antline until she caught sight of a millipede, or a caterpillar, something rather large and furry with many legs. It was lying on its side, looking dead, but strangely, the ants disregarded it, marching past as if it didn't exist. She hadn't known that ants were so particular about their diet, when all at once, the creature wriggled. Well, she thought, that explained it.

The ants didn't want it because it wasn't dead. When it righted itself, she changed her mind about what it was. Too big and broad and lumpy for a caterpillar or a millipede, and much too quick. It shot across the sand as if it were on wheels. And was it her imagination, or was it making some sort of squeaking sound?

A second later, it struck her chest, which was protected by her vest, then hopped from it to the open skin of her wrist. She tried to brush it off, but it had attached itself to her. She felt a little tingle, then all at once a razor-sharp, stabbing bite.

With a shock she realized what the creature was. Grabbing the bucket, she thrust her hand inside.

The Conk didn't like the juice one bit. Rearing up, it gave a piercing squeal, then released her and fled.

After that, she scoured the area around the tent for anything suspicious, then widened her search to include everything inside the boundary line. Finding nothing, she returned to the shade of the canopy. She had some water and dribbled half a cupful into Wyn's mouth, careful not to touch him. The blue Concretion had receded farther. Now it was no more than a knob, a mushroom cap, atop his meli.

She gave Payne water too, searching his face for information.

Overtly, he seemed at ease. His eyes remained closed, roving slowly back and forth beneath the lids as though he were dreaming. His breathing was deep and even, broken on occasion by a hissing sound on exhalation she hadn't heard before. His face looked poised between wakefulness and sleep, but overall he seemed calm. He might have been on the Lac du Lac, floating.

She recalled his speaking once about how healing required two states of mind, of consciousness, that on the surface seemed antithetical. One was complete subordination and immersion of oneself in one's patient, an engagement where that patient's needs, desires and pains did not merely become primary but were experienced, literally, as one's own. The other was separation and detachment, which allowed for objectivity. Without this there could be no hope for the proper perspective, no hope for reason and common sense to prevail. Both states depended on a systematic approach to healing. This, in turn, depended on a system.

The Seven Stages was Payne's system; it was every healer's system, as far as she knew. She wondered, though, if it was different when the healing was between Grotesques, if there was another stage, or another twenty. She wondered what stage they were in now. She wondered if they were making progress. Most of all, she wondered if Payne could do this thing that no one had ever done before.

She remembered taking care of Wyn after the abortive healing. She had brought him to her house on the Lac du Lac and tended to him, feeding him, washing him, reading to him, putting him to bed at night. In the beginning he had allowed these things, although it was never clear how much, if anything, got through to him. But she'd believed that if she was patient enough, good enough, penitent enough, she could reach him, and with time he would recover.

But he didn't. Instead, he became unmanageable.

At first it was little things. He'd lose his temper. He wouldn't sleep. He'd get all worked up for no apparent reason. He'd shout and carry on.

Gradually, the little things got bigger. He started throwing things: clothes, books, dishes. He broke a mirror and then a window. He tried to cut himself, and then one day he came at her. He bit her, once on the hand and once below the ribs, before she could fend him off. She had the scars to prove it, the one on her knuckle and the tooth-marked oval on her side, right in the spot where, had she been a tesque, her meli would have been.

After that she'd acted swiftly. She had Wyn put away and later transferred to the Pen. She had no choice. It was time to see things as they were, not as she wanted them to be.

What would she do, she wondered, if Payne became like that? If the man she wanted, or had wanted once, recovered, and the one who wanted her, to whom she would owe Wyn's life, did not?

In the afternoon a plume of smoke appeared, or what looked like smoke, except that it was moving against the wind. It seemed to be composed of interwoven tendrils, twined together like a braid of hair. She was half-asleep, and slowly it approached her, halting at the perimeter she had drawn, then edging forward, giving off a lilting, reedy sound.

Instantly, she was wide awake. Leaping up and grabbing her spear, she lunged at it, driving it back beyond the semicircle. She stood there, feet planted, spear point aimed at its center, daring it to return.

Not that she would have known what to do if it chose to do so, for if her spear had no effect, she had no idea what would. But it seemed to have settled where it was, a yard or two beyond the perimeter, neither approaching nor retreating.

It made her more than a little uneasy, especially its sound, which had become increasingly sweet and inviting. The heat, too, was getting to her, and the sleepless night, and not knowing how long she'd have to keep her vigil up, or the outcome.

And if Wyn did recover, what then? Certainly, he would be different, just as she was different from the woman she had been. Would he care for her? Would she for him? Would they go their separate ways? Would they try again?

At length the Conk condensed and darkened, and to her relief, like a cloud emptying itself of rain, precipitated on the ground. And there it puddled, slowly being absorbed by the burning sand, until it occurred to her that this was providential, this was manna that should not be wasted, it was juice that could be used against the likes of its own kind. She rushed to get the bucket, then scooped up what remained of the puddle, freshening her spear tip with it. After that, feeling both clever and more prepared, she returned to the tent.

That was the extent of her visitors that day. Bolt did not return, nor did any of the guards. She missed the company but was also relieved, for their return, she feared, would bode no good for Wyn.

At dusk the convoy rumbled into view, descending to the Pen in a whirlwind of dust. She used what remained in the bucket to fortify her circle, then watched with pike in hand as the day's cargo was dispatched. She was growing used to the Concretions, feeling less besieged, which was dangerous. Their multiplicity was astounding, their beauty awful and unique. There were dazed moments when she felt that she had found her niche, that these part-human, part-tesque creations were her family, and living among them was where she belonged.

In the west the sky turned orange, in the east lavender, as evening approached. The furnace sun finally dipped below the lip of the canyon. The wind died off. Two days and a night had passed since she had slept. Her eyelids fluttered like moths, then closed.

She had a dream. Seconds later, she woke with a start. The moon was up. Hours had passed.

Furious with herself, she rushed to Payne and Wyn. Something was different about them. Something was wrong.

Blindly, she swept her spear back and forth above them to drive away what she could not see.

Then stopped. And sucked in her breath. And stared.

Not wrong, but right.

The blue Concretion was gone. Wyn's side was clear, his meli dark and unburdened.

And his eyes were open; they were staring at the sky. By the feeble light of the moon it was difficult to be sure, but the blue opacity, the stony deadness, seemed gone from them as well.

She knelt beside him and called his name. He didn't respond. She leaned over him so that he could see her face, but he didn't respond to that, either. Nor to her scent, which had never failed to arouse him before.

His arm was trembling, the one that was bound to Payne. Except that it wasn't Wyn but Payne, she realized, who was trembling, trembling for the both of them, shivering and shaking as if possessed.

All at once he began to babble, loosing strings of words in bursts between labored breaths, as though he were conversing with someone. Wyn? But no, his brother was in another world. Her? Perhaps. But she couldn't understand a thing that he was saying.

He opened his eyes and sought her out, his speech pressured and urgent.

"What?" she asked. "What is it you want?"

He choked something out.

"Again. Say it again."

He did, then followed it with a medley of indecipherable, guttural noises.

She was at a loss. "I'm sorry, but I don't understand. Help me. Please. Speak clearer. Tell me what it is you need."

He tried again, but it was no better, and as her frustration grew, so did his. He raised his voice. He thrashed his head from side to side. He hissed at her.

She stiffened.

Turning his head and breathing rapidly, he pointed with his chin.

"Your hand? Is that it? You want me to free it?"

He nodded fiercely.

She hesitated. Wyn looked better, but Payne was not himself. And what had happened to the blue Concretion?

He pleaded with her to cut him loose, not in words but in sounds and gestures, so desperately that finally she gave in. With her knife she cut the thong that bound his hand, the one unattached to Wyn.

It seemed to calm him down. He flexed his wrist and then his elbow. He wiped his lips, then pointed to them.

She understood this to mean he wanted water, and she went to fetch some. In the half minute she was away, she heard a noise she took to be a Conk, then another one immediately after. It was dull and thumping, like someone pounding meat, and rushing back, she found Payne pummeling his meli. She grabbed his hand and forced it away from his body, then knelt on his forearm until she could knot the severed thong and get it back around his wrist.

He cried out.

"Too tight?"

But it wasn't that. It was his meli. In the pallid light she could see it throb. Something inside was trying to get out. Payne broke into a sweat and moaned.

The final stage began when the sickle moon was at its zenith and lasted through the dawn. The air around Payne darkened, as though the night had condensed, collapsing light. In this darkness appeared a faint blue luminescence, like a vapor or a fog or an exhalation of the ground. Gradually, it coalesced into a long and coiling spiral that wound around itself in a vortex of ever-tightening strands. It looked a little like a ball of string, but it was oval-shaped, like an egg. A large egg, fat and swollen at one pole. The other pole tapered to a tail-like thread that pulsed rhythmically from Payne's meli.

He spat it out like he was spinning yarn, and Meera watched from a distance, mesmerized, spear in hand. The extrusion, like all of them, was utterly unique. But it looked familiar, too, and perhaps it should have, having come of her through Wyn and now through Payne. It represented such a trivial malady, one she'd barely been aware of, and yet such grief had come of it, such pain. There was a lesson in everything: she believed this, and certainly there was a lesson here. But she did not believe, as many did, that everything had a purpose. For what could be the purpose in so cruel and harsh an outcome, so many years wasted, so much damage done, all for so innocent a mistake?

Hours passed, until at length the healing drew to a close. The extrusion had grown in all dimensions. As the sun appeared, its broad oval form hovered over the brothers, casting a faint shadow. By the thinnest thread it remained tethered to Payne's meli and began to revolve again, but in the opposite direction. Slowly and methodically, it unwound itself, until what had been dense and tightly coiled became long and sinuous.

Meera stood up and raised her spear. The Concretion took no notice. Rearing up its head, it let loose a frightening hiss.

Like a fish or a gigantic eel snagged by the tail, it whipped one way, then the other, thrashing wildly back and forth until at last, it tore free. Payne screamed at the unnatural birth.

The creature hovered over him as if to strike. Then blue as flame it fled.

BEYOND

ONE

H e had a dream. It was as close to reality as a dream could be, except for its strange, disturbing ending. In the dream he was roughhousing with his brother, and Wyn, as usual, was having his way with him. From the room next door his mother scolded Wyn to let him be.

"Yes, Mother," said Wyn, who sat astride Payne's chest, leering down at him. With his knees atop his younger brother's arms he had him pinned to the floor. "Give up? Give up?" he taunted.

Payne struggled to free himself but couldn't. Wyn was bigger, older and stronger. With a grin he worked his mouth, making spit bubbles between his lips, and was about to let Payne have it when their mother swept into the room. She pulled Payne up and brushed him off, then turned to her firstborn.

"Come here, you naughty boy."

While Payne looked on, she took Wyn in her arms and pressed him up against her chest. He seemed to disappear inside of her. All at once her eyes rolled back. Her scold gave way to a look of rapture. Alarmed, Payne cried out to her, but she didn't respond. He cried louder, and she heard him—he knew she heard—but she wouldn't listen.

When he woke up, he was in a room in the guardhouse on a bed, covered by a thin blanket. It was night, and on the other side of the room on a similar bed was Wyn, who by candlelight appeared to be asleep. Meera was perched on the edge of Wyn's bed. Her shadow flickered on the wall. She was stroking his hair and whispering words too soft for Payne to hear. Her eyes were red and puffy, as if she'd been crying.

He closed his eyes, and when he opened them again, it was day. Meera had a sponge in her hand, which she periodically dipped into a bowl, wrung out, then pressed against Wyn's cheeks and forehead. From time to time she gently raised his head and squeezed some drops of water from another sponge into his mouth.

On a stool beside Payne's bed was a small bowl of his own, filled with a salty broth. Propping himself on an elbow, he cupped it in his palm and sucked up some of the liquid.

Stirred by the sound, Meera turned her head. "You're awake."

"Am I?" He'd been rather hoping he wasn't. "How's Wyn?"

"Alive," she said. "But weak."

"Alive is good. Alive is what we wanted." He lay back down. "I healed him. I did it. May I have some water, please?"

Dutifully, she rose and left the room, returning with a pitcher and a cup, which she filled and handed to him. While he drank, she kept an eye on Wyn.

"He'll recover," Payne assured her.

"His meli's all torn up."

"All the better. He'll live a longer life if he can't use it."

The thought had crossed her mind, and she had put it aside, along with other questions better left for later.

"And you?" she asked. "How are you?"

His side was sore, all around his ribs and up into his armpit. His meli throbbed and ached. He was as thirsty and worn-out as he'd ever been.

"I'm fine," he said.

"Your meli?"

"Fine."

"That thing? The blue Concretion?"

"Gone," he said.

"It's over then. You did it. You're a hero." Out of gratitude, she took his hand in hers, pressed it to her chest, then kissed it.

There was a hint of reverence in the gesture, which was not what he wanted from her. As for her gratitude, he had hoped that that would lead to something else, that it would spark a deeper feeling in her heart for him, but the deeper feelings seemed reserved for brother Wyn. He should have seen it coming.

Before she could say another word, he pulled his hand away and thanked her for the water. "I think I'll rest a little now."

Poor man. What he wanted he could not have. What he had he did not want. It wasn't over. Not for him. The thing he'd battled and shaped and wrought was no Concretion. It was alive, extruded from his body but not gone. He would follow it. He had to follow it. There was nothing for him to follow here.

⋑⋑⋑

Two days later, revived and stocked with food and water, he set out after it, taking the trail along the fence until the trail gave out, then continuing up-canyon, the Pen now behind him. The going was slow, for the canyon bed was composed of a fine, soft sand that gave beneath his feet. There were also scattered outfalls of chalky rock that forced him into detours. He wore sturdy boots and a head cloth for protection against the sun. He carried no weapon.

Midday he stopped for water. The canyon had begun to narrow, and its walls had steepened. Soon he came to a stretch where they were nearly touching. It was the first shade he'd had since early morning, but he could not enjoy it, for the wind here was fierce. Funneled by the narrows, it picked up sand and flung it in his face. He pulled the head cloth down around his nose and mouth, then bent his head and like a mule plodded onward.

The wind and flying grit seemed determined to drive him back, but eventually the narrows ended. The canyon opened up and the wind died down, its roar falling to a whisper. Payne removed his head cloth, shook it out, and stretched his stiffened neck. He had some water, then wiped his face clean.

Ahead, like the bulb at the end of a thermometer, the canyon broadened, coming to a head in a little bowl. Here the cliffs were not as steep as before. There was vegetation on them, chiefly cacti, whose shallow roots found something to their liking in the thin, impoverished soil. There was also a smattering of gray-leafed, spiny shrubs. On one of these a branch lay dangling by a twist of stringy bark, as if a boulder or perhaps some careless animal had broken it. Sloping upward from this bush there seemed to be a path, although more likely it was just a wrinkle in the hill, a little cleft between two humps. Still, it seemed a reasonable way up, and Payne took it.

At the top of the slope was a ridge that snaked along for half a mile, climbing steadily to a rocky summit. Here he stopped to catch his breath. The Pen was not in sight, though half the world, it seemed, lay below him. He saw no sign of movement anywhere.

He had some water, then took his bearings. The sun was on his right and no more than an hour from setting. To his left, turning a dusky rose in the lengthening light, was a jagged line of mountains of which his ridge was but a low-lying arm. Behind him lay the canyon he had spent the day ascending. Ahead of him, falling off the summit at roughly ninety degrees to one another, were two daughter canyons. This seemed to be the way to go, but which, he wondered, should he take?

One seemed to run more or less straight into the mountains, falling then rising steeply before disappearing in the haze. The other wound around the mountains' ankles and looked more gentle. He couldn't decide and had more water and a little food, after which he promptly (and unintentionally) fell asleep. Several hours later he was woken by a troubling dream. The sun had set and the sky was full of stars. It was a grand display, but the aftertaste of the dream left him feeling cold and lonely. Unwrapping his head cloth, he pulled it around his shoulders, then lay down to wait for morning.

He tried to stay awake, for he didn't want more dreams, but an hour or two before dawn he nodded off. The next time he woke, the sun was staring him in the face. He'd had no dreams, or none that he remembered, and he felt better. This second sleep, more than the first, had restored his strength and cleared his mind. Without physical evidence to point him in the right direction, he resorted to common sense and reason. The right-hand canyon was the easier and more inviting, which argued for the left. Although maybe it was time to put that particular argument to rest, which argued for the right.

He pondered this a while. He had more food and water. At length he packed his small bag, shouldered it, then turned around twice with his eyes closed and pointed. It wasn't reason, but neither was it strictly chance. It was something in the realm of intuition that told him this was the right way to do it, and, satisfied with his choice, he descended.

What followed was a terrible day, which didn't necessarily make it a terrible choice, except for the effect it had on his confidence, which by midday was in a state of collapse. Distances in the desert, he discovered, were deceptive. What seemed close was far away, what seemed short was infinitely long. The bulk of the mountains kept receding. By afternoon he was barely halfway up the canyon, when all at once it split in two. Poised at the fork like a sentinel was a large boulder. It offered shade, if not direction, and he hunkered under it, hiding from the sun, faced again with a choice.

First, he had more water. His supply was getting low, and he allowed himself only a mouthful, not nearly enough to satisfy his thirst. On impulse he had a second. It was rash, but he was thinking of Meera, the only other thing he thirsted for, and he felt defiant. To die of thirst, if it came to that, would be ironic. But he didn't think that he would die.

He chose the right fork, this time on the chance that his intuition failing twice in a row was less than the chance of its failing once, which seemed reasonable but of course was not. After several miles the branch petered out, forcing him to scramble up a hill of jutting sandstone ledges, some of which undercut the canyon wall. He passed holes and pockets and even small caves in the rock. On the ceiling of one he found what looked like a petroglyph. Its wavy lines and cluster of tiny dots were similar to the spots and squiggly shapes that had been floating across his field of vision for the past few hours. He was exhausted, and it was possible that he was seeing things.

His meli had been aching ever since the healing, and now the rest of his body ached too. Every bone and joint was sore, his legs especially. The muscles of his thighs and calves quivered with fatigue and overuse. His feet felt as if he'd been traveling barefoot over stones.

He climbed a little farther, then had to stop. Instantly, he fell asleep and dreamed of water, then woke up and stole another drink. It was warm, but it was wet, and along with the nap, revived him a little.

Doggedly, he made his way forward, ranging ever deeper and higher up into the mountains and farther from the haunts of man. Rarely, he saw a sign, or what he took to be a sign, of the creature. But sign or not, it was never out of his mind. He sensed it ahead of him. Sometimes when the wind was still, he heard, or imagined he heard, its hiss. He and it seemed to be moving in tandem, it from him and he from Wyn and Meera, as well as from himself. He had done something no one since Mobestis had done, but now it seemed that he was leaving that identity behind. He had another future, and he didn't know what it was, but it frightened him.

On the third day his water gave out, and on the morning of the fourth he found a seepage in a cleft between two rocks. He'd been drawn to the spot by the unusual appearance of the cliff above it, whose horizontal cross-bedding was broken by a long, dark, vertical scar. It was lichen, he discovered, a living plant, which meant there was moisture. At the base of the cliff he dug a hole with a rock to form a basin, then sat back and waited for it to fill. It took forever, and the water was bitter and knotted up his stomach. It was also the best water he had ever tasted. He rubbed some on his face, topped off his bottle and reluctantly moved on.

Later that day, high on a pinnacled ridge, removing a stone embedded in his foot, he lost his boot. It was pure carelessness, and his heart fell as he watched it pitch and tumble down the slope, then disappear. He tried walking with one boot, but it was worse than none. Thereafter, he went barefoot, which was painful though not as painful as it would have been with sharper rock. The ridge was made of sandstone, pressed of ancient sediments and sculpted by the elements. It was soft as sandstone went, and while he sustained his share of scrapes and cuts, none was serious, and none became infected. The mineral-heavy dirt seemed to have antiseptic properties.

Higher and higher he climbed, through crumbling country where gnarled and stunted trees replaced cacti, and outcroppings of metaphoric rock began to appear along with the sedimentary stone. The daytime heat was not oppressive, as it was on the desert floor. Nights, however, were cold and increasingly uncomfortable. He'd been rationing his food, and now it was almost gone. He dreamed of it when he slept; when he was awake, he was always hungry. His meli, which had been throbbing like a toothache, began to prickle every so often with a sharper pain.

The next morning, an hour past dawn, he caught sight of the creature in a talus-sloped swale. It was far off, half a day at least, and in the distance looked small and harmless. He got a quiver of excitement, for it seemed the chase was drawing to a head. But then he lost it for the rest of the day, though not its hiss, which like the wind blew hot and cold, loud and soft, sweet sometimes and sometimes cruel. In this it was similar to other voices he had heard in his short, cobbled life—similar, in fact, to them all.

That night he saw it again, across a narrow defile on the crest of the opposing ridge. The moon was just rising, pale and yellow and fat, and the creature in silhouette seemed a thin cut across its face, a dark and crooked scar, a dribble. It paused in its flight and appeared to face him, emitting a long, piercing, high-pitched hiss.

He felt a stitch in his side, then a stab as though pricked by a knife. His meli had started to bleed. It was sticky and wet to the touch. He tore off a piece of his head cloth, wadded it up, and pressed it against the organ, stanching the flow of blood. But every time he moved, it started bleeding again, not a gush but an ooze, like a tree leaking sap, until eventually the ooze became constant.

There are wounds that bleed but don't hurt, and some that hurt less for the bleeding, but this was neither of those. Up to then he'd been able to put the pain out of his mind, but now that became impossible. At rest it was stabbing, and with movement it was worse. He walked with his hand clenched against his side; half the time he walked doubled over. He wondered what he'd done to deserve such a fate, and wondered at that, for he had never believed in pain as retribution.

He thought of Wyn. Beloved Wyn, whom he'd idolized. He thought of his mother and his father. His throat got tight, and then a sob escaped his lips. Soon he was weeping freely. It made the pain in his side worse, which to that point had seemed impossible.

Now he was groaning with every step, and every third or fourth step he stumbled. He lost his head cloth and then his ortine. His side was blood-soaked and wet. He tripped on something, caught himself, then tripped again and fell to his knees, too weak to get up. He was visited by the thought to fall farther. If he couldn't walk, he could slither belly-down, which seemed a reasonable mode of advancement for a man in his condition, though in the end he rejected it. Instead, head bowed like a beaten old dog, he crawled forward on his hands and knees, heading nowhere but driven by the thought that he had to keep going. A short time later he collapsed.

When he came to, he was sitting against a rock face, propped at the waist like a puppet. He felt better, which was strange, for in so many ways he was worse. Scraped up and bloody. Hungry, bruised and dying of thirst. At first he thought that he actually was dying, or about to die, that this sense of well-being was the prelude to his death. He waited for it to arrive, curious and without fear, but it never came. On the contrary, he felt more full of life than ever, and he couldn't understand it. Then all at once he did.

The pain in his meli was gone.

It still throbbed, but it was the throb of healing, not the throb of a worsening wound. To the touch it was dry. To pressure, just sore, like a bruise or a cut that was mending.

He wondered why and how this miracle had happened. He gave thanks, first silently, then aloud, the words spilling out in a torrent. He was not stingy in his gratitude and praise, but lavish, embracing the sun and the sky and the wind and whomever and whatever else he could think of. On the off chance he had been at fault, that the pain was, in fact, retribution, he swore to rectify his ways, to be upright and blameless and true, in short, to be and to do whatever was necessary to keep the pain from recurring. More than anything, he didn't want it back. It was a reckless, impetuous vow, and destined to haunt him, but such was the flavor of the moment and the immensity of his joy and relief.

When he was done, he stood up, and feeling light of head but lighter of heart, set out anew. He tracked the creature up into the heart of the mountains, and then, when it turned, back out. Down ridges and rockfalls and sun-bleached ravines, like unraveling a spool. In place of the pain in his side, he felt the thrill of the hunt and the chase. Without agony he found joy in being alive. The sky was more luminous, the air sweeter to breathe, the earth more replete and inviting. There was beauty wherever he looked, and the land was a garden of plenty. Cacti became a source of food and water for him. Lizards, too, though their horny bodies made for a stingy meal. The first time he ate one, and every time thereafter, he blessed them for giving him life and in the same breath asked forgiveness for taking theirs.

On the seventh day, while descending a flinty defile, he felt a twinge in his side. It lasted just a second, but then it returned, and then his meli went numb. It was a strange sensation to feel nothing, quite distinct from having no pain. When he looked, the organ seemed pale and pinched, like a mouth pursed against speech. He dabbed it with water, then, recalling something from his father, cut off a section of cactus and made a paste from the pulp. This, he hoped, would act as a restorative.

That afternoon, after rounding a broad shoulder of the mountain, he came in sight of the plain. It lay several thousand feet below him and looked as if it had spilled from the mountains themselves, a hazy brown liquid skimming the earth, vast and flat as a pan. In the distance, glinting like metal, was a line of gray-blue that seemed to separate the earth from the sky. Was this water? A mirage? The horizon? He rubbed his eyes and tried to blink it away.

The creature was still far ahead of him and, if it hadn't already, would soon be reaching the plain. The line in the distance did not disappear. It was water, he decided, and no trivial flow, but a river, or more likely, an arm of the sea. The creature was headed for the Lac du Lac: Payne had a premonition of this, and something told him he should hurry.

The numbness in his meli persisted, and despite his ministrations, the os kept constricting. It was now pinpoint in size, nearly closed. He forced it back open with the tip of a finger, which hurt like the stab of a knife. But before long it closed up again, tighter than before, and he couldn't get it open at all. And soon there was tissue bridging the lips, fresh, hymenal new skin. It crisscrossed the opening like the warp and weft of a cloth, until the os was completely covered. All that was left was a dimple in his side, a shallow depression like a thumbprint in clay, where his meli had previously been.

It was a puzzling and alarming development. When he had vowed to do anything to keep the pain from recurring, he had not thought of this. It was a price he was unwilling to pay. Healing was his gift, his one special gift. It set him apart. It gave him reason to live. He'd lost many things, but refused to lose this. Not his power to heal. Not his meli.

By moonlight he worked his way down a tongue of loose shale to the canyon where the creature had fled. In the dawn he found signs of its passage, broken branches and a winding, furrowed track in the sand. The drainage was dry but not lifeless. There was brittlebush, saltbush and stampon. There were cacti too, pin-cushion and beaver-tail, the pads of the latter studded with fruit. The swollen red globes had been pecked at by birds, who had spilled the black seeds on the ground. Mindful of the needles, Payne picked what was left, eating on the move. The fruit was juicy and sweet and more succulent than lizard, though not, he surmised, as nutritious.

While gingerly plucking one of these fruits from its spiny pad, he spied something half-buried in the sand. It was opalescent and looked like an egg, but after digging it up and brushing it off, he decided it couldn't be one. It was too big for one thing; no bird in the world could have lain it. And its surface was soft and rubbery, not hard like a shell. Thinking it might contain food, he tried to open it, but couldn't. Not with his hands and not with a rock. It resisted all attempts to be broken.

He threw it in his bag along with some beaver-tail fruit and resumed his pursuit through the canyon. A hundred yards farther he found another such egg, then another and another and another. All down the wash, like giant pearls, they were scattered, some nestled in sand, some exposed.

By day's end he reached the foot of the canyon, where its bed fanned out in a delta and its walls melted into the plain. He had gained on the creature; he could see its trail ahead of him, raising dust as it fled.

He set out after it, walking all through the night and into the day. It was a long and arduous journey. The plain was vast and not as flat as it looked from above. There were hill-sized dunes, some solitary and some part of ranges that were too wide to skirt, forcing him to trudge over them. The sand was like liquid and gave beneath his feet. In places it was so steep that he had to crawl. The sun was overpowering, burning his face and beating on his head and neck like a hammer. He rationed the cactus fruit, for it was his sole source of food and water.

He didn't rest because the creature didn't rest. He pursued it all day and all night. Finally, at dawn, he caught up with it, on the shore of the sea. It was gazing out over the water, as if waiting for him. Slowly it turned and faced him. It had taken the form of a human.

With a sweep of its arm it invited him to sit. Distrusting it, he remained standing. It assured him he had nothing to fear, and cordially asked what he wanted.

"My meli," said Payne. "Give it back."

The creature smiled with a smile that reminded him of Meera. Was he sure of this? it asked. His meli, that was what he truly wanted?

Payne eyed it warily and nodded.

The smile deepened, and for an instant the human face blurred, as if the creature had trouble holding its shape. When the face became distinct again, the smile looked different, less like Meera's and more like his brother's. The shape of the face was different too; less human and more Grotesque.

"Very well. Come here then. I'll give it to you."

Cautiously, Payne inched forward. The creature made no move until he was an arm's length away, and then it attacked.

It knocked him over, onto his back, and they grappled in the sand, throwing punches, clawing and kicking. Payne got in some blows, but he was no match for it, and before long the creature had him pinned.

It sat astride his chest, gloating. Enraged, Payne gathered every ounce of strength he had left, closed his eyes and with a surge of will, heaved the creature off. Then he rolled over and sprang to his feet, and before the creature could react, leapt forward. He pummeled it, first the body and then the face, furiously, relentlessly, sending it staggering backward. It held up its hands for him to stop, but he wouldn't stop, not until he had it pinned on its back.

The creature cried out to him. He was hurting it, wouldn't he please get off? Triumphant, Payne refused, but the creature whined and whimpered so that eventually he took pity on it and sat back a little, easing up the pressure of his knees. It was all the creature needed, and with a shove it threw him off and rolled away.

And now, abandoning its adopted form, it began to elongate, like glass being heated and stretched. Its arms and legs melted into its sides. Its tongue lengthened and narrowed into a featherlike whip. Its eyes lost their lids. Its skin turned thick and blue and scaly.

Payne was on his knees, staring at it, panting. Longer and longer it grew, until it loomed above him, blotting out the sun. It began to sway back and forth, languidly, almost listlessly, then coiled itself and prepared to strike.

Payne threw up his hands to protect himself.

Hissing, the creature reared its head and struck.

It was over in an instant. By the time Payne came to his senses, the creature had him wrapped up tight. Its skin was cool, which made it feel wet. Beneath the skin its body quivered with power and strength. Every time Payne exhaled, it tightened its grip on him. His breaths grew more and more shallow. Soon he would be out of air.

Its fat head floated above him, lolling side to side as if in time to a slow, sad song. Its tongue flicked out and kissed his cheek. Its blue eyes mocked him.

"Give up?" it hissed. "Give up?"

Crushed and starved for air, Payne could hardly think. He could barely speak. He drew what he knew to be his final breath.

"One wish," he choked. "One last wish. Then yes, I give up. Do what you want with me."

The creature's head stopped moving. Its tongue grew still. "What wish?"

"Dance," said Payne. "Let me dance."

TWO

He had no way to make music. The ortine was gone, and he didn't know how to sing. But his heart was beating and his blood was flowing, and once the creature released him, he could breathe again. He was alive, and that would have to do.

The first few steps were stiff and painful. He stumbled and tripped once over his own feet. His legs were weak, and it was hard to keep his balance in the sand.

He started over, widening his stance and bending his knees and paying attention to the ground's uneven contour with his toes. This steadied him, and he raised his arms. His shirt and pants had been torn off in the fighting. His naked skin was pale in the early light.

He lifted one foot, holding his balance, then slowly and carefully shifted his weight to the other. He repeated this motion, rocking back and forth, keeping his arms light, gaining confidence. He stomped his feet a few times, added a little hop to his landing, gradually picking up speed.

It was a clownish dance, but no one was there to call it that or ridicule him. It was silly, but what was that to him? Death was staring him in the face, coiled within striking distance, and here he was dancing. He glanced at the creature, and laughter bubbled out of him.

He had the rhythm now. He didn't need a drum to beat for him— he was his own drum, his own instrument. The music was in his body and his head. He flicked his tongue in and out and closed his eyes. The sun was bright behind his lids. Floaters shaped like worms swam across his field of vision. Tossing back his head, and stirring up these worms into a kind of spastic dance of their own, he started turning.

Sometime later he opened his eyes to discover that the creature was turning too. Tail planted in the sand, head ten or fifteen feet aloft, its lazy revolutions were timed to his. It remained coiled, and with every turn its coils tightened and its height diminished.

Payne kept dancing. The next time he opened his eyes, the sun was overhead, and the next time after that, it sat aflame atop the horizon. The sea glittered in its long horizontal light, and the beach blushed pink. The creature had contracted into a dense coil no taller than he was. Its head had flattened and its mouth had widened to the point that it seemed to be grinning. Its eyes were sleepy and glazed. The light in them was dying.

Payne felt a stab of pity and he slowed, prompting the creature to raise its head and speak.

"Don't stop. Finish it."

He hesitated, and the creature gave a hiss that made his blood run cold. With a sense of foreboding he resumed his turning. Not like before but fast this time, round and round until he dug a hole for himself in the sand, round and round until his head was spinning. He whirled and danced without a thought for the creature or himself, without a thought at all, until every bone and sinew in his body ached. He whirled with a sense of dread and then of ecstasy, until he was gasping for air. He whirled and danced until his heart was bursting and he had to stop. Staggering then, he clutched his chest and then his side, and it came to him that he was going to die, as surely as the creature was. It was the end of his life, and his eyelids fluttered and his eyes rolled back and he crumpled to the ground. He had danced the dance of death for both of them.

෯෯෯

When he came to, he was lying facedown in a shallow bowl. His mouth was full of sand. Nearby was another bowl, slightly deeper, filled with a dark blue liquid. He had only the faintest idea of what had happened and how he'd arrived at where he was, or for that matter, where he'd come from. His mind felt emptied, like the pages of a book torn loose and blown away.

He did feel tired, that he knew, and his eyelids drifted shut. When he opened them again, the material in the bowl beside him had changed. It was thicker now, and a darker blue, nearly opaque.

He brushed the sand from his face and got to his feet. In his bag was a clutch of eggs, as well as a partly eaten cactus fruit, which he finished. He filled his bottle with water from the sea, then returned to the pool of liquid. It had a sweet, nutritious, bloodlike smell. He crouched at its edge, arms around his knees, studying it.

At length he rose and went to his bag and removed the eggs, which he piled beside the pool. One by one, very carefully, he dipped them in. The liquid, he noted, was sticky and adherent. It coated the eggs in an elastic blue skin. When all of them were bathed, he carried them to the nestlike cavity in the sand where he had woken and gently placed them in it, close but not touching. Then he sat back and waited for them to ripen and mature.

The days passed, and from time to time he turned them, brushing off the sand that stuck to them before nestling them back in place. Occasionally, he wandered down to the water's edge, but mostly he stayed beside the eggs.

In time they hardened. The sun did its work, and the skinlike coating, which had been translucent, turned opaque. Not long after that, the eggs began to jiggle and shiver. Hairline cracks appeared in the shells. The cracks widened, pieces of the shell broke off, and one by one the eggs opened.

From each emerged a hatchling, boy or girl, hair wet and plastered to their heads, bodies glistening. The heads and faces of these boys and girls were neither tesque nor human but stranger than both, stranger than strange. Payne carried each of them down to the water, where he washed them off. Then he carried them back to the nest. The pool beside it had shrunk, but not completely. In the center a portion of it remained. Payne collected the now-viscous liquid in his bottle, which he brought to the children, dabbing the dark fluid on their tiny tongues. Later, when they could, he had them drink it. When there was no more left, he scraped the sand and broke off pieces of crust where the pool had dried and caked, and had them suck on these, and when they grew teeth, chew and eat them.

Before long, the children were walking, then running. They ran away from him, crying out that he should run after them, that he should give chase. But he had no desire to give chase, to them or to anything. He had chased enough. And when he didn't, they laughed and chased each other and sooner or later ran back to him.

With time their limbs lengthened. Their bodies filled out. They grew taller, smarter, older. To Payne it all seemed to happen in the blink of an eye. When they reached adolescence, he gathered them around him and said that it was time to leave. They had a journey to make, they were a tribe, and he would guide them.

And he did, over many years, out of the desert, over the mountains and beyond the sea. And in the fullness of time they came into a valley, fed by rivers and surrounded by deep forests. It was a rich and fertile land, untouched by tesque or human.

Here they settled. And they flourished and they thrived. They grew strong arms and legs, strong wills, strong minds, strong bodies. Strong faces too, strange faces, strangely featured, hideous but also beautiful, faces unlike any that the world had ever seen.

And like their father they were healers, every one of them, though none possessed a meli, nor did any of them need one. The skin where it might have been was no different from the skin around it. There was no os, no hidden organ, no internal gland. Yet they had the healing power to an advanced degree. A degree, in fact, that far surpassed any healer save their father who had ever come before. They healed through touch alone, touch and spirit, and they had no need to reify their healings, no need, that is, to make things concrete. They suffered no such earthbound limitation. Moreover, they had the power to heal tesques as well as humans, and animals if they chose. They had power to do a great many things, power, some said, commensurate with their monstrous beauty. Power that, despite the long and treacherous and often fruitless search to find their hidden valley, prompted many to seek them out. Tesques came, humans came, and as time went by, tesques and humans came together. For these healers born of Payne seemed to smile most on pilgrimages composed of both races. They seemed to love best the mix.

And Payne was proud of his children, and he was happy in his heart. But in time he grew restless and could no longer stay with them. And on the morning of the first day of the season they called Promise he left the valley and climbed the ridge to the east. When the forest was far below him and he could see in all directions, he stopped, and when night arrived, he built a fire and sat down. The sky above him was a sea of light, and there were shooting stars in great numbers. Each was swallowed quickly by the dark interstice between the points of light, all save one that arose from a long, serpiginous constellation in the north. This star seemed to fall forever. And in the hour before dawn a stranger appeared at the fire. Payne invited him to sit, and he accepted the invitation. The two of them shared the fire until daybreak, when the stranger stood, then rose. And Payne followed him.

ABOUT THE AUTHOR

ICHAEL BLUMLEIN is the author of *The Movement of Mountains* (St. Martin's Press, 1987) and *X,Y* (Dell, 1993), as well as the award-winning story collection *The Brains of Rats* (Scream Press, 1990, rereleased by Dell in 1997). A frequent contributor to the *Magazine of Fantasy & Science Fiction* and *Interzone*, his short stories have been anthologized many times, including several appearances in the prestigious *The Year's Best Fantasy and Horror Annual Collection* and *The Year's Best Science Fiction*. He has been nominated twice for the World Fantasy Award and twice for the Bram Stoker Award. He has written for the stage and for film. His novel *X,Y* was recently made into a movie. In addition to writing, Dr. Blumlein practices and teaches medicine at the University of California at San Francisco.